"A page-turner that's excitir mysterious. Delightful and de will give readers a
- Brenda Pandos, Bestselling

"*Devotion* had just the right amount of intrigue, mystery, and pulse-pounding action to keep me eating up the pages. All my favorite characters are back and there are a few new ones I fell in love with. The rich world building and deep emotional connection between the characters makes this addition to the series a must-read."
- Heather McCorkle, Author of *The Secret Of Spruce Knoll*

"The Soul Savers series grabs you and refuses to let go! I guarantee a few sleepless nights, racing hearts, and inappropriate fantasies while reading these books. This is the perfect series for paranormal fans who want to plunge into a world featuring a struggle between good and evil, an insanely strong heroine, and a plot that will keep you guessing."
- Jessica, Confessions of a Bookaholic

"There's no doubting the love that I have for the Soul Savers Series by Kristie Cook. Each book has kept me utterly captivated - with characters that are unforgettable and writing that sings to me. I highly recommend each of these books to anyone who loves strong characters, wonderful writing that tells a story of choices, love, good, evil, sacrifice, passion and so much more."
- Lisa, A Life Bound By Books

"The Soul Savers series is one about difficult obstacles, true love, soul mates, secrets, good vs. evil and everything in between. Kristie Cook has created a world full of fascinating characters, interesting twists and stressful situations. It's got all the great elements you want in a story and series, and Cook's writing flows without effort. It's captivating and full of fun (and sometimes scary) surprises!"
- Katelyn, The Bookshelf Sophisticate

Books by Kristie Cook

— SOUL SAVERS SERIES —
www.SoulSaversSeries.com

Promise
Purpose
Devotion

Genesis: A Soul Savers Novella

Find the author at www.KristieCook.com

Devotion

KRISTIE COOK

BOOK THREE

Ang'dora Productions, LLC

Naples, Florida

For my parents, Valerie, and Dan and Keena

Thank You

Acknowledgements

First and foremost, I thank God and His Son. You have truly blessed me. Let me count the ways…

Shawn, for being there when no one else was, in all the different ways that you have. My family—Zakary, Austin and Nathan, Mom, Dad and Keena, Terry, Grandma (RIP)—for your love, support and understanding.

Chrissi Jackson, we've come a long way and still have far to go. I'm so happy and proud to be sharing this journey with you. Thank you for picking up my pieces and holding them all together. Lisa Adams, thank you for lifting me up.

Author Brenda Pandos, your friendship means the world to me. We *got it* now (a little too much—haha!). Still living for the KM dream, but even if it never happens, this crazy journey brought us together and I am truly blessed for that. Thank you for your prudent picking apart of my story and my writing and for encouraging me to make it better. Thank you for all the extra help and, most of all, for your virtual shoulder when I needed it.

Lesley Turnpaugh, my sexy model, and Jennifer Trammell, the fabulously talented photographer, for bringing Alexis to life, and Brenda, for making my covers gorgeous. I can't stop staring and drooling. Thank you!

Author Heather McCorkle, Author Lani Woodland, Tina Moss, Judy Spelbring, Jennifer Nunez, for your time, patience and wonderful insight that has made this book shine. Heather Call and Patti Oaks, for taking your time to scrutinize each word and phrase.

Book bloggers around the world, for all that you do for authors and readers. Thank you to those who participated in my virtual tours and for taking the time to read my books and write your reviews. A special shout-out to Mindy, my favorite book whore *and* pimp, and to Lisa and Jessica, for your friendship. You all are much appreciated.

Last but certainly not least, I am blessed to have the best readers and fans a girl could ask for. Thank you for making my morning each day when I open my inbox to find your heartfelt fan mail or when I discover a new review posted online. I have had so much fun chatting and interacting with you. Oh, and your taste in men! Because of you, Tristan was the 2011 Indie Pick for Best Badass Hero and the Daemoni the 2011 Indie Pick for Best "Slimeball" Villain. You all ROCK! Let's see what we can do in 2012!

Chapter 1

I stood in the sitting room of the ancient Amadis mansion, stared at the giant tapestry spanning the entire stone wall and wondered how I could change the future it told for my son. A long vine, embroidered with gold and green thread and with leaves on each side, wound and climbed its way across and up the wall-hanging, a golden name on each leaf. These were the names of my ancestors. The Amadis Family Vine only showed the mothers and their children, the fathers deemed irrelevant in our matriarchal society—most had died young, long before their widows knew their real heritage.

Silvery-green thread outlined most of the leaves—the ones with female names, the daughters—but some were brown and separated from the vine. The names on the brown leaves were all male, a twin to a green-leafed sister, and each had an asterisk next to it. A seemingly insignificant little symbol ominously marking the fate of each boy. The meaning looked disproportionately large on this huge hanging: *Converted to the Daemoni.

A much smaller rendition of the image spread across the inside cover of the leather-bound book I hugged to my chest: *The History and Life of Alexis Katerina Ames Knight*. My history. The book explained that not only Angel blood coursed through my veins, but so did the blood of vampires, were-animals and mages. The book, which I'd already devoured beginning to end, was full of such fascinating details.

I stared at the enormous vine in the wall-hanging, however, because it better reflected the magnitude of my feelings than the tiny one in the book. At the top of the Family Vine, right above my leaf, scripted in gold like all the others, was the name Dorian, my son. His leaf, unaccompanied by a female twin, an anomaly in itself, was brown, though not separated from the vine. Yet, anyway.

I had no idea what I would do to keep it that way. I was too new to this Amadis life. But I vowed to do something. I could not let my son become part of the Daemoni, our innate enemies, servants to Satan himself.

"*Ma lykita*," murmured a smooth, sexy voice from the doorway, "staring at it doesn't change anything."

Tristan stepped behind me and wrapped his arms around my shoulders, sending electric currents under my skin.

"I know," I said with a sigh. "I'm just thinking about what we can do that *will* change it."

He kissed the top of my head. "We'll figure something out. Fortunately, we have a few years."

"According to the book and history, yes. But if he's anything like me or you, unique in so many ways, he could go early."

"But not tonight or tomorrow or anytime soon. Right now, we have more pressing matters to worry about."

"More pressing than our son's life?"

Tristan sighed. "Nothing is more important than Dorian's

life. But there's a difference between important and urgent and, for now, the issue isn't urgent. We have time. But tomorrow morning—in a few *hours*—we have a council meeting and I expect it'll be intense. It's late and you have to be tired."

My body did feel heavy with exhaustion, not surprising with the combination of jet lag and a lack of sleep. Excitement to learn about my heritage combined with being overwhelmed by my new mind-reading ability prevented me from sleeping on the flights from Miami to Athens. I'd been awake for nearly forty-eight hours, which included fighting a psycho vampire intent on killing me. I didn't think I could shut my mind down, though. Between all the information I just learned about my history and my genetic make-up and figuring out what to do about Dorian, there was too much to think about.

"How am I supposed to sleep?"

"I put Dorian to bed. Let me take you. You might be surprised once you let yourself relax. And, if you can't relax," he kissed my ear, giving me goose bumps, "I can help with that, too."

"That's stimulating, not relaxing," I said, my body already trembling for his touch.

"Hmm . . . good. After all, we do have that other matter and the council will want to know we're working on it." He nuzzled his face into my hair, pressing his lips against my neck. As usual, my body immediately responded. I couldn't help it—he'd always been irresistible to me.

"We do need to keep trying," I conceded with a smile. "And it *has* been a while."

"It's been way too long." He took my hand and led me up the stone stairs, lit by torches affixed to the stone walls.

Two days certainly felt like a long time, for us, anyway. We'd never before gone more than twenty-four hours without making love—if you didn't count the seven-and-a-half years while he was held captive by the Daemoni. Our eight-year anniversary was less than four months away, but we were still newlyweds in a very real sense, having had a total of three weeks together as husband and wife.

We also had a mission to accomplish: we needed a daughter for the survival of the Amadis—my family, our society. And if the Amadis didn't survive, neither would humanity. It would be lost to the Daemoni.

"Can't we flash to our suite?" I asked as we continued up the stairs to the third floor.

"If you flash everywhere, you'll get lazy and I won't have a lazy wife," Tristan teased. "More importantly, you don't want to create bad habits. We'll have to mainstream soon and you can't be flashing all the time around the Normans."

"Normans," I'd recently learned, meant normal humans. They'd been keeping much from me all these years, including the jargon of this world.

"I know. But I'm not being lazy." I slid my hand down his back and over the perfect roundness of his ass and gave it a squeeze. I finished the thought telepathically. *I'm just horny.*

"*Ah. Why didn't you say so?*" He picked up the pace and we practically flew through the long hall.

As we entered our wing, I slowed. A door on the left led to Mom's suite and I sensed she was still awake, probably reading. I stopped at the door on the right—Dorian's room.

"I stayed until he was sound asleep," Tristan whispered, but I cracked open the door anyway, needing to see him. A little-boy snore rattled in the darkness and his dream appeared in my head—he was swimming with his dad and happily fighting sharks. I could only imagine the embellishments Tristan had added to Dorian's favorite bedtime story. With a smile, I closed the door.

We entered the front room of our suite at the end of the hall, and once we were alone, I was instantly in his powerful arms, locked into a kiss.

"Not in here," I reminded him, remembering Mom's warning of the antique furniture in the front sitting room.

We made our way to the bedroom, which was specifically designed for our kind, completely bare except for a large, stone platform with a two-foot thick pad and lots of pillows—the bed. A stone pillar stood at each corner and blue gossamer hung in curtains between the posts. The bedding was either easily reparable or replaceable—a necessity considering our kind tended to destroy things in moments of passion.

Tristan lifted me with one arm and carried me to the bed, his satiny lips never leaving my tingling skin. Making love with him had always been intense, but since the *Ang'dora*, my heightened senses made it so much more sensual and our powers made it so much more *fun*. With expert skills, Tristan quickly took me over the edge. The loss of control crumbled the mental wall I so carefully held up to block out others' thoughts . . . and to protect my own.

All at once, my feelings flowed out as the mental images flooded in. Thankfully, Dorian still dreamt of sharks, but Mom stiffened in her reading chair then shook her head, thinking, "Alexis!" Solomon and Rina, in their own bed, exchanged knowing looks. Owen felt surprised and confused and . . . excited? The sheet over his lap began to rise. *Oh, shit!*

My mental wall flew up, feeling more solid than ever, in fact, solid as steel. I could almost hear a metallic clang as it slammed into place, like the thick, heavy door of a vault. Everyone's thoughts disappeared. Mine were my own again. I panted, my body as rigid as the steel wall in my head, as I still clung to Tristan, who was pressed against the ceiling. I forced myself to relax and let go, fell to the bed and lay there on my back.

"Oh, shit?" Tristan said as he joined me on the bed, his expression a mix of satisfaction and amusement. "That's a new one. I think I prefer 'Don't stop' or 'Right there' or even 'Love you, baby' to 'Oh, shit.'"

"Did I say it out loud?" I asked hopefully.

"Mmm . . . no."

I groaned, automatically reaching for the necklace that no longer hung around my neck. Playing with the ruby pendant Tristan made for me had been a nervous habit for years, but now Vanessa the evil vampire bitch had it.

Tristan rolled onto his side, facing me. He took my hand from my neck and kissed my palm. "What's wrong? I thought that was pretty great myself."

"Of course it was." I brushed his hair, still long and darker than usual, away from his face, to see the gold in his hazel eyes sparkling brightly with my affirmation. I dropped my hand with a sigh. "And that's the problem."

He lifted an eyebrow. "That's a problem?"

I threw my arms across my face, trying to hide. "Everyone in the mansion heard me!"

He chuckled. "Their hearing isn't that good, especially through stone walls."

"That's not what I mean. You heard me, right? In your head?"

"Ah," he said with understanding. And then he laughed.

"Tristan, this is so not funny! I'm . . . *mortified*."

He kept laughing, though. I dropped my arms from my face and stared at him. I wanted to hit him. He took in my glare and, a smart man, silenced his guffaws.

"Lexi, there's nothing to be embarrassed about. They all expect it. In fact, they *want* us to do it. They want a daughter, too."

"But, Tristan, you know how I can make you feel what I'm feeling through my thoughts? I just did that with them!"

"Then I'm sure they enjoyed it." He flashed my favorite smile, then pulled me into his arms. "I bet Rina and Solomon are having their own fun now, Sophia won't care and Owen . . . well, at least he'll have good dreams."

I didn't know about anyone else, but I didn't sleep long enough to dream. Although exhausted, I tossed and turned throughout the night, my mind unable to turn off. The words of my history book churned in my head, particularly those pointing to the fact we would lose Dorian. Every male of the direct Amadis bloodline went to the Daemoni. Every. Single. One. Since the beginning, when Jordan, the first male twin purposefully sought them out and eventually became leader of their army.

Obsessed with the idea of gaining immortality and any other powers he could have, he and a witch created Jordan's Juice. The powerful potion infused the best qualities of vampires, were-animals and mages—the magical race encompassing witches and wizards, the more powerful warlocks and the strongest of them all, sorcerers—into my ancestors' DNA. For the girls, the *Ang'dora* brought into full effect the creatures' endowments, as well as powers given by the Angels.

The boys, however, were different. And ever since, all of the boys followed Jordan's path to the Daemoni. With Tristan born and raised by them and my own sperm donor one-hundred-percent evil, Dorian had a lot more Daemoni blood running through his veins than he did Amadis. Everything told me he was doomed—nothing in the book provided any kind of escape clause or even the mention of one—but I couldn't believe it. I rolled over again. *There has to be* something *we can do.*

જ

The next morning, I procrastinated in our suite as long as I could, not wanting to face everyone. If I had any chance of talking to Rina, my grandmother and the only other telepath to exist in many centuries, I would have been the first one downstairs, asking her to teach me better control. But with the council meeting, I knew she wouldn't be able to help much today.

"Alexis, I don't know about you, but I'm starving," Tristan said. "Can we please go eat breakfast? This meeting could last all day."

I leaned against the doorway to a small balcony wrapped with wrought iron, a white sheer curtain puffing around me in the spring breeze. The hem of my dated sundress—one of the few items of clothing I owned—fluttered against my thighs. Our suite was on the third floor of the mansion and the mansion on a hill, so I could just barely see the blue-and-white-capped Aegean Sea beyond the ancient cypress treetops.

"Go on and eat. You don't have to wait for me," I said without moving.

He placed his hands on my shoulders and turned me to face him. The wide ring of emerald green in his eyes shone brightly, the gold sparkles surrounding the pupils glinting. His skin almost seemed to glow, as it had on our honeymoon, the morning after our first time. He was happy. This place was good for him. He'd literally been to Hell and back and he needed the Amadis power—you could almost feel the energy pulsing from the island itself—to strengthen his goodness.

"I see what you're doing," he said with the devastating smile that made my heart flip. "You have to face them some time. Do you really want to do it by yourself or would you like me next to you?"

"Of course I'd like you next to me. Always. But . . ." I hesitated.

"But what?"

I dropped my head, staring at the floor. "But you think this is funny. I can already hear the jokes."

"Hmm . . . yeah, I'm not the least bit ashamed of what I can do to you." He lifted my chin with his fingers, brushing his thumb across my lower lip. Then his hand trailed down my neck, between my breasts, along my stomach . . . and lower. I shuddered. He smiled proudly. "So I guess I'll go down by myself and we can all have our laughs without you."

He kissed me and winked, then turned and walked out the door. I stared after him in a daze, and when the fog cleared, I hurried after him.

"Don't forget I can do the same to you," I said when I caught up to him.

He chuckled. "Trust me, I'll *never* forget. And I'm not ashamed of it, either. But I do promise to behave."

He took my hand, his touch automatically calming me, but right before we entered the dining room, I stepped behind him.

"Dad!" Dorian bounded from his chair at the table and leapt into Tristan's arms. "I've been waiting *forever* for you to wake up!"

He threw his arms around Tristan's neck in a tight hug.

"Guess I don't count for anything anymore," I said with mocked pain.

He peeked over Tristan's shoulder with the same hazel eyes as his father's. "Hey, Mom. I missed you, too."

"Sure you did," I said, ruffling his blond hair. I didn't blame him for his enthusiasm for Tristan—yesterday was the first time they'd ever met. They had a lot of catching up to do.

Rina, Mom and Owen sat at the table, coffee mugs and breakfast plates in front of them, their conversation we'd heard from the hallway suddenly silent. I barely glanced their way, just in time to see Owen turning his head and dropping his sapphire eyes, his face as pink as the half-eaten grapefruit on his plate. The image of the rising sheet popped into my mind, and my face heated, probably turning darker than Owen's. I studied the tablecloth, wondering if anyone would notice if I crawled underneath it and stayed there the rest of my life. Or at least until Owen left. *How can I ever face him again?*

As soon as Tristan and I sat down, a woman who looked as old as the ancient mansion came through a door with a tray of coffee, mugs and condiments. She placed everything in front of us, and I reached for the coffee pot, but she grabbed it first, pouring our coffee for us. I wasn't used to this.

"Alexis, this is Ophelia," Rina said with her Italian accent. She was over a century-and-a-half old, but Rina appeared to be in her late twenties, not much older than Mom looked. Her wide, mahogany eyes, nearly identical to mine and Mom's, warmed with appreciation as she regarded the elderly woman. "She has served the Amadis for over two-hundred years, since the days of my great-grandmother's rule. Ophelia, I'd like you to meet our Alexis."

Ophelia dipped into a curtsy. I definitely wasn't used to that.

"Nice to meet you, Ms. Alexis," she said, her voice soft and smoother than I expected, compared to her severely creased face. She turned to Tristan. "Nice to see you again, Mr. Tristan. It has been a long time."

Ophelia returned her attention to me, her gray eyes surprisingly clear behind the many folds of her eyelids. Doing the math, I realized she was nearly the same age as Tristan. *Ew. That thought's . . . discomforting.* I banished it immediately.

"What would you like for breakfast, dear?" she asked me.

"What are my choices?"

She smiled. "Anything you'd like, Ms. Alexis."

"Anything?" I asked with surprise. "Chocolate croissants? And strawberries?"

She curtsied again. "Certainly. Mr. Tristan?"

I stared at him as he rattled off a list of eggs, bacon, sausage, biscuits and practically every other breakfast item known to mankind.

"I told you I was starving," he said once Ophelia disappeared.

"I thought we were in a hurry," I muttered. "It'll take forever for her to cook all that."

But as soon as I said the last word, Ophelia came through the door again, another tray on her arm. I wondered if the kitchen always had food ready to go and then the truth hit me—the chef probably prepared it with magic. And then I realized, with mild shock, Ophelia herself was probably a witch. I'd only just learned the basics of the creatures that made up the Amadis, and mage made the most sense. Since she served the royal family domestically, she couldn't have been a warlock, who'd be out fighting, even at her age. Although . . . she might have been a Were, explaining how her frail-looking body could hold all that food, but then I noticed she wasn't actually carrying it. The tray hovered just over her arm, so it only *looked* as though she carried it. *Yep, a witch. Weird.*

Dorian eyed her, apparently not seeing that magic held the tray. "How are you so strong, Ophelia? You're so old!"

"Dorian!" I hissed, my face even hotter than it had been. "That's not nice."

"He's simply saying what he sees—I *am* old," Ophelia said with a chuckle as she doled out all of Tristan's plates. Then she winked at Dorian. "Bat wing soup and lots of vegetables."

"Ew," Dorian said, wrinkling his nose. "Good thing I'm strong because of my dad."

"Vegetables help," Tristan said as he pierced some kind of decorative leaf on his plate of eggs and shoved it into his mouth.

He dug into all his food while I pulled my croissant apart, picking at it more than eating it. My stomach remained knotted with worry, not helped by the embarrassment for my loss of control last night. I couldn't ever have felt any more awkward than I did at this moment, sitting at a table full of people who had all experienced my orgasm right along with me.

"*Alexis!*" Rina's voice said in my head, sounding very nearly like her regular voice but loud as a shout. I nearly jumped in my seat at the urgent tone and my eyes shot up at her. Her brows drew together as she studied me then she finally said, "*I need to talk to you about your gift.*"

Had she heard my thoughts about last night? I blushed.

"*Yes, we will talk about that, but it will have to wait,*" she said. "*I need to discuss a few things with you regarding the council meeting.*"

This way or in private? I asked her.

She rose from her chair. "We need to be at the Council Hall in ten minutes. Sophia, Alexis, please come with me, yes?"

I dropped the fist-sized strawberry I was eating onto the plate next to my half-eaten croissant, wiped the red juice from my fingers onto the cloth napkin and stood up.

"I'll stay with Dorian during the meeting," Owen offered. He wasn't a member of the council—just my bodyguard, though I thought of him more like the big brother I never had but always wanted. Similarly, he was like an uncle to Dorian. They adored each other. Dorian, who'd been pouting because he wanted Tristan to himself all day, grinned at the idea of at least getting to hang out with Uncle Owen.

"No, Owen, I would like you at the meeting," Rina said. "You will continue to serve as Alexis's protector, so you need to know everything. Ophelia will take care of him."

"We'll go toad hunting," Ophelia called from the kitchen, just as Dorian was about to frown again. His eyes lit up. He jumped off his chair, gave Tristan and me quick hugs and ran for the kitchen.

I followed Rina and Mom out of the dining room and down a long hallway. Rina's deep-violet, floor-length gown swished at her legs as we entered what appeared to be her office. It was large and beautifully decorated, with polished wood furniture, including a desk and ceiling-high bookshelves, full of ancient-looking books and knickknacks. A leather sofa and two high-back chairs created a sitting area near the fireplace, where crackling flames danced, as they did in every fireplace in the cool stone mansion. *Everything* was antique.

"Alexis, use your mind to determine if anyone is nearby," Rina said after Mom closed and locked the door.

This was something she could do herself, of course, so she was either allowing me to practice or testing me. I probed outwards with my mind, careful to keep my mental wall in place. I sensed no other thoughts nearby and shook my head.

"Before we go into the council meeting, you need to know we have not disclosed your gift of telepathy to anyone," Rina said, moving to the chair behind her desk. Mom and I took the seats in front of her. "Only the three of us, Solomon, Tristan and Owen possess this knowledge, and I want it to remain so for as long as we can keep it secret."

I nodded. She had told me this before, at the beach house in the Florida Keys, implying it had to do with the video I'd received showing the Daemoni beheading Tristan. The video was, obviously, a fake.

"I do not even want the council to be made aware at this time," Rina said.

"Okay . . . but why? I thought you figured out the Daemoni had hacked your email and sent the video to me—"

"That was a guess," Mom said. "It makes the most sense they would send it, but we're still investigating. Rina has reason to believe—"

"I would like you to listen to the council members' minds during the meeting," Rina cut in, her eyes flashing anger at Mom.

My eyebrows shot up. "Um . . . I could be missing something here . . . but isn't that a big invasion of privacy?"

"You *are* missing something," Mom said, leaning back in her chair and crossing her arms as she glared at Rina.

"What?"

"I—" Rina broke Mom's gaze and began shuffling and stacking papers on her desk. "I just need you to listen."

"But why me? Can't you do it?" I didn't mean to sound so demanding, but her request made me uncomfortable. As did the tension between the two of them.

Rina abandoned her papers and clasped her hands together. Her chest rose and fell with a deep breath and she shook her head slowly. I'd noticed yesterday, while she provided some of the answers I'd been waiting to hear for so long, a new shadow over her I'd never seen before. Something different—less confidence, I supposed, as if something had seriously shaken her. I thought my mention of Noah, her son and Mom's twin, had caused it, but today the gloom was more pronounced. Her face appeared tighter than normal, and she held her shoulders at a more defined angle, as if stress locked her muscles in place.

"Someone might be blocking her power," Mom said when Rina didn't answer me.

"But not mi—? Wait—they can *block* your power?"

Rina sighed, the sound pregnant with profound sadness. *What's making her so unhappy? What can I do to help?*

"There is a possibility a mage might be able to shield me from entering his or her mind," she finally said. "A slight possibility, but a possibility nonetheless. I would have thought only a sorcerer would be powerful enough, but the witch, wizards and warlocks on the council are among the most powerful in the world, nearly rivaling any sorcerer."

"Then they could easily block mine," I pointed out.

"Not if they don't realize they need to," Mom said. "Our reason for keeping it secret."

"Well, there aren't any guarantees it'll stay secret. I don't exactly have the best control." I anxiously pawed at the base of my throat, once again coming up empty, no pendant hanging there.

"I only need you to keep your wall up and listen, just listen," Rina said. She implored me with wide, pleading eyes, and I wanted to make that look go away. *But could I do what she asked?*

I stood up and walked over to the fireplace, gnawing on my lip and staring at intricately designed glass eggs lining the mantle.

"Alexis, I would not ask you if I did not think you could handle it," Rina continued. "You have excellent control of protecting your own thoughts. I cannot hear them without your allowing me to."

I glanced over my shoulder at her and lifted an eyebrow, hoping it was enough to remind her of last night.

"Yes, well, that is a different matter," she said dismissively.

"You and Tristan won't be having sex at the council meeting," Mom said more bluntly.

"No, but what if something else happens?" I asked, throwing my arms in the air and nearly knocking over one of the eggs. I steadied it before it fell, turned and began pacing. "So many people . . . all those thoughts . . . I nearly had a mental breakdown on the flights over here! I'm not ready yet. Can't it wait until I'm better at this?"

"No," Mom and Rina said in unison.

Rina stepped in front of me, forcing me to stop pacing. She took my hands into hers. "I need you to do it now, darling, or I would not ask you. It is quite urgent."

I blinked at her desperate words. "What's going on?"

She pursed her lips together as if trying to hold the words back. "I cannot imagine who . . . or why . . . I trust them all immensely . . . perhaps too much . . ."

"Who? What?"

"Just say it, Mother," Mom said with obvious impatience.

Rina sighed and I thought I could see tears building in her eyes. "I have received a message from the Angels. I can only interpret it to mean . . ." She cleared her throat, blinked away any moisture gathered in her eyes and lifted her chin. ". . . to mean there is a traitor in our midst."

"A *traitor*?" I asked. "On the *council*?"

"We're not positive," Mom said. "It could be anyone in the Amadis, but it's most likely someone on the council. We're praying it's not true, but if it is . . ."

"I am hoping you may be able to find out, Alexis," Rina said. "Since your power will not be blocked, you may be able to learn something I cannot. My hope is you will find nothing, that I have interpreted the message inaccurately, but I must ask you as a precaution."

"And you think this traitor sent the video?" I asked. "It was Amadis, after all?"

"We have no conclusive evidence. If there really is a traitor, however, it might be the person who sent the video. They might be planning something worse. It could mean the destruction of the entire Amadis if not addressed."

I took a deep breath and let it out slowly. *Wow. No pressure there.* I didn't know anything about the council, but as the matriarch's advisors, I assumed they'd be the best and most loyal of all the Amadis. So who would want to betray us? Why? What did they have planned?

"Alexis?" Mom said. She and Rina stared at me expectantly.

"I . . . it's just . . ." I stammered. I wanted to help, to relieve Rina of this pain that seemed to be stabbing her right in the soul. I wanted answers, too. But could I handle the pressure?

"You will be fine, Alexis," Rina said. "You are very powerful. I trust you with this task."

"Honey, you're one of us now," Mom said. "Sometimes that means doing things we don't always want to do, things that push us beyond our comfort zone. We're only asking you to *try*. We need you." She placed her hands on my shoulders and gave them a squeeze. "If it becomes too much, you can leave. We'll alert Owen to keep an eye on you, in case you need help."

The mention of Owen's name made my stomach take a dip. How could I rely on him when I felt so awkward just hearing his name?

"Tristan is aware, too," Rina added. "I shared all of this with him at breakfast and he immediately saw the best solution— your involvement. Either can help, if you need it."

Tristan and Owen both were familiar with my breakdowns when the "voices" in my head became too much. They both knew how to distract me, how to give my mind something to "tune into" while blocking out everyone else—they'd helped me survive the long airplane flights, where there was no escape if the thoughts bombarded me. Surely Tristan could get me through this meeting. And Owen, too, if I could bring myself to let him.

"Okay," I finally said, throwing my hands in the air with defeat. "I'll do my best. But I make no promises."

Chapter 2

Rina inclined her head in appreciation and Mom gave my shoulder another squeeze, then Rina asked me to tell the men we were ready. Either more practice or another test—one I wasn't sure I could pass. I had never reached out to multiple people at once or someone so far away before. Not on purpose, anyway. In fact, the other person had always been only a few feet away. I concentrated on the image of a black cloud in my head and pushed it outward. I extended it beyond the confines of my skull, while keeping it from enshrouding Mom or Rina—I would hear the thoughts of whoever came "within" the cloud. I continued pushing it out, beyond the room to search for Tristan, but the force was too much. My wall fell and I heard a jumble of everyone's thoughts. I sucked the cloud right back into my head and raised the wall.

"Sorry," I mumbled, shaking my head.

Rina's brows furrowed for an instant, reminding me of the look she'd given me at breakfast, then calm returned to her face.

"Do not worry, dear," she said, "you will learn. Right now, however, we do not have time."

She fell silent while she "called" for Tristan, Solomon and Owen.

"How far out can you go?" I asked her while we waited for them.

"If it is to pick up any random thoughts from anyone, a few kilometers, though without proper control, it can be quite painful if it is a crowded area. If it is to communicate directly with someone in particular, much farther, especially if I am very familiar with them. You can identify your mother, Dorian or Tristan across a large, crowded room simply from a laugh or a single spoken word, yes? It is easier because you are attuned to their voices."

I nodded with understanding. Then I thought I must have been using my gift all wrong, with the visual of the cloud—it wasn't a good enough analogy. I sighed with frustration. This was the worst time to be confounded.

"Rina, I don't think I can do this yet. I have too much to learn."

"You *can* do this, Alexis," she said. "You were able to save Tristan, even with all the Daemoni and Amadis soldiers there. You blocked them out and focused only on him, no?"

Only a few days ago, I'd protected Tristan from a Daemoni attack on his soul, partially by talking him through it telepathically. I had no clue how I pulled it off so well, though, how I was able to keep out everyone else and only talk to him, without anyone but Rina, Mom and Owen aware of what I was doing.

"That is all you need to do during the meeting," Rina said. "Hold your wall and focus on one mind at a time. Just listen. That is all."

There was no more time to argue. Mom opened the door right as the men reached it. Tristan took my hand and "led" me for the flash—all I had to concentrate on was going where he was, since I'd never been to the destination before. There were other ways to flash somewhere new, but I hadn't learned them yet.

I was starting to feel like an alien, learning the ways of a whole new world.

We appeared next to Rina and Solomon in a small area that must have been a holding chamber and had been empty until we arrived. The room reminded me a little of the green rooms when I did television interviews, though the stone walls indicated the building pre-dated television by millennia. The chilly air—no fire in these grates—might have caused a mage or a Norman to shiver, but no one here noticed. Mom sent Owen out to see if all the council members had arrived.

I stepped over to the single window and was surprised to see a whole village outside below us. We were at the top of a hill, at one end of a main road that ended with a pier jutting out over the sea. Between here and the beach, people bustled in and out of an eclectic collection of shops and other buildings lining each side of the road, many with brightly colored awnings, others blank and austere. The rooftops of houses—some steep and pointed, some flat and others rounded, all in various shades from white to blue to fuchsia—spread out beyond them.

"Where are we?" I wondered aloud. We had to still be on the Amadis Island since it was shielded—we could only flash within shields, but not through them.

"The Council Hall in the island village," Tristan said from right behind me. "All those people out there are Amadis."

"You mean . . . witches and wizards and vampires and everything?" I asked with awe.

"Yes, your very characters."

Of course, they weren't the exact characters in the books I'd written about witches, werewolves, vampires and various other supernaturals. I thought I'd been writing all fiction, not knowing these creatures actually existed, but *my* fiction came somewhat close to reality, which I'd learned just last week.

Seeing the people out there—*my* people, the Amadis—was like seeing my characters come to life.

"I want to go meet them!" I said, momentarily forgetting the whole reason we stood at this particular window in the first place.

Tristan chuckled. "You'll meet some today, don't worry."

Oh! The council members themselves aren't exactly human. The cold-water effect of this realization doused my elation. *How can I possibly concentrate on my task now?* I'd be too distracted, overcome with excitement of meeting real-life creatures I'd been so fascinated with since I was a kid. My stomach fluttered with anxiety—I was doomed for failure.

"Tristan," Rina said from the other side of the room and we both turned toward her. "I have just learned some of our members have been delayed with . . . a situation. You may take Alexis into the village to orient her."

"*Alexis!*" Why did she seem to be yelling my name all morning? I tilted my head, acknowledging her. "*Please practice listening while in the village. It will give you the confidence you need before going into the meeting.*"

I nodded as Tristan took my hand. He led me out of the large, stone building and down a path to the main road through town. As we meandered through the business district, I gaped with amazement at everything, keeping Tristan quite amused. The many shops sold a wide variety of goods. In one window, dried herbs hung from the ceiling and shelves contained jars of other reagents, some unidentifiable and others I wished I hadn't been able to identify (lizard eyeballs!), for the mages. Others displayed bottles of thick, red liquid with pretty labels similar to wine bottles, but instead of "pinot noir," "cabernet" or "merlot," they advertised "O+" and "B-"—donated blood for the vamps. Live animals roamed one window display, imitating a pet shop, but these weren't pets. Rather, chickens, rats and hogs waited to be selected for were-creatures' meals. One shop sold wands and another enchanted armor for the warriors. People, dressed in a variety of fashions, present-day and not, frequently appeared and disappeared, flashing around the village.

I couldn't help but wonder what my fellow fantasy authors would think if they ever saw this place. Many had described similar villages in their works, but what would they do if they actually saw it in person? Probably be like me . . . ambling about with their mouths hanging open.

"Are they scared of you?" I whispered to Tristan at one point, as we walked down a residential street by ourselves. "Everybody bows their heads and no one looks us in the eye."

"Maybe," he said with a chuckle, "but that's not why they do it. You're royalty, my love. We both are. They do it out of respect."

"Oh, right. I wish they wouldn't. It makes me feel . . . weird. I thought this would be the last place I'd feel unusual, surrounded by all these mythical creatures that aren't really mythical."

He slid his arm around my waist and pulled me close to him. "Stop worrying about what everyone else thinks."

"Easy for you to say. You've been beautiful and you forever. You're used to it."

"And *you've* been beautiful and you forever, too. Your forever is shorter than mine, but you should be used to it by now."

"I've only been beautiful and royalty for a few days and I don't think I'll ever get used to it." In fact, every time I caught my reflection in the mirror since the *Ang'dora*, I had to stop for a moment, making sure it was really me. So I stayed away from mirrors as much as possible. It was too much to accept.

Tristan kissed the top of my head. "You've become self-conscious on me again. You remind me of when I first met you."

I remembered how uncomfortable I'd been with him, torn between wanting him to know the real me and trying to be "normal" because I thought he was. It felt like several lifetimes ago.

"Sorry. I just feel so out of place here," I said as I contemplated the odd assortment of houses lining the street.

Some were painted in vibrant colors or with wild patterns, and others appeared to be from the ancient Greek era, perfectly preserved. The mish-mash looked as though houses from Whoville were picked up by a tornado and randomly dropped into a neighborhood of Parthenon-like buildings. Various odors carried on the air, some pleasant, some not so much, making me wonder what kinds of concoctions were being created in some of the more eccentric homes. A few people were outside—one cutting herbs from a garden, another walking a pet tarantula the size of my head on a leash, making me shudder—and they all inclined their heads as we passed by.

"I'm the alien but they all treat me like . . ."

"Royalty?" Tristan finished for me.

I sighed. "Yeah. At this rate, I'll be ready to get back to normal life sooner than I thought. At least in the normal world, I know how to behave, what to do."

He gave me a squeeze. "We'll be leaving soon enough, I'm sure. But first you have a lot to learn. You need to train. Have you been practicing at all, or just gawking?"

"Pretty much just gawking," I admitted and then I frowned. I hated listening to people's thoughts, and it felt especially intrusive when the people close by thought they were in the privacy of their own homes. At least on the main street, people would be thinking fewer intimate thoughts and more about their business at hand. "Let's go back downtown, or whatever you call it, so I can be with more people."

As we walked, I pushed my cloud out to people we passed long enough to hear a brief thought, then quickly pulled the cloud in as soon as I'd succeeded. I kept to only one person at a time, afraid I'd lose control if I tried more. Fortunately, what I heard was mostly mundane, except . . .

"Can't stop thinking of him as Seth. Look at him, walking around as though he owns the place, his hands all over the real royalty, as though he owns her. He's such a traitor. He'll be the downfall of the Amadis."

As we walked by, the man—I picked up the thought he was a were-animal of some sort—inclined his blond head like everyone else, and hurried past us.

"Wow, he's not quite a fan of yours," I muttered to Tristan. "He thinks you're a traitor."

"Yes," Tristan said with a hint of steel in his voice, "there are some who think I shouldn't be here . . . and especially shouldn't be with you."

Before I could say what those people could physically do to themselves, my brain rattled with an agitation that exceeded my own. Somehow my mind followed the disturbance to pick up the disjointed thoughts.

"This meeting . . . a farce! . . . What to believe! . . . Another daughter? . . . And the boy? . . . Martin ruling? . . . Is it possible? . . . Tristan—a traitor! . . . Something needs to be done . . . the Amadis . . . Decimated!"

I peered over my shoulder, sensing the owner of such mental chaos behind me, but no one was there. Whoever had been so upset had disappeared.

My own mind spun. The fragmented thoughts made no sense. Were his thoughts really so disjointed or did the telepathy cut in and out like a poor cell phone signal? Did he mean my future daughter? And Dorian? Who was Martin? And, most importantly, how many people thought Tristan would betray us and how could they possibly still believe that after everything he's done for the Amadis?

I opened my mouth to tell Tristan what I heard, but he cut me off. "Rina's asking for our return."

"She told you? But not me?"

Tristan shrugged, took my hand and led me back to the big white building at the top of the hill, the Council Hall. I wondered briefly why Rina had only spoken to Tristan as if I was inferior, but my mind quickly returned to the commotion I'd heard.

The man had mentioned the meeting being a farce, but didn't specify *which* meeting. The council meeting that was about to begin or another one? Thinking he might possibly be a council member, I knew I needed to gather my wits and courage and do a damn good job of "listening" for Rina. Something was definitely going on.

❧

"You can't go in there!" Owen's bark came from the other side of the door to the little room where we waited with Mom and Rina once again for the council meeting to begin.

"Owen, I am your mother. You let me in right now," commanded a stern female voice. The door burst open. "Sophia!"

"Sorry," Owen muttered, following the woman in.

Mom grinned widely. "It's okay, Owen. I doubt your mother is trying anything sneaky with us."

The woman slid out of her leather jacket and tossed it to Owen as she strode over to Mom and embraced her. She wore black leather from head to toe—a bustier, pants and combat boots—and though her build was slight, the confident way she moved and held herself would make a bully cower. She appeared to be in her mid- to late-thirties, but she had to be nearly three times older: Owen appeared to be twenty-five, but was actually sixty-eight and this woman, apparently, had given birth to him. With shoulder-length, straight hair the same shade of blond as Owen's and eyes the same sapphire blue, the resemblance was obvious.

"I know I'm breaking protocol, but I couldn't wait a minute longer to see you or to meet Alexis," she said, already advancing on me. She didn't wait for introductions. "Ah, yes, you are as beautiful as I've heard. Hello, Alexis, I am Charlotte Allbright."

It took me a moment to recover from her straightforwardness. "Um, nice to meet you, Ms. Allbright."

She laughed. "You can call me Charlotte or Char."

"Or Charred or Charcoal," Mom said.

"You'll never let me live that one down, will you?" Charlotte gave Mom a mischievous smile at some private joke.

"Alexis, this is Owen's mother, as you've figured out," Mom said. "And, I have to admit, a long-time friend of mine."

"I apologize for my son's irresponsibility while he was supposed to be protecting you. Sometimes I wonder why Sophia insists on him having the job. He should really—"

"Oh, no, please don't blame him," I quickly interrupted. "That was totally my fault. Owen's great at his job—when I let him do it."

Charlotte eyed me. "Hmm . . . well, I suppose I can understand, if you're anything like your mother."

"Worse," Mom muttered. I tilted my head in question. "Charlotte has been my protector from time to time and she thinks *I'm* hard-headed and rebellious."

"Of course you are! I wouldn't love you if you weren't," Charlotte said with a laugh.

Mom shrugged. "So, maybe I am."

"You think I'm hard-headed and rebellious . . . worse than you?" I asked, not sure what I thought about that.

"Of course you are. And *I* wouldn't love you if you weren't," Tristan said from behind me as he placed his hands on my hips. Mom and Charlotte chuckled.

"Alexis, we will have our hands full with you," Mom said.

I frowned. Charlotte placed her hands on each side of my face and looked me directly in the eye, an impish gleam in hers.

"These are admirable traits, Alexis. There are dark days ahead and we'll need your spunk and spirit. Martin says we all need to be prepared, especially you." With that cryptic message—there was that name Martin again—she planted a kiss on my forehead. What did she mean by dark days ahead? And why especially me? I didn't get a chance to ask as she turned away. "I suppose I should let Owen kick me out. I'll see you soon. We have some catching up to do, Sophia."

Charlotte held her arm out to Owen and he took her elbow, pretending to forcefully escort her out of the room. She hooked her boot around the door, pulling it shut behind them.

"She's a handful herself," I muttered and her laugh echoed from another part of the building.

Mom laughed, too. "Yes, she is. But she's a great friend to me, a powerful warlock and an excellent addition to the council."

"She's on the council?" I asked. She acted as though she hadn't seen Mom for a long time, but Mom had been at the island for nearly a week. She and Rina returned before us so they could debrief the council on the recent events in the Florida Keys—my *Ang'dora*, Tristan's escape, the Daemoni's attack . . . and everything else.

"She is now. Martin, her husband, took Stefan's place, but Char is a new addition. She's been fighting in the Middle East and returned last night," Mom explained. "Rina will swear her in this morning."

So Martin was Char's husband and Owen's dad, and their family was apparently close to ours. Which made everything I'd already "heard" today much more confusing. This meeting may or may not be a farce, but it seemed as though it would certainly be intense, just as Tristan had predicted. I pressed my hands against my stomach, which twisted and turned with anxiety over Rina's request.

"We're ready to begin," announced a low, booming voice.

Solomon stood at the door, beckoning all of us. I tried not to stare at him, but it was nearly impossible. After all, he was a real, live (or real, dead?) vampire. Now that I knew what to watch for, I realized he *did* look like a vamp, something I hadn't noticed the other times I'd seen him. His complexion was an exotic ash color—the vampire paleness of someone who'd originally been dark-skinned. His features were broad and beautiful, his hair in cornrows, the front pulled back into a ponytail, and he had an accent I was sure originated somewhere in the Caribbean. He smiled at us and his fangs were short, barely longer than a Norman's eyeteeth, much less threatening than Vanessa's and the other vampires' fangs had been.

Solomon wasn't the first vampire I'd seen in person, but he was the first *good* one I knew. Yet, as he continued smiling, my stomach tightened more with fear.

Rina joined him at the door, winding her arm with his. Mom stepped behind her and Tristan and I stood behind Mom. Tristan took my hand as Owen led us through the door and down a short hallway. Seeing Mom alone between Solomon and Rina and Tristan and me made my heart ache for her. She'd given up any chance for a real mate—one who could handle her love and passion—to stay with me in the normal world. She'd had a handful of Norman boyfriends throughout my childhood, but none could give her true companionship. Even if she could have revealed her true identity, they would have never understood . . . and never survived.

We stopped at a doorway as Owen stepped inside and announced the matriarch's entry. Wood scraped against stone—the sound of people rising to their feet—and then silence reigned. Rina and Solomon led us inside. Pillars lined the long sides of the rectangular room and on the walls at each end hung a large, ornate cross centered between two angels. But not peaceful, praying angels or cute cherubs—these angels brandished swords, daggers and other weapons, their expressions fierce and their muscles large and defined, as if tensed for a fight.

At the center of the room stood a giant, round, wooden table with throne-like seats surrounding it. In front of all but five chairs stood an Amadis council member, their heads bowed. Rina and Solomon led us to the empty seats. Solomon sat on Rina's left and Mom on her right. Mom and Tristan indicated I was to sit between them. Owen stood behind me. I felt as though I sat at King Arthur's Round Table right in the middle of Athena's temple.

As soon as the five of us took our seats, everyone else sat down, too.

Rina launched the meeting with a prayer, followed by swearing Charlotte in as "the second's chosen confidante." I'd gone through the *Ang'dora* and also had Tristan by my side, so Mom no longer needed to give me her full-time attention and protection. She would become a more permanent fixture on the council and, apparently, had chosen Char to be her personal advisor. Rina then introduced me to the council and Tristan officially as a member of the royal family. As soon as she said this, the room temperature seemed to drop a degree or two while the air thickened. I thought I'd imagined it until—

"Ms. Katerina," murmured a man across the table from me. Well, not a man. A vampire, with dark, shoulder-length hair swept back from his lovely face, and an accent that rolled the "r" in a way that would make most women's thighs tense.

"Yes, Armand?"

"Are you sure—"

Rina didn't let him finish. "I am aware of your feelings. You have made them clear to me. And yes, I am sure. Do not forget we have given *you* a second chance."

Armand pursed his lips and stared at the wooden table. Rina had effectively silenced him. The tension remained in the air, however, and I had a feeling Armand wasn't the only one who had an issue with Tristan and his place at the table or in the family. Whoever I'd heard in the village was definitely one of these people at this table. I scanned the unfamiliar faces until my eyes landed on one I had seen before—the first guy, the blond Were, who had called Tristan a traitor. His dark eyes narrowed at me for a brief moment. It was time I went to work.

But Rina immediately distracted me when she mentioned a coronation ceremony—as in the official crowning of Tristan and me. In front of a crowd of strangers. My insides squirmed. The conversation didn't last long, but my stomach still spasmed as Rina moved on to the next subject.

"Are there any regional updates since our last meeting of a few days ago?" she asked.

A woman of Asian descent, wearing a silver kimono and a ridiculous green hat the Queen of England would admire, stood first and delivered her report. I listened, taking time to become acclimated to the council before starting my task. That was my excuse anyway, but to be honest, nerves kept my mind from going there. The council members—not just creatures from my books, but the most powerful ones of our society—were intimidating enough. What if I screwed up? What if my wall fell and everyone found out what I was doing? I didn't have the best control under ideal circumstances, and now I'd been thrown to the wolves. Part of me wanted to know what was going on, but the other part hid like a coward.

The Asian woman said the Daemoni had pulled back, with the last two attacks in China and Vietnam nearly twenty-four hours ago, about the same time Vanessa found Tristan and me in the Aegean Sea. Finding us was easy for the vamp—she'd drank my blood, creating a connection between us. It wouldn't last, though. As she burned through my blood, consuming it as a fire consumes fuel, the connection would weaken and disappear. That's what Tristan had told me, anyway.

Other council members simply said they'd experienced the same in their regions, although two had suffered rogue attacks. One this morning had delayed two council members.

Amadis all over the world were on edge, knowing attacks could resume at any time, and the council briefly discussed options for fighting back, but I tuned them out. The *Ang'dora* had enlarged the capacity of my brain, or, at least, allowed me to engage those parts most humans never do use, but I still had difficulty following the conversation, being unfamiliar with my new world—or with war strategy, for that matter. I observed my subjects a little longer, needing to gain a better understanding of them before tapping into their minds.

Besides Solomon and Armand, the French vampire who'd been shut down by Rina, the only other vampire on the council was Julia, who I recognized from the Keys. As Owen had mentioned, Julia definitely appeared to be a closer advisor to Rina than the rest of the council, besides Solomon. Rina looked to her often and I suspected they exchanged silent communication frequently, though Julia never spoke aloud. The dark-haired vampire had eyed me during the meeting's opening, more closely than everyone else, scrutinizing me just as she had done at the beach house. She still felt *wrong* to me, though I couldn't explain the feeling.

Armand, it became apparent, oversaw the Amadis equivalent of the police—the group who ensured Amadis people managed themselves responsibly, whether within the Amadis society or while mainstreaming in the Norman world. In other words, that they didn't bite or curse people.

My gaze skimmed over the were-animals, who were nearly as mesmerizing as the vampires and easier to identify than I expected. I couldn't distinguish by sight exactly what kind of Were each was—by possessing animal bodies, the Ancients had created a Were bloodline in the form of every predatory animal on Earth. I thought one woman may have been a bird, perhaps an eagle or falcon. With thin limbs but powerful-looking shoulders and chest, round eyes and a long nose, she certainly looked like a bird.

I identified the mages easily, too—not only because they obviously weren't vamps or Weres, but while in the village, Tristan had pointed out their eccentric tastes, including their fashion styles. It wasn't so easy determining what kind of mage each was—a female witch, a male wizard, or a more powerful warlock. All I knew was they weren't sorcerers because according to Owen, the Amadis didn't have any.

"Martin," Rina said, the name catching my attention, "your intelligence update, please."

The man sitting next to Charlotte stood and I bit off a small sound of surprise. I'd expected to see an older version of Owen, but my protector definitely took after his mother, except his stature, which was exactly like his father's—tall with long, sinewy muscles wrapping their lean frames.

"Yes, Ms. Katerina," Martin said, giving her a nod. He scrubbed his hand through his shoulder-length, black hair, just as Owen would do, and, like Owen, three lines appeared between his eyebrows when he pushed them together in thought. The resemblance stopped there, however. Besides his dark hair that was nearly opposite Owen's blond, Martin's blue eyes were several shades lighter than Owen's and set into a fine-boned face that made me think "pretty boy."

Martin pressed his long-fingered hand down his white, button-down shirt, as if straightening it, pushed his shoulders back and lifted his chin. He spoke with a faint trace of an Irish accent and lilt, as if he'd had many years' practice in hiding it. "As we expected, the Daemoni are preparing for war. Their attacks on Amadis villages may have stopped for the time being, but they're making plans to grow their army."

The statement sent a chill up my spine. Building their army meant attacking and infecting Normans—changing them into vampires and Weres. Of course, that meant the Amadis must fight back by converting the newly turned as quickly as possible, saving their souls and growing our own army at the same time.

"They won't let Tristan—or Alexis—go easily, of course," Martin added. "They will fight for them, harder than ever. Since we have them protected here, they appear to be in the midst of making plans for flushing them out. I recommend we keep them here on the island as long as possible, for their protection."

"I disagree," Armand said. "They need to mainstream. The boy is getting old enough to remember what he sees here. He cannot know our secrets, since he will . . ."

I didn't hear the rest of Armand's sentence—I didn't have to, though, to understand he and others would want to protect the Amadis secrets from Dorian, their future enemy.

Rina broke into my mind.

"*Alexis,*" she said, again sounding as though she yelled in my head, automatically grabbing my attention. "*Have you started?*"

I pressed my lips together and wiped my palms on my dress as tendrils of anxiety slithered in and around me.

"*Focus on the mages,*" Rina instructed. "*They are the only ones who could block me. You do not need to worry about the others.*"

I pulled in a deep breath, tried to blow out the tension inside me and commanded myself to proceed. The discussion of when we'd need to mainstream resided in one part of my brain, while I used another part to conjure my cloud. I envisioned enlarging the black cloud beyond my head, which took more effort than ever before, probably because nerves tried to hold it in. With effort, I pushed it out to enshroud Charlotte, who I thought would be a good start. Nice and safe.

She wasn't completely focused on the conversation either, but silently cussed at Mom for dragging her onto the council with all of its hellishly boring meetings, when she could be out fighting. Although, she also admitted to herself, she was happy to be paired up with Mom again and couldn't wait for the paybacks Mom owed her for this meeting. Paybacks that involved margaritas on the beach and working with me. *Hmm . . . what does that mean?* I couldn't linger on that last thought, though, and forced the cloud to Martin, but didn't stay long with him, either—his mind was focused completely on the discussion, and he was Owen's dad, after all. A pang of guilt stabbed at me for invading his parents' thoughts in the first place.

My head already began to ache as I concentrated on moving my cloud along to Armand, and then, following Rina's instructions, onto the next person, the were-falcon (a brief dip into her thoughts confirmed my theory of her being a bird). As everyone else discussed exactly how long we should stay on the island, I continued coercing my cloud around the table, taking my time with the mages. I learned nothing from their thoughts.

"We do not know for sure about the boy," said a beautiful woman with raven hair and eyes, and skin the color of smooth caramel. Wearing an intricately embellished, gold sari, I figured she came from India and discovered she lived part of her life as a leopard when I checked her mind. I couldn't help the intrusion, although she wasn't a mage, after that statement about Dorian. *Did she know something the rest of us didn't?*

"Of course we do, Chandra," said the Italian blond man I'd seen in the village earlier. They had called him Savio and,

I learned now, he was a were-shark. He and Armand were definitely on the same team, a team against Tristan. And, apparently, against Dorian. I didn't like the French vamp and the Italian Were. Not one bit. "You are always optimistic, but all boys go to the Daemoni. That's how it is, how it's always been."

"*There is nothing wrong with having hope,*" Chandra thought, but she didn't respond aloud to Savio's dismissive statement. I supposed she didn't know anything, but simply wanted to hope, as I did.

"We will give them as much time as they need. Alexis needs to learn our ways before returning to the Norman world," Rina said, putting that line of conversation to a temporary end. Surely they'd give us a move-out day sooner or later.

Although I hadn't learned anything useful, I needed a mental break and allowed my cloud to disintegrate before my head exploded.

"As long as they're trying for a daughter, who cares where they are?" Minh, the Asian witch with the green hat, asked. If she hadn't been talking about me, I would have giggled with surprise at this little, soft-spoken woman bringing up the topic of sex. But she *was* talking about me. And her topic wasn't sex, not really. It was the daughter I'd failed to give them.

The next daughter was a hotter topic than I expected. Everyone had something to say. They were more concerned about this subject than anything they'd discussed so far, even more than they were about the Daemoni's preparations for war. After all, without a daughter to rule in the future, the Amadis would fall, regardless of what the Daemoni did. Having to face everyone in person made me feel worse than ever about this failure.

Armand went so far as to demand proof that Tristan and I were proactively working on this.

"Armand, you are not in France at the moment," Martin said. "That is not an appropriate question."

Armand banged his fist on the table. "We deserve to know."

"We are working on it," Tristan said. "I personally guarantee it."

My face heated and surely became redder than the tomato on Minh's hat. To add to my complete embarrassment, Solomon spoke up as a witness to confirm we were, indeed, working on it. Once again, I wanted to crawl under the table and never come out again.

My head pounded. The concentration of listening to everyone's minds, the frustration of not learning anything and the tension of this topic were like hammers taking turns on my brain. I felt so inadequate, in more ways than one, and didn't want to disappoint Rina again. Since I hadn't brought her the next daughter, I could at least do better with my so-called gift. So I tried once again, painstakingly pushing the cloud to only the mages, besides Owen, Charlotte and Martin.

The conversation heated, though, making concentration on anyone's thoughts difficult. Voices grew loud and hands waved about as everyone's emotional investment in this became clear. I tried to ignore the feeling of being personally attacked, even as my breaths grew shallow and my soul felt as though they physically pounded it. *Just focus on your task. Don't worry about them. Tristan will take care of it.*

But it was too much. The emotions—mine and everyone else's—overwhelmed me. My wall I kept so carefully in place crumbled. The thoughts came crashing in, wave after wave beating at my mind, swirling and tumbling about, pulling me under. I couldn't distinguish thoughts from spoken words, let alone specific voices, except those I was most familiar with.

"Give them two years."

"Too long. One year."

"No, six months."

"There are other possibilities to consider, too."

"Not Tristan. Never right. Shouldn't be here. Owen . . . the right mate."

I gulped for air. My heart raced. I had no idea what thoughts Rina could hear or if she totally depended on me, but I was failing. A silent scream to her or Tristan or Owen that I needed help clawed at my mind, but I held it back, afraid I'd lose control and everyone would "hear" me, ruining everything.

"We don't need deadlines or other possibilities," Rina said. "Tristan and Alexis are supposed to be together, their souls are *made* for each other. We must trust the Angels. They have told me there *will* be a daughter after Alexis."

"I *feel* that truth. Tristan and Alexis have a daughter in their future," Mom added.

"Not good enough. We need a daughter now!"

"We must take this into our own hands."

"Stupid women. Basing everything on their feelings and non-existent messages from the Angels. Of course Alexis won't get pregnant. We already have the girl. We just need to keep her hidden a little longer . . ."

Chapter 3

I gasped, choking on a swelling rage. My eyes burned with angry tears and my throat constricted. The words ricocheted around my mind like an angry wasp desperate to find its way out. "*We already have the girl. We already have the girl.*" I gripped my chair tightly, trying in vain to control the tremors racking my body. Trying to control the urge to jump to my feet and demand answers. But I couldn't say anything. I couldn't even acknowledge the words. I had to bear the sting each time they hit me.

Tristan laid his hand on mine, and I took his and squeezed it hard. I couldn't breathe. My vision swam. *I have to get out of here. Now!* I knew there was a way to escape, but the how wasn't coming to mind. My brain lost all function as it remained stuck on those five words. I looked at Tristan with desperation. He nodded and took me in his arms. The air whooshed out of my lungs and the meeting room disappeared.

We appeared in our suite at the mansion, and I sucked in a

lungful of oxygen and fell to my knees. My heart still raced and my body still shook. And my mind still reeled.

"Holy . . . shit," I whispered between pants. "Holy. *Shit*."

Tristan sat on the bed in front of me. He placed his hands on my shoulders and studied my face.

"You heard something?" he asked. I nodded, slowly, my eyes bugging. "What?"

We already have the girl. The words echoed in my head.

Before I could share them, though, a *pop* came from the sitting room. I froze. *What had we left behind?* I'd lost all control at the end. I might have shared everything I'd been hearing with everyone else. If whoever had blocked Rina—the traitor—knew I'd heard that thought and came after me . . . but no. Tristan didn't hear what I heard. And I recognized the familiar scent in the front room.

"Owen," Tristan and I both said as my protector appeared in the open doorway to the bedroom.

"At your service," he said. "Is everything okay?"

"Do they know anything?" Tristan asked.

Owen shook his head. "Sophia told them Alexis gets all whacked out about the next daughter and she probably needed air." He peered at me and then Tristan. "Well, not those exact words. I think she said, 'especially sensitive.' So . . . what happened?"

Tristan studied my face and must have seen I wanted to tell him first. Alone. "Guard the door," he told Owen. "Just in case."

Owen narrowed his eyes for a brief moment, but then he shrugged and disappeared to stand outside the door to our suite. Tristan turned back to me.

"So?" he asked.

I stared at him, suddenly unable to say it. Unable to put the words in the right order. Unable to believe them. Owen's appearance and the threat of the traitor had been enough to distract me from the urgency of the actual words. From the reality of hearing them.

"Tristan . . ." I started. I swallowed, hard, my throat dry and tight. "We . . . we might already have . . . a daughter."

He lifted an eyebrow. "Explain."

I recalled the chaos of the meeting, everyone yelling aloud and in their heads and how I heard all of it. The energy and urgency returned in full force. I sprang to my feet and paced while rehashing for him everything I'd heard . . . including how it had sounded as though we already had a daughter and someone kept her hidden from us. By the time I finished, he was shaking his head.

"That's absurd, Alexis. No one on the council would have done that."

I stopped pacing and put my hands on my hips.

"I know what I heard. Would you ever think anyone on the council would be a traitor in the first place? Of course not! But that's exactly why I was listening."

"But hiding a daughter . . . what would be the point?"

"You tell me. You're the great seer of the best solution to everything."

He leaned his elbows on his knees and pressed his hands together, resting his chin on the steeple his fingers formed. He sat silently for a moment, his eyes far off as he considered the options.

"I guess it would make sense," he finally said, "to keep her safe. If the Amadis weren't aware of her, then the Daemoni wouldn't be either. But it's impossible. Rina and Sophia would know."

He was right. Although I'd had a difficult time giving birth to Dorian, actually passed out for part of it, Mom and Rina had been present the whole time. I thought they had been, anyway.

"What if they stepped out of the room while I was out of it? What if someone else flashed in there?"

Tristan shook his head again. "They would have been too protective. They wouldn't have left you. And that's not entirely what I meant. Rina would have heard someone's thoughts about it. Sophia would have felt the truth there was already a daughter."

I paced again as I considered this and stopped in front of Tristan. "But if they can block Rina's telepathy, they might be able to block Mom's power, too."

We stared into each other's eyes as we continued to consider this possibility. Mine filled with tears. *What if I do have a daughter?* She'd been out there for seven years without me, someone else raising her. Did she know about us—her parents, her twin brother? Who took care of her? How did they treat her? *Do they love her?* The tears fell.

Tristan took my hands and pulled me into his arms. I fell into his lap. "Don't cry, Lexi. If it's even true, it's good news. But we don't know if it's true. His thought wasn't that specific, right?"

"Hers," I corrected.

"Hers what?"

"*Her* thought. It was a female voice."

"Well, that narrows it down. The only female mages on the council are Minh, Galina and Charlotte."

"It definitely wasn't Charlotte."

"I wouldn't expect so. Of course, I wouldn't expect any of this. You're sure that's what you heard?" His hazel eyes pierced into mine as if he expected I'd suddenly give a different answer.

"Yes. 'Of course Alexis won't have a daughter. We already have the girl. We just need to keep her hidden . . .' And then the thought trailed off."

"Trailed off or you lost it?"

I considered his question and realized I wasn't exactly sure. I'd been quite upset by then, so I may not have heard the rest.

"I don't know," I admitted.

"So maybe there was more . . . something that explains it better."

"And what could that be? It sounds pretty clear to me."

Tristan blew out a heavy breath of frustration. He had no answer.

"What if she's out there, Tristan? What if we have a daughter after all this time?"

He squeezed me tighter against him. "Then we find her."

I nodded. *Yes, we would certainly find her.*

Though Mom, Rina and Solomon were among the most graceful people on the planet, I could hear the whispers of their footsteps coming down the hall. The meeting must have ended. There was a soft knock on the front door of our suite, then they all, along with Owen, entered. I quickly moved out of Tristan's lap to sit in the middle of the bed against the pillows. Mom and Rina sat next to me, on the other side from Tristan, and Solomon and Owen stood at the end.

Rina took my hand. "What did you hear, my darling?"

I inhaled deeply and blew it out slowly. Then I told them.

"That's ridiculous!" Mom said.

"Impossible," Rina added. "We would know."

Tristan and I explained all the reasoning we'd already considered.

"We were there for the entire birth," Rina said. "No one else was close."

"You're absolutely sure?" I asked. "Not even a brief moment, when someone could have flashed in and out?"

"We would figure out you'd had another baby, though," Mom said. "And it would have to be longer than a moment. Long enough for you to give birth and them to cut the cord and then flash—*with* someone in their arms, which only Tristan can do—without Rina or me knowing."

"I also had the house shielded," Owen added. "There's no one powerful enough to break my shields . . . except maybe sorcerers. *Maybe.*"

Solomon rocked back on his heels. "We have no sorcerers, so it would have to be Daemoni."

Everyone fell silent. I guess because I was allowed to be ignorant, I asked the question they all had to be thinking.

"Could there be Daemoni on the council?"

Everyone stared at me as if I were crazy. Okay, maybe they weren't thinking the same thing.

"Of course not," Rina finally said. "We all have senses for Daemoni."

"It would mean they infiltrated us over seven years ago, which is impossible," Solomon said. He crossed his arms over his broad chest. "They would have exposed themselves by now. They don't have that kind of self-control."

"So if it's not Daemoni, it must be Amadis," I said. "And it's not just the video. There's a girl . . . possibly my daughter."

Rina's fingers picked at something invisible on her dress. She shook her head slowly. "I do not understand why or how this would happen. The Daemoni have never succeeded in killing the youngest daughter. Why would anyone think this daughter would need more protection than usual?"

"And why would they do it without the matriarch's knowledge?" Solomon demanded. "If there is reason to think this daughter's life is in more danger than usual, why wouldn't they tell their leader?"

Mom shifted toward me. "Honey, are you sure that's what you heard? Are you sure that's his exact thought?"

"*Her* thought," I said, and Tristan explained it had to have been Minh or Galina.

Mom's shoulders relaxed as she let out a breath she may have been holding since I first broke the news. Solomon dropped his arms to his sides. And Rina laughed. I think it was the first time I ever heard her laugh.

"That cannot be right," she said, a new, almost joyful tone to her voice. "Their thoughts are always completely clear to me. I know what they are thinking before they do. They have no desire to block me, even if they could. It cannot possibly be them."

"Charlotte is the only other female Mage," Tristan pointed out.

Owen leaned forward and glared at us. "If you think—"

Tristan held up his hand, shaking his head. "Of course not, Owen."

"Your family is like our own," Rina said.

"It definitely wasn't Charlotte," I said. "I already know her voice well enough. Is it possible for someone else to block you, Rina? A Were or a vampire?"

She shook her head. "They do not have enough magic. Even as a full-blooded mage, they would have to be very powerful." She took my hands into hers and beheld me with wide, brown eyes. "I think we must have a misunderstanding, Alexis. I am sorry to have put you through this."

"What do you mean?" I asked, fearing I already knew.

"I put too much pressure on you, darling. You must be exhausted from all of the recent events and the travel, and I understand this adjustment is overwhelming. You must not have heard everything or the thoughts must have come through distorted. Based on who it could have been and what you thought you heard . . . it is impossible." She patted my hands. "I am sorry. I asked too much of you too soon."

"You don't believe me?" I blurted, my voice rising with anger and frustration.

"I do not believe what you think you heard."

"You're calling me a *liar*?"

"I am sorry. I—"

"What the hell? Why did you ask me to listen if you won't believe what I tell you?"

~ 44 ~

"Alexis," Mom said in a one-word warning.

I bounded off the bed and spun to face them all. "I don't understand! I didn't even want to listen, but you all thought this was such a great idea. There was no point to it if you won't believe what I say!"

"I thought I would be able to listen to you," Rina said. "I thought I would hear what you heard. But you have erected a very strong, effective shield, blocking me from entering your mind. I must shout your name to capture your attention."

I inhaled a deep breath, trying to calm myself. At least I knew why she seemed to be yelling in my head all the time. "Are you sure it's not part of the traitor's block? Maybe she kept you out of my head, too."

Rina pursed her lips. "I felt it at the breakfast table. It is you, darling."

"Well, that's good then. At least it means I can't broadcast my thoughts and expose our secret. So I guess you'll just have to believe me."

Rina's gaze broke away, and I knew then it didn't matter what I said. She trusted her council members—the very people she asked me to spy on—more than she trusted me.

"Again, I am sorry to have put you through this," she said, rising to her feet. "We will work together to strengthen your gift and your control."

I blew out an exasperated breath and turned my back to her, trying not to lash out with the words that nearly choked me. I wanted to tell her how much I hated this stupid gift, how much I hated her for putting me through that, how everyone could go to hell for all I cared.

"I don't see the point if you won't believe me," I muttered instead. "It'll be a waste of time and energy."

Nobody said anything at first. The only sound came from

the open balcony door—birds singing in the distance and a breeze swishing the sheer curtain against the stone floor. A small hand landed on my shoulder.

"Alexis—" Rina started.

"Just leave me alone," I said, shrugging her off. Her hand fell away.

"I *am* sorry. I hope you will change your mind about working with me. It will not be a waste." Her words were followed by two faint popping sounds.

When I turned, she and Solomon were gone. Tristan and Owen stared at the wall or floor, doing everything possible not to look at me. As if I might go off on them, too, if they muttered a sigh or dared to glance my way. Mom scowled at me, her disappointment clear in her stormy eyes.

"You don't believe me either." It wasn't a question. Her expression said it all.

"I feel the truth you heard what you did, but I believe what you heard doesn't mean what you think it does."

I returned her scowl. "A convoluted way to say you don't believe me."

"Alexis," she said, "you are an Amadis daughter. You have—"

"*Really?* You're going to lecture me about responsibilities now? I did what you asked me to do, even when I didn't want to, and for no reason. I don't want to hear about responsibilities!" I glared at her but she had no response. "Just go. Please. I need to be alone."

She pressed her lips together, then nodded before slipping out the door. Owen followed her without a word.

As soon as they left the suite, I noticed a considerable difference in my head. It was like pulling a cotton ball out of my ear, but more like a big handful of it out of my head—my mind immediately felt lighter and more open. Although I had this telepathic gift for barely a week, for most of that time I'd been with only Tristan and sometimes Owen. I realized now how used to them I'd become—I could easily tune their thoughts out without having to think about it at all. When there were others nearby, that one part of my brain had to work harder to hold my mental wall up. And when there were several people or a crowd, it took immense effort, especially when under stress, such as at the council meeting.

If I wanted a clear head, I'd have to spend the rest of my life with Tristan and Dorian and forget the rest of the world. An attractive idea at the moment.

Tristan opened his arms to me and I rushed into them. He held me tightly, his muscles hard underneath my body. I leaned my chin on his shoulder and he stroked my hair as we held each other in silence.

"They'll come around," he finally said. "They just need to get used to the idea of there being a traitor. It must be difficult for them to wrap their heads around it."

"I can see that with Owen. He has such a strong belief in the Amadis. But my mom? She's never trusted the council, but now she's defending them."

"I'm not so sure about that. I think she might already believe you. I imagine she's trying to be more objective, though, now that she's taking her place as second."

I supposed that sounded reasonable. Mom took her responsibilities seriously, especially to the Amadis. After all, she kept secrets from me my entire life because of her loyalty to the Amadis, regardless of how much she did or didn't trust them.

I pulled away to see Tristan's face. "So you believe me?"

"Of course."

"Because you really do or because you're supporting your wife?"

He rolled his eyes. "Rina asked you to listen for a reason. We already knew the betrayal was a strong possibility—we just didn't know who or how. There's no reason for me *not* to believe you. I hope there's more to it, but I trust you."

"So what are we going to do?"

"You work with Rina, learn better control and try listening again."

With a sigh, I pulled away and walked over to the balcony, noting how things changed so quickly since standing in the same place only a few hours ago.

"So you think I'll 'hear' better—differently—if I have better control. You really don't believe me, do you?"

Tristan came up behind me and his arms encircled me. His breath fluttered my hair.

"Of course I do, my love, but if you can listen again, maybe you can find out more. Something we can use to convince Rina—"

"She'll never believe me, Tristan. Not when she doesn't *want* to hear it. And I don't think I can stand to be in the same room with her."

"But if you don't master your power, we may never know the truth. Even if Rina doesn't want to believe you, we can find out on our own if we have more information."

"You mean, go searching for this girl?"

"If she exists, definitely. If we have a daughter out there, we will find her."

I leaned against him, suddenly feeling exhausted, the strain of the last several days, the lack of sleep and last night's tossing-and-turning catching up with me. I had no energy to think about this new idea of his—a reason to work on my power. Or maybe I didn't *want* to think about it, being as stubborn as Rina because I didn't want to see her at the moment.

"In the meantime . . ." He kissed my ear and neck.

"We keep trying."

"Exactly," he murmured.

"But not now."

His lips moved against my cheek. "Why not? Dorian probably doesn't know we're out of the meeting yet."

"Honestly, because I'm so exhausted I might actually fall asleep in the middle of it."

He recoiled and gave me a dramatically pained face. "I can't believe you said that. You'd really—"

"No, probably not," I said with a laugh. His expression didn't change. "Okay, definitely not. I would not fall asleep in the middle of it. But I *am* really tired. Besides, I can't do that again. Not after last night."

"Mmm . . . I'll have you convinced by tonight," he promised, moving his mouth along my jaw. And I thought he might be right—he could be quite persuasive. "But I guess Dorian's been told we're back."

Two seconds later, our son burst through the door.

After we settled him down, we spent a few moments of quiet family time for the first time ever. Dorian told us, again, about the airplane trips from Atlanta, where he, Mom and I had been living up until a week ago, to Athens, and then the boat ride to the Amadis Island. Then he updated us on all the fun things he'd been doing in the days before we arrived. Based on his stories, Rina, Mom and the others protected the Amadis secrets—he seemed to know nothing about the magic of the island, the village or that the people around him were any different than Normans.

The quiet time lasted about fifteen minutes. In most regards, he was a normal six, nearly seven, year old boy, and fifteen minutes was about as long as he could sit still. We steered the conversation to his birthday, less than two weeks away, but he grew too excited as he told us what he wanted—a puppy and a dog and a puppy and, oh yeah, a dog. He didn't care what kind and bounced all over the room as he rattled off every possible color. Finally, I urged Tristan to take him out and do some father-son bonding. They deserved it. They needed it.

As I watched them leave the suite, Dorian's tiny hand wrapped in Tristan's large one, happiness surged inside me. But, instantly feeling completely alone, I started wondering what it would be like to see the boys leaving to do their boy things and to still have a daughter here with me, to do girl things. *What would we do? Paint our nails? Bake brownies?* I had a feeling a daughter of ours—the so-called ultimate warrior and fierce protector—wouldn't be interested in those girlie things. She would probably be more of a tomboy, wanting to go off with her dad and brother. *I could do that, too.* Either way, I'd be happy, to have my family . . . my complete family.

I fell onto the bed, stared at the blue gossamer canopy, which someone must have repaired after last night's escapades with Tristan that now felt like years ago, and mentally recapped the council meeting. The end had been so emotionally violent. Could Rina and Mom be right? Did I twist the thoughts, jumbling them because of my inexperience? Once again, though, the traitor's thought came loud and clear in my head, as if I were hearing it again. *No, I know what I heard.* Maybe the traitor was right—Mom and Rina relied too much on their feelings and couldn't see what was right in front of them. After all, they'd been so sure I'd been pregnant with twins, based on their *feelings.* They'd even had me convinced, but I obviously hadn't been. *Or had I?* As I drifted off to sleep, I didn't know what or *whom* to believe anymore.

❦

I awoke several hours later, the late afternoon sun casting an orange glow over the cypress trees outside our window. I felt like a brand-new person, which was exactly what sleep did for us—it completely regenerated our cells. I took a bath in a marble tub large enough for a party . . . or a lot of fun for just two, which made me wonder where Tristan was.

He and Dorian were not upstairs in our wing, so I meandered down the stone steps to the main level of the mansion. I refused to use the telepathy to find anyone and instead used regular old Norman thinking. The sitting room and the kitchen made the most sense for where they might be and the sitting room was closer. I heard someone moving about inside and headed there first.

As soon as I entered, I regretted it. I didn't find Tristan and Dorian. Rather, Rina stood by the coffee table, holding Tristan's and my history books. I didn't want to talk to her yet, but I didn't want her to take our books, either.

"I'm sorry," I muttered, moving into the room and reaching my hand out for the books. "I didn't mean to leave them lying around. I can take them—"

"Oh, no, darling. They must be returned to the Sacred Archives."

"We don't get to keep them?"

"I am sorry, dear, but as your stories continue, they can only be written in the Sacred Archives."

I silenced a growl building in my chest. "But I'm not done reading the past."

"You have read the whole thing, no?"

"Well, yeah, but that's not what I mean. I want to study it more."

She shifted the books into one arm and lifted her free hand to tap my temple with a finger. "If you have read its entirety, its entirety rests in there."

I scowled, not understanding.

"Look into your own mind, Alexis. It is all in there."

Then I realized what she meant. I didn't simply *remember* what I'd read last night enough to summarize, but I could actually visualize the entire contents of my history book, word-for-word. *Wicked.*

"Rina?"

She was headed out the door and turned in the doorway. "Yes, darling?"

I hesitated, annoyed at all the "darlings." How could she be so warm after accusing me of being a liar? I thought about quelling my curiosity, but the question came out before I could stop it. "Who writes the books?"

The corners of her mouth turned up in a slight smile. "It is the secret of the Sacred Archives, but I imagine the Angels write them."

"Oh." I said no more. She didn't believe me earlier, so I definitely didn't mention what I'd been thinking.

"I am sure you are hungry, no? I will have food brought to you here." She disappeared before I could say anything.

I gnawed on my bottom lip as I walked the perimeter of the sitting room. Like the rest of the mansion, the walls were made of stone; only a single, narrow window interrupted it, showing the darkened sky and grounds. A blazing fire in the hearth produced the only light, casting dancing shadows on the walls from the antique furniture and filling the room with a relaxing, woody scent. Besides the family vine hanging, which covered the entire wall it hung on, other tapestries decorated the remaining walls. They appeared to be old, yet well kept, each depicting a glimpse into ancient battles between angels and demons.

When I turned around from one, I sucked in a breath. The coffee table displayed a spread of food. I'd never heard anyone bring it and Rina had only been gone a few minutes.

"Ophelia?" I asked—she couldn't have been far already. The old witch *popped* right in front of me.

"Yes, Ms. Alexis?"

I'd expected her to come through the door, and she surprised me with her sudden appearance. "Um . . . where does all this food come from? I mean, is it brought in by boat every day or what?"

She nodded her gray head. "We grow some on the island, but most of it is brought in as regular deliveries."

"Who knows the island is here?"

"Only the Amadis. The Daemoni have an inkling of its location, but cannot see it for themselves."

"Because of the shield?"

"Shields protect. Cloaks make the item or area invisible," she clarified.

"Right. Must be a powerful shield and cloak," I said, thinking of the size of the island.

"Oh, yes. Mr. Martin is more powerful than any of us."

"Owen's dad? He powers the shield?"

"Yes, Ms. Alexis. He is our strongest mage by far and no one but himself can break his shields. Not even the Daemoni. The rest of us mages keep it reinforced, especially when he is off-island."

The tight belt of stress constricting my chest loosened a notch. Knowing Martin's shield protected us and kept the Daemoni out—kept them from taking my son—was a bit of a relief. I gave Ophelia a small smile.

"Thank you, Ophelia."

She curtsied. "Certainly, Ms. Alexis. Is there anything else?"

"No—wait. Do you know where Tristan and Dorian are?"

"They finished their evening meal a few minutes ago. I believe Mr. Tristan took Mr. Dorian upstairs for a bath."

I thought about joining them, but the spread of food beckoned me. Father and son needed their time together anyway, and I'd see Dorian before bed. So I sat on one of the old couches, its leather soft and supple from age, and began loading a plate with sausage, cheese, grapes, apple slices and bread that was crusty on the outside and soft and warm in its center. Except for the couple bites of croissant and strawberry at breakfast, I couldn't remember the last time I'd eaten, and I devoured two plates full, along with two glasses of red wine. Then I lay on the couch, closed my eyes and perused the mental pages of my book.

I found no mention of my daughter or of a girl. Not that I'd expected to—I'd studied the book for hours last night. I would have remembered anything about a daughter, but the book only mentioned the lack of one. If it had been written by the Angels, messengers of God, the story surely would have mentioned my daughter if she truly existed. Right? Why wouldn't they include her in the book or on the vine?

Which meant I either misheard at today's meeting or I didn't get the full story. Perhaps Mom and Rina were right. And even if they weren't, even if I really did hear Tristan and I already had a daughter, we had no information to use to search for her. If I wanted answers—

"I've been looking for you." Tristan's lovely voice broke into my thoughts. I opened my eyes as he lifted my legs to sit on the couch with me and then dropped them to drape over his lap.

I sat halfway up. "Is Dorian with you?"

"He's in bed."

"So early?"

"It's not that early. It's nearly ten."

I hadn't realized I'd been lying on the couch, lost in my own mind, for so long. My heart sank as I sagged back against the cushions. "I miss him so much and I've barely spent any time with him since we've been here."

"I think I wiped him out. He crashed pretty quickly."

"I'm glad you at least got to spend time with him. He's great, isn't he?"

"The best." Tristan smiled proudly. "He loves me."

"Of course he does. What'd you expect?"

"We're practically strangers. I suppose I thought he'd be more leery or shy."

"Hmph. Dorian is afraid of nothing. Besides, I've been telling him stories about you since he was born. He's missed you, too."

"Thank you," Tristan murmured. He bent over and brushed his lips across mine. "So what were you thinking so hard about?"

I didn't answer him at first, still sorting out my thoughts, and when I did, it wasn't exactly what I'd been thinking. "You flashed with me again. At the council meeting. You're getting pretty good at that."

Leading in a flash and following someone's flash trail were fairly common, but flashing with someone else was supposed to be impossible. Tristan had done it with me four times in the last week.

He shrugged. "You obviously needed help. Why didn't you flash yourself?"

I sighed and dropped my face into my hands.

"I . . . forgot . . . that I could," I mumbled, feeling like an idiot. I waited for his chuckle, but it never came. I looked up at him expectantly.

"I think you had your mind on something else," he said and I nodded. "But you do need a lot of training. You can't forget things like that. Flashing is paramount to your survival."

"I know, but . . ." I didn't finish, not able to excuse my own failure.

"That's what you were thinking about when I came in?"

I sighed again. "Sort of. I was thinking about how much I don't know. How much I have to learn. Including how to use this damn power I've been given."

"So you'll work with Rina after all?"

"I haven't decided yet. I'm still pretty mad at her."

"Mmm." His hand brushed tingles along my shin and calf and his jaw muscle twitched as he seemed to be lost in thought for a minute. "You don't really have much choice."

"What do you mean?"

"We're not leaving this island until you're trained, and Rina's the only one who can help you with this particular power."

I opened my mouth but he cut me off.

"*And* we need you to listen to the council again if we want the information we need to find this girl."

I shut my mouth. He knew how to get to me.

He took me to bed, and I lay in his arms, unable to sleep after putting the brakes on sex. Although Rina said my shield was nice and tight, I wasn't about to risk that humiliation again. *Another reason to learn control.*

I groaned internally and rolled over on my side. *Why me? Of all the powers a daughter can be given, why did I get this one?*

I wanted to ignore this gift. To squash it. To pretend it didn't exist until it disintegrated into nothing from lack of use. It caused way too many problems and was completely worthless since I couldn't use it properly. Which, of course, was exactly the problem.

Tristan was right. I had no choice. I couldn't return or exchange the power or re-gift it to someone else. The Angels had given it to me for a reason and my job was to make the most of it. As much I hated it, I'd better learn to control it and use it. I blew out a breath of resignation and closed my eyes.

Rina? I silently called out, hoping she wasn't asleep yet.

Chapter 4

The next morning, Ophelia served us breakfast again, which included a note from Rina that Tristan and I were to meet Charlotte in the gym and Rina and I would work together afterwards.

"I wonder what we're doing with Char," I said.

"Who's Char?" Dorian asked.

"Uncle Owen's mom," I said.

Dorian's mouth dropped open, as if I'd just told him Owen was with a pink elephant in a tutu. "Uncle Owen has a *mom*?"

"Of course, silly. Everyone has a mom."

"She has some skills to teach you, I do believe," Tristan said.

"Sounds boring." Dorian crinkled his nose. "I'm gonna go play games. Uncle Owen said we got a new Harry Potter game."

He gave Tristan a hug, smacked a wet kiss on my cheek and ran off.

"Games?" Tristan asked.

"If there's a computer anywhere in this mansion, Dorian would find it and all the games on it, too. Kind of like you and your toys," I said, then something occurred to me. I couldn't believe, being a writer and usually tied to my laptop, I hadn't thought about it before. "*Are* there computers here?"

"Of course. In the media room."

My brows furrowed with another thought. "How do they run? And how come I just now realized I haven't seen any electricity since we've been here? I'm a disgrace to my generation."

Tristan chuckled. "The island does that to you. Especially this mansion. You feel like you've stepped into another world and another time."

"It feels so . . . natural, though." This place—this world—seemed to become stranger every time I turned around, yet it still felt like . . . home, I supposed. Almost as though I belonged here. Almost, but not quite.

"There's a power plant on the island. Fueled by magic, of course."

"Of course," I muttered.

"Rina prefers to keep things old-fashioned." Tristan rose from the table and held his hand out for mine. "You ready?"

I placed my hand in his, and he led the way. We left the mansion through the front door and walked along a path lined with sixty-foot-tall cypress trees and a series of ancient stone arches overhead.

"I can't believe this place is so old," I said, awed by the huge arches. The island and the mansion had been a part of the Amadis since the beginning.

"A couple of millennia," Tristan said. "About as old as anything in Greece."

"It's been well taken care of." I ran my hand along the smooth marble of one of the arches as we passed through.

"It's protected by the Otherworld. This place—the mansion and the whole island—is practically sacred."

We turned off the main path and down a narrower one through the trees that led to a short, stout building. The two-story stone structure was a miniature replica of the huge mansion, bigger than Mom's cottage in Cape Heron had been, but smaller than our beach house in the Keys. The wooden door stood ajar.

Tristan led me into a room that took up nearly the whole building. The walls and hardwood floor were bare and a grid of wooden beams stretched overhead where a second floor would have been, with the roof far above the beams. The grid was multi-dimensional—the beams weren't level with each other but set at different heights. Sunrays streamed in through open skylights and created an interesting pattern of shadows on the floor.

"I'm in here," Charlotte called from our right.

We followed her voice into a small area near the door and my jaw dropped. Weapons of every kind imaginable except firepower lined the walls and floor—short knives, daggers, curved sabers, long swords, stars, chains, axes and other things I had no names for.

"No guns?" I asked, trying to hide my bewilderment.

"Guns are pretty useless in our world," Charlotte said. Instead of the leather of yesterday, she wore a tight black tank, black spandex pants and black boots, and her blond hair was pulled into a ponytail. And she was still intimidating. "Unless you're were-hunting, which is outlawed for the Amadis. Remember: our goal is not to kill unless there is no hope or if it's absolutely necessary to protect yourself or someone else."

Her blue eyes traveled up and down my body as though sizing me up, and then she wrote something on a clipboard.

"These are practice weapons," she said, casually waving her hand in the air. "Sophia put me in charge of training you. We'll figure out your strengths before deciding on your weapon of choice."

Ah. Charlotte wanted *to train me.* This was one of her rewards for Mom dragging her onto the council.

"But we have powers. Are they not enough?"

"You always want choices," Charlotte said matter-of-factly.

"Especially with vamps. They're nearly impossible to kill," Tristan added.

I regarded the weapons, intimidated by the number and variety. The idea of actually using them, practice or not, made my stomach lurch. I hated fighting. I hated watching it and I sure as hell hated doing it. I'd already had enough violence in the last week with Vanessa and Tristan and wished I'd never have to fight again.

But I had to be logical, and I knew those weren't my only battles. Apparently, everyone thought I needed to improve my skills, which I couldn't disagree with, although I could think of other training I'd prefer to be doing. Like with my telepathy. Now that I'd decided I wanted to learn how to use it, I was anxious to begin my lessons with Rina.

"So where do we start?" I asked, wanting to get this over with.

Charlotte eyed me again and wrote something on her pad. "We start with hand-to-hand combat."

She flicked her hand and pointed us toward the main space. What had been a bare room only a few minutes ago now held various sized punching bags on stands and hanging from the beams. I glanced down at the sundress and Mom's borrowed cardigan I wore.

"Mom could have warned me," I muttered. "I don't have many clothes that fit, but I do have running wear."

"No worries. You both have training clothes in there." Charlotte pointed to a doorway next to the weapons area. "And you should have new clothes in your suite by the end of the day, by the way."

Tristan and I changed together in the little room that contained only a bench with two piles of clothes on it. I held up a black sports bra and black spandex pants—the only clothes for me—and nearly groaned, until I remembered my new body. Tristan had been given nothing but a pair of loose black pants. With his hair pulled back in a ponytail, he looked as though he belonged in a martial-arts film, ready to fight in a tournament or take on his self-righteous teacher. In other words, he looked delicious.

"I'm supposed to concentrate with you in that?" Tristan asked, his eyes traveling up and down my body. I couldn't help it. I shivered.

"Ditto," I muttered and forced myself to tear my eyes from his very bare, very lickable chest. I contemplated our feet instead. "But no shoes or boots?"

"Not necessary yet," Charlotte answered as we returned to the main room. She stood by a hanging bag. "So, we start small and we'll get as far as we can, while we can. I could be called to the field again at any time. Tristan can always take over for me, but it's easier to have us both here."

"Okay, then let's do it." I had nowhere else to be except with Rina, so the sooner we finished today's training, the sooner I could work with Rina and the sooner I would learn about the mysterious girl.

We started with various punches: jabs, hooks, crosses and uppercuts, as well as martial arts chops and strikes. Tristan demonstrated the moves and Charlotte watched my form.

"Some inaugural meeting for the two of us, huh?" Charlotte asked as I practiced my right hook.

"Hmph," I grunted as my fist slammed into the bag. "Are they always so intense?"

"Martin says they can be. I guess it's better than boring. I could have killed Sophia for making me go to those meetings."

An "I know" almost slipped from my lips, which would have required an explanation, so I simply hummed in agreement.

"I think she did it just so she wouldn't have to be alone with all of them," Char continued as she circled me and the punching bag, eyeing my technique as I threw the punches. "They can get . . . intense, as you said. Especially when it comes to the next daughter."

"So I noticed," I muttered.

"Now practice with your left," she said.

I threw what I thought was a left hook. Tristan said it was more of a jab and showed me the correct way, then put me to work, repeating the move.

"I don't see why they're so uptight about another daughter," Charlotte went on. "If Rina and Sophia say it's going to happen, we need to let it happen when it's supposed to. Otherwise . . ."

I slowed my moves when she didn't finish. "Otherwise what?"

She tapped her finger against her lips. "Well, there's a reason Dorian came by himself, right?"

I stopped my punches and stared at her.

"Charlotte," I said, "do you know Chandra very well?"

"Sure. I often work under her when I'm in India or the surrounding area. Why?"

"She mentioned something about Dorian not going to the Daemoni."

Char pressed her lips together and nodded. "Some people want to believe that. In fact, some think he might even be able to lead the Amadis."

"*What?*" My eyebrows flew up. I glanced at Tristan, but skepticism darkened his eyes.

"Martin has mentioned it, but I don't see how. We've always been a matriarchal society." She shrugged. "It's not my forte and it's pointless to speculate. *My* job, at least for now, is to teach you how to protect yourself. Tristan, let's show her some kicks."

After I practiced a variety of kicks, we moved on to combination moves. At first it was exhilarating, even fun, but eventually it became tedious as they made me practice the same moves over and over again. My body, into the rhythm, did everything on its own, while my mind wandered, thinking about Dorian, the council meeting, the "voices" and what the one said about the girl. Then I thought about Rina and wanting to work with her instead of doing these silly exercises.

"Alexis!" Tristan's bark snapped me out of it. "Pay attention!"

My mind returned to my surroundings. The punching bag I'd been working with swung violently on its chain, its insides bursting out of a huge hole.

"Did *I* do that?" I asked, jumping out of its way as it swung toward me.

"Yes! Because you're not focused." Tristan's angry growl bemused me.

"I'm sorry. I'll fix—"

"The bag's not a problem," Charlotte said, her voice much calmer than Tristan's as she waved her hand. The stuffing sucked back inside the bag and the hole closed itself. "But your lack of concentration is."

"Yes, it *is* a problem," Tristan said. "You have to focus. When you're in the middle of a fight, your mind must be one-hundred-percent directed on what you're doing. You *can't* let it wander."

"But I'm just doing the same hits and kicks over and over—"

"You need to learn the moves. Your muscles must memorize them."

"Which they seem to be doing very well," Charlotte added, more kindly than Tristan's tone, but then her voice became firmer. "But you must be alert and aware at all times, regardless of how mundane the situation seems."

I shook my shoulders and arms out. "I'm sorry. I'll focus more."

Tristan walked away from the punching bags, over to an open area. "Practice on me, not the bags. Maybe then you'll pay attention."

"I *said* I'd focus." I didn't understand why he seemed so upset. You'd think the punching bag might suddenly grow arms and fight back when I wasn't watching.

"I want to see how much strength you're putting into it."

I blew at the hair that had escaped my ponytail and fell in my face. "Fine."

"Do the jab and roundhouse combo," he said. "Full strength."

I did the move several times. He could take my full strength, although his balance faltered more than once.

"Good. You could probably knock out a large man with that kick. But you don't always need to make them unconscious. Sometimes you only want them on the ground. Use less strength."

So I did. Tristan's anger ebbed as we did the moves several times and I controlled my strength.

"Now," Charlotte said, "pretend Tristan is a Norman about to enter danger and you only need to scare him so he'll run away. Hardly any force. Just enough to grab his attention."

I lightened up more, barely striking Tristan with my hand or foot. I continued the moves as long as they kept saying, "Go!" and, as I swung my leg around in what felt like a lazy roundhouse, I wondered how much longer we'd be at this because it really was ridiculous. *Fist fighting? Really? When I could shoot a lightning bolt out of my hand?* This was a waste of time I could be spending with Rina.

The next thing I knew, my leg became trapped and my body suddenly flipped over, my stomach flipping with it. The hand released my leg and two arms caught me right before I hit the ground, breaking my fall. Still, they felt like two bars of steel against my back, knocking the wind out of me. The beams above swam in and out of focus. So did Tristan's face as he laid me on the ground and stood over me, his hands on his knees, his arms braced as he glared down at me.

"I said *harder*," he snarled.

"I didn't hear you." I meant to match his ferocity, but I was still catching my breath.

"Exactly." He turned and walked away.

I forced myself to my feet and found disappointment written all over Charlotte's face.

"If you don't focus, you can easily be taken out," she said, her voice low and calm.

Tristan spun around and suddenly stood in front of me. "In other words, you let your mind wander and you could be *dead*."

"I'm pretty sure, in a real fight, I would be completely focused. This just seems pretty freakin' stupid. As if we'd ever fight this way."

"How did you fight Vanessa?" Tristan asked, his voice still venomous. "Wasn't that hand-to-hand?"

"Of course it was. I didn't have powers then, remember?"

"You can't always rely on your powers!" He whirled again and paced.

"Alexis, you have to be prepared for any situation," Charlotte said. "We're not gods who can go around wielding powers out in the world. Sometimes we go face-to-face, mano-a-mano. Sometimes we use weapons. Sometimes we use our powers. You must know how to handle every situation. You must be prepared."

"Okay, I get it."

Tristan appeared in front of me again, too fast to see him move. "Are you sure? Because that just now, in the real world, would have been the end of you."

"I said I *get* it. Sorry if I have a lot on my mind!"

He opened his mouth, but Charlotte interrupted him.

"I think we've done enough for today," she said.

"I agree!" I stomped to the changing room to retrieve my clothes then stomped out of the building, toward the mansion. Tristan appeared next to me, pacing his strides to mine.

"Lexi," he said, "I'm sorry."

"You should be!"

"I had to get your attention. Your mind—"

"Was elsewhere, I know. You didn't have to throw me on the ground."

"Well, technically, I didn't. I threw you into my arms."

I gave him a sideways glance and saw the smirk I expected. "I sure hope that's not your idea of romantic because if it is—"

He stepped in front of me, cutting me off both verbally and physically. I blew out a breath of exasperation and stared at our feet. He lifted my chin with his fingers to look me in the eye.

"The thought of you fighting scares the hell out of me. If something happens to you . . ." His voice trailed off. He shook his head, as if erasing a horrible thought. "I can't lose you, my love. I *need* you to be prepared for anything."

The pain in his eyes, dimming the gold flecks, engulfed me. My throat worked to swallow the lump in it.

"I'll try harder next time," I murmured. "I'm just anxious to see Rina. If I can get the telepathy thing under control, we can find out about this girl. She and Dorian are all I can think about."

Before Tristan could respond, we were ambushed by a six-year-old. Dorian came out of nowhere, flying into his dad's arms.

"Can we play now?" Dorian asked. Tristan looked at me.

I waved my hand, as if shooing them away. "Go. Have fun."
They took off, Dorian jabbering away.

After a quick shower, I rushed downstairs, picked up on Rina's mind and followed my sense to her. I hadn't realized what I'd done—picked out her "voice" or brain wave or whatever it was—until I raised my hand to knock on the door of her study. I paused to consider that. *I hadn't heard her thoughts, but I knew it was her I was sensing. Maybe . . .*

"Come in, Alexis," Rina called aloud from the other side of the door, interrupting my near epiphany.

I entered and closed the door behind me. Seeing Rina renewed my frustrations, but I pushed them aside. She had her reasons for her behavior, as did I. Besides, she was my grandmother and I didn't have much family. I needed to forgive her. Or at least move on.

"Is this a good time?" I asked.

She put aside whatever she'd been working on and moved, graceful as always, to the sitting area.

"Yes. Learning to control your gift is a priority."

She sat in one of the high-backed chairs, and I sat on the small leather sofa, nervously groping for the non-existent pendant. My hand dropped with a heavy sigh. *Something else to worry about, too.* Tristan had made it clear we needed to recover the pendant from Vanessa. He'd said it couldn't be in the Daemoni's hands.

"Alexis, darling, we face many challenges, but we cannot solve them all at once," Rina said. "But working on your powers is a good first step."

"So, what am I doing wrong?" I blurted out. "It was so easy before, when we were at the beach house. Even with the Daemoni attack and Vanessa and everyone, I could still focus. Now I can barely control myself."

Rina nodded. "You had just gone through the *Ang'dora*. Your power has probably strengthened since, becoming more difficult to control. But, it is really more about your self-confidence. When Tristan was trying to kill you, you knew what you needed to do for him."

I thought about that day, waking up and feeling all-powerful. I'd been so excited to finally be like Tristan, and I *did* believe I could conquer pretty much anything. My confidence had wavered, but not nearly as much as now. The feeling of being an alien, combined with all the problems nearly overwhelming me, weakened my spirit.

"A lack of confidence is understandable," Rina said. "You have been uprooted and replanted in a very strange place. It has been over one hundred years, but I remember well when I was brought to the Amadis and went through the *Ang'dora*. It takes time to become accustomed to it all, especially to your powers."

"I feel like we don't have much time, though. There's so much going on."

"You still measure time with a Norman perspective." She shifted in her chair and folded her hands into her lap. "However, you are right. We have little time regarding the traitor. We must identify him as soon as possible, before any serious damage is done."

So she still didn't hold an ounce of belief in what I heard at the council meeting. She searched for someone else, a "him," and some other way someone was betraying her. If that motivated her to help me sooner rather than later, though, I would let it go.

"So what am I doing wrong?" I asked again.

"Let us focus on what you are doing right first," she said with a small smile. "You still have the wall I taught you to raise?"

"Yes, but barely. It seems to fall so easily anymore."

"Mmm, yes. The wall is . . . how do I say it? It is what you call training wheels on a bicycle, yes? I taught you to envision it as a temporary solution to help you learn control. However, to use this gift to its fullest potential, you will eventually have to stop using the wall."

I hadn't realized I'd been leaning closer to her until now, when I shrank back with anxiety. "But I like the wall," I protested. "It keeps everyone's thoughts away and protects my own from jumping into their heads."

"You are mistaken, Alexis. The wall only keeps others out. You protect your own thoughts. You can only share those if you want to and you are already very good at that."

I fidgeted uncomfortably, but I needed to discuss this with her if I ever wanted to have a sex life again. "And the other night? Every time we have sex?"

Rina lifted a shoulder in a graceful shrug. "There is not much you can do about it. To truly enjoy the moment, you must be willing to completely let go. If you inhibit this part of you, you hinder other parts, too, such as the physical enjoyment."

"So I'm doomed to either no sex, bad sex or letting everyone 'hear' me?"

She sat back in her chair. "I would say that is your decision to make, but truthfully, it is not. You need to be having sex. As often as possible."

If I'd been drinking anything, I would have spewed it in her face. *Did she really say that?*

"I apologize for being so blunt, but we need a daughter. But do not worry. Your thoughts are shielded." She pursed her lips and tilted her head. "In fact, your shield is *too* heavy—it protects your vulnerabilities, but it also inhibits the power of this gift." She paused, rearranged her expression and waved her fingers dismissively. "It will resolve itself on its own, I am sure. In the meantime, let us concentrate on controlling the many voices in your head and eliminating the wall."

My heart jumped. "Already?" I squeaked.

"Not completely. We will practice—you will practice—extensively first. Eventually, you will feel comfortable with letting it go."

I took a deep breath and nodded. "Okay. So how do I practice?"

I explained my usual technique with the black cloud that gave me something to focus on as I opened my mind to others. It worked well when it was only Tristan, Owen and me, but not so much anymore.

"Yes, that is an imperfect way to envision it," Rina agreed. "I expect it is easy with Tristan and Owen because you know their voices so well. You probably do not need that vision with them anymore. You are able to identify their specific mind signatures."

"Their what?"

"Mind signatures. That is what I call them. It is difficult to explain, but if you have felt it, you understand what I mean. It is like a thought current I receive, but I do not actually hear the thought yet."

"Oh! That's kind of how I just found you. I didn't hear your thoughts, but I did pick up your voice or your brain wave or something, and followed it here to your office."

She smiled. "Then you are becoming more familiar with me. You identified my mind signature. What you felt is produced by every brain, and each one is unique. Rather than sending out your cloud, imagine identifying the signature you want and then focus on it until you receive the thoughts. The signatures are already out there. Simply let yourself feel them and decide which one to focus on."

"And I have to let the wall go to feel the signatures."

"Correct. To start with, imagine the wall as a screen, letting only the signatures through, but not the thoughts. Become accustomed to the mind signatures, then learn to find the thoughts behind them, letting only one person's stream of thoughts through the screen at a time. If too many thoughts start flowing through the screen at once, you can solidify the wall. When you are not practicing, you can keep the wall up. You will learn, however, to function almost normally without the wall or screen, letting the signatures . . . hmm, how do I say? . . . float—I suppose that is a good word—around you."

"So how long do I have to practice before I get another chance with the council?"

"The council will not gather again until the coronation ceremony in three months."

Three months! That was too long. *If I had a daughter out there . . .*

"But I will try to provide you with opportunities to be near council members individually before then," Rina added. "I need to know if my interpretation of the Angels' message is correct sooner rather than later. First, however, you need to practice as much as possible."

I promised her I would. This was just as urgent to me as it was to her, although for different reasons.

"Let us start, then." She paused for a moment, her head tilted to the side as if listening for something. "It is only you and me here. Dissolve your wall and make it into a screen."

I stared at her for a long moment, then inhaled a deep breath. *Please be okay. Please be okay.* I so did not want to do this, but the thought of a little girl reminded me I had no choice. With my eyes closed, I imagined the wall as a big, black structure in my mind and visualized the tiniest of holes puncturing it all over. I held my breath, waiting for something to happen, but nothing did. No thoughts from the other side came crashing into my mind. So then I imagined the holes disintegrating the wall even more, into a screen. Still, no one else's thoughts invaded.

"Okay," I said.

"Can you feel my mind signature?"

The visual in my mind was too clear and I tried to actually see a wave of something floating through the screen. I wiped my mind clean of the image and made myself *feel* the screened wall instead, and then feel for Rina's signature as an energy current, just as I had felt it earlier without realizing it. I detected her signature immediately. She must have sensed me.

"Now focus on it and allow yourself to receive my thoughts."

I mentally pulled the signature toward me and her thoughts slowly became defined until I could hear them loud and clear.

"*Very good, Alexis.*"

Next, she explained how to let go of the thoughts and let the signature float. As I practiced this, I realized her signature was no longer the only one nearby.

"I think someone's coming," I said.

Rina smiled and nodded. "Try to focus on the thought and you will identify the owner."

"Solomon," I said as soon as I focused. His low voice rumbled in his head.

"See how his mind signature is different than mine? Become familiar with it."

Recognizing the difference was easy—Solomon's mind signature was as dissimilar to Rina's as I imagined their handwritten signatures would be. With Solomon approaching Rina's door, I excused myself to leave.

"Wait a moment, dear," Rina said. "I think you will want to see this."

Chapter 5

Solomon came through the door, one arm loaded with a stack of newspapers. He handed some to Rina and some to me. The datelines showed yesterday's date. My breath caught as I read the large front-page headline on the top issue:

A.K. EMERSON BELIEVED DEAD IN BOATING ACCIDENT
Divers Searching for Author's Body in Aegean Sea

I fell back onto the couch, feeling as though Tristan had flipped me again. I knew this was the plan—to fake the author's death because I could no longer be A.K. Emerson—but it still caught me by surprise. The words in such large print, official and publicized to the world, drilled the finality of it into my core. *She's really gone.* I never enjoyed playing the role of the wildly successful author—the fame and attention wasn't my thing—so I had actually expected to feel relief at her death. But she was a very real part of me, a very *big* part of me. She had pulled me through my darkest times. Only my writing and Dorian kept me going through the years without Tristan.

After recovering from the initial shock, I skimmed through the article. It reported my trip to Athens, Greece, with a "Jeffrey Wells," who they believed to be the father of my son and new husband, and an explosion of the boat we'd rented for pleasure. Such a tragedy to come, the reporter wrote, when we'd just been reunited. A diving team continued searching for our bodies. Of course, they wouldn't find them, and my guilt surged because they tried so hard. The rest of the article told about my books, their record-breaking sales numbers and speculation of whether the last book of the vampire series would ever be published.

"What *will* happen to the last book?" I wondered aloud.

"Once the commotion of her death diminishes, we will announce that she finished it right before her untimely death, so it will be published," Rina said happily.

"Sales of the whole series will probably break their own records," Solomon said with a grin. "Art is always more attractive after the creator has died."

"I currently am planning a funeral," Rina said, flipping her hand toward her desk. "Some Amadis members in America will masquerade as your family. After the funeral and other formalities, Sophia will contact the publisher."

The moment felt so surreal, Rina speaking about planning a funeral—my funeral, in some ways—with such a matter-of-fact tone. To her, A.K. Emerson was a vehicle, a means to an end. The author's life and death marked an accomplishment for the Amadis. For me, though, her death marked the ending of life as I'd always known it—not just the death of the author, but the death of me as a somewhat normal human being.

I flipped through the other newspapers Solomon had

brought. They were mostly American, from various cities in the States, although a few hailed from major cities throughout the world. AP sourced the article, so they were all the same, as was the photo, a headshot from my last book cover, over a year old. Though I didn't look as old and fat as I had toward the end, right before the *Ang'dora*, the picture made me cringe. I had seriously let myself go over the years, and I appeared to be much older than my real age—more like forty-something—even with the professional touch-up to the photo. I now looked nineteen or twenty, there was life to my eyes and face, and my body was hard and fit.

"At least no one will recognize me as her," I muttered, pointing at the ugly picture. Rina and Solomon chuckled.

I left them to plan my funeral. As I meandered through the mansion, I made my wall into a screen and sought out mind signatures, searching for Tristan and Dorian. The first ones that floated by me were staff members'. As soon as I realized this, I let go of their thoughts, not wanting to invade their privacy. By the time I'd wandered through almost the entire first floor, I was able to feel mind signatures from throughout the mansion. None were Tristan's or Dorian's, but I did identify Mom and Owen. I followed the "currents" to a large room at the end of a short hall.

Unlike the rest of the mansion, which felt primeval with its stone walls, antiques and torches for light, this space reflected the 21st century. Computers lined one wall and flat-screen TVs hung on another, with a theater-style seating area in front of them. I'd found the media room. And I also found Mom and Owen, watching several American news channels at once. It was early morning in the States, so America was just waking up to the news of my probable death. Some of the screens scrolled information across the bottom, while a few showed my picture, apparently the topic of the moment. According to the text running across the bottom, the Greek authorities had officially called off the search for my body.

"Hey, Alexis," Owen said, "you look better dead than you did alive."

Unlike yesterday, when he avoided my eyes as much as I avoided his, he looked at me and grinned. If he could act as though nothing ever happened, so could I.

"Very funny." I punched his arm lightly. Well, I thought it was lightly, but I forgot my new strength. He gave me a face while rubbing his bicep. "I'm sure you will, too, because you can't look any worse."

"Maybe, but at least I never looked that bad," he said, pointing at my picture on one of the screens.

"I can fix that." I held my left hand up, palm facing him. He flinched, then narrowed his eyes. "I may have looked bad then, but I'm quite *shocking* now."

"Ugh," Owen moaned, rolling his eyes.

"That was quite horrible," Mom said. "You're a writer— surely you can do better."

It was, admittedly, a bad pun.

I sat down on the couch next to Mom, as far from Owen as possible. Although I could joke around with him, it still felt odd—almost wrong—just to sit next to him. I hadn't been able to bring myself to tell anyone, not even Tristan—*especially* not Tristan—what else I'd heard at yesterday's meeting: the opinions that I should be with Owen rather than Tristan. The thought was nauseating. Owen was too much like my brother. He was also Tristan's best friend, and I didn't want to think about what this would do to their friendship.

Trying to ignore him, my eyes skimmed over the many TV screens. Some had moved on to other news, but some still had my face plastered on them.

"Kind of weird, huh?" Owen asked.

"Very."

My life had always been strange, but it seemed "weird" had now gone to a completely new level.

"Watch this," Owen said pointing at one of the screens. "It's hilarious."

He waved his finger and the sound switched from another TV to the one he indicated. After watching for a brief moment, I realized the news station was from Atlanta. The reporter spoke off-screen about receiving a tip with my home address as the camera panned out, showing the full length of our street. We could only catch a glimpse of my house through the privacy fence and hedges, but what I did see . . .

"Holy crap! What the hell happened to my house?" My first thought was a Daemoni attack. Last time we'd had to escape, right after our wedding, they had torched our houses and Mom's bookstore. "I thought Rina said to save it."

Owen laughed. "It's cloaked. That's just an illusion."

"Cloaked? An illusion?"

"Your house still stands and we have people staying there," Mom said, "keeping it protected. They're actually using it as a secondary safe house, too. The primary Atlanta house is full, with so many seeking refuge from Daemoni attacks."

"I thought the attacks had stopped."

"The rogue attacks continue, because they can," Mom said. "Enough of them to scare some of our more vulnerable into hiding."

"And Sheree's at the main house, still in detox, so that limits how many others can safely be there," Owen added. "We were lucky the Daemoni didn't find your house before our people got there."

I watched the screen as the camera focused in on the rubble. The reporter ran a continuous commentary about the fire diminishing my house to nothing but a few charred four-by-fours, my probable death and the authorities considering whether it was all a coincidence or foul play. A mystery, I knew, they'd never solve. It was kind of funny, to know the house really stood there and there were people inside. Then a feeling of discomfort poked at me, thinking about strangers sitting in my house, roaming the halls . . . our bedrooms.

"I packed anything important or meaningful before Dorian and I left," Mom said. "It's all been shipped here. We don't really have many personal belongings, especially you. I think you took with you what you really wanted?"

I considered it and nodded. My laptop, Tristan's old bag, Mom and Dorian were most important to me. I hadn't owned many clothes and brought most of them with me to the Keys, so there really wasn't much in the closets or drawers for anyone to pilfer through. What was there, they could have. It still felt strange, though.

"That's what we mean," Owen said, pointing to a screen showing a yellow-bagged body being wheeled out of a home on a gurney. "And that." Another screen displayed pictures of a woman and a man, both in their mid-twenties, side-by-side, and the word "MISSING" labeled across the top in large, bold letters.

"You think those are Daemoni attacks?" I asked.

"Probably," Owen said.

"How do we stop them?"

"We're doing what we can," Mom said. "We have troops out there, but the Daemoni outnumber us. It will probably get worse before it gets better."

"Why?"

"Because they're waiting for you and Tristan. Once you leave the island—and you will have to eventually—they'll be distracted from the Normans."

My stomach tightened into a ball and bile burned my throat. Mom was right, of course. We would have to leave eventually, and Dorian with us, and we'd probably always be under attack. On the other hand, if they weren't chasing us, they kept themselves entertained with innocent people. I jumped to my feet, the need to escape squeezing the breath out of me.

Mom eyed me. "What are you doing?"

"I'm going . . ." Leaving the island was out of the question, but I at least needed to be outside. "I'm going for a run."

"Ah. I'll go with you."

I thought I wanted to be alone but after the first half-mile, I was glad to be with Mom. We hadn't had any one-on-one time since before I went nearly insane with the *Ang'dora*. Besides Tristan, she was still my best friend, and I could talk to her about things I couldn't bring myself to discuss with him. Such as this mess with Owen.

"I thought you didn't like the council, but you agreed with them, didn't you?" I asked as she took us along a path through the woods behind the mansion.

She gave me a questioning look. "Who?"

"At the meeting, there were at least one or two who thought I should be with Owen. You used to think that."

With the grace of a gazelle, Mom hurdled a log lying across the path. I jumped it, too, but surely not as elegantly as she did.

"I admit at one time I thought Owen was safer for you."

"Is that why you wanted him to be my protector? To try to get us together?"

Her eyes cut sideways at me. "You don't miss anything these days, do you? I wondered if you'd caught that meaning from Char."

"I guess my mind's finally in a place where I can pay attention."

"I wanted Owen to be your protector because he's a powerful warlock, possibly the most powerful we have after Martin. I saw that truth the day he was born."

I stopped short for a second with surprise, then blasted forward to catch up with Mom. I had no idea how fast we ran, but I was pretty sure Olympians would hate us. "You've known him that *long*?"

"Since his birth. He's always shown impressive potential. I wouldn't be surprised if he out-powered even Martin one of these days."

"So that's why you and the council thought he'd still be a good mate. Not quite the same as Tristan—"

"But one of our best, yes."

"And you agree with them? You're on their side? I thought you didn't like them."

"I'm not on anyone's side but our own, Alexis." She ran a few paces before continuing. "I don't like the council. Not in general. I don't appreciate how they try to control our lives. Sometimes they forget they're advisors, not the decision makers."

We ducked under a branch and burst through the edge of the trees onto a meadow about a half-mile long and at least half as wide. The other end sloped upwards into a hill. Mom ran for it and I stayed by her side.

"The ones I truly didn't like," she continued, "when you were an infant and they were planning your life—your mate—for you, are mostly the same ones who now think you should be with Owen. They're temperamental and impulsive, either following everyone else's lead or doing whatever suits their best interests at the moment. I don't trust them because I can't feel the truth in their beliefs."

"So they're like all other politicians."

"Basically, yes. But not all of them. And they don't have any final say. That's left to the matriarch. She can't be vetoed or overruled."

"And if they try?"

"No one ever has. As Amadis, they serve—and trust—the matriarch. Their devotion and service to her represents their devotion and service to God. She's ordained to be their leader, and they understand that."

We came to the end of the meadow just before it sloped more sharply upwards and stopped for a break. We'd probably run at least eight miles, by my guess. A white stone building stood at the top of the hill and I realized it was the Council Hall, which meant the village was right on the other side. A figure—Julia, upon closer inspection—rounded the corner of the building and ducked inside a low doorway in the back.

"They don't seem to be so devoted to her now," I said, starting a jog up the hill to see where Julia had gone. If there was someone on the council I specifically didn't trust, it was her. Mom's hand gripped my shoulder and spun me around.

"I admit something's going on," she said, "but we're not going up there."

I opened my mouth to protest.

"No, Alexis. You can't keep running off on your personal whims, as you did when you went to Key West."

"I didn't do that for *me*. I did it to keep Dorian and everyone else safe."

"Honey . . . remember you're not in this by yourself." She glanced again at the Council Hall. "Besides, you're not ready. Not yet."

She turned and took off down the hill, back toward the woods, expecting me to follow. I examined the Council Hall again, curiosity about Julia so strong, I almost couldn't control my feet from heading up there. But Mom was right—I would need my telepathy, and I wasn't nearly ready to try to use it again. I raced across the meadow to catch up with her, and we ran in silence for a while.

"You said something's going on, so do you believe me now?" I finally asked.

She slowed down, and I slowed with her. "I believe *in* you, honey. I know you will eventually be able to use your gift to find out the whole truth."

My jog diminished into a walk. Mom stopped and waited for me to catch up to her. She still didn't completely believe me, but at least she didn't outright deny anything as Rina had.

"And do you still believe in Tristan?" I asked because I really needed her on my side when it came to being with him. Surely Rina would fight for us, but I needed Mom, too.

She swung her arm over my shoulders. "Of course I do, honey. I've always felt the truth about you two, even when I didn't want to admit it. Besides, I can't deny my own gift . . . or the Angels . . . or the *Book of Prophecies & Curses*."

"The book of what?" *Did she really say what I thought she said?*

"Prophecies and curses." Yes, she did. "It holds all the prophecies received by the Amadis and all the curses the Daemoni have made. There's a prophecy about you and Tristan in it."

"Really? Where is it? I want to see it."

"In the Sacred Archives, but—"

"And where is that?"

"In the mansion."

"And the message Rina received about Tristan and me is written in there? How does she get their messages, anyway?"

"They're written in a form only the matriarch can translate. So the message about you and Tristan is between Rina and the Angels. It's not in the *Book of Prophecies & Curses*."

I furrowed my brow, confused. "So the Angels' messages aren't the same as prophecies?"

"Prophecies are messages the Angels *might* have given to others besides the matriarch, usually in a dream or trance.

There's no way to verify if they're real or imagined, though, so we consider them . . . strong suggestions or useful information." She pushed a low branch out of her way and held it back for me. "The Angels' messages, however, are much more direct. They're only delivered when they need us to do something or behave or respond in some way we otherwise would not have. The Angels don't interfere unless they feel they must and then it is only with the matriarch."

"So there was a prophecy *and* a message about Tristan and me?"

She cleared her throat and looked away. "Apparently, some didn't take the prophecy seriously enough, so the Angels made sure we understood."

I suppressed a smile. She'd been among the "some" who didn't take it seriously, all the way up until Tristan and I were practically engaged. We walked past the gym and soon were on the arched path leading to the front of the mansion, but Mom stopped and took my hands into hers, stopping me, too.

"Alexis, you know you can trust Rina and me, even if you feel like you can't trust anyone else?"

I could probably trust her. Rina . . . I still wasn't sure. I nodded anyway.

"Rina will do what's best for the Amadis, but, unless it's absolutely necessary, she won't sacrifice us, her own flesh and blood. It's sometimes hard to believe or accept, but she does act in our best interests, okay?"

I nodded again.

"We each have our place and purpose. I'm learning mine as a support to Rina. You need to learn yours. Remember—this isn't only about you, Tristan and Dorian. You need to keep the big picture in mind."

I nodded a third time.

"So let her handle things the way she needs to. Forget about books and needing to know every little thing. Mind your own business and stay out of trouble. The best thing you can do for you and Tristan and Dorian—for all of us—is to concentrate on yourself and your powers so we can get to the bottom of this."

I understood her point, but I didn't nod this time. I wouldn't make a promise I didn't intend to keep. I would find out everything I could, even if it meant finding and reading this *Book of Prophecies & Curses*.

When she concluded that I wouldn't reply to this last order, she sighed and turned back for the mansion. Just as we separated ways in the foyer, Tristan's voice thundered in my head, the loveliness distorted with anxiety. "*Alexis!*"

I froze in place, focused on Tristan's signature and followed it to his thoughts. Through his mind, I saw Dorian crumpled on the ground, his leg twisted at a sickening angle.

Chapter 6

My heart stuttered. My lungs felt as though an elephant collapsed on my chest.

Where are you?

Tristan glanced at their surroundings, showing me a single mulberry tree among a copse of five cypress trees close to the mansion. I recognized the place—the view from our suite's window—concentrated on it and flashed. I fell to my knees next to Tristan and Dorian's unconscious body.

"What happened?" I cried, gingerly touching Dorian's arm. He began to stir.

Tristan's explanation came out in a flurry. "We were racing back from the beach and I was keeping pace with him and he was right next to me, but then he was gone. As if he had flashed. As soon as I realized it, I turned and he was hitting the ground so fast, *I* couldn't catch him."

That was odd. Tristan's reflexes and speed were faster than anyone's on Earth. Literally. How could Dorian pull such a feat?

I looked down at him and his eyes fluttered open.

"Hey, Mom," he said, watching me with wide hazel eyes. He started to sit up, but I gently held him down.

"Don't move, little man. You're hurt pretty badly." His leg was obviously broken, but I didn't know what else. *His spine?* I panicked at that thought.

"It's just my leg," he said calmly. "Nothing else hurts."

Tristan peeled Dorian's eyelids back and peered into his pupils. He moved his hands along Dorian's body, using his medical background to check for any other injuries.

"It's only his leg," he confirmed.

I stared at the grotesque bend of it.

Can you heal it? I asked Tristan silently, not wanting Dorian to hear me. Any kind of power, including Tristan's ability to heal other people, we had to keep hidden from Dorian.

"*There's no open wound, so only by giving him my blood.*"

I grimaced. Not only was the thought nauseating, but the idea nearly impossible. Unless we could do some kind of transfusion, the only way for Dorian to receive Tristan's blood would be to drink it. How would we get a six-year-old to drink blood? It turned out to be a non-issue. Dorian sat up and, as Tristan and I watched, he twisted his leg into a normal position, then he shook it, as if waking it up from the numbness of a lack of blood flow. We stared at him in shock.

After a few long moments, Dorian stood up and said happily, "I feel better. Wanna see what I did?"

Tristan and I both still sat there staring, amazed Dorian could *heal* himself. Already. And from such a bad injury. Before the *Ang'dora*, I couldn't heal a deep cut on my own, let alone a broken bone.

"NO!" we finally shouted together in a delayed reaction.

It was too late. Dorian bent his knees and sprang upward, landing lithely on a tree branch about fifteen feet above the ground.

"I almost fell last time, so I went too fast and landed really hard," he said from the branch. Then he stepped off.

"Dorian, *NO!*" I shrieked, my heart leaping into my throat. Tristan blurred to where Dorian would land, this time poised to catch him.

But Dorian came down too slowly, completely breaking the law of gravity. He kept his body straight and stiff, his arms held slightly out from his sides as he seemed to *float* toward us. His light blond hair ruffled in the breeze and the gold in his eyes sparkled with excitement. He circled Tristan and then landed softly right next to me.

"It's okay, Mom," he said, beaming. "I've done it lots of times."

It took a conscious effort to close my gaping mouth.

He'd never shown any powers before. He'd learned to walk when most babies learned to scoot or crawl, ran faster than kids twice his age, and consistently tested at least three grade levels above his in all academics. But actual powers? No. I didn't think so, anyway. And he was way too young. Having powers this strong already . . .

Tristan, this is so not good. If he's getting his powers already . . .

According to history, the sons converted to the Daemoni shortly after they began receiving their powers. Usually this didn't happen until they started puberty. Unlike Amadis daughters, who received their powers with the *Ang'dora*, sons changed as they grew from boys into men, receiving their powers gradually, and then they stopped aging in their early twenties. Dorian was a long way off from puberty.

"*I know, my love. But it might just be the power of the island. Maybe he'll lose some when we leave.*"

I clung to that hope. Though the worry that Dorian, like Tristan and me, would be more powerful than usual at an early age was part of the fear constantly gnawing at me, I'd been banking on having a few more years, counting on it more than I realized. We needed that time to come up with a plan to protect him, to keep him with us.

"What are we going to do?" I asked Tristan that night as we lay in bed.

"I have plenty of ideas of what we can do," Tristan said, nuzzling his face against my neck.

I sighed. "You know what I mean. Dorian."

He leaned up on his elbow and tucked a loose strand of hair behind my ear. "You worry too much, my love."

"I can't help it. He's my *son*." I searched his eyes, wondering why they weren't filled with the same fear I felt. "Do you not care?"

"Of course I care!"

"Then how can you be so calm? My stomach rolls every time I think about it."

"I never *stop* thinking about it, trying to figure out a solution—"

"And?" I asked a little too excitedly. "What have you come up with?"

One corner of his mouth curled back in a grimace. He shook his head. "Nothing. There might not be anything we *can* do. It happens to every Amadis son, almost naturally. Or automatically. As if it's inevitable."

"And you tell me not to worry." It wasn't a question. I crossed my arms over my chest and scowled.

"If there's nothing we can do—"

My breath caught. I sat up and stared at him. "You're giving *up*?"

"If there's nothing we can do *right now*," he continued, "worrying only takes energy from realizing the solution."

"There must be something," I said. "Something must cause this . . . this defection, or whatever you call it."

"The Daemoni call the Amadis sons the 'Summoned.' As if they're called over to the other side. But what they do—the Daemoni, with the boys—isn't really forceful. Persuasive, perhaps, but not forceful. When they discover he's gaining powers, they seek him out and explain to him what's happening, that it's more than normal puberty he's going through, and tell him they can help. They tell him about the Amadis and how he'll have no future with them but he will with the Daemoni. The ones I've actually witnessed . . . the boys don't even stop to really think about it. It's as if they were compelled. Almost like they suddenly thought they had no other future. The Daemoni was their only future."

"Wait—did you know Noah?" I'd wanted to ask about Mom's twin since I found out she had one, but I couldn't bring myself to inflict the pain on Mom or Rina by bringing up his name.

Tristan's jaw clenched and his eyes hardened. He lay back on his pillow, not answering me.

"You did, didn't you?" I whispered.

"I did," he finally answered. His voice came out low, full of guilt and disgust with himself. "I was partially responsible for his summoning."

I stared at him as the questions raced through my mind, and I debated whether to ask them. He never talked about his past life, when he was Daemoni. He probably wouldn't answer them anyway. But he surprised me when he started telling me more.

"I created the fire, the explosion that supposedly killed him," he said so quietly that if I had been a Norman, I wouldn't have heard him.

"But he didn't die, right?"

"No, it was a cover. But Rina and Sophia thought he had . . ." He closed his eyes, but the grimace on his face reflected the pain in his heart. "How they can even look at me . . ."

"But they know it didn't kill him, right? Is he still alive?"

"Yes, but that's not the point. I—"

"They obviously forgive you, though. Tristan, I've told you, you need to—"

"Alexis." He opened his eyes and turned on his side to face me. The gold flecks were dim, barely visible, the green dark and muddy. His pain silenced me. "Noah wasn't in the bakery. I didn't know anyone was in there. It was only supposed to *look* like Noah had been there when I started the fire. But . . ."

I swallowed. The one-word question came out silently. *Who?*

"Their father . . . Rina's husband . . . your grandfather. He died. Because of me."

My hand flew to my mouth. Tristan rolled over and stared at the ceiling. I didn't have to enter his mind to know he replayed the scene. I had no idea what to say. I thought of Mom and Rina and how devastated they must have been to lose a father and a husband, a son and a brother all at once. Only the two of them left . . .

"But that's how it's supposed to be," I finally said. "They're Amadis. That's how it is for us. The sons go to the Daemoni. The fathers, at least the Norman ones, die young. All so the daughters can come to the Amadis to serve their purpose. And, like I said, they obviously forgive you."

"Do you see my point then? You just said it yourself."

The sons go to the Daemoni. I did say it myself, as if it's a given. Natural. Unchangeable.

I lay down in the crook of Tristan's arm, my head resting in the soft space right below his shoulder. A heavy blanket of guilt and sorrow lay over us.

"They do forgive you, Tristan," I whispered. "You have to forgive yourself."

He didn't answer. It wasn't the first time I'd had to tell him this. I wanted to cry for him, for Dorian, for Mom and Rina, too. Instead, I changed the subject.

"Does someone in the Daemoni have the power of persuasion, like my mom? Is that how they do it?"

Tristan didn't answer at first, but I felt his body relaxing under mine as his mind shifted gears. The guilt blanket lifted. "Sure, but it doesn't matter who speaks to the boy, whether they have that power or not. That's not what's causing it."

I sat up again and pulled my knees under my chin. "We *have* to figure it out, Tristan. I just got you back. I can't lose him."

"We will, my love. But you really do need to relax." His hand slid up my spine and massaged my neck. "You're so tense. We can't solve this tonight, and as I've said before, we have time. You can't be like this for the next several years."

"You still think we have that long? Even after today?"

"It's hard to say. I guess we have to have faith, don't we? We have to trust, Lex."

I snorted. "Trust is not exactly my strong suit."

"I'm not asking you to trust a stranger. You know who you need to trust for this. Let it go. You *need* to if you're going to do any of us any good." He pulled me down into his arms and nibbled my ear lobe. "I'll take your mind off of it."

I cringed from the tickle—and the total turn-on. "I can't, Tristan. I just . . . can't."

"Again, you're worrying too much." His lips traveled along my jaw. His hand slid along my side, under and up my new pajama top that had magically appeared along with a pile of other clothes in our suite this afternoon.

"Please?" I nearly begged.

"I thought so," he murmured against my chin.

"No . . . I mean . . ." I could barely talk, my heart rate and breath already speeding. I tightened my hand over his arm and pulled it away. "Please. Don't."

"Are you sure?" His lips lightly pressed against each corner of my mouth, then dead center. My resolve melted into the kiss. And he was right—this would take our minds off all our worries. Except one. One that was screaming louder and louder. The horror of the other night.

I placed my hands between us, against his chest. "Yes, I'm sure. I don't want to be. But I am."

He lay down and intertwined our fingers, then pressed the back of my hand against his lips.

"Okay. I can be patient," he said.

"Let's make a deal. If you don't pressure me on this, I'll try to relax about the other things."

"I wouldn't pressure you anyway, my love. I want to relieve you of worry, not add to it." He wrapped his arm around my waist and turned me so my back pressed against his chest—and my butt against his still-hard groin. I sighed. "We'll figure out something. For all of it. Relax, Lex. Get some rest."

I tried to relax under his normally calming touch, tried to melt into his embrace, but what he didn't say, what he knew would only make me feel worse, lurked with everything else in the corners of my mind: no sex meant no baby girl. And we had to try, in case I had completely misunderstood the thoughts about the mysterious girl. How could I ever humiliate myself like that again, though?

❦

Life on the island fell into a routine. While Mom and Rina taught Dorian history and languages in the morning, Tristan and Char taught me how to fight. At least, that was the goal, they said, but, so far, everything was about training my muscles until things became automatic—things such as punches, chops, kicks, handsprings and flips. I'd yet to learn any real fighting or anything about weapons, and I wondered if Tristan purposely prolonged the training process, not wanting me to learn them. He'd said he wanted to prepare me for anything, but he could have fooled me. In the afternoons, Tristan taught Dorian math and science while I practiced my telepathy on anyone who was nearby, then I took over with Dorian, working on his English, reading and grammar. Not exactly a Norman's routine, but regardless of how different the actual tasks were from real life, routine still became mundane.

Dorian's birthday broke up the monotony. Mom and Char threw him a big party—big for him, anyway. With Tristan and me, Mom, Owen, Rina, Solomon, Char, Martin and Ophelia, it was the biggest birthday party Dorian ever had. He didn't care no other children attended. He'd never been one to hang out with kids his own age anyway. In fact, he could barely get along with them.

"Dad said I can get a puppy!" Dorian exclaimed as he ran circles around my chair on the lawn.

I turned toward Tristan to throw him a look of annoyance, but had to fight a smile instead. Wearing jeans, a t-shirt, an apron and a chef's hat and flipping burgers and steaks on the grill, he could have been any Norman dad on a Spring Sunday afternoon. Though, unlike most dads, he looked more delicious than any food and sizzled hotter than any steak. I almost giggled at the thought, giddy with how perfect today felt. Life had been nearly normal like this once not too long ago, before the *Ang'dora*. Yet, without Tristan, it had been incomplete. Now I felt emotionally whole . . . almost. A daughter was the final missing piece.

"Oh, really?" I said.

Tristan grinned and shrugged. "Sure. Why not?"

"I've been good," Dorian said, making a figure eight around Mom and me. "You and Mimi said I could have a dog if I didn't get in another fight before my birthday. Now it's my birthday and I didn't fight."

I laughed.

"You haven't been around any kids to get in a fight with," Mom pointed out.

That didn't matter to Dorian. He practically sang, "I'm getting a dog! I'm getting a dog!"

"We said we'd talk about it," I reminded him. He stopped dead in his tracks, and the big grin turned into the saddest frown I'd ever seen. His bottom lip started to tremble.

"That's what you say when you mean no," he said, his voice quavering.

My heart broke. I didn't want to tell him no. In fact, I wanted to give him anything in the world I could, even the moon, if it meant he'd stay with us and never leave. I wasn't beyond bribing him. But a dog was too impractical for our crazy lives. How could we make such a promise? What was Tristan thinking?

"No, it means we have to wait until we have our own house," I said, taking his hands and pulling him into a hug. "We can't have a dog at Rina's and we don't know when we'll be moving to our own house. But, when we do, if our house is good for a dog, well . . ."

"We'll get you a dog, little man," Tristan said. "We just don't know when. Okay?"

Dorian looked at me and behind me at Tristan, then nodded. Then he was bouncing out of my arms toward Owen, who held the football he'd given Dorian for his birthday. Ophelia took over the grill so Tristan could play with them. Char, Martin, Solomon and Mom joined in the game, and I stood up, too.

"*Alexis.*" Rina's voice rang loudly in my head. I peered over at where she stood, off to the side of the party. Even at a child's birthday party on the lawn, she wore a long, sequined ball gown that sparkled like champagne in the sun. "I would like you to practice with me."

The group had already divvied into teams and started their game. As I headed toward Rina, I hoped Dorian wouldn't get an urge to do something . . . unusual.

Okay. What do you want me to do?

"*Let down your wall. Hear their thoughts. They should be harmless enough while they are playing. How many can you hear at once?*"

I dissolved my wall into a screen and let everyone's mind signatures float in and around me. I latched onto Dorian's thoughts, which were single-minded and simple at the moment. Understanding what Rina meant, that they would be focused on the game and their thoughts wouldn't be threatening or overwhelming, I felt enough courage to try another. Keeping Dorian's thoughts running in one part of my mind, I grabbed onto Tristan's and then Owen's, but I couldn't focus on any of them. Tristan had many thoughts running through his mind at once, and all of them jumbled together with Dorian's and Owen's into a mind-piercing cacophony. I instantly pushed them all away at once without realizing I did so until a deafening silence filled my head. Then came Rina's voice.

"*Take a walk with me,*" she said.

I strode off after her into the woods, toward the beach where Tristan and I had first arrived on the island. We walked several minutes in silence until we hit sand, when Rina stopped and gazed out at the sea. Waves came and went, spraying foam as they crashed their way onto the beach then swirled in their retreat, building up for the next attack.

"You have been practicing and have become stronger," Rina finally said. "Do you feel it?"

"I think so. I mean, I can identify every mind signature of everyone at the mansion—all of us, the staff . . . I can tell when Charlotte comes on the grounds for training."

"How far out can you go?"

I shrugged. "I sense when Charlotte's in the gym before we leave the mansion. But I haven't sensed anyone beyond that. I don't know if I can't or if there just isn't anyone to sense . . . if there's anyone else farther out."

Rina nodded. "You have been confined, I understand. It has been good practice for you, but I believe it is time for you to be among new people, new mind signatures."

"Really? Who? The council?"

"I believe so. Do you think you are ready?"

I didn't know, but I wasn't about to tell her that. This was the moment I'd been waiting for—excitement crackled through my veins. "Yes."

"I will bring only one in at a time, as they are available," she said. I tried to hide my relief. All of them as a group would probably still be too much for me. Rina broke her gaze from the ocean, turned to me and took my hands into hers. Her eyes pierced into mine. "Alexis, you will be among people with whom you are unfamiliar."

"I think I'll be okay. You said my shield was strong, and I haven't had any problems controlling that part."

Rina's lips pressed into a thin line. "No, you have not. I am actually concerned about that. I thought you would have relinquished that shield by now."

My brows furrowed. "What do you mean? I thought it was good."

"Just now, with the others, you had a difficult time listening to more than one, no?"

"Yes," I admitted. "I had Dorian, Tristan and Owen, but all together, all at once, it became too much, and I panicked."

"You closed them off without meaning to, yes?"

My eyes widened. "Yes. How—? Were you in my head?"

Rina shook her head. "No, darling. You would not let me in. You were surrounded by people you know and love, and still, you would not loosen your hold."

"So why is that bad?"

"It means you are not comfortable with your gift yet. You cannot relax enough to use it properly, not even when surrounded by those closest to you. The tight control you keep on it prevents you from using the real power it contains." She freed one of my hands while holding the other as she turned back down the path toward the party. "Do you remember during the battle many years ago, when we were in the cellar of the safe house, and I shared what I saw through others' minds?"

I nodded. How could I forget? It had been the worst day of my life, watching through Rina's mind, which saw through soldiers' eyes, people destroying each other on the battlefield outside the safe house. Tristan even probed straight through one soldier's mind, past Rina's and right into mine to say his last goodbye. Rina had used her gift far beyond any capabilities I had. *Oh! That's it!* The thought hit me as though Rina had actually slapped me. That was the only way to convince her of what I heard from the council—I needed to be able to share with her, let her hear it for herself!

"How do I do that?" I asked.

"It is not too difficult. If you are at ease with your gift, that is. Not only one-on-one with those closest to you, but comfortable in various situations. With strangers, especially in groups, in any kind or size of crowd." We'd returned to the lawn and the barbecue. She stopped walking and made her next words slow and deliberate to ensure I understood. "Comfortable enough to let your shield down without losing control. You will have to *allow* it, Alexis. It is up to you."

With that, Rina slid off her heels, hiked up her sequined gown and ran for the football game.

"You are going down, big man!" she yelled as she plowed into Solomon, who chased Dorian, the ball carrier. Rina tackled the vampire to the ground, but right before they hit, he swung her around so his body would take the impact while she landed on top of him.

Although my mind still chewed on what she meant—"you will have to allow it"—I couldn't help but laugh at them, along with everyone else. Who would have thought with those two? Dorian rolled on the ground with whole-body hysterics. But then I caught something in Martin's eyes that didn't match the grin on his face.

Was that a look of disgust? Or annoyance at the matriarch's behavior?

He caught me watching him and whatever I saw disappeared. His eyes were just as warm as the rest of his face as his smile widened. I returned his grin before realizing I did so.

Chapter 7

Were-birds were freaky. At least the one on the council was. Her name was Robin. No joke. She morphed into a falcon, which she inherited by birth, not by being infected, so her parents knew what they were doing when they named her. *Why do parents do that to their children?* Robin was the first council member I was able to listen to and her thoughts were . . . uh . . . flighty. I felt sorry for her, though. She seemed to have similar problems as mine during sex—she couldn't let herself completely go or she'd turn into a bird. My issues weren't so bad after all. At least I could enjoy it when (if ever again) we were alone. Robin and her husband, who wasn't a Were, had to deal with it every time, feathers flying as she reached her orgasm. I picked this up while Robin sat in Solomon's office waiting for him to begin his meeting with her while I sat in Rina's office to mentally eavesdrop. TMI was the part I hated about my gift.

Guilt for invading her mind and discovering her intimate issues stabbed me in the gut, but the need to find the traitor and the little girl gripped my heart and soul.

Robin was basically useless, though. As Solomon subtly interrogated her about a traitor, her thoughts bounced around, never focusing on anything for long, especially not on the subject of betrayal. She dismissed this idea, her thoughts giving me the impression she knew nothing of the traitor. Her only concern was she hoped I would have a daughter sooner rather than later so she could have her own children—she didn't want to bring young into the world if the Amadis would not be here long enough to protect them. I couldn't help but wonder if she'd give birth or lay eggs.

As the weeks passed, Rina brought in other council members as they were available. I couldn't help but notice that besides Robin—who Tristan thought was likely a test or warm-up for me because Rina knew she'd be harmless—the only others who came in were mages. First there was Shihab, a wizard from Arabia, followed by Jelani, another wizard, from Africa, and Attair, an Arabian warlock. They were all men, so not the person I sought, and Rina realized they weren't who she sought either. With obvious reluctance, she eventually brought in Minh, a Vietnamese witch, and Galina, a female Russian warlock. I understood Rina's trust in them immediately. They couldn't have been more faithful, trusting Rina and standing behind Tristan and me.

The others, however, each had their own opinions about the direction the Amadis should be heading. Shihab and Attair thought I belonged with Owen, and Jelani felt as though Dorian might be able to lead, believing that was the reason he came alone. These were fleeting thoughts, however, especially the one about Dorian. There was nothing to back it up, and I could only chalk it up to wishful thinking.

Frustration and uncertainty battled for dominance within me as time passed with no mention at all of a hidden girl. Not an inkling of a thought. Nothing. Each meeting with this nothingness only solidified Rina's argument that I hadn't heard what I thought I had at the council meeting, and I began to wonder myself. When impatience nearly drove me to madness, Tristan reminded me there was nothing we could do until we had more to go on, because all we had now was a fleeting thought that even I was beginning to doubt was real. The only way to find out was to continue listening to the council members.

If only Rina would have let me.

"It is time to move on," she said one afternoon nearly a month after we'd started as we sat in her study. Galina, the final mage to be interrogated, had just left Solomon's office. "I need to progress with a wider investigation. I need to involve the council."

"But what about the rest of them? Shouldn't I listen to everyone?"

"There is no reason. They cannot be blocking me, and I have discovered nothing from them. I cannot spend anymore time on this."

I dropped my head and stared at my hands in my lap. I couldn't help but agree the last month had been a waste. All she'd needed to do was bring in Galina and Minh, and I would have known immediately they didn't have the voice I'd heard at the council meeting. I could have told her—tried to tell her—but she refused to listen. And now she was giving up, leaving me with no way to access the other council members until the coronation ceremony.

"Have you at least overcome your problem?" she asked me.

I shook my head, then sighed. Her point was clear—why bother with the rest of the council members if I couldn't share it with her? If I couldn't prove anything anyway?

"What's wrong with me, Tristan? Why can't I control this damn shield?" I fell onto the bed and blew out a big breath of frustration.

We'd just returned from an evening walk through the village, which Rina had convinced me to take to practice my power around more people. "The more you practice, the more comfortable you will become," she'd said before I left her office this afternoon. The walk had done nothing to ease my mind, though. Several of the townspeople harbored serious anxiety—I couldn't help but pick up their indignant thoughts that reflected some of the council members'. No, it wasn't a relaxing stroll. And it definitely did nothing for my shield.

I'd shared everything with Tristan, including Rina's disappointment in me and her implication of the last month being a waste of time.

"I don't think she really sees it that way," he said. "You at least had a lot of practice, which is probably why Rina continued with it for so long. If she'd truly thought it a waste, she would have ended it long ago."

"But that's it—it *was* a waste because it didn't do what she'd hoped. It didn't help me get comfortable enough with this power. I'm still strung so tight, and I can't shake the freakin' shield!"

Tristan took my hands and pulled me up into a sitting position. He knelt in front of me and lifted his hand to push my hair back from my face. A small smile played on his luscious lips.

He made his voice low and sexier than ever. "I have an idea about that."

"Oh, really?"

"That first night we were here . . . the last time we really made love—"

I grimaced, humiliation and guilt both tugging at me. "Yeah, I remember."

"Do you think that's when you blocked—"

My eyes widened. "Oh! Maybe you're right! I was so freaked out, I threw up my wall so hard and fast . . ."

His fingers trailed along the side of my face and across my cheek to my lips. "So maybe that's how we take it down."

Before I could think about it for a second, his lips pressed hard against mine, and my body immediately went into hyperdrive. I wanted him so badly, it hurt, and his lips and his touch against my skin heightened the ache until I couldn't stand one more second of not feeling him inside me. And if this would bring down my shield, I would take the chance of humiliation. *This is right. This is what I need. This is what I want!*

Or so I thought.

First I felt the wall crumbling. Felt the mind signatures coming through. Then, when Tristan moved just right and nearly sent me into oblivion, I felt the shield tremble. I knew I needed to let it fall. Let it go. But if I did . . . *No!* My whole body went rigid. So did my mind. I refused to share this intimate moment again. I refused to let go.

Which meant no loss of control, not of the shield or of myself . . . and no orgasm for me, either.

"That . . . was inadequate," Tristan muttered as we spooned afterward.

"I'm sorry. I just . . . couldn't. But at least you—"

"Yes, my love, but it's no fun without you. It's not the same."

My heart sunk. I never thought I'd become one of those women who faked orgasms. Now I understood why they did it. I wanted him to enjoy it, even if I couldn't.

He gave me a squeeze that didn't make me feel any better.

"Did it at least work?" he asked.

I sighed. "No. That was the whole problem. I couldn't bring myself to let go."

"Hmm," he murmured in my ear. "Don't worry. We'll figure something out."

He said that a lot lately. There was a lot to figure out. But for someone who has the best answers, he kept coming up short. Our problems seemed to be too big for even him.

✌

Tristan woke me up at the crack of dawn, wired and excited.

"We have to talk to Rina immediately," he said, pacing along the side of the bed. "Hopefully she hasn't said anything to the council members about a traitor yet and we have to stop her before she does."

I sat up and stretched, the sheet falling into my lap. "What's going on?"

Tristan stopped his pacing and his eyes lingered on my chest, still bare from last night. Then he frowned. I frowned, too, self-consciously pulling the sheet up to cover myself.

"What?" I asked.

"I . . . uh . . . forgot what I was saying." He picked up his shirt from the floor, the one he'd worn yesterday, and tossed it at me. "You're too sexy for my own good."

I smiled to myself as I pulled his shirt on. "Better?"

He grinned beautifully, which made me lose *my* train of thought. "Yes. Thank you. So what was I saying?"

"Um . . . something about Rina, I think."

"Right. She wants to start an investigation outside of the council, which means notifying the members of her message about the traitor. She can't do it yet. I had an idea this morning. She needs to let you have a chance with the rest of them."

"I doubt she'll do it. She wants to move on. I've already wasted her time, remember?"

"We have to convince her, Alexis. You need to do this *before* you lose that protection. Right now, with your shield so tight, you couldn't expose your power if you wanted to." He dropped onto the bed in front of me and held my eyes with his. "There's a lot of discord and not only on the council. Rina *does* need to expand the investigation, but it'd be in her best interest—all of ours—if you can feel out the council members first. Find out who's fueling the fire."

As soon as we finished breakfast, Tristan and I went straight to Rina's office, but she wasn't there. He asked me to mentally find her, but it only took me a moment to notice her mind signature was nowhere in the mansion.

"She's not here, but Char's about to—"

A faint *pop* was followed by Charlotte's appearance at the other end of the hall. Her fists rested on her hips and her eyebrows lifted high.

"Do you plan on training this morning or were you going to ditch me?" she asked.

One hand shot up and her wrist flicked, then something sailed through the air at us. Just as they trained me, I eyed the object, identified it and timed my movement to pluck it safely out of the air. I held the knife by the hilt and stared at the gleaming blade that could have done some serious damage.

"We start weapons training today. Are you coming?"

I tilted my head at Tristan.

"You go," he said. "I'll find Rina. I'll join you as soon as I can."

Tristan disappeared with a *pop*, leaving me to explain his abrupt exit to Charlotte without telling her too much. Not one to waste time, Charlotte flashed to the gym and I followed. With her announcement about weapons training, I expected to find the full gamut of practice weapons spread out in the main training room, but only glinting discs, some star shaped and others round with razor-sharp edges, waited for me. At the other end of the room stood various sized dummies. She taught me the different ways to throw the discs, and I practiced with the dummies, Char correcting my form whenever necessary. Which was embarrassingly often.

"Has Owen taught you everything about mages?" she asked after a while.

I glanced at her as I let go of the disc I was about to throw, and it went wild, bouncing off the stone wall. She lifted an eyebrow.

"It should have cut the stone, not bounce like a rubber ball. You're still not putting the right amount of power into your twist." She clasped my hand in hers and demonstrated—again— how to hold the disc and how to flick my wrist. The motion felt unnatural, but I kept trying. "Sophia says you've been working on learning all about the Amadis, but you haven't asked me anything about mages. So, has Owen told you everything you need to know or do you have questions?"

"Actually, I haven't seen Owen much since we've been here."

She made a noise in her throat. "Yes, I'm afraid Martin has kept him busy."

"Are they close?"

"They used to be, when Owen was a kid. Martin made him stay in school longer than he should have, though. First primary school to learn his ABCs and 123s, then mage school—"

"Mage school?" I interrupted, surprised to hear such a thing existed.

"Of course. The kids have to learn how to use their magic. They start at twelve years old and it's another ten years. Then Martin made Owen attend mainstream high school and college for many more years than necessary so he could learn as much as possible about Normans and their ways. Stefan finally said he'd had enough, that Owen needed more hands-on practice."

"No wonder he hates school so much."

Charlotte sighed. "I think he resents his father, and now Martin is trying to make up for it. It's good for them to have this opportunity to spend some time together."

"Mom says Martin is the most powerful warlock we have and Owen's a close second."

"It's very true, but I'm not too far behind," she said with a wink. "Actually, Martin is surprisingly powerful. I tease him that his parents must have been sorcerers."

"But Owen said his grandparents were all warlocks, converted by Rina's mother."

"The ones he knows of—my parents and Martin's adopted parents."

I threw her a look. "*Adopted?*"

"After completing their conversion to Amadis, they took their first tour of mainstreaming and found a baby by a stream near Martinstown, Ireland. They sensed his powerful magic, even as little as he was. What could they do? They couldn't leave him for Normans to find. And definitely not for the Daemoni. So they took him and raised him as their own."

"So *could* Martin's parents be sorcerers?"

She chuckled. "It would explain a lot, but I highly doubt it. He's not powerful enough to be full-blooded, and sorcerers have become too arrogant to mate with anyone less than themselves. In fact, in my 106 years, I've never heard of any leaving their lairs. As far as I know, it's been centuries since they've reproduced at all."

"No sex for centuries? That sucks for them."

Charlotte laughed. "I guess they're even beyond that. Their earlier children diluted their blood and magic by breeding with Normans, which is probably the worst thing possible in their eyes. I imagine they've given up on everyone by now, including each other, hiding out in their caverns and castles."

"Unless . . ." I remembered some of what Owen had told me on the long flights, while he kept my mind busy, and an idea occurred to me. "Owen did have a chance to tell me a little and he said there are legends that sorcerers can shape-shift, even into other people. So maybe—"

Charlotte's odd expression cut me off. I was about to ask her what was wrong when she shook herself and let out a chuckle that sounded forced before plastering on her normal don't-screw-with-me expression.

"Impossible. Those are just *legends*, Alexis," she said, her voice firm and deliberate as she handed me another disc. "Very *old* legends."

Damn. I'd thought I was onto something.

"So old, only a handful of people still remember them," Tristan said, appearing in the doorway. The deflation of my hope and the surprise of Tristan's appearance caused my hand to slip again right as I threw the disc. Thankfully, he ducked and the blade soared out of the door over his head. "Trying to tell me to get a hair cut?"

"Sorry," I mumbled.

"I guess discs aren't your strong point," Char said, jotting a note on her ever-present clipboard and seemingly happy to change the subject. "No worries, we'll figure out your best weapon. We're just getting started."

❦

"Did you find Rina?" I asked Tristan after training finished and Char disappeared to the village.

"Yes, but it was too late. She's already sent messages to the council members so they can start investigating."

My shoulders sank. Tristan had me convinced this really was the best timing.

"But she did agree to give you a chance with the rest," he said. "She still doesn't believe any of them are the actual traitor, but I was able to convince her that whoever is the traitor is influencing at least some of them and listening would give you valuable experience while freeing her to work on other matters."

And so we resumed our interrogations, er, meetings. We still learned nothing about the hidden girl—in fact, none of the females had the same voice as the one I'd heard at the council meeting. I told Tristan it must be Julia then, because she, Martin and Charlotte were the only ones who hadn't been in for questioning, but Tristan pointed out the most likely possibility: whoever I'd heard before knew about my power and now blocked me or had altered her mental voice enough to throw me off. She would be paranoid and extra cautious, avoiding any thoughts about the girl at all.

We sorted all of the council members into three camps: total support for Tristan and me, whether we had a girl or, somehow, we discovered how Dorian could lead; support for me, but not Tristan, believing Tristan was the traitor and would bring the Amadis down; and the belief that Tristan, Dorian and me, and possibly Rina and Mom, too, were dangerous to the Amadis, and it was time for new leadership. Rina heard many of these thoughts for herself, but she didn't seem too worried, not even about this last one.

"The instigator of such ideas is probably a new convert, not a council member, who has not had time to adjust and understand our structure," she said. "Sometimes they do not appreciate all of our rules and try to change our ways. Eventually, they realize their mistake. I will have Armand investigate our recent additions. We do not need such ideas to spread and take root."

"You don't think it's the traitor denouncing you? You're not worried about a coup or anything?" I asked.

"Alexis, darling, no one can take over the Amadis. The Angels have given our family the responsibility to lead them. Not anybody else. Until they say otherwise, we lead with the power they have given us, trust their instructions and have faith in God's plan."

"But they've sent you a message about a traitor. That has to be who's spreading the idea of new leadership, trying to gain power."

"Which is exactly why the Angels have forewarned us, so that we may identify the perpetrator and—" She peered at me and her eyes sparked as a small smile tugged at the corners of her mouth. "—We squash them down until they understand who rules whom around here."

With such surety as that, I could almost believe she had total control over the situation. Almost.

But then I'd catch a slump in her shoulders. Saw light shadows under her eyes. Heard something in her voice that made her sound unlike herself. The changes in her became a little more apparent as those who didn't support Tristan—and sometimes me—became more vocal about their concerns the closer the coronation ceremony approached.

Did she rely too much on her senses? On the Otherworld? If the Angels' messages were so hard to interpret, how could she be so sure about any of this? The words "prophecies" and "curses" had popped up a few times over the last few weeks wrapped in thoughts about Dorian and my daughter. I couldn't help but wonder if a certain book held clues everyone had forgotten about, including Rina. Maybe it was time to find out for myself.

After a morning of dodging Tristan's excellent swordsman skills while failing epically with my own sword, I hastily showered and did a quick scan for mind signatures in the mansion. Tristan and Dorian had already started their math lesson in Dorian's room, Rina and Solomon were nowhere to be found, perhaps having gone to the village with Mom. I knew that was Mom's plan for the afternoon—to spend some time with Charlotte—but I didn't know if the matriarch ever made an appearance in the village. I didn't care. I saw the opportunity and seized it.

Quietly, I made my way to the hallway leading to Rina's office, figuring the Sacred Archives would be nearby. Only a few doors led off the hallway, all of them closed. I paused next to Rina's to confirm her office was empty. Still feeling no one nearby, I continued to the end of the hall and rounded a corner into another corridor—the mansion was a maze—where a door stood open into a vast area full of books.

I hesitated at the opening and peered inside.

No light source hung from the ceiling or walls or stood on any tables, yet the room . . . *glowed*. As if everything in it gave off some Otherworldly shine that provided a natural light. *This is it. The Sacred Archives.* As soon as I crossed the threshold, the atmosphere completely changed. The air felt different, heavier in a way, but cleaner, too, as if the room wasn't really part of our world. The air smelled as I imagined sunshine would smell. The whole space felt special.

Silvery shelves lined the walls, edge to edge, floor to ceiling, with exactly the right number of books to fill the entire space with no overspill and no open slots. Every book had a pearly white leather binding that gave off a soft glow, contributing to the room's light. I stepped to the closest wall, intending to make my way around the room until I found the book I sought. As soon as I eyed the top shelf, however, my heart sank to the pit of my stomach. I surveyed the rest of the shelves and found the same thing: none of the books had titles imprinted on their spines. How would I ever find the book I wanted among these hundreds of others?

With a tiny bit of hope, I randomly selected a book and pulled it off the shelf. The front cover remained untitled, too, so I opened it, and my heart sank all the way to my feet. No words scrolled across the pages. Only unfamiliar symbols. I flipped through the book and every page was full of these strange graphics, kind of a combination of Oriental and Middle East writing, but less defined. I'd never seen anything exactly like them, although the closest might really be tattoo art. If this was what Rina received in her messages, no wonder she had a hard time interpreting them. I returned that book to its place and selected another from a different shelf, hoping to find something more familiar, but, again, only symbols. *Crap. I just want the* Book of Prophecies & Curses. *I need to see for myself*. . .

A faint noise sounded behind me and I spun around. Completely on its own accord, a book had slid off a shelf and now floated toward me. My breath caught in my throat. The book stopped inches in front of me and simply hung there, in midair, all shiny and beautiful like a ginormous mother-of-pearl. I stared at it for a long moment, waiting for my eyes and brain to make sense of it or for the book to fall to the floor or . . . for *something* to happen. But nothing did. I glanced around and peered into the hallway behind me, expecting to see a mage playing a trick on me, but no one was there. Still no mind signatures anywhere on this level.

I made a slow circle around the book as it hung in the air, keeping my distance, afraid to touch it. Finally, with shaking hands, I reached out and grabbed it. The heavy book fell open in my hands, and at first I was relieved to see it didn't contain those strange hieroglyphics. I recognized both Greek letters and the Latin alphabet. Unfortunately, I couldn't read any of it.

From research for my own books, I knew enough about the Greek alphabet and how Greek words formed the basis of many English words, so I was able to figure out the title on the cover page: *The Book of Prophecies & Curses*. The exact book I wanted. How did the room know? Who was behind it? I only had to think the title, and it came to me as if sensing my desire. *Who cares? Find what you need and get out of here.*

I flipped through the pages, hunting for at least something in English. Numbers—the universal language—headed each entry. They were dates, going back to Before Christ, and increasing chronologically, with the last one dated many years ago. Prophecies and curses weren't very common. Under each date, Greek letters lined the page, followed by lines of Latin letters in a foreign language, probably Latin itself. I skimmed the last pages, hoping to find something I could make out, perhaps a familiar name. Two lines seemed to jump out at me as if somehow bolder than the others, but not, and I started sounding out the letters, hoping to understand—

The snick of a door closing sounded down the hall. Followed by barely audible footsteps. Panicking, I slammed the book shut. What if I wasn't allowed to be in the Sacred Archives? Mom had told me to leave it alone, but was it because there was some rule about the Sacred Archives or the *Book of Prophecies & Curses*? Or did she just want me to "behave"? In case I'd violated the Angels' space, I didn't want to be caught.

I let go of the book, hoping it would return to its place the way it had come because I had no idea where it belonged. It fell to the floor. Nearly bouncing on my feet with anxiety, I held my hand out and the book flew up into it. I examined the shelves in the direction from where it had floated, but didn't see an opening anywhere.

"Go *home*," I whispered with desperation. The book jumped out of my hand, floated over to a bookshelf in the far corner and slid into its home.

I turned toward the door to sneak out, but it was too late. No way to escape, and no place to hide.

Chapter 8

Martin stepped around the corner to my left at the same time Solomon appeared outside the door to my right. They stopped in the middle of the corridor, right in front of the Sacred Archives—right in front of me. Frozen in place, my heart pounding against my ribs, I waited for their demands of why I was in there. They both glanced my way, but neither of them said anything. In fact, they gave no indication of even seeing me, though if I were any closer, I'd be invading their personal space.

"Martin, good to see you," Solomon said. "Did you bring news from the field?"

Martin licked his lips. His hand slid down the front of his shirt. "Not exactly. I met with Katerina."

Really? How come I hadn't sensed their mind signatures? Did Rina have a way to shield her office? Or maybe Martin did. Interesting . . .

"And?" Solomon asked, swinging his arms to clasp his hands behind his back.

Martin's eyes darted around, as if ensuring no eavesdroppers hid in the shadows. Yet here I was, and he still acted as though he didn't see me. He lowered his voice when he spoke.

"I'm concerned about Julia," he said in a near whisper, his Irish accent stronger with his apparent worry. "She's been a bit dodgy. I think she's . . . being influenced or something of the sort."

Solomon lifted his brows. "What is your basis?"

"The messages she relays between Katerina and me—they're bloody wrong. She's missing facts, not telling Rina everything, but lets on that it's my doin'. Something is goin' on with her."

I knew it! I'd always felt wrong about Julia, and now Martin confirmed she was hiding something. From Rina, no less.

Solomon rocked back on his heels. "And what did Rina say when you brought this to her attention?"

"She was flummoxed at first but then denied it, of course. Claims I'm being paranoid with the news of the traitor." Martin leaned closer to Solomon. "Keep a sound lookout on that vampire, Solomon. She's not right, and I worry for Katerina."

Solomon nodded. "I will keep this in mind."

Martin clapped Solomon on the shoulder, then disappeared with a *pop*. Without even a glance my way, Solomon headed on down the hallway. I remained in the Sacred Archives for only a moment, my mind spinning with what I'd heard. Was Julia really the traitor? What exactly was she trying to accomplish? And how could she, a vamp, possibly block Rina's power? I stepped out of the Sacred Archives, trying to be as silent as possible, and the air of the real world hit me as I crossed into the hallway. Solomon spun on me.

"Alexis?" he said, his voice its normal boom again. He peered behind me then narrowed his eyes. "Where did you come from?"

With the sound of stone sliding against stone, the door to the Sacred Archives slid shut as if telling me my time in there was over. Solomon paid it no attention, as if he didn't hear it, and I realized he must not have seen it, either. Could only Amadis daughters see the Sacred Archives? Because only we could enter it? Not something I could waste time thinking about at the moment.

I swallowed. "Um, I came from my suite. I was, uh, wondering if I could talk to you."

Solomon studied me for a long moment, and I fought the desire to shiver under his gaze. No matter how much time we spent in the same house with the same loved ones, even knowing he was a good man, I just couldn't relax around him.

"Of course," he said, his face breaking into a wide smile, white teeth against ashy skin. "You've been avoiding me. Have you finally gathered your courage?"

He teased me. I could see it in his dark, gleaming eyes. He knew I was supposed to have spoken with him weeks ago to glean direct knowledge about vampires. Although they were my favorite of all the creatures, I'd been too scared to be alone with him.

"I promise not to bite," he said.

I couldn't help it. A nervous laugh burst out of me, and Solomon chuckled, too. And with that, I relaxed. A little, anyway. He led me to his study, right next door to Rina's. Solomon twitched his finger, the door swung open, and he disappeared within, expecting me to follow.

I took a tentative step inside, drinking in the vampire's semi-private space. He and Rina shared similar tastes in décor— dark wood antique furniture decorated the room. Like Rina, he had a large desk, floor-to-ceiling bookshelves and a sitting area next to a fireplace. On closer examination, however, their preferences were also completely different. While books and beautiful statues of angels and other feminine ornaments filled Rina's bookshelves, Solomon's displayed interesting carvings, tribal masks and weapons, crude and ancient-looking.

"That wall is from my time in Africa," Solomon said, following my gaze, then his eyes slid to another wall, where more wood carvings, ceramic pottery, wooden necklaces and dolls that looked alarmingly like voodoo dolls decorated the shelves. "Those are from my home country."

"Where are you from?" I asked, studying a carving of a duck or, perhaps, a pigeon. The crudeness made it hard to tell.

"What was once known as Hispaniola. When I left, it was Ayiti. You know it as Haiti. I was part of the *gens de couleur*—free men of color who helped emancipate my brothers in the Revolution. I almost did not survive the battle. Some would say I did not survive at all. The Daemoni found me near death after a particularly bloody fight and made me a vampire. So here I am."

I looked up in surprise, not expecting to hear such personal information. Not that he shared his whole life story, but, at least in my books, being turned was usually not something vampires preferred to talk about.

"Enough about that. You are here to learn about my kind, not me specifically."

"Everyone says the more knowledge I have about each of the creatures, the better I'll understand the enemy."

"Everyone is correct."

"So you don't mind this interview? Because I have all kinds of questions. Vampires have always fascinated me." Heat rose in my cheeks with the admission. Would Solomon tease me like Tristan does?

Both understanding and a bit of arrogance flicked in Solomon's eyes. "Of course not."

He gestured toward the seating area, and I sat on the edge of a chair upholstered in red leather with bronze rivets outlining its contours. Solomon sat across from me and, admittedly, it made me feel more comfortable. Perhaps because I didn't have to crane my neck up to see his intimidating face. Or perhaps because when he sat, he somehow seemed more human. Solomon flicked his hand, and the door slid closed.

"How do you do that?" I blurted. "I mean, you're not a mage or have Amadis blood . . . right?"

"Before we start—I believe you have been instructed to practice your telepathy?"

I nodded.

"It will be easier and more effective if I simply share my thoughts."

I inhaled a deep breath and let it out slowly, imagining my wall disintegrating into a screen again. I sensed Solomon's signature immediately and latched onto his thoughts.

Um . . . hello? I asked, hesitating with the strangeness of looking right at him, but not talking to him aloud. It didn't feel natural as it did with Tristan. But I expected nothing would ever feel natural with Solomon.

A small smile played on his lips. "*Rina has said it is sometimes easier when she closes her eyes.*"

I nodded, leaned back in my chair and closed my eyes. A small part of me kept behind my shield couldn't help but wonder if this was a trick. After all, vamps could quite easily convince their prey to relax, to turn their backs or shut their eyes so they couldn't see the attack coming. Not able to help myself, I barely slit an eyelid open to peak at Solomon. He, too, sat back in his chair, his eyes closed. *This is Rina's mate; he won't hurt me.* I closed my eyes again and opened my mind to him.

Visions appeared in my head of vampires buying blood by the glass, bottle or box, as if it were wine. Solomon explained how Amadis vampires didn't drink directly from the source. Mages provided vamps their life-force by donating blood, and vampires absorbed many of their magical powers. The older they were and the longer they fed on mage blood, the more powers they gained and kept.

So that's how you can flash or close the door without touching it? I asked.

"*Yes. Almost all Amadis vamps receive such basic powers.*"

Are Daemoni vamps the same?

"*Not exactly. They prefer to drink from the source, not only because it is fresher, but more for the thrill of the bite and the drain.*" Disgust filled Solomon's silent voice. "*They prefer the sweeter, unadulterated blood of Normans.*"

So they're not as powerful?

He explained that because their souls had not been saved, their demonic powers were naturally stronger than Amadis vampires. When they had seen the Amadis vamps' new powers, however, they tried taking blood from the mages. Their lack of self-control killed many, and they could not afford to lose any others.

"*Occasionally they feed from the mages, but only in controlled situations and only when necessary, such as when they are preparing for battle,*" Solomon continued. "*They do not need any more powers than what they already have to serve their primary purpose: preying on Normans.*"

Do they always kill?

"*Not always. But often. The fresher the blood—and the more human it is—the more difficult it is to not drain the source completely. The Daemoni are not known for self-control, and vampires are worse than the rest. Sometimes, they are able to prevent a total draining so they may create a new child.*"

Before I could ask how new vampires were made, Solomon's thoughts came to me visually. A vampire nearly—but not completely, he emphasized—drained a human and then replaced the human's blood with his own. The vamp's blood healed the body and infused it with Daemoni magic, bringing the victim back to near-life. Because the master could only replace a small part of the body's blood without draining himself, the newborn came into its new life starving to the point of madness.

"Once they taste their first victim, the bloodlust becomes deeply ingrained. After time passes—for some, a few months, for others, several years—they need blood less often and begin to behave more civilized. Until then, they are wild animals with no fear, no control and only one thing on their minds. Their masters are supposed to parent them, but not all vampires, like humans, are very good parents."

Have you . . . ? I couldn't finish the thought, not wanting to imagine Solomon as Daemoni at all. He understood the question, though.

"I have no children. I had no desire to bestow this terrible lifestyle on another being. I was turned against my will. It astounds me anyone would purposefully want this."

Are there many who do?

"More than you would think. Many Normans believe vampirism provides the solutions to their problems, not realizing all it entails. If they choose to be turned, their soul is more easily lost to us—we usually cannot save them. However, if they are turned against their will . . . if they really do not want to exist as a monster . . ."

They keep their souls, and we can help them.

"Correct."

Are there many turnings these days?

"At this very moment, no. But, the Daemoni plan to build their army. They will take dying soldiers, as usual, but with the recent infatuation with vampires, they will likely find many who are willing. More Normans will be reported missing, never to be heard from again, their bodies never found."

I gasped. My eyes flew open, and I jumped to my feet.

"Solomon!" I cried aloud, forgetting the telepathy.

He was on his feet so fast, I never saw the movement. His body tensed, and his eyes surveyed the area with alarm. "What?"

"My books! They helped create that infatuation. And now people will be turned because they *want* to be vampires. What have I done? What was everyone *thinking?*"

Solomon was suddenly sitting again, lounging in the chair. He waved his hand dismissively. "Relax, Alexis. You know the reason for your books—to create more awareness of evil so Normans will better prepare themselves. And they *will*. Those who *want* to be turned would want to anyway. You have done more good than harm."

"But can't we do something?" I demanded as I plopped into my chair.

Solomon's gaze swept over my face. "We try to prevent vampire turnings—and Were infections, too—whenever possible. We place our soldiers on the same battlefields the Daemoni target, and Martin's intelligence group tracks those vamps who have a history of turnings. We also maintain a heavy presence where Daemoni vamps prefer to gather."

"Such as Key West?"

"Key West has not had a turning in more than a decade because of our presence," he confirmed with a nod. "The vamps favor tourist havens, because their victims are often drunk, making them easy prey. The older ones, those with more control, can drink from the sources without draining them, and the Normans have no recollection the next morning. They remember—what is the modern saying?—a one-night stand."

I thought of the vampires in my books and how they could not only feed off fear, but also off lust. Biting and blood during sex provided the greatest satisfaction to both parties. The magic in the vampire's saliva entered the victim's bloodstream through the bite, creating a sense of euphoria. I had thought, at one time, I had taken that idea from when Tristan had helped me heal the deep gash on my leg, the night I learned who he really was. His mouth on my leg had nearly brought me to my first real orgasm. Now, I realized, Tristan's ability to do that—both heal me and excite me in such a strange way—came from the vampire DNA embedded in his genes. I suddenly wondered if Solomon and Rina . . . I blushed. No way could I ask him that.

"Do you drink only mages' blood?" I asked instead. "I mean . . . have you ever drank Rina's?"

Solomon's brows arched, creating several horizontal lines across his forehead. "Blood from an Amadis daughter is very precious. Very powerful, but very precious. I've only had her blood once, when I was dying, and only because she forced me."

An idea occurred to me. "Did you absorb any of her Amadis powers, such as telepathy? I mean, the same way you absorb mages' magic?"

"I did not drink enough. I do not know if it is possible, and it is best not to find out."

"Well, how much magic can you gain from a mage? Can you become as powerful as them?"

Solomon seemed to consider the question, rubbing his chin.

"I have never heard of a vamp gaining that much magic," he finally said. "Perhaps if they fed off a powerful warlock for an extended period of time or from a sorcerer . . . but we cannot risk our most powerful, and I doubt a sorcerer would allow a vamp within arm's length of their blood." He made a sound that almost sounded like a snort. "Thank goodness, too! We do not need a vampire loose with that much power."

Hmm. Could perhaps a vampire, such as Julia, block Rina's powers if they'd had the right kind or amount of blood? A possibility, although Solomon didn't seem to think so.

"So, what would make you so weak for Rina to give her

blood to you? How can you die? Tristan and Char say it's nearly impossible to kill a vampire."

"Vampires and enchanted silver," he said. "Another vampire can greatly weaken us without killing. So can silver, and if it has been enchanted, the metal can kill us. We need blood to regain our strength. Without blood, we continue to grow weaker until we eventually dry up into corpses . . . until blood regenerates us."

"Only vamps and silver blades can kill you? There's no other way? A stake to the heart?"

Solomon chuckled. "Vampires started that legend, as well as allergies to garlic and the need to be invited into a home. These stories give the Normans a false sense of security, and vampires embrace it. They pretend to be frightened away, only to return later for the unsuspected attack. Vampires enjoy playing with their food."

And it was such statements, along with the wide, white grin on Solomon's face, that made him so frightening.

I swallowed, pushing down the unnecessary fear. "And the myth of not being able to come out during the day?"

"Started by the Amadis. The idea was to make Normans more fearful of being out at night, alone in the dark when vampires prefer to hunt."

"So the sun has no effect at all?"

"I would not say that. It can weaken us. And most prefer the night because it is easier to hunt. Many come out *only* in darkness, and the longer they live nocturnally, the more the sun affects them. Some can be weakened to the strength of a mere man at the sun's full height at noon."

I lifted an eyebrow. "That's how Bram Stoker's Dracula is."

Solomon nodded. "Yes, he had some details right. Whether they were guesses or an actual vampire gave him the information, nobody knows."

"What about beheading?"

"Only with an enchanted blade. With such a blade, you can slice a vampire into pieces, the only way *you* can kill one. You must burn all the pieces, however, or the vampire will put himself back together."

My stomach rolled at the thought. "And you said silver hurts?"

"It weakens us, but it does not necessarily kill. Silver affects all Daemoni to a certain degree."

"So are you affected by silver now? After becoming Amadis?"

"No. That is the strange thing about the metal. Many believe the Angels enchanted silver in the Earth's beginnings to protect people against evil. Some believe silver is an element brought to us from the Otherworld. But that may just be a story . . . fiction."

I lifted an eyebrow. "Fiction? There seems to be truth in much fiction."

Solomon chuckled again. "Yes, there does, doesn't there? The best stories—and the best lies—are woven around the truth. It is up to us to discover which is which."

Chapter 9

"Well, Alexis," Charlotte said a week later, pressing her palm to her forehead as she studied her clipboard, "the discs are out, you're not bad with knives, but your swordsmanship skills are quite lacking."

I grimaced, feeling as though I'd been given a big, fat F. The coronation ceremony was only a few days away and afterward, Char would be back out in the field. She'd pretty much come as far as she could with me, and I'd disappointed her. "Sorry. I can't get comfortable with the sword. Tristan says to make it one with me, but I just don't feel it."

Char waved her hand in dismissal. "No worries. It takes years to become an excellent swordsman. Besides, swords are impractical in the Norman world anyway. They can be cloaked, of course, but they're cumbersome when you're mainstreaming." Her hand darted into her cleavage and, in a snap, she produced a long-bladed, double-edged knife. She grinned at my surprise. "Which is why I prefer daggers." She handed it to me. "Let's see what you can do with this. Tristan?"

Tristan selected his favorite weapon—himself. With all the talk he'd given me about not completely relying on my powers, and about needing to be able to fight in all kinds of situations and with whatever tools I had, he used nothing but the gifts he'd been given. Of course, he'd had centuries of training and could paralyze someone in an instant, making weapons virtually pointless, although new ones were being made for him, "to be prepared for anything" as he put it.

The only way to evade his power was to be behind him, but he was so alert and so fast, it was nearly impossible to be behind him long enough to make a difference. I was the only one who'd been able to take him on and match his power, although he'd still nearly won. In fact, it hadn't really been me who beat him that day. It had been the Amadis power boosted by a miracle.

In training, however, my Amadis power was useless, having only a positive effect on other Amadis, and I hadn't been allowed to use my electrical power except a few times when Charlotte needed to see what I could do and then see how it had strengthened over time. So practicing with the dagger with Tristan meant using only my speed and agility.

The dagger felt more natural in either of my hands than any other weapon we'd tried. I easily danced around Tristan with it, twisting and turning without tripping myself up as I had done with the sword. Right when Tristan lunged at me, I did a spin and a hop and landed on his back, the dagger at his throat.

"Perfect!" Charlotte said with a laugh. "The dagger it is. And the beauty of the dagger, Alexis, is we can have yours made to take your powers, both the electricity and the Amadis. Whatever you want to use, you can pass it through the dagger. You will have a most formidable weapon. I'll put the order in today, but you'll need to go in tomorrow so the blacksmith can be sure he has the right measurements."

I hadn't really expected an actual blacksmith, just the old-fashioned title given to whomever used more advanced technology in today's age. But when Tristan and I went to the village the next day, he took me to a space that resembled a blacksmith shop straight from the Middle Ages—rustic and smoky, with the only light coming from several hearths with blazing fires. Except, unlike a traditional blacksmith, herbs and other reagents hung from this one's ceiling or were kept in jars on shelves near the fires, I assumed to enchant the weapons and armory forged here.

At the hearth in front of us, a stooped, white-haired man tossed some kind of powder into the unnaturally green fire. The flames shot up, turning from green to silver, and he thrust a long piece of metal into the heat. His hands flickered with pink sparks as he turned the metal in his palms and whispered a spell. Finally, he pulled the staff from the flames and dropped it in a vat of water. He squinted up at us and then ducked his head.

"Ms. Alexis. Mr. Tristan. I've been expecting you," he said, his voice gravelly as if he'd been inhaling the smoke in the shop for hundreds of years. With his dark, lined skin, perhaps he had been. He gave us a nearly toothless grin and held his hands out toward me. "May I?"

I stared at him with uncertainty.

"It's okay," Tristan said. "Ferrer needs to take your measurements. Just give him your hand."

I hesitantly placed my hand into the old man's rough and calloused ones. After a few long moments, his knobby fingers released mine, and he asked for my other hand.

"Very good. I will have your dagger and your knife ready to be presented at the coronation ceremony," he said.

"That's it?" I asked with surprise. *What, exactly, did he measure?*

"Yes, that's it. Do not worry, Ms. Alexis, they will be splendid weapons. I told Ms. Charlotte the dagger would favor you, but she insisted on testing you, all the same. I have already the one meant for you to hold." Ferrer gave me a wink and then turned to Tristan. "I will have yours ready then, as well, Mr. Tristan."

As we stepped out of the shop into the bright daylight, an uneasy feeling overcame me. I stopped and studied the mind signatures surrounding us. Some felt familiar from the many trips we'd taken to the village, yet one, in particular, really stood out. Not because I knew it—I certainly had never felt it before—but because it was so different. Everyone's signatures were unique, but they also had similar qualities, especially among the same species. This one was nothing like any of the others. I grabbed Tristan's hand and pulled him up the road, following the signature.

"What's going on?" he asked.

Someone new . . . different. It's weird and I want to know who it is.

He sighed, but indulged me. The signature headed up the sloped road, and right where the business district ended and the road climbed higher to the Council Hall, the owner made a sharp right. A moment later, we rounded the same corner. The Council Hall was up the hill to our left and a storage shed stood in front of us, aligned with the rear of the shops on the main road. But no one was in sight. The mind signature had disappeared.

"Huh. They're gone," I said, turning in a circle to be sure.

"Maybe they flashed," Tristan said as he tugged me back toward the road.

"Yeah, I guess—"

A sound came from behind us. We both jerked and turned toward the shed. Martin, Julia and Armand were exiting the little building, Martin forever smoothing his shirt, his face pale and distressed. As soon as he saw us, though, he straightened his spine and smiled. But this didn't distract me from seeing Julia's tongue run across her lips or Armand's eyes narrow suspiciously. What was going on? They weren't feeding off of Martin . . . were they?

"Tristan! I need to speak with you." Martin's voice came out a little more cheerful than normal, and he hurried toward us, as if extremely relieved to see Tristan . . . or, more likely, to escape the vampires. Armand disappeared, and Julia headed up the hill, toward the Council Hall. "Owen and I have a theory and I was thinking . . ."

I stopped paying attention to Martin and focused instead on Julia, who peered over her shoulder, as if checking to see if she was being followed. When she blurred around the corner, headed for the rear of the Hall as I'd seen her do months ago, I wondered what she could possibly be doing that required her to sneak in through the back door. Nothing good, I was sure. Not with that kind of treacherous behavior.

Out of the corner of my eye, I peered at Tristan and Martin. Their heads were close together, deep in discussion. Martin had told Solomon to keep a careful watch on Julia, but he wasn't watching at the moment when she was obviously up to something. I could have read Julia's mind, but I saw the opportunity and flashed to the rear of the Hall instead.

Just as I appeared, two backs stood in the doorway—Julia's and another: Ophelia's. The witch held a copper flask in one hand and perhaps something else in front of her that I couldn't see. Julia's hand pressed against Ophelia's shoulder, pushing her downward until they were both lost to the gloom inside. *What are they doing?* Was Ophelia delivering something to Julia? Did the flask hold more blood? Was Martin's not enough for the gluttonous vampire? I wondered whose blood it was. Perhaps Ophelia's, adding more magic to Julia's system. Or . . . perhaps Rina's. *Solomon could be wrong. Julia could be gaining enough power.* I had to find out.

I inhaled a deep breath to gather my courage, blew it out slowly and stepped through the open door onto a narrow landing at the top of a steep flight of stone stairs. Below was darkness and strange noises, as well as Julia, Ophelia and another mind signature. I suppressed a gasp.

This mind signature surprised me. It somewhat reminded me of Dorian's—intense and animated—but not quite the same. A sharper edge to it. Yet, still childlike. A soft moaning floated up the stairs, the sound of a girl's whimper.

I froze. My pulse pounded loudly in my ears. *Could it be?* I hesitated. Although I was Amadis Royalty, there were still boundaries I couldn't cross yet, and I was sure this was one of them. Especially if . . . *Exactly why I need to see for myself!* The girl's voice came louder, more of a wail. I hurried down the steps.

A corridor stretched out before me, most of it dark and dank with a coordinating musty odor, doors spaced evenly apart along each wall. A triangle of light lit the end of the hall, an open door allowing it to shine through. I took a single step, then stopped, debating whether to proceed or to enter Ophelia or Julia's mind first to see what—

Whoosh! Air rushed past me. A bar of steel pressed against my stomach and a board against my back. My body flew up the stairs. Literally. My feet didn't touch the ground. Then I stumbled as I was dropped into the brightness outside.

"You can't be down there!" Julia seethed at me, her voice more screechy than I expected. I couldn't, at the moment anyway, ever remember hearing her speak aloud. I cursed myself for letting her catch me off guard.

"Why?" I demanded. "What's going on down there? Who is—"

Pop! Tristan appeared by my side.

"What's going on?" he asked, looking from me to Julia. He took in her expression and stepped protectively in front of me.

~ 131 ~

"It's too dangerous, especially for you!" Julia hissed at me. And then she disappeared with a *pop*.

Tristan turned to me. "Are you okay? What—"

"Julia's hiding a girl down there, Tristan! With Ophelia! What if it's *her*? Our daugh—"

Tristan shook his head. "Lex, that's where they keep Amadis who have broken the law and unstable converts. You probably sensed a young Were or witch who lost control. Who can hurt you. They're delivering food and water. That's all."

"I want to see for myself. How do you know it's not *the* girl—the hidden girl?"

"Right under Council Hall where anyone can find her? That's not exactly hidden."

He had a point. And because I knew he would be honest with me, I gave in, let him take my hand and lead me for the flash to our suite.

But the girl's wail continued to echo in my mind.

ↂ

The morning trip to the village threw off our schedule and when we returned to the mansion, we discovered Charlotte had been called away to an emergency. So after putting Dorian to bed, Tristan suggested a workout in the gym.

"Let's see what you can really do with this when you put your mind to it," he said, handing me a dagger from the practice weapons. His eyes sparked with excitement.

I narrowed my eyes, suspicious of his motives.

"Oh-kay," I said with hesitation, taking the blade from him.

"I mean, use your *mind*. Char's not here. You're free to use the best defense you have." He grabbed a sword, the blade as long as me.

I lifted an eyebrow. "You never use a weapon."

He flicked his wrist, making the long, thin blade bend and twang. "I thought I'd make it interesting."

He winked at me, and I stared at him in a daze. Until I saw the glint of his sword swinging for my legs.

"That's cheating!" I squealed, jumping over the blade.

"I use whatever advantage I can," he said with a sublime grin that made my knees weak. The sword swung at me again and I parried it with the dagger. "You have a bigger advantage than anyone, *ma lykita*. Use it."

Just as I had done when we'd seriously been fighting each other in the Keys, I read Tristan's thoughts and knew every move before he made it. I ducked, twirled, twisted and danced around his swipes and lunges, blocking or dodging most of his attacks. We blurred around the room, sprang off the walls, and flipped, jumped and cartwheeled over each other. Tristan jumped for an overhead beam and, knowing what he planned to do, I landed on it at the same time as he did and our fight continued. We jumped from beam to beam and through the open skylights, briefly sparring on the roof, then back inside again. Then Tristan threw his sword down and lunged at me. I dove for the floor, planning to tuck into a somersault for the landing, but he grabbed me in mid-air, encircling me in his arms and turning to take the impact. He rolled me over to my back, pinning me to the floor. I squirmed, trying to break his hold and thought about shocking him.

But then his mouth was on mine, and I immediately surrendered.

"You cheated again," I breathed when he finally pulled away. "That kiss wasn't very fair."

"You know what's not fair?" he asked, the gold in his eyes sparkling brightly. He leaned his head down again, his lips near my ear, as he took my hand and moved it to his hard groin. He whispered against my ear, "What you do to me isn't fair."

His soft lips traveled along my jaw line and to my throat as I rubbed his erection through his thin workout pants. My back arched as his lips moved to my chest, my breasts aching for his touch. He nibbled my nipples poking through the sports bra then moved lower to kiss my bare stomach. His fingers slipped under my waistband and I gasped. He moaned. He'd moved too low for me to reach anymore, so I took his head in my hands and pulled him up.

"I can't, Tristan," I whispered, my body screaming "yes, you can!"

"Not even out here?"

"We're too close. I can contact anyone in the mansion from here."

His eyes penetrated mine and I could almost see the gears turning in his head. A wide grin spread across his face, then he wrapped his arms around me. "I have an idea."

He flashed, taking me with him. We appeared in a tiny clearing, surrounded by ancient cypress trees that seemed to touch the black sky, leaving just enough to show a moon uncomfortably close to being full.

"We wouldn't be able to do this in a couple of nights—too many Weres would be running around," Tristan said. "But right now, I don't sense anyone for quite a ways. Can you?"

I dissolved my wall and the mind signatures I felt were too far away, making them distorted and indistinguishable. However near the closest person was, they were beyond my mind-reaching capabilities. A smile stretched my mouth wide. I jumped into his arms, my legs encircled his waist, and I pressed my lips against his.

My hands tangled into his hair as I pulled him into me,

separating my lips to taste his tangy-sweetness . . . mangos, papayas, lime and sage. *Mmm . . . delicious.* I thought I might devour him, if he didn't devour me first.

Keeping my legs tight around him, I only let go with my arms long enough for him to pull my bra over my head. I pressed my naked breasts against his bare chest, but not for long, as he slipped his hand between us, caressing and squeezing. His mouth traveled down my neck, and I leaned backward, his hands supporting me, so his lips could move lower, while I ground my pelvis against him.

"*Alexis!*" My name thundered in my head, but not in Tristan's voice and definitely not in mine. I stiffened. My wall had already fallen, and someone had moved into range. I immediately zoned in on the mind signature and picked up the thought. ". . . There's something about her . . ."

"What's wrong?" Tristan mouthed against my breast.

"Stop," I whispered. I let go of him with my legs and dropped lightly to the ground. "Someone's coming."

Tristan groaned quietly. "Are you sure?"

I listened for a moment and didn't hear anything—in my head or with my ears. I shook my head.

"Just wait a sec. Maybe she stepped into range and out again."

After maybe a minute that felt like an hour, I still didn't hear anything and neither did Tristan. He pulled me back into his arms.

"*She's more powerful than expected.*"

I pressed my forehead against Tristan's chest and concentrated. The mind signature felt strange, unlike any of the others. She definitely wasn't a Were or a vamp. The texture was similar to the mages' signatures, but not quite the same. I thought maybe distance distorted it, but that didn't make much sense, since I could hear her thoughts clearly. Another moment of focus brought recognition—it was the same signature I'd noticed in the village earlier today . . . and the same voice I'd heard at the council meeting.

I picked up my bra and pulled it on.

"Seriously?" Tristan asked, barely making a sound, but I could still hear the defeat.

"Sorry," I mouthed. Weres and vamps had super-human senses and could hear the tiniest sound a mile away, so I explained telepathically. *I think she's coming closer. Let me listen.*

He nodded reluctantly, disappointment filling his eyes.

"*But is she powerful enough? Is she as intelligent as they say?*" I could almost hear what felt like a snort. "*Nah, she is nothing. We have our leverage over her. Over Katerina and Sophia, too. We'll take care of them easily and the plan will go perfectly. We just need to keep the girl hidden long enough.*"

My hand flew to my mouth, and my eyes practically popped out of their sockets. I stood frozen until the thought was long gone. Then nothing. The signature traveled out of range again. I plopped to the ground, dumbstruck.

Tristan sank to his knees in front of me and placed his hands on the sides of my face, tilting mine up to his. He whispered only loud enough for my keen ears to hear. "What is it?"

I told him what I heard. "And it was the same council member. The same voice."

"But she still didn't say a daughter, just a girl."

"What other girl would anyone want to hide? And both times she's mentioned it, she paired it with my name."

Tristan shrugged. "At least we know for sure this is the traitor and there's some kind of plan."

"I need to figure out who it is so I can learn as much as possible. And I need to let go of this freakin' shield so I can give Rina proof."

"We can try again . . . return to what we were doing . . ." No enthusiasm filled his words, though, as he gave me a half-hearted smile.

I frowned, and he nodded with understanding. Our moment ruined, he took my hand, and we flashed back to the suite.

୧୨

I couldn't sleep. Visions of Sheree and how I'd almost killed her while trying to save her soul flashed in my mind, mixed with images of an auburn-haired, brown-eyed young girl trapped in a jail cell. With Julia's suspicious behavior and the voice I'd heard tonight, I couldn't help but think that's whom they kept in the Council Hall cellar. My daughter. Taken from me at birth and hidden away.

Tired of tossing and turning, I slid out of bed and tiptoed into the bathroom, closing the door behind me before lighting the candle by the sink. Tristan surely couldn't have slept through my restlessness, but I didn't want to wake him in case he had. I stood in front of the mirror, pushed my fingers through my hair and pressed my palms against my temples while staring into my own eyes.

"What if . . . ?" I whispered to myself. And the answer came right back. *I have to know.*

I grabbed my spandex workout pants from the hamper and quickly pulled them on, along with the T-shirt Tristan had taken off before our trip to the gym. It hung to my knees, but I didn't care. No one would see me. *No one but . . .*

Without anymore thought, I flashed to the Council Hall cellar. Darkness filled the corridor, now that the door upstairs and the one at the end of the hall were both closed. My eyes adjusted quickly and skimmed the five doors lining each side of the hall. I was only interested in one. The last door on the left, the one imprisoning the only nearby mind signature.

Before I could talk myself out of it, I crept down the corridor. No handle, no indication of a lock or anything interrupted the stone face of the door, except a small opening toward the top with bars and a metal screen covering it. Magic probably kept the door closed and locked the prisoner inside— magic I wouldn't be able to break through. I stood on my toes and peeked through the barred window.

A girl with stringy, matted blond hair and eyes such a pale gray, they were almost no color at all, huddled in the corner. She must have been about twelve years old—not my daughter—but looked younger, so pathetic and harmless.

"*You can open it,*" a girl's voice sounded in my mind. "*You're Royalty. And you can help me get out of here. If that vampire comes back . . . I can't take it again. What she does to me . . .*"

I blanched. She couldn't have known I could read her mind, so she simply thought words she couldn't bring herself to voice, but her fear of what Julia did to her alarmed me. She flipped her arm out and red indentions marked her skin in the crook of her elbow. I sucked in a breath. Bite marks. That was enough for me. I flicked my hand and, as she'd expected, the door slid open.

The girl sat motionless for a long moment, as if she wasn't sure what to do. I stood perfectly still, not wanting to frighten her. When she still didn't move, I took a step and crossed the threshold.

A high screech rented the air.

A blur of motion flew at me.

Her ears suddenly pointed up beyond the top of her head. Her eyes glowed pink. Her lips disappeared, exposing rows of pointed teeth filling her mouth. Hairy claws stretched out in front of her, aimed for my face. I noticed all this in a fraction of a second as she sailed toward me.

My hand flew up and an electric jolt shot at her, throwing her to the corner she came from. She flew at me again. But a force jerked me out of the cell, and the door slammed shut, her body crashing against the other side. She let out a feral wail, muffled by the stone. Strong arms engulfed me, trapping me against a hard body.

"Damn it, Alexis. Don't you listen?" Tristan growled. His voice was full of anger, but his hand gently stroked my hair.

"What was that?" I whispered. My heart still pounded against his abs.

He flashed us to the suite before answering. "Remember the potion Jordan and the witch created, the one that mixed the qualities of all the Daemoni creatures?"

I nodded.

"And you remember no one knew the exact recipe for it after his witch-lover died, but the Daemoni kept trying to recreate it?"

I nodded again.

"They've been experimenting all this time. For centuries. They finally came close with Lucas, but he was a grown man when he drank it. They thought giving the potion to a man and a woman before conception would allow them to create the strongest, most powerful warrior ever. And they did."

"You," I whispered.

"Yes, me. But Lucas and I were the two exceptions. Every other experiment has gone wrong, producing *things* of your worst nightmares."

"And that was one of them?" My voice came out hoarse, filled with horror.

"Over the years, the Amadis have found a few experiments, abandoned by their creators. They keep trying to see if they can ever get through to them, overcome the evil and find any humanity, possibly convert them. They haven't succeeded yet."

I dropped to the bed, my hand over my mouth.

"But why would Julia feed off of her?" I asked.

"Julia would never—"

"I saw the marks."

"You also saw what you thought was a harmless, young girl," he said softly.

I nodded with understanding. "Illusions. Deceit. She's still just Daemoni."

Was this the girl being hidden? Did the traitor have some kind of plan to use her against us?

Tristan sat next to me and folded me into his arms. "Do you remember, in the beginning, how I had to fight to keep control so I wouldn't kill you? That's why they created me, why they keep trying to create warriors—to hunt down and kill the Amadis. I had nearly twenty years of being Amadis before I met you, twenty years to learn control, and I still hadn't mastered it." He tightened his arms around me. "She would have killed you without a thought."

Chapter 10

The day I'd been dreading for three months—the day of the coronation ceremony—dawned bright and beautiful, mocking my dark mood. Every time the ceremony had been brought up, my insides squirmed uncomfortably, but I tried not to think too much about all the attention it would bring. As if the curtsies and the head-bows weren't bad enough, the whole island would be paying tribute at once. I wanted to run away and hide. When Mom brought me the dress I was supposed to wear, I silently and profusely cussed at the fact that I couldn't flash off the island.

The dress looked very much like my traditional Amadis wedding dress, only it was lavender instead of white. The straps on the leather bodice were slightly different and amethysts, rather than diamonds, lined the band encircling my neck. The silk, A-line skirt was surely shorter, though, several inches above my knees. I loved the color and the stones—my favorites—but nothing else. And this time I'd be seen in it by more than family and a handful of strangers.

"So why do I have to wear *this*—" I flipped my hands at myself, particularly my boobs, which were about to fall out of the bodice "—and you get to wear *that*?" I asked Tristan when I saw him dressed and ready to go.

His outfit was comparatively simple—black dress pants and a black, silk, button-down shirt—though he looked especially stunning in it.

He eyed me appreciatively and grinned, the gold flecks in his eyes shining brightly. "Because I pulled some strings so I'd get to see you in something like that again."

I narrowed my eyes, but he was teasing. He shrugged unabashedly.

"So I had nothing to do with it," he admitted. "It is traditional. But if I did have any say, I'd definitely choose this for you."

I stuck my bottom lip out. "I thought you loved me."

"I do." He brushed his lips across my forehead. "And I love showing you off."

"This is so unfair," I muttered, tugging at the top of the bodice. As with every other part of me, the *Ang'dora* enhanced my boobs, and whoever made this dress must not have taken that into account.

We flashed to the little holding room in the Council Hall, where Solomon, Rina and Mom waited. The fact that Mom's and Rina's dresses were similar to mine—Mom's was a darker purple with both amethysts and diamonds around her neck and Rina's was a deep violet with large diamonds—didn't make me feel much better. They surely felt just as uncomfortable as I did, even if they didn't show it. Rina favored floor-length gowns and Mom was more casual, like me, though Mom preferred dressy jeans and blouses, while I believed life should be lived in shorts, T-shirts and flip-flops. They both looked exquisite, of course, making me wonder how I could ever think I was now as beautiful as them. It simply wasn't possible.

Before we could go to the arena for the ceremony, we had to wait for all of the council to arrive. Many had been delayed because they'd been helping Martin with a situation in Italy. As I wondered—and wished—if they might cancel the ceremony, I noticed Rina's head cock slightly, and a second later I, too, picked up on the new mind signatures in the building.

"I will be back in a moment," Rina said. "Julia requires me."

With the mention of Julia's name, I identified the vampire's mind signature. She waited in the large, archaic meeting room with the round, wood table. Another mind signature hovered nearby as well, though Rina didn't mention anyone accompanying Julia. It was the same signature, with the same strange, almost-mage-like texture, as I'd heard the other night in the woods. Rina was gone before all of this registered. *Should I warn her the traitor was there, too?* I hadn't told her about the incident in the woods, and there was no time to explain now. So, I listened to see what I could learn.

Rina and Julia didn't speak aloud. Too many people had way-too-good of hearing, and I was sure neither of them wanted eavesdroppers. My impenetrable shield wouldn't allow me to listen to both of their thoughts at once, but since they "spoke" to each other, I didn't have to. I listened through Julia's mind—Rina would sense my presence in her head.

"*What is so important it cannot wait until after the ceremony?*" Rina asked.

"*Many people are restless with Tristan here,*" Julia said. "*Some of the council members, and others, demand that he leaves the island soon. Alexis and the boy, too. They want to know today when they'll be leaving.*"

"*I am well aware of some feelings against Tristan. Do you*

~ 143 ~

share these feelings, too, darling?" Rina's tone, though warm, held the edge of a challenge to it.

"*I believe it would be wise to remove the child from the island and from all the Amadis,*" Julia said, not answering the question. "*I have seen him use powers.*"

My breath caught in my throat, and I fake-coughed to cover it up. Tristan wasn't fooled. I gave him an I'll-tell-you-later look and refocused on the telepathic conversation.

"*Dorian is too young to have powers,*" Rina said.

"*I have seen it myself. We cannot have him near our people or our secrets. The Daemoni will be hunting him soon.*"

"*They already hunt him and his parents. We must keep them protected as long as possible, not send them out to fight on their own.*"

"*We cannot keep them here!*" The intensity of Julia's thoughts escalated drastically. "*Their presence on the island is a danger to all of us!*"

"*What ever is the matter, darling? You seem quite upset all of a sudden.*"

"*It is not all of a sudden. I have my doubts about all three of them. The people who question Tristan's loyalty make excellent points. How do we know he's not actually betraying us by being here? He could be the traitor! Even Alexis—her father is Daemoni! We have no guarantees—*"

Rina cut her off, her own thoughts full of anger. "*This is ludicrous, Julia. I will not stand for this.*"

"*There are too many unknowns with those three.*"

"*I have assessed them myself. They are Amadis. Both of them!*"

"*Are you sure about your assessments?*" Julia sneered. "*Maybe you want them to be with us so much, you're not being completely objective.*"

Julia's eyes showed the shock on Rina's face.

"How dare you!" Rina seethed, her beautiful face contorted with a mix of emotions. She took a moment to regain her composure. *"Where is this coming from? What is wrong with you, Julia? Questioning me? This is not like you at all!"*

"Everyone questions you. They think you make poor decisions based on emotions rather than fact or past experience."

Again, Rina's face showed shock. Then her expression melted into . . . *defeat?* No, it couldn't have been defeat, but I wasn't sure what Rina was feeling, and I couldn't take the risk to hear her thoughts.

"I sense a division in my council," Rina finally said. *"I will take this all into consideration. Thank you for being forthright with me, Julia. I can always count on you."*

Rina's tone was amicable, but the disappointment and dismissal came loud and clear.

At that precise moment, Owen barged through the door to our room and bellowed, "Attack!"

We all spun at him with surprise, and he explained in a rush.

"The situation in Italy has escalated. The Daemoni have attacked our village in Tuscany, along with a Norman town nearby. They surround our island now!"

"What do they want?" Solomon demanded.

"Tristan and Alexis, of course," Owen said. "They say they'll continue attacking until Tristan and Alexis come out of hiding."

"Absolutely not!" Solomon barked, the rage in his eyes blowing away any doubt that a good vampire could be frightening. I was glad he was on our side.

Julia's voice rang in my mind. *"I told you there would be trouble,"* she said to Rina in the grand room. *"They need to leave. Immediately."*

Tristan's voice brought me back to our room. "What exactly happened? What do you mean by attacked?"

~ 145 ~

"An old-fashioned raid," Owen said. "Dad arrived a few minutes ago and said they set fire to the Normans' homes and businesses and attacked the citizens. All to provoke us. Our people lifted the village's shield to flash to the Norman town and fight, but Daemoni were already waiting for them. We've lost several lives—both Amadis and Normans. Including a few . . . children." Owen's voice cracked with that last word.

My stomach rolled as if I'd plunged over the highest hill of a roller coaster. I clutched at my chest, finding only leather straps instead of the missing necklace.

"People . . . *died* . . . for us?" I gasped breathlessly. "We can't let them keep attacking. Tristan, we have to get out of here."

"You cannot leave," Solomon said. "If the Daemoni surround us, you cannot get off the island without being captured . . . or killed."

I stared at him with disbelief. "We can't let them kill anyone else because of us."

Julia piped up again, reminding me I remained connected to her mind. *"Even Alexis knows they can't be here, Rina."*

"Yes, she is concerned about everyone else's safety, but we must keep her protected," Rina insisted.

"We must let her leave! Let them go, Rina. It is best for everyone."

Next to me, Tristan murmured, "Give me a moment, my love."

I let him search for the best solution while Rina and Julia continued in the back of my mind.

"Her safety is paramount to our survival," Rina said.

Julia blew out a breath. *"I didn't want to do this, but if you don't let them go, if they don't leave immediately, I will expose your secret."*

My full attention jetted back to the other room in time to see Rina's eyes narrow. *"What secret?"*

"Your secret about the next daughter."

My breath caught again. *Rina knows? She knows about the girl?*

"Yes, we should go," Tristan said at that moment, covering the noise in my throat. "It's the only way to keep everyone safe."

I barely heard him, still reeling, as though I'd been punched.

"We're getting out of here," I said, again sounding breathless.

"No!" Rina commanded as she burst through the door. "You cannot leave our protection!"

"You choose your own blood over all of the Amadis?" Julia's thought followed her in, though her body did not. *"Do you forget your role?"*

Rina's face blanched, but I didn't feel sorry for her. Not when her betrayal stabbed me like daggers in the heart. She knew something about our daughter—the very one she dismissed after the council meeting, saying it was a ludicrous idea.

"Yes, I think that's exactly what we need to do," I said, trying with everything I had to keep my cool. "We don't need your protection. Tristan is the most powerful creature on this planet. According to you guys, I might be the second most powerful."

I didn't personally believe that last part, but, hell, everyone else did, and it supported my argument. I'd say anything to get out of here.

"Where will you go?" Mom demanded. "You'll be attacked everywhere."

I didn't have an answer, but Tristan did.

"The States, as we'd originally planned," he said.

"And if she is recognized as A.K. Emerson?" Rina challenged. I knew she didn't believe that possible. She grasped at straws. Why did she want to keep us from leaving, especially if her secret would be revealed? I didn't understand her anymore—no, I never really knew her at all.

"We all know I look nothing like the author's pictures."

"We'll use disguises, if necessary, but that's where Alexis wants to go," Tristan said. "It takes us away from the direct center of the current action here in Europe, and it's a place where they likely won't search for us. They won't expect us to go anywhere near where we once lived."

Just then, I realized Julia's mind signature was still close by—she was listening to our plans. And so was that other signature, which I'd nearly forgotten about.

"Rina, who was with Julia?" I demanded, seemingly out of the blue. She looked caught off guard.

"Nobody," she said.

"Bullshit!" Everyone gasped but I ignored them. "There was someone else."

I wanted to tell her about the other mind signature, but I couldn't. Too many people in the building weren't aware of my power, and I wasn't about to try telepathy with her while still minding Julia and the other signature. Too many thoughts to manage safely.

"I do not know what you speak of, Alexis," Rina said, sounding offended. "It was only Julia. I would have sensed anyone else, would have heard their thoughts."

Again, I couldn't say what I wanted to—that it was the traitor who could block her. I had no idea why I felt the need to protect her and her plan, after what I'd heard and the betrayal I felt, but I didn't push it anymore. Instead, I zeroed in on the other's thoughts, trying to gain any additional information before we left.

"*It does not matter if they go to America. Yes, they may come dangerously close, but as long as they do not suspect, we can keep the girl right under their noses, as we have been all these years.*"

That was enough for me.

"We're going to Australia," I blurted for some instinctual reason, and without hesitation, I flashed to our suite. I was already hurling clothes out of the closet, not with my hands but using my powers, when Tristan appeared in our bedroom, followed by Mom and Owen.

"Alexis, what happened?" Tristan asked.

"Pack! We're getting the hell out of here," I seethed. My eyes cut across each one of them and they all just stood there, including Tristan. He wasn't packing. "Fine! You really want to know what happened? Are you really sure? Because you're going to be pretty fucking disappointed."

"Alexis!" Mom admonished.

"I don't want to hear it, Mom. Not after what I heard. This Amadis thing is a bunch of fucked-up shit. I thought the Amadis were *good*, unified under the Angels to do good in the world. But it really is nothing but a bunch of politicians looking out for their best interests. Including Rina!"

"Alexis," Tristan murmured, taking my hands and trying to calm me down. The clothes I'd been sending to the bed fell from mid-air to the floor. "That's rather harsh. Tell us what you heard so we can make sense of it."

I told them everything, including Julia's silent comment about Rina's secret and the other mind signature.

"I didn't sense anyone but Julia," Mom said. She looked at Tristan and Owen, and they both shook their heads.

"Because she's blocking you! I didn't sense her presence, only her mind signature. She was there." I shook my head. "It doesn't matter. Julia may not be the traitor, but she's in cahoots with her. They're holding something against Rina, and it happens to be the secret of my daughter."

"You're saying Rina knows you already have a daughter?" Owen asked with skepticism.

"That's absurd," Mom said. "You're jumping to conclusions and making a fool of yourself."

"Thanks for your understanding and support, Mother. I guess you're just like the rest . . . sheep following fools. I know what I heard, the first time and today. Everyone's stabbing each other in the back, and my own grandmother's knife is between my fucking shoulder blades."

Mom glared at me. "That's enough, Alexis. This behavior is unbecoming for your position."

I started hurling clothes through the air again. "I don't give a shit about my behavior or my position. Right now, I don't even want my position. I'm going to take my family out of here so you all can be safe again, and then we're going to go find *my daughter!*"

Mom sighed heavily. "You don't have a daughter yet. That's not what Julia meant."

"*Mom*. I thought of all people, *you* would believe me. Since you don't, go. We don't have any more time to waste."

She stood there, staring at me as I stuffed the pile of clothes on my bed into my suitcase.

"Take Owen with you," she muttered, and she disappeared.

I turned to Owen. "We don't need you. I don't want you along if you don't believe me."

He chewed on his lip. "I believe you . . . all except for the Rina part anyway. I can't see her doing such a thing. But my job is to protect you and Dorian, and I want to help you get to the bottom of this."

"And we *do* need him," Tristan said. He shared his plan with us while I finished packing for both of us. Which ended up being useless because we couldn't flash with luggage and flashing was our only means of escape, from the Daemoni *and* from the Amadis.

"Okay, so there are two things I don't get," Owen said ten minutes later as he started the boat's engine.

He paused as he backed the boat from the pier and turned it away from the Amadis Island. Away from my son. Tears still stung my eyes from saying goodbye to Dorian. I was leaving him. Again. But it was part of Tristan's plan, the only way to get us—all of us—off the island. Owen would follow with Dorian, but Tristan and I had to distract the Daemoni first. Keep their attention away from Dorian. At least I was able to say goodbye this time, to hold him and kiss him one more time. I prayed Tristan's plan would work.

"First," Owen continued, "you said the person in the woods the other night had leverage over all of you, and you couldn't know about the girl until the plan had been executed. You think the secret of the daughter is the leverage they're holding over Rina, right? So how could they hide the girl from Rina? Or do you think the plan *has* been executed?"

I stared at the afternoon sun glinting off the steel-blue water. "She thought *they* couldn't know about the daughter, not any of us specifically, so maybe she only meant Tristan and me . . . or anyone besides who knows already. Or maybe Rina knows *about* the girl, but doesn't know where she is."

It came out convoluted, but Owen seemed to understand my points.

"So you don't think this Daemoni attack is part of the plan?" Owen asked. We all looked at each other with the same coldness in our eyes.

"That would mean the Daemoni are involved in all of this, which means the traitor is working for them, not just against us," Tristan said.

"And that's impossible," Owen said. "Like Solomon said, they don't have enough control to pull it off this long."

"I think the plan is simply to gain more power," I said. "They're making Rina doubt herself. Julia was laying that on pretty heavily. And the other leverage they have over all of us is Dorian's powers."

"Yeah, that's my second thing," Owen said. "Dorian has *powers? Already?*"

"Yep, which means you need to keep an extra-close eye on him," I said. "We've told him he can't do those things around other people because it would make them feel bad that they can't do it, too. But that doesn't mean he won't try or do something accidentally."

"We're hoping it's the power from the island, and he loses his abilities, or at least the strength diminishes, when he leaves," Tristan added.

"Or he could be a freak like his mother," Owen said.

I narrowed my eyes and held up my left hand threateningly. "Not in the mood."

Owen got the message and focused on steering the boat. My eyes probed beyond the shield that stretched about a mile out from the island, and my stomach dropped. A whole fleet of boats spaced evenly apart, waiting for us. *Idiots. They'll attract Norman attention.* A few gigantic birds hung in the sky and, knowing now there were Were marine animals, I wondered what might be in the sea. I told myself it couldn't be bad—Tristan wouldn't have let us swim in it before if there was danger. That's what I told myself, but I didn't believe it one bit.

"Are you ready, *ma lykita?*" Tristan murmured in my ear. "As soon as we pierce the shield, they'll be aiming for us. Be ready for my 'go'."

I nodded, though my stomach felt as though flopping goldfish filled it. I suddenly wanted to flash back to the island and hide out with Dorian tucked safely between us. But then

I imagined his face among the dead in the Amadis village or the nearby Norman town, and my heart broke for the mothers of the children who'd died. We couldn't let that happen again. Not because of us. At least if we were away from the island, the Daemoni could enjoy a game of cat-and-mouse with us, rather than terrorizing innocents.

"Please, please, *please* keep Dorian safe, Owen," I begged. "Your parents, Jelani, and Chandra are all on his side, even think he could lead some day. Use them if you have to. I'm counting on you."

"Don't worry. I'll do *anything* to keep you from going back to the way you were. Besides, I'd never survive the wrath of both you and Tristan."

"Use your magic if necessary," I said. "I don't care who's around. Protect him, Owen. That's an order!"

He saluted me. "Ready? About ten seconds."

Tristan took my hand, and we both stood in the center of the boat as it flew through the shield. We waited just long enough to be sure some of the Daemoni saw him and me, then Tristan said, "Now!"

A blue streak of some kind of magic sailed past my ear right when I flashed.

Chapter 11

A string of profanities flew out of my mouth when we appeared at the Athens airport, right in front of a mirror in a bathroom.

"How could you let me leave in *this*?" I hissed at Tristan as he checked the stalls to make sure we were alone.

He'd brought us to this particular bathroom because it was only used by employees, so it was often empty. And now I had to sneak out of it dressed as a gladiator-slut from the 1300s—I still wore the traditional Amadis dress. We could only flash with what could fit in Tristan's pockets—passports, a cell phone and money—so I couldn't change.

"Thought you were keeping it on for a reason," Tristan said with a shrug. "You could get your way with any warm-blooded male wearing that. Although . . . you could probably do the same wearing sweats and a T."

I rolled my eyes. "This is so not cool. I need normal clothes. At least you *look* normal!"

He was also still dressed for the ceremony-that-never-happened. Though I wished our escape from that mortifying event wasn't because of these more terrifying circumstances, the timing couldn't have been more in my favor. Of course, here I was in this scanty dress about to be seen by a lot more people than would fit on the Amadis Island. And they'd be staring more because they wouldn't be bowing their heads. *Who wears a gladiator costume on an airplane?*

Tristan sighed. "Stay here. I'll go find something. Lock the door behind me and be ready for *anything.*"

I nodded and held my hands up, palms out, ready to fire electric bolts and move objects. "Thank you."

Tristan wasn't gone five seconds when musical laughter rang somewhere nearby. I froze. *Vanessa.* I bent my knees, kept my hands in position, and waited for her appearance, my heart pounding against my chest. If she was alone, I could beat her, but I might have to kill her, and Amadis weren't supposed to kill if there was hope for the soul . . . unless it was our lives or theirs. And between Vanessa and me, it would always be to the death. Even if she knew she couldn't beat me, she'd die trying. Only Tristan could scare her away, and I didn't know how long he'd be.

I wondered how she found us. It'd been three months since she'd ingested my blood, so she had to have burned through it already, severing our connection. I dissolved my wall and felt for her mind signature. Two signatures came at me—two females, both Norman. I relaxed and blew out a breath of relief, and then the door rattled in its jam, making me jump. The two women simply needed to use the bathroom. *Crap.* I couldn't open it for them, as much as I wanted to.

"We have to get out of here."

I jumped again at the sound in my ear, though I knew the lovely voice better than anyone's. Tristan stood next to me, empty-handed. The two women gave up and left—or heard the male voice and went for security.

"Too many Daemoni here," Tristan said. "They prepared for us to try to fly out of here."

"But surely they wouldn't attack in the middle of a busy international airport?"

"They don't usually attack Norman towns or our villages, either. Come on, I'll lead." He held his hand out and I took it, needing the touch to follow his flash.

We flashed our way to the Skopje Airport in Macedonia, roughly one hundred miles at a time, pressing the distance limits of our flashing abilities. This time, before letting Tristan leave the hidden area he had brought us to, I probed outwards, carefully but quickly roaming through the mind signatures, searching for danger. When I gave him the all-clear, Tristan disappeared again, still on the hunt for clothes. He returned with a white, wool sweater. I raised my eyebrows. There was nothing wrong with the sweater—I just hoped to change into jeans, too.

"It's all I could find. It's a tiny airport, and they don't have boutiques, only a couple of duty-free and souvenir shops. Unless, you want me to raid someone's luggage?"

I sighed. "No, we're not stealing someone else's clothes."

Since I wasn't wearing a bra under the leather bodice, I kept it on and pulled the sweater over my head. At least the white didn't clash with the lavender skirt. And at least I didn't feel as though I wore smexy lingerie in public.

Three flights, two days and nearly five thousand dollars later, we arrived in Sydney, Australia, all as a show for whoever might have been following us . . . friend or foe. Because I'd said we were going to Australia instead of the States, Tristan thought we should actually go and see who, if anyone, pursued us before we rejoined with our son and headed for our real destination.

So far, we'd only detected Daemoni, nothing more—and they didn't take the chance of attacking with all the Normans around. I didn't have the same problem of listening to their thoughts as I did with Normans or Amadis. At least, not ethical issues of invading their privacy. On the other hand, their thoughts disgusted and terrified me. By listening, though, I learned a lot, such as Lucas, my sperm donor, had ordered them to take us alive, with as little Norman attention as possible. But, of course, Daemoni didn't always follow orders.

Julia, the traitor and any other Amadis against us didn't send anyone in pursuit. Apparently, they really did just want us off the island. I was sure, though, it was more than because they were concerned for everyone's safety. They had a plan.

We spent the night in a busy hotel in Sydney and checked in with Owen. I'd been worrying about him like crazy, feeling guilty for abandoning him on the boat in the middle of Daemoni fire. He'd held his own, though, and left the Amadis Island with Dorian the day after we did. He couldn't tell us where they were, in case of eavesdroppers, but Tristan's plan remained on track. We'd rendezvous in Kuckaroo, an Amadis village in the Outback, in a couple of days. We were able to talk to Dorian briefly, and he asked several times when he would see us again. Of course he was scared of losing us. He'd lived nearly seven years without his father and now was ripped apart from him again. I lied through my teeth and told him everything would be okay, and we would see him soon.

I sorely missed my mom, too, but we couldn't take the risk of contacting her. I wasn't sure if we could trust her right now. I didn't think she was in on Rina's secret, but she'd made it clear she believed Rina over me.

The sting from Rina's betrayal bit again as I stared out the hotel window at the lights of Sydney's nightscape, my turn to be on watch while Tristan slept. Tonight was the first time we'd really slowed down since leaving the Amadis Island, and the constant action had kept my mind off of what had happened, focused instead on what lay ahead. Downtime meant thinking time, and tears burned my eyes as I wondered how Rina could do this to me. I'd always had so much respect for her and, though slightly frightened of her at first, came to love her dearly. She always believed in me, even when I was young and (nearly) a Norman. She was this powerful matriarch who admired me, loved me . . . and betrayed me. She even lied about the other person who'd been in the room with her and Julia. I thought she protected love, but my mistake was now painfully obvious. Julia and Mom were wrong. Rina protected the Amadis first, family and love second.

I'd actually been mistaken about the Amadis in general. Mom, Tristan, Owen . . . all of them emphasized over and over that the Amadis were *good*. Over the years, I'd created this high expectation of them—the society and the council, expecting the council to be almost like Angels. But they were nothing but typical, slimy politicians. They might fight for good against evil, but they weren't above fighting each other out of greed—greed for money, power, or whatever it was that motivated them.

I woke Tristan with kisses, wanting to finally make love to him, to take me to another, blissful place away from my reality. After months of holding back, I was so ready. I didn't care who heard me when my wall crashed—the hotel guests and employees were all Norman strangers who'd never know what hit them. The inevitable destruction of the room was a concern . . . but a minor one at this point. We'd just have to leave money to cover the damages.

He awoke immediately and responsively, his luscious lips kissing me back. The gold in his eyes sparkled with anticipation, the green shining beautifully as he looked into my eyes. Once again, I couldn't believe how breathtaking he was and how lucky I was to be with him. His strong arms enveloped me and held me against his hard body, making me feel safe and loved . . . and desperate for him. But apparently the stress and exhaustion of the last several days was more than I'd realized—some time before I was even naked, I crashed.

At least in my dream we made love. We were in our beach house in the Florida Keys, destroying the Caribbean room once again, our bed in shambles, the rest of the furniture in pieces. I moaned with pleasure, so close to euphoria . . . and then that musical voice chimed in: "Sweet dreams, little bitch."

I bolted upright in the hotel bed, my eyes darting around wildly and my heart pounding in my chest.

"Sorry to wake you from such a hot dream, but we need to go," Tristan said.

"Vanessa," I replied. The musical voice had been real and close by.

BANG!

The door burst open, bounced off the wall and slammed back in the white-blonde's exquisite face. Her lightning-quick reflexes caught it just in time, the metal door molding to the shape of her arm. Tristan took my hand as she threw it open again and, after catching a glimpse of Vanessa and her brother Victor flying into the hotel room, we flashed.

They came close enough. We appeared on a deserted beach, and Vanessa and Victor appeared right after us, catching our flash trails. They were stupid to think they alone could defeat us—they couldn't beat Tristan even without my help—but Vanessa's pursuit was always based on emotions, not on the obvious facts. And it wasn't Tristan she wanted to beat. She only fought him because he protected me. He shot fireballs at her, and I shot an electric bolt at Victor, singeing a hole through his shirt and into his chest, turning his white skin purple.

"Now!" Tristan said, and we flashed again, now somewhere inland and desert-like. The sickeningly sweet smell of burning vampire flesh still filled my nose.

"Son of a witch!"

Vanessa and Victor followed us once again, immediately lunging forward when they appeared. Vanessa's hand grasped my right wrist like a steel vise. I shot a constant flow of electricity at her, the current traveling through her arm and back into me, then into Tristan, who still had a grip on my upper-right arm so I could follow his flash. Victor, the idiot, wrapped his arms around his sister, trying to pull her off me. The electric current charged violently through all of us.

Rather than electrocuting me, though, it boosted my power. Tristan could take it. Vanessa and Victor could not. Their bodies convulsed, and purple tendrils of smoke rose from their skin. They knew what would happen from the last time I nearly smoked the vampire bitch, and she finally released my wrist. Both of them fell to the ground, their bodies still writhing. Tristan and I used our powers together to send them flying back twenty yards, too far to follow our trails.

"*Again*," Tristan said, and I followed him to a new place, more remote than the previous one.

We stood back-to-back, our knees bent in fighting stance, palms held out. My heart thrummed erratically as adrenaline and lingering electricity shot through my veins. Hundreds of beats thundered in my chest as we waited . . . and waited. When the two vampires didn't appear, the air imprisoned in my lungs finally released with a whoosh. I leaned forward with my hands on my knees, panting, trying to slow everything down to a normal rhythm.

"That was . . . fun," Tristan said, swinging around to face me. I looked up at him and lifted an eyebrow. A wide grin filled his face. He meant it. "You weren't really scared of those two, were you? They're not a real threat."

"She wants to kill me. That's a real threat in my book."

"She missed her opportunity, *ma lykita*. You're too strong for her now. I think you could have fried all of us and still be left standing." He squatted in front of me and lifted my chin with his thumb to look into my eyes. His sandy-brown hair still crackled with a trace of electricity. "Just make sure I'm there when you fight her. I've been looking forward to watching that for a long time."

I rolled my eyes. I wasn't sure if he wanted to see me beat Vanessa or just watch two women fighting . . . especially because it was over him. Well, I was sure it was both, actually. He wanted me to beat her, but he wouldn't mind a show of it.

My heartbeat and breathing returned to normal, I finally stood up straight and caught a glimpse of movement out of the corner of my eye. I spun, instinctively holding my palm out. A kangaroo stood a hundred yards in the distance.

"Oh!" Without a thought, I sprinted after it.

"Alexis, NO!" Tristan shouted but I ignored him, wanting to see it up close.

The kangaroo sprang away from me, but I was too fast for it. I was nearly close enough to touch it when it spun on me, leaned back on its tail and lifted its powerful legs. Its huge feet slammed into my face. I landed hard on my back and the breath flew out of me. *OW!* I panicked. Power shot out of my hand, and the kangaroo soared ten yards away before landing on its tail and feet. I lay in the dirt, dumbstruck, as it bounced away.

"What the hell are you thinking?" Tristan asked, his voice full of amusement as he appeared in front of me.

"Was . . . it . . . a Were?" I asked breathlessly as I struggled to sit up, mentally kicking myself for being so stupid and not checking first.

Tristan helped me to a sitting position. "No. Only a kangaroo."

"Really? Are they always that . . . mean?"

"Yes, especially when they feel threatened. So don't do that again. You'll ruin my favorite face in the world. Look what you've done to it." He knelt down in front of me and gingerly touched my nose and cheekbones. I flinched. Of course, I couldn't *look* at it, but I could *feel* it—my nose and cheeks hurt like hell. I groaned. The blood flowing from my nose had already stopped, and I could feel the broken bones mending themselves, but I would have serious bruises for a day or two.

Tristan lowered his mouth to my cheek and kissed across it, over my nose and to my other cheek.

"There's no open wound. You can't heal it with your saliva," I pointed out.

"Thought it might make you feel better, though."

It did, actually, eliminate the pain. My skin tingled rather than throbbed.

"My lip is cut," I whispered, and he moved his mouth to mine, his tongue running over my lips that had already healed.

"Would you like to pick up where your dream left off?" he asked.

I stiffened, staring at him. "*What?* You know what I was dreaming? Was I sharing it?"

The idea of my dreams seeping out of my head and into someone else's never crossed my mind. *How mortifying!*

He chuckled. "No. Looks like I'm right, though."

"Are you sure? Even Vanessa said something about my dreams."

"Hmm . . . could be coincidence . . . but your sexy little moans and movements made it obvious to me."

I groaned. "How embarrassing."

He chuckled again and brushed his lips across mine. "I was personally enjoying it, my love. But the real thing would be better."

I sighed. "Sorry about last night . . ."

"You can make it up to me." He kissed across my cheeks again, opening his mouth, his healing powers taking away the pain and replacing it with bliss.

"I will," I promised.

"Right now?" he whispered against my ear, sending goose bumps across my skin.

I glanced around at our surroundings. Not a soul around, not even any animals. But it was dry and dusty, and the thought of that dusty sand making its way into certain places was not exactly romantic or sexy.

"Hmm . . . follow me." He took my hand and flashed.

We appeared in a grassy area, surrounded by trees and the bank of a smooth pond in front of us. Its surface duplicated the trees and sky above so perfectly, it was difficult to tell where the real world ended and the reflection began.

"Crocodiles?" I asked but I already knew the answer. The only mind signatures I sensed were birds and a couple of snakes in the distance. Like the night in the woods on the island, I jumped into Tristan's arms and crushed my mouth against his. And pain shot through my face. I gasped. "Crap."

"Take it easy, my love." He lowered me to my feet and took off his shirt, spreading it on the ground. He kissed along my collarbone as he undressed me, then lay me down on his shirt. His lips moved against my breasts, sending electric currents downward. "You've taken care of me all this time. Now I can finally take care of you."

I pushed my hands in his hair as his mouth caressed my breasts and his tongue flicked over the tips. He sucked, pulling my nipples erect between his teeth, making me moan and writhe. He moved his mouth along my stomach, kissing and sucking every inch. Electricity shot through my lower body as he continued moving down, his hands on my breasts, sliding along my sides and then underneath me, raising my pelvis. His tongue danced expertly against me, doing things that should be illegal, making me cry out. His mouth took me over that elusive edge and into oblivion.

When the convulsions subsided, I pulled him up, then took him into my hand, stroking him as I guided him into me. He shuddered before he even entered. He looked down at me, his eyes sparkling, as he slid inside. I ran my hands over his chiseled chest and hard abs, around to the perfection in back, and then thrust my hips against him, pulling him into me at the same time. We both moaned and moved with urgency. It'd been way too long. We built up quickly and soared away together. There was no time for messing around, playing games with our powers, destroying whatever lay in our path. This time was relatively normal—except for a few bruises, of course.

But they were nothing compared to—

"Holy crap!" I stared at the water's smooth surface, perfectly reflecting my battered face as I leaned over the edge of the bank. I looked like a damn raccoon, one large bruise creating a mask around my eyes and across my nose and upper cheeks. "How could you want to make love to this?"

"I won't acknowledge that idiotic question," Tristan said, considering me. "But I have a good one: Did it work? Your shield?"

I had to think about it. "I don't know. I don't think so, but without anyone else around, I can't tell."

"Hmm." He shrugged it off. "Let's clean off, and we'll get moving again."

He led me into the water, and although the ripples distorted the reflection, it was still hard to see what hid underneath. I felt around with my feet, and finding nothing, I dipped down and immersed my shoulders. The water was cool and refreshing, especially since I hadn't had a chance to shower this morning, thanks to Vanessa and Victor. Tristan was already out, buckling his pants, and I was splashing water against my face when I sensed the mind signature and saw the movement under the water at the same time. I hadn't been paying enough attention.

The eyes broke the surface first, and then the long, broad snout. As its head emerged, its mouth opened widely, exposing rows of teeth several inches long.

"Waaaaah!" I screamed, punched its nose as hard as I could, and literally flew out of the water, clearing twenty-five feet over the bank before I landed behind Tristan. My fingernails dug into his arm as I peeked around him. The oversized, white crocodile sauntered out of the water, snapping its jaw. My superhuman strength didn't slow it. "What the hell! What do we do?"

"Shh . . . it's okay. Can't you tell?"

Of course it was okay to him. He'd been fighting sharks and probably crocodiles and various other monsters for centuries.

"Yeah! It's a freakin' Were! Do something already."

Tristan lifted his hand, but instead of attacking, the crocodile began transforming.

Chapter 12

"Please don't," the half-man/half-croc begged, the words distorted as he finished morphing. "It's me—Jax."

Amadis! That's what Tristan meant: he was asking if I could tell the were-croc was one of us.

Jax and I both stood there naked, Tristan between us. Jax's arms hung at his sides, completely relaxed, not at all embarrassed that I could see every bit of him. And there was a lot to see. Although quite a bit shorter than Tristan, he was otherwise large—*every*where—too over-muscled for my liking, but it was probably natural, his being part-crocodile and all. Scars ripped across his darkly tanned skin in several places, including his bald scalp. With my keen eyesight, I couldn't see a strand of hair anywhere—not even eyelashes or . . . never mind.

"G'day," he greeted, a toothy grin crinkling a scar that cut from above his brow, down his eyelid and to his cheekbone, though his brown eye looked undamaged. He saw me peeking at him from behind Tristan and winked at me.

Tristan's chest rumbled. He held his hand out to his side, and his shirt flew up from the ground. He pushed it back at me. It covered me better than the Amadis dress, but I still stayed behind Tristan and kept my eyes only on Jax's face—I'd seen enough of him already.

"Who are you and why were you sneaking up on me?" I demanded.

"You're a feisty little sheila, aren't ya?" Jax rubbed his nose, smiled wider and nodded toward Tristan. "I'm an old mate of his."

Tristan crossed his arms over his chest. "Hmph. *Mate* isn't exactly the right word. Or did you forget who gave you that scar over your eye?"

Jax laughed. "Naw, not forgotten."

"You must not have learned your lesson, then, sneaking up on us again. Or were you getting a little thrill from my wife?"

Jax shrugged. "She *is* a bloody ripper. Cracked a fat, all right."

Tristan's chest rumbled louder, and he leaned slightly forward. I didn't understand what Jax meant, but apparently it wasn't a compliment.

"Just giving ya a compliment, mate," Jax said.

Okay, maybe a compliment, but derogatory.

"Do you realize who she is?" Tristan growled.

"Hmm . . . you said your missus, right? Why don't ya make introductions?"

"Jax, this is Alexis," Tristan said, that familiar steel undertone in his voice, though on the surface it sounded polite. "Alexis *Ames*. As in Sophia's daughter, Katerina's granddaughter."

Understanding dawned on Jax's face, and he grinned warmly again. "Ah. So that's why you're throwin' such a wobbly. Didn't mean to disrespect ya, Miss Alexis. I don't get out among the Amadis much. So what brings ya out here to the bush?"

Neither Tristan nor I answered at first. Suspicion waved off Tristan's body, making me uneasy. Jax's being Amadis no longer meant what it used to. I focused on his thoughts, ensuring Julia and her posse hadn't sent him. He was mentally kicking himself all over for being *"such an arse around royalty,"* though a very basic man part of him was thinking about how hot I was, even with the racoon face. I squeezed Tristan's hand.

"Just passing through," Tristan finally said.

"Where you going? I hope not west—you'll end up in the never-never. You can't flash ya way to the west coast before dark."

All three of us automatically looked up. The sun hung in the western sky, not far from setting.

"No worries about us," Tristan said.

"Probably not, but since you are Amadis Royalty, I'll worry anyway. I don't spend much time around them—not around anyone, really—but mates are mates. You can stay the night at my place. I don't have much to offer, but it's better than being out in the bush overnight."

"Are there Daemoni around?" I asked.

"Naw. Haven't seen them in donkey's years. But that doesn't mean it's not dangerous out here at night."

I looked at Tristan, relying on his knowledge and experience, since I had little. He still looked suspicious. I probed Jax's mind again, looking for any ulterior motive.

He's okay, I told Tristan after listening. *A little lonely, wanting to do the right thing for us, but not dangerous.*

Tristan glanced sideways at me. I squeezed his hand again, and his shoulders relaxed.

"We're headed north to Kuckaroo," he told Jax.

"Hmm . . . you could make it before dark, if you know where you're flashing and don't show up in the middle of a dingo fight or a roo cave. It's risky. Up to you. Offer's there for you."

I shuddered at the thought of appearing in a kangaroo cave uninvited. I'd be admiring them from a distance from now on. Of course, we were just as likely to appear right next to a variety of unfriendly animals during the day and, realizing this, flashing our way through the Outback sounded less and less appealing.

My desire to stay out of the great outdoors at night may have been irrational. After all, we could see just as well in the dark, and Jax said Daemoni hadn't been around for ages. But somewhere in the recesses of my mind, I thought I remembered learning that Australia's nocturnal animals outnumbered their day-loving cousins. I could probably easily defend myself—animals could be electrocuted—but that didn't relieve the feeling of fear of the unknown. Especially after being pounded in the face by a kangaroo. Besides, a real bed was always a nice draw.

I want to stay, Tristan. He narrowed his eyes at me. *We'll be okay. Whatever your past is with him, he wants to help now. Unless you want to hear me whining all night, because I won't get an ounce of sleep out here.*

Tristan sighed and shook his head slowly. I could hear the reluctance in his thoughts. *"Fine. Maybe we'll learn something."*

"Give us a minute, and we'll go with you," Tristan told Jax.

Jax returned to the water and when he was out of sight, I quickly removed Tristan's shirt and put my own clothes on. When we reached the bank, Jax the person was gone, but the crocodile hovered under the water's surface, only his eyes and a slice of forehead showing. He swung his large head to the right, motioning for us to follow him. Though the croc was still a bit frightening, even knowing it was Jax, I was glad he changed—he may not have been embarrassed by his nakedness, but I was. We followed the croc half-way around the pond, to its feeder stream and up the stream to a tiny shack.

Tristan and Jax caught fish from the stream and we grilled it over a fire for dinner. It took a couple prods from Tristan to get Jax talking, but once he did, he chatted incessantly about his life in the bush. I didn't have to listen to his thoughts—he told us everything and then some. He stayed in the bush because it made living easier as an Amadis Were; in other words, if he wasn't around people, he wasn't tempted to eat them. He was changed by a Daemoni were-croc that bit him when he was a teenager out in the bush by himself. A warlock, who we figured out to be Charlotte, converted him, and he lived in Kuckaroo for a while. But full moons made control difficult, and he eventually moved out on his own.

He rarely saw people and preferred it that way. A female were-eagle visited him during new moons only, when he had the most control over his instinct to eat her. He'd learned to live entirely off the land, usually eating as a crocodile because it made the hunting easier, but when he needed supplies, he went to the nearest Norman town. He only visited Kuckaroo every few years. Except for the eagle, none of them came to visit him and he hadn't seen or sensed Daemoni since shortly after his own turning. He called the surrounding area within a two-hundred-kilometer range his home and knew it as well as he did his little one-room shack. He told us a handful of other Amadis Weres lived similarly in the Outback.

He asked about my face, and Tristan shared the story of my brief encounter with the kangaroo. Jax laughed for several minutes. We told him we were on the run from Daemoni, but little else about our situation. Now that we reminded him, he said he remembered hearing some of our story—the reason for the Daemoni's desire to have us, Tristan's capture—but hadn't heard about Tristan's escape.

"I don't trust any authority, including the Amadis, but you two seem all right," Jax said. "Anytime you're in my part of the bush and need anything, just sing out and I'll find ya."

"And your maker? Is he still around?" I asked, not particularly wanting to run into him.

"You mean 'she' and she's dead. After I converted to Amadis, she attacked me, and we went into a death roll. She gave me a lot of these scars, and I gave her death. I'm the only one of my kind now. If I were on the registry of animals, I'd be labeled as extinct."

Jax divided a pile of hides and blankets into two, creating two beds—one for Tristan and me and one for himself—in front of the fireplace. I didn't get a real bed, but it was still much better than being outside in the wilderness.

"Sorry, princess, it's the best I have," Jax said with a wink.

I told him it was fine. Tristan must have warmed to him during the evening—he didn't growl this time at Jax's wink. But he did put me on the opposite side from Jax, placing himself between us, and kept his arm tightly around me through the night.

∾

According to Tristan, by saying "Australia," I'd sent us to both the best and worst place for our escape. Before meeting me, Tristan spent nearly twenty years hiding from the Daemoni by blending into Norman society. He said the hard part was shaking them in the first place. It would be fairly easy by becoming lost and "vanishing" somewhere in the great Australian Outback. If we could give them the slip here, we could go just about anywhere, including the States. The problem with Australia, though, was getting off the continent—the few major airports would be watched, and we'd have Dorian with us, which meant no flashing or swimming. It wouldn't have mattered, though. The only places within flashing or swimming distance would be watched, too.

At the moment, I understood what he meant about becoming lost in the bush. We left Jax's shack at first light, flashing north toward Kuckaroo, and supposedly we were somewhere close. But we couldn't find it. We walked and walked and walked . . . and walked some more. We probably walked right by it, around it, possibly through it, for all I knew, but they kept a heavy shield and cloak over it.

"You would think other Amadis could see it or at least have some way to detect it," I complained after we'd been searching for the village for nearly two hours in the blazing sun. It was early winter Down Under, but an unusual warm spell brought summer heat, especially the farther north we traveled.

"We *should* be able to sense it, but they're probably on high alert after the attacks. And they must have a powerful warlock or two to create a shield this heavy. You're sure you can't pick anything up?"

"*No.* I already *said* I couldn't." I didn't mean for it to come out so harshly, but I was hot and dirty and tired of walking aimlessly, searching for the invisible. We may as well have been searching for the lost city of Atlantis in the middle of the Mohave. Our bodies adjusted to extreme temperatures, but within the last several minutes the heat became increasingly annoying, pushing down on us, creating a thrum in my head. Besides, it was the fourth time he'd asked me about mind signatures in the last fifteen minutes, and his own tone was full of impatience. "Are *you* sure you can't get a cell signal?"

I'd asked him the same thing more than four times. For some reason, pushing buttons felt like the solution for relieving the pressure in my head.

"We're in the middle of fucking nowhere, Alexis. Do you *see* a tower anywhere nearby?"

Apparently, he felt the need for an argument, too, and the overwhelming urge to fight consumed me.

I threw my arms in the air. "You're the big toy collector. Why don't you have one of those fancy satellite phones that get signals everywhere . . . *even* in the middle of fucking nowhere?"

"And when did I have time to buy one since leaving *Hell*?"

"Well, let's see . . . maybe during that whole week doing whatever the hell you wanted before you came back to me?" I yelled.

He shot a vicious look at me and, for a brief moment, I expected to see the old fire in his eyes. That was a low blow, and I knew it. I didn't apologize, though. I didn't feel like it right now. I wanted to strangle anything I could get my hands around.

"So what now?" I asked sharply. "Should we go back to Jax's?"

"Yeah, you'd like that, wouldn't you?" Tristan sneered.

"*What?* What's that supposed to mean?"

"I saw you ogling him out at the pond."

"I wasn't *ogling* him! He was naked and standing right in front of us!"

"Which you didn't mind one bit, did you? Or the way he looked at you?"

I stopped in my tracks and stared at him as if he'd slapped me. *What's wrong with him?* This was not my Tristan. My Tristan was sweet and caring and definitely not jealous. He had no need to be. He was the center of my world, and absolutely no one could ever compare to him.

"I spent seven-and-a-half years *waiting* for you," I spewed. "It's always been you and no one else. How *dare* you!"

I glared at him, my fists balled on my hips. He glared back. *Well, if he's going to be that way . . .*

"At least Jax would be able to find this place. I *trusted* you to know what you're doing, and now we're lost."

That did it. Tristan's perfect face twisted and contorted as several emotions tried to take over at once. The gold in his eyes sparked—not like they used to, with real flames, but like anyone's eyes when they're overcome with anger. My trust in him was sacred ground, not something to be thrown around lightly.

But before he could settle on any single emotion, something behind him caught my eye. The air itself wrinkled. I first thought it was the heat rising from the ground, but as I watched, it did it again and it was definitely . . . not normal.

"Oh! Tristan! I think we found it," I shouted, my anger replaced by surprise and jubilation. "Over here!"

I tugged on his hand, pulling him with me. We took two strides toward the wrinkle when a large Jeep burst out of that space, charging right at us. A musical laugh chimed over the grinding of tires on sand and gravel as the Jeep slid to a stop twenty yards in front of us. Tristan and I spun back around, but had nowhere to go. We were surrounded. Six Jeeps encircled us—some drivers and occupants with fangs, some with wands and yet others quivering, about to transform.

"Sorry to spoil your spat," Vanessa chimed. "I was quite enjoying it, and it kept you nicely distracted."

Tristan squeezed my hand, and I knew he was about to flash and I was to follow him. But before we had a chance, the air around us whooshed upward and our surroundings suddenly changed, like an abrupt scene change in a movie. We stood in the center of a wide road, a handful of old, brick buildings and squat houses spread out beyond the Jeeps. *Kuckaroo.* Vampires, Weres and mages surrounded the jeeps that surrounded Tristan and me.

"These two are mine but the rest are fair game," Vanessa yelled.

Chaos erupted. The vampires became blurred streaks as they flew at each other. Daemoni Weres changed on the fly as they lunged at their enemy cousins, bits of skin and goo—were-pulp—raining down on us. Magic spells shot around and across the circle. Jaws snapped. Buildings and Jeeps burst into flames. The screech of metal against stone echoed off the buildings.

Vanessa laughed maniacally, then lifted her arms and jumped toward me, flying across the twenty yards between us.

I knew what she planned to do before she did it, but I saw a chance to retrieve my necklace wrapped around her gloved arm, so I didn't stop her. Just as she was close enough to touch, her fangs bared for the bite, I ducked out of her way and reached for the pendant. My fingers brushed her ice-cold shoulder, and a spark crackled as they barely touched the ruby. Damn it! I missed, but her fangs didn't—they sliced across the inside of my arm, from wrist to inner elbow.

I didn't have vampire skin, but close enough, and, just as they can cut through their own skin, vampire fangs could cut through mine. Vanessa's left a deep gash that didn't heal instantly, and they couldn't have been more precise on the vein. Blood spurted to the rhythm of my speeding heart.

And I was suddenly surrounded by ravenous vampires. Including ours.

If there was any blood even Amadis vamps with the highest control couldn't resist, it would be mine. Owen had called it an energy drink for vamps—and that was before the completion of the *Ang'dora*. Now it was more powerful, and the vamps could smell it. They closed in on me.

Tristan growled deafeningly, and the vampires flinched. At once, he held one hand out and hit the Daemoni vampires with his power, and with his other hand, grasped my wrist, lifted my arm to him and ran his tongue along the gash. I could feel it starting to heal before, but his saliva sealed it instantly, stopping the blood flow.

"Well, isn't that sweet," Vanessa sang right before Tristan swung his hand toward her. She disappeared with a *pop*.

Her retreat signaled the rest of the Daemoni. The vampires, disabled by Tristan, disappeared first. He hit the Weres the best he could without hitting our own as they fought, and the evil Weres ran away. We both aimed at the mages who shot spells everywhere, some hitting buildings, some hitting our people. We blasted them together, cutting off their spells, and they finally flashed, too.

The air hung still and silent long enough for me to take in the destruction—burning buildings and Jeeps sending smoke plumes skyward, injured Amadis moaning with pain and crumpled bodies lying motionless on the ground. But not long enough for someone to finish yelling "Shield!"

Popping sounds filled the air as a new round of Daemoni appeared. After all these years, I still recognized the leprechaun face of Ian, the former Amadis who'd told me about the arranged marriage between Tristan and me, and the narrator of the beheading video. He quickly threw his hands in the air, as if in surrender, as he'd done with Tristan so many years ago.

"Just deliverin' a message," he said with his Irish accent. "You two stay 'ere, we keep attackin'."

"You have no right," Tristan yelled. "These are innocents!"

Ian laughed his sick ogre's laugh, his red hair shaking and his pale blue eyes crinkling. "But *you* ain't! And . . . so's ya know . . . the boy is ours."

My breath caught. *Dorian!* The realization that he and Owen were supposed to be here slammed into me like a Mack truck. The thought of them in a burning building or among the bodies drained all of my sensibility.

"Dorian," I yelled, turning around in circles, the obliterated village spinning in blurs. "Owen! Dorian!"

A female vampire knelt in front of me and took my hand. "They're not here, Miz Alexis."

I turned to Tristan, jerking my arm away as the vamp sniffed at the drying blood. The gold in his eyes was dim, the green dark, his expression unfathomable.

"They *have* him?" I shrieked with near hysteria.

Ian laughed. And I couldn't help it. Every time I saw the disgusting ogre, he was laughing at my heartbreak. I didn't electrocute him, though. Ian hated the Amadis in a different way than other Daemoni—he held a vendetta for his own heartbreak by my mother, who rejected his advances. So I pushed all my Amadis power through my hand and directed it right at his chest. Love, hope and faith . . . everything good wrapped into a thick rope of energy that I jammed into his heart. He fell to the ground, writhing.

Maniacal laughter—laughter at *his* misery—bubbled in my chest, but I managed to suppress it. I'd torture Ian until he begged for mercy and would only let up long enough to take what I needed from his mind. *And then I might kill the bastard.*

The other Daemoni advanced two steps toward me as I continued with the force on Ian. I held my left hand up.

"Don't. Make. Me. Fry. You."

A warlock held his own hands up, threatening me with his magic. "Leave then."

"We leave after you do," Tristan said. "We're not abandoning these innocents."

"We're watching," the warlock warned. "You don't leave, we attack. Again. And again. And again . . . until you do."

Tristan cocked his head and I heard what he heard—with my ears and my mind—and my breath let out with relief. I let Ian go.

"Not a problem," Tristan said.

An old, rusty truck appeared down the road, heading straight for us and swerving for the Daemoni. They popped out of sight.

"Need a lift?" Owen yelled from the driver's side.

"Get in, princess," Jax called from the passenger's seat as the truck slowed down enough for Tristan and me to jump into the back. But I didn't move until I saw the little blond head wedged between Owen and Jax. *He's safe.* I sprang into the truck's bed.

"Take cover," Tristan yelled at the Amadis and the burning village instantly disappeared. "The truck, too, Owen!"

Owen thrust his hands up to shield and cloak the truck and then yanked the wheel in a hard left turn, throwing Tristan and me against the side of the bed. Several figures popped into existence in the direction we had been heading, but not able to see us, they gave up and disappeared again. Then the truck back-fired, slowed and stopped.

"Is something wrong?" My voice cracked on the last word as panic tried to grip me.

"Nah. This is where I get out, princess," Jax said. "I only came to show warlock here how to find Kuckaroo. He would have never made it in time, the direction he was going."

"How did you know?"

"My bird friend brought me a message about the Daemoni. It doesn't take a genius to figure out what they're looking for." He peered back the way we'd come, as if he could still see the hidden town. "I guess those are the closest I got to mates. I can't abandon them. Better see what I can do."

He took off down the road, no time for any of us to say long goodbyes.

"Thank you for everything," I called out.

"Any time, princess."

Owen jammed the truck into gear, and it lurched, then rumbled on. I jumped to the front of the bed and pulled Dorian through the open window to the cab, welding him against me, never wanting to let him go. I kissed all over the top of his head, every part that wasn't buried against me.

"Mom . . . can't . . . breathe," Dorian gasped against my chest.

I laughed, an unfamiliar sound mixed with joy and grief—joy to have my baby in my arms, grief for what we left behind.

"You have a plan, Scarecrow?" Tristan called over the truck's ear-splitting engine.

"You're the plan man," Owen yelled back.

"Can you still fly?"

Owen laughed. "Oh, yeah! Those were the only classes I didn't mind sitting through."

"There's a private air strip about a-hundred-and-fifty kilometers due west."

"Gotch'ya! It'll take a while with old Bertha here," Owen said, slapping the ancient truck's dashboard, "but we should get there before dark."

We rumbled along through the bush on no apparent road. The benefit of Owen's shield, besides the fact that it made us literally disappear in the Outback and lose the Daemoni, was that it magically protected us from the dust. Not that I could be any nastier with dirt stuck to the dried sweat and blood from the morning.

Tristan leaned against the front of the truck's bed, wrapped his arms around us and pulled us between his legs, Dorian still in my lap.

"I love you, *ma lykita*," Tristan murmured against my ear. "I'm sorry about earlier."

"Me, too. I have no idea what overcame me."

"Could have been Vanessa's mages messing with us before we saw them."

"Ah." I closed my eyes. *Bitch.* "You know I love you more than anything, right?"

"Of course."

"More than me?" Dorian asked.

I thought for a moment. *How do I explain the difference to a seven-year-old?* "Hmm . . . more than anything but Dorian. And Dorian, I love you more than anything but Dad. Okay?"

Dorian considered this for a moment. "Awesome. I'm the same as Dad."

I leaned my head against Tristan's chest and closed my eyes, tears silently seeping through my eyelashes. *Another village attacked, more people dead. Because of us.* And we couldn't even stay to help them. The best thing we could do for them was leave. And never return.

We were on our own.

Chapter 13

Tristan wiped my tears away and whispered in my ear, "At least we're together."

I nodded against his chest.

Those were the last words spoken for nearly two hours as Bertha bumped through the wilderness, her rusty moans and creaks filling the silence. Dorian fell asleep in my lap, my body cushioning him on all but the worst of the bounces while Tristan's body cushioned mine. After grieving for the Amadis we left behind, my thoughts switched to our escape, and I hoped Tristan was concentrating on the best solution to get us off this God-forsaken continent. My experiences so far marred my perception of Australia—wild, dirty and frightening.

Owen must have grown bored after two hours of driving through the barren terrain—he broke into song. He had an unbelievable voice I never knew about, imitating the singers perfectly, from Elvis to Chester Bennington, and even the instrumental parts. It was the closest we had to a radio, so we didn't mind. As he finished *Shadow of the Day*, the sun already low in the western sky, he slowed Bertha, eventually bringing her to a stop.

"Is this it?" Owen asked.

I opened my eyes and almost whooped out loud when I saw the homestead. Bertha sat in front of an old farmhouse, facing a faded red barn. My mind was already inside, drinking a cold glass of water and then standing under a hot shower. But as I looked around more closely, my heart sank to my lap. Siding hung off the dilapidated barn, and the roof was caved in. The fields and stock pens were overgrown and unkempt. Paint peeled off the walls of the house, and grime tinted the windows a yellowish-brown color. A tiny, old airplane sat at the end of what once may have been a dirt runway, but now was littered with overgrown weeds and potholes nearly the size of Bertha. *This can't be it.*

"Yep, this is it," Tristan said, pushing me forward so he could stand up.

Owen turned in the driver's seat, and his face looked how I felt. "Dude . . . seriously? I think the owners abandoned this place decades ago. Probably ran away scared."

"Perhaps. I haven't been here in . . . a lifetime." Tristan hopped out of the truck. "Come on. Let's check it out. There's nothing here *you* can't fix, Scarecrow."

"True," Owen agreed, sliding out of the driver's seat, "very true."

Somehow, Dorian slept through the loud screech and bang of the truck's door closing. I stayed with him in the truck bed and listened while Tristan and Owen explored. Their discoveries didn't sound good. Based on their comments, Owen was right— the owners apparently took off years ago, leaving everything behind as if they were going to the store, including trash and dishes in the sink. The pipes creaked as they tried to turn the water on, but it sounded as though only a few drops actually dispelled from the faucet. *So much for a drink or a shower.*

Tristan suddenly appeared beside the truck, and various screeches, pops and bangs came from the house. I stiffened. It sounded as if Owen was *fighting* something.

"You left him in there?" I whispered anxiously to Tristan.

"Sure," he said with a shrug. "He's fixing it up."

Of course. Some things—such as Owen being a warlock—I still had a hard time remembering as real. To me, he was simply . . . *Owen.*

"Running water?" I asked, my voice mixed with doubt and hope at the same time.

"That's most of the noise—the pipes are a disaster. If Owen can't fix it, though, no one can."

"Good to go," Owen said, emerging from the house. He raised an eyebrow at me, questioning my doubt in him. "Including running water."

"Dibs on first shower!" I handed Dorian to Tristan and scurried out of the truck.

The house still looked the same on the outside, but when I walked through the front door, it could have been a model home . . . from the 1970s. Though outdated, the plaid-upholstered furniture appeared as though it'd just come off the delivery truck, and the avocado-green carpet as if it'd recently been laid. The orange kitchen appliances gleamed, and water poured out of the faucet . . . brown water.

"Ew. Can you fix that?" I asked.

"You sure do ask a lot," Owen teased with a grin. "It already looks better than it did. Just give it a few minutes."

The water eventually ran clear and hot, and I finally became clean and felt human again. Well, as human as I could be. With the dirt scrubbed away, my face looked perfect—no more bruises or any sign I'd been whacked by a kangaroo. *Whew.* A raccoon face wasn't the best disguise for our escape—a little too memorable. The gash on my arm from the morning's fight had also disappeared. I was as good as new . . . almost. Some decent sleep would take care of the rest.

Dinner consisted of snack food Owen and Dorian had in the truck, and as soon as he finished eating, Owen crashed in one of the bedrooms. Besides Dorian, he'd need the most sleep, and we had to leave in the middle of the night and travel in the dark. After putting Dorian to bed, Tristan and I loaded the luggage Owen had brought for us in the six-passenger airplane. I didn't know how it would ever get off the ground—it looked as though it'd been sitting for decades. Tristan and Owen had worked on it while I showered and then bathed Dorian, but they could do nothing about the old fuel. Tristan told me to have faith.

Though a little crowded in the queen-sized bed with Tristan and Dorian, I slept amazingly well and was wide awake after four hours of sleep, my body feeling completely regenerated and renewed. The guys could sleep another hour before we had to take off, so I crept outside and sat on the front porch steps. I gazed at the unfamiliar sky with more stars than I'd ever seen, feeling close enough that I actually reached up and waved my hand across the sky, nearly expecting to scatter the sparkly jewels. Of all the places in the U.S. Mom and I had lived, no starry night compared to that of the Australian Outback. The beauty mesmerized me.

But the diamond-studded sky couldn't distract me from the anxiety of the search. I couldn't wait to return to the States and begin looking for the girl. For our daughter. The last four days of escaping the Daemoni were four more days lost, four more days we were separated. Every day seemed to count now.

Just as Dorian had celebrated his seventh birthday less than three months ago, so had she. Seven years . . . *How long would they have let it go? Would I have ever known?* Surely I would have learned at some point, but they might have kept her hidden until she went through the *Ang'dora*—thirty, forty, even fifty more years.

I licked my lips and tasted the salt of stray tears. I still couldn't believe the betrayal by Rina and some of the council. And then the sadness turned to quiet anger. Those same council members who hid our daughter suspected both Tristan and me as traitors. They accused *us* of betrayal when *they* hid the hope for the Amadis' future from the very people they served, the people whose lives depended on that future.

I heard a soft catch of the door's latch behind me and expected Tristan, but Owen sat next to me.

"Pretty insane stuff going on, huh?" he said quietly when he saw me wiping my eyes.

"It's nothing like I expected. I knew we'd be on the run a lot and I knew we'd have to fight to be together, but I never thought it'd be this bad."

"It won't be for long. The Daemoni are still throwing their tantrum after Tristan's escape. They'll get bored, quiet down and abandon the hunt, especially when they won't be able to find us."

"That would be a relief. We have other things to focus on without worrying about them." I sighed. "They're not the only ones we have to fight for our love. Some of the Amadis don't want us together. Some don't want us at all. They'd probably celebrate if the Daemoni captured us."

"I wouldn't go that far . . ."

"They think we'll betray them, Owen. For some reason, they think I have more loyalty to the sperm donor I've never met than to the Amadis, to my only family. And they think Tristan will go back, too. Why do they doubt us?"

Owen scrubbed his hand through his hair and scrunched his eyes. When he spoke, the seriousness of his tone and his word choices gave a rare indication of his true age. "There are some who always worried about both of you. You have strong Daemoni blood. So does Tristan. Some believe that even if he *wanted* to convert, it's not possible. When he tried to kill you after the *Ang'dora* . . . that only fuels their beliefs there's still something under the surface, waiting for another opportunity to attack. And then there are a few who think he never wanted to, that he's pulling the ultimate spy job on all of us . . . and that you'll go along because you love him so much."

"What? That's completely absurd. How could they . . . ?"

He shrugged. "He was such a formidable Daemoni warrior for so long, attacking our people, humans . . . *innocents*. That's how they remember him and they can't believe he could ever change."

"That was Seth, not Tristan," I said.

"You and I know the difference, as do most of the Amadis. The ones who don't knew him much longer as Seth. Some served him before their own conversions and saw the worst of him."

"But he didn't like himself then. He *never* wanted that life. You'd think they'd know more than anyone how much he wanted out of it."

Owen cut his eyes sideways at me. "Alexis, the Daemoni are cunning deceivers and Tristan was the best. He did what he had to do to make them happy just to stay alive. If you think he sulked around and defied them all the time, you're fooling yourself."

I pressed my fingers to my temples and squeezed my eyes shut, pushing away the images trying to surface—images of Seth's horrible acts, which Tristan had inadvertently shared with me the night I tried to save Sheree, the were-tiger. "I don't want to talk about this. My point is that's *not* him now. How can anyone not see that?"

"Some people need time. Others . . . well, they might not ever believe. They might not want to believe. Just as in the Norman world, there are always a few who like to stir the pot."

"I don't get it, Owen. I thought the Amadis were all *good*."

"We *are* good. We find good, and we protect it. But it doesn't mean we're all perfect, that we don't screw up." He shifted, turned toward me. "Listen. We'll find out what's going on and take care of this mess, and I'll bet you the *truly* good people will be proven right . . . including you and Tristan and Rina. Remember what I keep telling you . . . in the end, good always wins. *We* always win." He patted my knee. "Have some faith, Alexis."

That was the second time I'd been told to have faith tonight. But my faith was waning.

☙

After Tristan strapped a sleeping Dorian into his seat, Owen rubbed then thrust his hands at the airplane's propeller to start the engine, at which point I had no choice but to at least have faith in him . . . because we were going to fly with magic as our fuel.

As I walked through the house one more time to make sure we left nothing behind, Tristan came jogging in.

"Thought I should leave a note, tell them where their plane is," he explained, finding a scrap of paper and a pencil nub in a drawer.

"Um, I could be wrong—I usually am anymore—but I really don't think they're coming back," I said.

He shrugged. "With these people, you never know. They're kind of like that."

He wrote a one-sentence note detailing the town and

country where the plane would be and then paused before signing it—as Seth. I lifted an eyebrow, trying to ignore the tingling down my spine. He grimaced.

"Trust me—that was harder for me to write than for you to see. But that's all they know me as."

I nodded silently then flashed to the plane, trying not to think about it. But I couldn't help it, especially since Owen and I had just been discussing Seth. I held an entire, silent conversation with myself, trying to convince myself that it meant nothing more than he knew the owners a long time ago. But the paranoia gnawed at me for most of the flight. *He wouldn't . . . would he?*

He looked back at me from the front seat right then, as if he'd heard me ask myself that question, but our minds weren't connected. I mentally slapped myself when I looked into his eyes. He loved me. The look in his hazel eyes, all over his face, made it perfectly clear. I smiled warmly at him, and he grinned and winked. I forgot my doubts.

When we landed at the tiny airport, I realized we weren't even in the same country Tristan had left in his note, and he immediately arranged for the plane to be flown to the location where he'd said it would be. A mental slap wasn't enough. I deserved to be physically punched. *What is wrong with me? I can't doubt him! We have to stick together.* I couldn't let other people's ignorance and prejudices get to me. That would only make things worse for us.

Two days later, we arrived on U.S. soil without incident, and if it weren't the L.A. airport, I might have dropped to my knees and kissed that soil. Until we'd left the Keys for Greece, I'd never been out of the United States. My publicist had wanted me to do an international signing tour when my books became popular overseas, but I refused—the U.S. tours were difficult enough. Though California was one of the few states I'd never lived, I felt as though I was home. Just hearing (mostly) English with American accents gave me a sense of normalcy. And to make it better, no one looked at me with an ounce of recognition.

"Are we almost home?" Dorian asked while we studied the departure boards, trying to decide where to go next—where to start our search.

Hmm . . . home? I wasn't quite sure where "home" was yet.

"We can't go to your old home," Tristan said. "We talked about that, remember?"

"I know we can't live there anymore, but can we go visit? I want to show Joey and everyone else at school that you're real and not a shithead."

I fought the urge to laugh. Tristan raised an eyebrow.

"Watch your mouth, little man," I warned, hiding my smile.

"But that's what Joey called Dad, and it's not true!" He lifted his chin and stuck his lower lip out in a defiant pout. "Maybe Dad can beat up their dads. They're the real shitheads."

I couldn't help it. This time I full-out laughed, and Tristan and Owen joined me. We all had a hard spot in our hearts for the publicity and rumors about Dorian's father abandoning me when I was pregnant.

"We're going to do the right thing and leave them alone," I finally said. "If there's something you miss from home, though, we can get another one."

"Naw. I got Dad now." He took Tristan's hand and grinned. "And I'll be getting my dog soon."

He apparently hadn't forgotten about that birthday present.

We still didn't have a real plan, but traveling was obviously a necessity. Whether we'd establish a home base first or tow

Dorian around with us on our search, we hadn't yet decided. Now that we were at least in the States and hadn't been detected by Daemoni so far, Tristan should be able to concentrate on a plan. But first, we had to get out of L.A., which held a certain attraction for Daemoni, and it was only a matter of time before someone sighted us. We decided to fly to Salt Lake City first—it was safe, convenient and one of the first flights available after we passed through customs.

Salt Lake was convenient because Tristan happened to have the key to the safety deposit box he had there, one key of only a few he picked up before we left Miami. Along with a nice stash of cash, the box held a false ID for him, so we could check into a hotel under a different name. It was also convenient because "one of his guys," who created false identification, lived nearby. Leave it to Tristan to know the one guy who was probably the only shady character in the whole state of Utah.

While Tristan focused on our plan, Owen and I taught Dorian the rules of the game—if anyone asked, he was to give them his pretend name and say he was Tristan's brother and I was his brother's girlfriend. Owen was their cousin. We helped him memorize everyone's fake names, and he practiced calling me "Angela" instead of "Mom." I felt bad for him—just as he would grow used to this game, we'd have to create a new one, with different names and relationships. At least he was intelligent.

"How's it coming?" I asked Tristan a while later, sitting behind him on the bed and rubbing his shoulders. Owen had left to retrieve dinner, and Dorian sat in front of the television, engrossed in a cartoon.

"I've considered the options, and the best one for Dorian's safety and protection is to give him a home. Our search might be dangerous—too risky to have him with us. We should also be near a colony, for extra protection."

"A colony? Is that what you call a village in the New World?"

He chuckled. "No, silly. A village is *only* Amadis, living together, usually under a shield. A colony is where many Amadis have settled in close proximity to each other, but among Normans."

"A Chinatown for Amadis?"

"Exactly, but not so obvious. Normans don't see anything unusual."

"Do Daemoni?"

"Some. But colonies aren't isolated or cloaked like villages, so the Daemoni would be stupid to attack in front of so many Norman witnesses, if they even found us. And there are a lot more colonies in the U.S. than there are villages. So . . . where would you like to live, my love?"

I stopped kneading his shoulders in mid-motion. I hadn't expected to be able to choose where we lived. I was happy to be in the U.S. "*Any*where?"

"Pick a place and I'll tell you if it's an option."

"Hmm . . ." I moved my hands down his back as I considered. I thought about the many places Mom and I had lived over the years and the many more where we hadn't, but at this point, I sought comfort and familiarity. My first choice probably wasn't possible, so I hesitated before finally blurting it out. "Florida?"

"We can do Florida. If the girl's been hidden under your noses, I think she's in the Southeast, so Florida works." He paused. "But not the Keys. Not the beach house."

"Okay."

"And not Miami. In fact, probably not the east coast at all."

I smiled. "Even better. Because I really liked Cape Heron, but I know we can't go there."

"No, but . . ." He grinned.

"But?" I asked, excited by his smile and the promise in his tone.

"There's a colony near Fort Myers."

I bounced into his lap. "Really? We can really go that close?"

"It's not all that close to Cape Heron." He kissed me on the forehead, his eyes sparkling brightly. "And you will love it."

"Close to the beach?"

"*On* the beach."

I threw my arms around his neck. "Thank you, thank you, thank you!"

"My pleasure." His mouth found mine, and I wouldn't let him go, at least, not until Owen returned with the perfect welcome-home meal: cheeseburgers and fries.

Our conversation with Mom later that night killed my buzz. After a series of ring signals, we called her from a pre-paid cell phone Owen picked up at the drugstore, set on speaker so we could all three participate in the conversation. She delivered good news first: we lost the Daemoni after leaving Kuckaroo, and they had no idea where we were. But the Daemoni staked out the Amadis villages worldwide—they couldn't see them, but they knew their general locations and stood guard in case we tried to seek their protection.

They'd given up watch on my Atlanta house, so Mom and Charlotte were planning a trip to retrieve a few things and convert it to a permanent safe house. Then Mom said they had Amadis business to watch over in the States, so they'd be here for a while. She was concerned about leaving Rina, though, and that was the bad news: the situation among the council had only worsened.

"I never fully understood Rina anyway, but she's acting very strange," Mom said. "When she's alone with Solomon and me, she's normal. Concerned about all of you, wanting to send protectors out for you, missing you. But when she's with the council members—which is a lot, they've been holding so many meetings lately—she's completely different. She doubts herself and even agrees with some of their points about you two not being entirely trustworthy. She's been spending a lot of time with Julia, and I'm not sure that's a good thing."

"Of course it's not! Julia and her little group are the problem," I said. "They're obviously a negative influence on her."

"Julia's always been supportive, though," Owen said. "She and Rina have been close almost since the day she came over to the Amadis."

"I think Solomon is the only vampire you can fully trust, though," Mom said.

"Very true," Owen admitted, and Tristan nodded in agreement.

"I've never been able to lock onto any truths with Julia," Mom said, "which tells me her loyalty changes with her best interests."

"That's exactly what I get from her," I said. "You knew that and still doubted me?"

"At the time, yes, and I'm sorry, honey. Rina's always trusted Julia so much. Even if I didn't trust her completely, I never thought she would betray Rina so blatantly. I'm still not so sure . . ."

"I am," I said firmly. I had no doubts at all about Julia. "Has she told anyone about Dorian yet?"

"Is it true? Does Dorian really have powers?"

"We don't know, actually," Tristan said, glancing at Dorian's sleeping lump under the covers of one of the beds. "He revealed a couple things when we were on the island, but hasn't since then. We were hoping the magic of the island was boosting what little bit he had, and he'd lose it after we left."

"Hmm . . . hold on." She kept silent for a few seconds. "I'm not feeling that truth."

Mine and Tristan's eyes locked with dreadful understanding.

"Keep an eye on him," Mom said. "You'll be in even more danger if anyone finds out. There are already nasty debates about providing you protection at all. Many of the village mayors say they won't take you in. People are scared, and it will only be worse if Dorian has powers. The Daemoni's hunt will intensify."

"So Julia and the others still have two threats they're holding against Rina—Dorian and our daughter," Tristan said.

Mom started to say something—another denial—but I interrupted her. "Did you ever find out who else was with Julia and Rina in the Council Hall, right before we left?"

"There was no one else," Mom said. "None of us sensed anyone and, in private, when Rina is more herself, more honest and direct, she still says there was no one else there—not in body or in mind. She didn't detect any other thoughts."

I looked at Owen and Tristan, and they both shook their heads.

"She's a powerful blocker, then. I heard someone else in that room. Or at least in the building."

"Things are such a mess here, I honestly don't know what to believe," Mom admitted. "But I do know you misunderstood at least one thing. Rina is not hiding your daughter from you."

"She may not be hiding her. She may not be aware of her location," Tristan said, "but it sounds like she knew the girl exists."

"No, you have it all wrong. If you heard right, Alexis, if they're even blackmailing Rina in the first place, that's not the secret she's been keeping—" Mom paused. "Someone's coming. I have to go. I don't want anyone knowing I've talked to you. It's not . . . stable enough here."

The line went dead.

"Son of a witch!" I pounded the table, cracking it in half. "What the hell was she saying?"

"Rina's not part of the conspiracy," Owen said with an I-told-you-so tone. He thrust his hands at the table and fixed the damage.

"But she is hiding something," Tristan said. "Something about our daughter."

Chapter 14

Trees, rocks and land blurred into streaks of green, brown and gray beyond the rental car's window as we raced along the highway pointed southeast. Once our identification documents were finished in Utah, we flew to Nashville, and now we headed toward Chattanooga. Tristan wanted to make a stop before heading south to Florida.

"We all need to be on alert," he said as we began climbing into the foothills. He kept his voice low enough so only Owen and I could hear—too low for Dorian's still-human hearing. "You can't trust faeries."

"Then why . . . ?" I started to ask. "Wait—did you say *faeries*? We're going to see real-life faeries? They *exist*?"

Tristan chuckled, apparently finding it amusing that I could still be shocked at some things. I found it annoying.

"We'll only see one, maybe two, if they're there. They come to our world more than most faeries, but they're also in the Otherworld a lot."

"There were no faeries in my history book," I said, hoping no one else heard the growl in my tone. I'd been living in and studying our world for three months, and still I hadn't learned everything. Still I felt like an alien. Or, at least, like an idiot.

"Because they're neither Amadis nor Daemoni, and they haven't played a significant enough role in your life or history." Tristan peered at me. He probably heard the annoyed growl after all. "They're spirits, usually evil, but some are . . . not good, exactly, but more neutral. But even those enjoy wreaking havoc among humans."

"People are their playthings," Owen muttered from the backseat. "Good thing they spend most of their time in the Otherworld."

"Why?" I asked. "I mean, why do they prefer the Otherworld?"

"In the Otherworld," Tristan said, "they can be free spirits, not bound to physical bodies."

The Otherworld was a concept I found difficult to grasp. I imagined it as a different dimension—my history book called it the spiritual realm—occupied by Angels and Demons (and apparently faeries, too). From what I'd learned, those in the Otherworld could see right into our physical realm. Be close enough to touch us without our realizing they were there. To watch over us. To spy on us.

"So if they're not good and we can't trust them, why on earth are we going to see some? What if they bring the Daemoni?"

"Faeries, like most denizens of the Otherworld, tend to stay out of our earthly wars. Besides, these two lean toward our side and they might have answers, information from the Otherworld that can help us."

"If they want to share," Owen said. "Or tell us the truth."

I didn't know what, exactly, I expected. Admittedly, the images of a tiny, winged Tinkerbell-like creature and a ghostly, disembodied presence crossed my mind. But that's not what we found.

Tristan turned the car into a driveway in the mountains and pulled to a stop at a cute little cottage hidden in the woods. Ferns and other plants hung in baskets on the front porch and wine-colored tulips lined the beds in front of it. The late afternoon sky hid behind tall pine and oak trees, and little lights twinkled among the greenery—I wasn't sure if they were lights or magic, because I couldn't actually see the source.

"Who's come to say may?" chimed a sweet voice from inside the cottage. She'd really said "see me"—her southern accent was heavy, and that was the first thing that caught me by surprise. Then she appeared in the doorway, and I stared at her stupidly as she bounded down the two steps toward us. "Oh, yay! Ah'm so happy to say ya'll!"

I barely noticed the glance Tristan and Owen exchanged, mesmerized by this . . . completely normal human. Or so she seemed, at first glance. She stood several inches taller than me, perhaps five-eight or five-nine, and had a body that belonged in bikini ads. Her blue hair hung in ringlets past her shoulders, and her silver eyes were bright and playful. But something about her was obviously different, besides the blue hair . . . I just couldn't pinpoint what it was. Something Otherworldly, I supposed. She *looked* normal, yet somehow you knew she wasn't.

"Say, I knew ya'll were comin' when I saw you leavin' Nashville. I was in the Otherworld, but it only made sense that you'd be comin' to say may. And it's about time." She eyed Tristan as she said this. "Last time you came, you had all kinds of questions I couldn't answer."

"Couldn't or wouldn't?" Tristan muttered.

She shrugged off the question. "Now I do have answers for you. So come on in, ya'll. I'll get you some sweet tay."

She turned and sauntered back into the cottage, long legs moving gracefully under a mini-skirt that swooshed side to side to the rhythm of her swinging hips. She obviously had no doubts we would follow.

When I looked at Tristan for guidance, amusement colored his face as he eyed Owen. "Maybe you should stay outside with Dorian, Scarecrow, before you get into any trouble."

I turned to Owen and had to suppress a giggle. His mouth hung open as he stared at the space where the faerie had stood only a moment ago.

"I think you're drooling," I said.

"Huh?" He finally looked at us, as if just now remembering we existed. He shook his head. "I, uh, think I'll stay out here. With Dorian. At least you have Alexis."

Tristan explained before I could ask. "Faeries are irresistible to the opposite sex, but especially to singles. My love for you dilutes her power drastically. Owen doesn't have a chance, and his involvement with a faerie is the last thing we need right now."

He took my hand and led me up the steps to the cottage, leaving Dorian and Owen at the car. Even if Owen hadn't reacted to the faerie like a teenager in a strip club, I'd be leaving him outside with Dorian. I already felt vulnerable, regardless of the faerie's preference for good or evil. No way would I leave my son unattended. I glanced over my shoulder at him, still sleeping in the car, before entering the cottage.

"So I know who you are, Alexis, but you don't know may," the faerie called from what I assumed was the kitchen. She appeared in a doorway, carrying a tray with three glasses of brown liquid poured over ice. "I'm Lisa."

I stared at her. *Lisa?* Such a Norman name.

"Well, that's not mah real name, of course. That one's too long and hard to say. It's easier to go by Lisa here . . . in this world." Maybe she didn't intend it, but I thought I saw her nose crinkle when she referred to our world. She placed the wooden tray of drinks on a coffee table and motioned for us to sit on the sofa. She plopped into a chair. "Where's Owen? He's not stayin' outside, is he?"

She looked disappointed when Tristan nodded, but then she laughed, a bright, joyful sound. "Ah, well. We have business to take care of anyway. First, I heard you were askin' about somethin'."

"Yes, our daugh—"

"No, no, not that," Lisa said, waving her hand. "Not yet. I mean this."

Another woman glided into the room. She struck quite a resemblance to Lisa, but with purple hair instead of blue. A tight white blouse, shorts barely longer than a bikini bottom and knee-high boots clad her killer body. She held a small animal in her hand.

"It wasn't easy, these are so rare, but Jessica was able to find this one," Lisa said.

"Who? What?" I asked, thoroughly confused.

"This is my sista, Jessica. And she found ya'll this."

The purple-haired Jessica strode over to me and deposited the little animal on my lap. *Whoa!* Was this some kind of faerie creature? Though it had a canine body shape and a wolf's face, light-gray lines marked its white fur, similar to a tiger's stripes. And closed tightly against its sides were feathery, shiny-white wings. *Wings!* It was the most beautiful creature I'd ever seen with the silkiest, softest fur I'd ever felt. I peered sideways at Tristan.

"I promised Dorian," he said.

I lifted an eyebrow. "Um . . . this isn't a dog."

"No. It's a Lykora."

My mouth dropped open. "You mean . . . ?"

"What I nicknamed you, exactly."

Ma lykita, he had told me once, meant "my little Lykora," a supposedly mythical creature that appeared to be tiny and non-threatening, but when it felt its loved ones were in danger, it would grow to the size it needed to be to protect them. I stared at the little animal in my lap, and it stared back with big, puppy-like eyes. Its tail wagged, and its wings fluttered slightly. The smell of baby powder engulfed me. It even smelled good. And then a blue tongue darted out of its mouth and licked my hand. *Crap. Crap, crap, crap.* I was already in love. But there was no way we could keep it. Dorian couldn't *see* it.

"Tristan, this is *not* a dog. Dorian can't have this."

"Sure he can." He scooped the little creature out of my lap, and with one hand, held it up to his face. "Hide," he told it.

The Lykora didn't run away and disappear. In fact, it didn't seem to obey at all. But then I noticed . . . its wings and stripes had disappeared, and its face had softened. It now looked like a little white puppy. I smiled as it licked Tristan's nose.

"She's been cared for by a wizard in Juneau," Jessica said in the same Southern drawl as her sister's. "She's about sixty years old, so still a pup, but well trained. You tell her what you want, and she'll do it. It'll take a few days for her to relearn her loyalty, though. She's yours."

Tristan's eyes narrowed. "In exchange for what?"

"Oh, come now, sweetie, why would you say that? What could we possibly want from ya'll?" Jessica asked.

"You faeries never do anything for nothing."

The faerie giggled. "Ah. I guess that's true. But there's nothin' I need from ya'll . . . not right now anyway."

She sauntered out of the room the way she'd come.

"So is this what we get instead of information?" Tristan asked Lisa. "This is your so-called answer? Something I didn't even ask of you specifically?"

Lisa shook her head. "No, no. I have other answers for you, too."

"So you'll tell us about our daughter?" Tristan asked, placing the Lykora back in my lap. "Are you willing to tell us who has her, where she is . . . ?"

A strange look crossed Lisa's face, her expression unreadable, almost confused and mischievous at once. It was time to tap into her thoughts. Her mind signature felt completely different than anything I'd come across yet—a bit of human, but filmy, not quite there—and when I focused on her thoughts . . . they weren't there at all. I concentrated on the signature harder, followed it to her mind but nothing. Nada. Zilch. I couldn't hear her thoughts. *Crap. Not good.*

"I feel you in ma head, Alexis," she said. "You can't hear me, though. My thoughts are not of this world."

It took a conscious effort to keep my mouth from hanging open. Tristan glanced at me, and I shook my head. His lips pressed into a hard line. He'd hoped I'd hear what she might refuse to say aloud.

"Anyway, I don't know what you mean about your daughter," Lisa finally said, dismissing that awkward moment.

"I thought you said you had answers for us," Tristan reminded her.

"I do . . . but my answers aren't to that question. I don't know about your daughter yet. I'm not a prophet."

"You can't see her from the Otherworld?"

Lisa's eyes twinkled. "I can't see what doesn't exist yet."

Tristan and I stared at her for several beats. I hated not being able to tell if she was lying. Not being able to listen to her thoughts.

Tristan stood up and held out his hand. "Come on, Alexis. This was pointless."

"You don't want your answers?" Lisa asked as I cupped the Lykora in my hand, stood and followed Tristan as he headed for the door. I gladly followed, ready to be moving again. I didn't feel safe here. For all I knew, she could have been stalling us, waiting for Daemoni to arrive.

"You don't have the ones we want," Tristan said without turning.

"But I do. If ya'll are searchin' for a daughter, you're lookin' for the wrong thang." She paused. "Where's your stone, Tristan?"

We both stopped abruptly, turned and stared at her again.

"The stone you were supposed to give to Alexis. Where is it?"

My pendant? Is that what she meant? The ruby in the pendant was the only stone he'd ever given me, besides the obvious one on my finger.

"You don't have it. And that's what ya'll *should* be lookin' for. It'll give you what you seek, what you *need*."

"How do you . . . ?" Tristan asked with that familiar steely undertone in his voice.

"Oh, I know. Do you remember what you were told?"

I looked at him when he didn't answer. His eyes were dark, the gold dim.

"Have you spoken with Bree yet?" Lisa asked.

"Who?"

"Ah, I guess not."

Something flickered across Tristan's face.

"Who's Bree?" I demanded.

She didn't answer for a long moment, but something showed in her face, too. *Sadness?* When she smiled, it didn't reach her eyes. "Bree is who you need to speak to, Tristan. She has your answers. Find the stone and find Bree. That's what I have to tell you."

We stood there for several more beats, but Lisa didn't explain any further.

"Are you going to tell us where to find this Bree?" I finally asked. Perhaps she was only distracting us from finding the girl, sending us on a wild goose chase for something else. From Tristan's and Owen's descriptions of faeries, it'd be something she would do. But if she was serious, if this Bree had our answers . . .

Lisa laughed, that same delightful sound from earlier, the humor reaching her eyes now. "There's a reason Bree has survived all these years—because she can't be found. But Tristan knows. He just needs to reach deep down in his heart, into places he refuses to go."

I looked at Tristan, and his expression was incomprehensible. His eyes were hard stones, the gold sparking with anger. He shook his head at me. *He has no idea what she's talking about.*

"So you're saying the answers to the questions about our daughter are buried in Tristan's *heart?*" I asked.

Lisa laughed again, then said cryptically, "Always were . . . in more ways than one."

Her riddles had become quite annoying and were getting us nowhere. I took Tristan's hand and turned for the door. "Come on, Tristan. You're right. This was pointless."

As soon as we were in the car, Dorian squealed with delight when I gave him the Lykora-puppy, but he instantly silenced when Tristan slammed his hand against the steering wheel. Fortunately, he reined his strength in before hitting it; otherwise, he would have jammed the wheel all the way into the engine compartment.

"Fucking faeries," he growled under his breath as the car peeled out of the driveway and sped the winding roads to the highway. Not daring to speak aloud, I silently reminded him that Dorian and Owen might not heal from an accident.

"Did any of it make sense to you at all?" I finally mustered the courage to ask once we were on the highway, headed south.

"The stone is in the pendant I gave you," he said, that steely undertone still in his voice. "The one Vanessa has now. I have no idea about the rest of it."

"So you don't remember what you were told?"

"I just said I have *no idea*. It's all bullshit. She's making it all up, playing with us. Forget about it, all right? Seeing her was a waste of time."

"So you don't think this Bree—"

"Damn it, Alexis! Drop it already!"

I flinched at the roar that filled the car, and his eyes flew to me, then returned to the road. He growled with frustration and swung his hand down toward the steering wheel again, but I caught it before he hit it. I was pretty sure he wouldn't restrain himself this time, and we were driving over a hundred miles an hour. I held his hand between both of mine in my lap, feeling him relax with each passing mile. His jaw muscle stopped twitching by the time we crossed the state line into Georgia.

We drove in silence all the way through Atlanta. Even Dorian and the puppy knew to keep quiet. At least, until Dorian's stomach growled loud enough for us all to hear, and he finally said he was hungry. Food lifted all of our moods.

"Faeries are hot, but totally not worth it. Women are hard enough to figure out, but could you imagine being married to that?" Owen asked as I handed him a burger from the fast-food bag. Tristan and I laughed, and the car's atmosphere immediately changed. "So what's next, big guy?"

"We'll get to Fort Myers tonight, and tomorrow Alexis and I go house-hunting. We need to get settled as soon as possible, but while we're doing that, I need you to check around. See if anyone in the state can tell you anything helpful."

"Shouldn't Alexis be in on that, so she can—?" Owen glanced at Dorian who was totally enthralled with the puppy, but he didn't need to finish his sentence for Tristan and me.

"We have too much to do right now," Tristan said, "but I don't want the time going to waste. Hopefully, you'll learn something that will give us a better starting point when we're ready."

❦

The morning after we arrived in Fort Myers, the first thing we did was go to the Harley-Davidson dealership, and Tristan paid cash for a pearl-white Fat Boy with the "necessary" extras. I drove the car to the hotel for Owen, then hopped on the back of the bike, wrapped my arms around Tristan and immediately felt as though the last eight years had never happened. The familiar rumble under us, the smells surrounding us, and the rush of wind as we cruised over the causeway took me to our early days, when we used to ride to Gasparilla Island.

This time, however, he took us to a different island. Sanibel was an undiscovered paradise, lush and green, many of its streets canopied with oak, banyan and palm trees. We drove along the main road through the island, passing restaurants, shops and inns, and then followed signs for Captiva Island.

Much of the road at the northwest end of Sanibel was undeveloped, lined with trees whose branches stretched over the road but not quite creating a canopy. The only indication that we crossed over to Captiva was a sign mounted on a small bridge. Then we started passing large homes and small mansions with signs on the mailboxes displaying names such as "The Unicorn's Lair" and "Magpie's Delight."

Eventually the homes became a little smaller and closer together, but even the more developed area of the tiny island wasn't overdone. Brightly colored townhouse clusters, quaint boutiques and ice cream shops were surrounded by tropical plants, bushes and palm trees that survived the hurricanes. It was here the textures of the mind signatures changed. There were just as many not-quite-human signatures as there were Norman ones.

"The colony," I breathed against Tristan's ear. He nodded.

Unsuspecting Normans would see the island as a sweet little beach resort, with people walking and riding bicycles and visiting the shops and cafes—enough people to feel neighborly but not overly crowded. They would never know the shop owners were witches and wizards or their waiter might morph into a wolf or the bartender preferred blood to wine. Not even the local Normans knew. The Amadis lived among them, served them, but with the security, support and camaraderie of being near each other.

Captiva was the perfect name—it captured my heart and soul.

"I told you you would love it," Tristan said.

As soon as we walked into the real estate broker's office back on Sanibel, Tristan cursed under his breath and turned around to leave. The office was small, with an unmanned receptionist's desk in front of us and two sets of French doors leading off the lobby into two offices. One was dark and empty. A plump woman, in her mid-thirties and with short, bleached-blond hair, stood from her desk in the other office.

"Can I help you?" she called out to us as Tristan opened the front door. He stopped short and quietly cursed again.

"I was looking for Don," Tristan said, nodding toward the darkened office. Don was the real estate broker and another of Tristan's "guys," one of many he had throughout the world.

"He's on vacation, but I can help you," the woman said.

Tristan blew out a breath of resignation and led me toward the woman. As she took a good look at us, recognition flickered across her face.

"Do I know you?" she asked. *Oh, crap. The first person to*

recognize me. Then she shook her head, and her expression changed, a smile spreading across her face. "Never mind. That would be silly. You look like someone I met many, many years ago."

Neither Tristan nor I said anything, though my chest tightened with an eerie feeling. I fought the urge to listen to her mind, to find out who she thought we were because she obviously wasn't thinking A.K. Emerson. But she was a Norman. She wouldn't know about us or our world. So I granted her privacy, even when, the closer I looked at her, the feeling that *she* seemed familiar grew. But who could she be? For some reason, my mind kept morphing her into someone with dark hair and a much thinner body. Perhaps she'd been an instructor at the college where I met Tristan, now with bleached hair and a few extra pounds. That had to be it—it would explain the recognition both ways, and she would quickly dismiss it because we shouldn't look exactly like we did then.

Tristan relaxed with her, probably coming to the same conclusion I did, and we began our house hunt. The woman showed us a few McMansions on the southeast end of Sanibel and two closer to Captiva, but none of them felt right. Tristan admired the architecture of some and criticized others, but he left the final decision to me. As soon as we drove up to it, I knew right away: I was in love. A charming wine-colored house nestled in the trees between the main road and the beach, on the Sanibel side of the bridge that crossed to Captiva, putting several miles between the colony and us. It wasn't unnecessarily huge like its neighbors, but with four bedrooms and a separate office, it was plenty large enough for the three—and one day soon, four—of us. And it felt like *home.*

"One of these days, we'll build our dream home," Tristan murmured as we stood on the beach while the agent started the paperwork inside the house. "I'm sorry you have to settle on this for now."

"Yeah, because this house is such a dump."

He chuckled. "Not exactly what I would design."

I turned in his arms and placed my hands on each side of his face. "Anything you do would be perfect. But I *love* our new house. Thank you for it."

"My pleasure," he said with my favorite smile, his eyes sparkling. As he dipped down for a kiss, I said a little prayer that we weren't making a big mistake and bringing our deadly problems to this slice of paradise.

By the time we arrived at the hotel, our offer had been accepted. Of course it had. It was a generous offer, especially because it was all cash. We weren't even tapping into my money, which Tristan had moved around into various accounts before we left the Keys. With his ability to see all possible options and the best solution, he had an uncanny investment strategy that worked exceedingly well, even when unmanaged for over seven years. He lost some—everyone had, especially in the last couple years—but it was a small dent in what he had accumulated over the previous decades.

We spent the next couple of weeks living out of the hotel and shopping for our new household, starting with a family car. By the time we closed on the house and after buying everything from furniture to clothes to electronics, I felt like a gluttonous pig, and we only bought the basics—beds, a couch and TV, a kitchen table and chairs, two laptops and living necessities.

Owen bought his own motorcycle and a condo on Captiva. The Amadis bankrolled his party. I wondered how long they would pay him to protect Dorian and me, or if they would cut him off if he continued to help us. I didn't *think* Rina would let it go that far . . . but who knew anymore?

The time wasn't an entire waste on the search for our daughter . . . well, depending on how you looked at it. Owen checked around for us and talked to a lot of Amadis people, though he couldn't go anywhere near the villages because the Daemoni still watched. He didn't find any leads for us, which meant it was either a waste of time or that we should start our search outside the state.

"I haven't been able to reach everyone, though," he said our first night in our new house. We sat on a blanket on the balcony, watching the sunset after a picnic dinner. Dorian and Sasha, the Lykora, had already run off to his room. "A certain witch coven refuses to talk to me, and I haven't heard from one of the wolf-packs either."

"What'd you do to them to make them so hostile?" I teased.

Owen snorted. "It's not me they're afraid of. You and Tristan, however . . . they've been warned to keep their distance from you."

Well, that wasn't good. How would we find the girl if no one would cooperate?

"Did you take care of the real estate agent?" Tristan asked, abruptly changing the subject, which meant he wasn't too worried about the witch coven or the wolf-pack.

"Sure did," Owen said.

"What did you do to her?" I demanded, all sorts of ideas going through my mind.

"She was very helpful—I really don't think you had anything to worry about," Owen said without answering me. "She said her daughter's available to babysit that cute little boy of yours, though."

"What did you do?" I asked again.

"She needed to forget some things about us," Tristan said flatly.

I opened my mouth to ask what that meant, although I already knew deep down—knew it meant Owen messed with her memories and also knew it was probably safest for all of us, including her. But the doorbell silenced me. We all stiffened.

"Amadis," Tristan and Owen said at the same time.

They could sense the person on the other side of the door, but they could only identify people they knew, usually by scent for Tristan and magical qualities for Owen. So they both looked at me, and I felt for the mind signature.

"She's a witch. And she brought us a cake as a welcome gift. She wants to be friends."

Tristan and Owen followed me to the door. I didn't know if it was to protect me, or because I said "cake."

A pretty blond stood on the other side of the door, with the biggest eyes and boobs I've ever seen. Okay, maybe not the biggest boobs, but they were disproportionately large on her slender frame—too big not to notice. I peered at the guys on each side of me, smiling inside at what I expected to see. Tristan surprised me—he stared at the cake, actually. Owen, though, was no surprise. He stared above the cake in her arms . . . and not at her hazel eyes. I was thankful for my mental wall, because I didn't want to know what ran through his mind at the moment. *Poor guy. We really need to find someone for him.*

She smiled warmly and held the cake out toward us. "Hi, I'm Blossom. Welcome to our neighborhood. Well, I live over on Captiva, but close enough."

Owen continued staring, and Tristan took the cake from her and carried it off to the kitchen. I shook my head with embarrassment.

"Come on in, Blossom," I said, stepping aside and purposely knocking Owen out of the way. "Sorry about these guys. They're just . . . uh . . ."

"Guys?" Blossom said.

"Yeah. Exactly." I held my hand out. "I'm Alexis."

She pushed my hand out of the way and gave me a hug. "I know who you are. Oh, I guess I'm supposed to curtsy."

"Oh, no! Please don't," I begged. "Really. A hug is fine."

"Yeah, hugs are perfect," Owen said from behind me. I jabbed my elbow into his ribs.

Blossom eyed him. "Hmm . . . maybe if you're good, I'll give you a hug goodbye."

Owen became a perfect gentleman. He introduced himself and Tristan, then helped Tristan bring plates and silverware out to the balcony so we could enjoy Blossom's cake. I liked Blossom. She gave Tristan a once-over, then looked at me with a "nice catch" expression, but she didn't ogle or drool as most women did around him. After hearing an unusual thump in Dorian's room and checking on him, I brought him out to meet our guest, and she proceeded to rave about how great he was—the poor kid fell hard with his first crush—and I beamed with pride. And once I took a bite of her heavenly chocolate cake, I liked her even more.

"Oh, my! This is the best cake I've ever eaten." Part of me wanted to devour the whole piece on my plate and then the rest of the cake itself, and part of me wanted to savor every single crumb. I hadn't had good sex since . . . since Australia, but I thought the cake could be a perfect replacement. It was orgasmic. My "mmm's" and "ooh's" that kept escaping my lips with each bite were met with "that" look from Tristan.

While we ate, Blossom told us all about the colony—which business owners were Amadis, where they hung out at night, how they managed their secrets, etc. She said they were a big, happy family . . . until we came to town.

"There have been threats, and we heard about attacks. The colony will fight for you if they have to," she said, "but they really don't want it to come to that. They like their lifestyle here. It's comfortable and laid back. The tourists aren't crazy drunks looking for trouble and attracting Daemoni attention. We want to keep it that way."

"The Daemoni don't know we're here," I said. "We chose this place because it's safest for us *and* the people surrounding us."

She tilted her head. "You're like a catch-22. No one else can protect us better in these times . . . but, well, we probably wouldn't need your protection if you weren't here in the first place."

"We'll keep them away from the colony," Tristan promised. "We want to call this place home, too."

Blossom nodded, but she didn't seem entirely convinced. I couldn't blame her—if I were her, I wouldn't want me living nearby either, even when we were five miles from the colony. By the time she left, I didn't know if she still wanted to be friends, and I didn't check her thoughts to find out. If any friendship were to develop, I wasn't going to start it by being a snoop.

I had the same dream that night as I'd had every night since visiting Lisa, and the repetition began to annoy me. I'd always been a dreamer before the *Ang'dora*, and often my dreams were meaningful. It was part of being a writer, I'd always thought. But since the *Ang'dora*, I'd hardly dreamt at all, and when I did, they were random and vague. Now I dreamt every night about faeries, my pendant and Vanessa, endlessly chasing and searching but never quite grasping any of them. I woke up frustrated. The dreams meant something, and there was only one person who, supposedly, had the answers. If only I could get him to talk.

Chapter 15

I opened the door the next morning, wishing the furniture deliverymen waited on the other side, but I already knew Owen stood on the front steps.

"It's your mom," he said as my new iPhone rang. The phone was an early anniversary gift from Tristan, who was playing with his own at this exact moment. I glanced at the number on the phone's screen.

"Are you psychic and not telling me?" That wasn't the first time he'd done that.

"No. I just got off the phone with my mom." He walked past me to the kitchen. Apparently, he hadn't bought his own food yet.

"Hey, Mom," I answered.

"Hi, honey. How's your new house?"

I glanced around. "Pretty empty right now, but our furniture should be here any minute."

"I won't keep you then. Did you happen to buy a bed for the guest room?"

Uh-oh. "No. Why?"

"That's okay. I can sleep with Dorian or something. We'll work it out."

"Are you coming here?" I tried to sound excited, but my emotions were mixed. I missed her, but I still had to wonder whose side she was on.

"Charlotte and I will be there next Friday. We have an investigation into a witch who's learned how to enhance breasts, and she might be planning to sell that as a service. We'll stay for the weekend. Char can stay with Owen, of course."

So we'd both be buying guest beds.

"That's great, but Tristan and I might not be here. We're going . . . out of town."

I couldn't tell her where or why; she'd disapprove and probably try to stop us. Tristan decided Owen's phone calls and investigations weren't enough—we'd be paying a personal visit to either the witch coven or the wolf pack. He just hadn't decided which one yet.

"Out of town? Do you really think that's a good idea?" Mom paused, and I should have known not to try to keep anything from her. "Alexis, you need to get off this wild goose chase! Until the Daemoni settle down, you're endangering your lives every time you go out in the world."

"They'll never settle down. You know that as well as I do. In the meantime, there's a girl out there . . . maybe our daughter—"

She cut me off. "We'll talk about it when I get there. In fact, we have a lot to talk about. See you next week."

"Love you, Mom," I muttered, but the line went dead.

I sat next to Tristan on the living room floor and watched him download finance and stock-tracking apps onto his phone.

"Great timing on their part," he said, referring to Mom and Charlotte.

"Yeah, I know." I sighed.

"No, it is good timing. They can stay with Dorian, so Owen can come with us."

"Sweet!" Owen called from the kitchen.

That improved things. Owen and his shield were always good to have along, but until now, we thought he'd have to stay home to protect Dorian.

"What do you think about Blossom?" Tristan asked, his head still bent over his phone.

"She's hot," Owen chimed in.

I ignored him. "She seems cool. Why?"

"I was wondering how much we can trust her. It wouldn't hurt to have a witch along with us."

"That means telling her everything," I pointed out.

"Not necessarily. I'll think about it more, but if she comes around, check her mind out."

I made a face.

"For me? Please?" He grinned and winked. I must have nodded while the fog clouded my brain because he thanked me.

"If I do that, then you owe me," I said when my head cleared.

"I don't have to owe you, because you can have whatever you want from me. *Any*thing for you, my love."

I rolled my eyes—I was pretty sure it wasn't going to be so easy. "Then tell me what Lisa was talking about. About my pendant."

He scowled. "Except that. I told you, I have no idea."

"I think you do, especially if you do a little digging." When he didn't reply, I tapped my head with my finger. "I can find out from you if I really wanted to."

He narrowed his eyes. His voice came out low. "You wouldn't."

"I really don't want to, Tristan, but I feel like this might be important. You can't think of anything? What about what you were told? Surely, you remember that. You have a perfect memory."

"It's irrelevant," he growled. "Just bullshit that we're not going to bother ourselves with."

"So you do know." It wasn't a question. He knew and refused to tell me. Usually, I'd let it go, not wanting him to relive any pain or guilt from his previous life, but unlike his other memories, it seemed as though this one had to do with us, not only him.

He jumped to his feet. "Furniture's here."

I heard the truck about a mile down the road.

"You said anything for me," I pushed.

"Not this! It's not worth it, Alexis. Trust me."

He strode toward the door, and I sprang up. "You can't keep secrets from me, Tristan!"

He turned on me, his face hard. "You'd really invade my private thoughts?"

"No! I meant we're married, that we're in this together. We can't survive with secrets. We need to *trust* each other."

His face softened, and he wrapped his arms around me.

"I'm sorry." He kissed the top of my head. "But I do have secrets, my love, things you really don't want to know."

"If they have to do with us, with our daughter, then I do want to know. Anything that might help."

He sighed. "It won't help, *ma lykita*. It'll only make things worse. Please trust me on this."

The doorbell rang, and I had to let it go. For today, anyway, because the rest of the day was full of furniture deliveries and cable installers, then Tristan setting up the television and Internet service. And, finally alone with only Dorian sleeping soundly in the other room, we were able to make love. Another reason for choosing to live away from the colony was that I didn't have to worry about anyone hearing us—with their sharp ears or minds. Only Normans surrounded us, so if my thoughts reached out farther than our property, they'd only think they were having good dreams. We couldn't get too crazy—the sounds of our bedroom being destroyed would wake Dorian—but we still broke our new bed. Owen would have to fix it, and I had to brace myself for the embarrassment . . . but it was worth it.

"Hey, Mom," Dorian said sleepily the next morning, snuggling between Tristan and me on the floor, Sasha under his arm. "What happened to your bed?"

Um . . .

"Mom was jumping on the bed and got out of control," Tristan answered with a grin.

I bit my lip to keep from laughing . . . because it was very near the truth.

❧

Blossom came over nearly every day with another to-die-for cake. She usually dropped the cake off and chatted for a few minutes, but once the following week, with the guys out on the beach, she stayed, and we had some girl time. It was strange for me. Besides Mom, I hadn't hung out with a female since I was ten years old.

"You're going to make me fat," I mumbled through a mouthful of strawberries and icing.

"You can't get fat," she said matter-of-factly. I gave her a questioning look. "When you sleep, your cells regenerate, and your body goes back to exactly the way it was after the *Ang'dora.*"

"Uh, yeah, right. Is that common knowledge, though? I mean, around the Amadis?"

She gave me a sheepish grin. "Not exactly. When I found out an actual Amadis daughter had moved in, I did some research, you know, to find out exactly what you are. You're really kind of badass—vampire, Were, mage and angel all rolled into one. Of course, you could eat an entire cake every day and not gain an ounce, so that makes me want to hate you. But . . . well, I can't. You're too cool."

I stared at her in disbelief. She researched me? Well, then, that gave me permission to research her . . . even if it wasn't exactly the same method. Within a minute of listening to Blossom's thoughts while she talked, though, I felt ashamed, yet fascinated. I'd never heard a mind work so fast.

I'm so freaked out, this investigation will be the death of me, but I just hope Eduardo doesn't get dragged into it—the image of a man with dark hair and eyes showed in her mind—*he's so great and hot and even though it was his idea, asking me if there was a spell to make tits larger, I was the one stupid enough to see if I could create one and it's a good thing I used myself as the guinea pig because anyone else would have killed me!*

She barely paused before moving on.

I still need to figure out that last ingredient to the potion that should cure the neighbor's cough and hopefully it will turn out better than this enlargement spell, if I can just control myself, but it's so dang exciting to create new stuff and I know I'm a good witch—wait, no, I'm a great witch!—just a little enthusiastic is all, like with these boobs, and, really, everyone needs to get over their stupid fears because I like Alexis and the rest of them.

"So what are you doing this weekend?" she asked without a break in the conversation—that's how fast she processed all those thoughts.

I pulled completely out of her head, my own spinning. "Going out of town, I think. My mom's coming, though, so plans might change."

"Yeah, I know." She chewed on her lip as she looked out the window. "She's coming to investigate me."

So . . . she's honest.

"I got a little excited with my experiment and ended up with these." Returning her gaze to me, she smushed her breasts together with her hands. "I didn't mean to. I was pretty happy with my girls before, actually. Now they're way too big. They get in the way all the time, and it's impossible to find cute tops that fit right. But Eduardo—he's the vamp who owns the coffee shop on Captiva—likes them, so maybe it'll be worth it. He's really yummy. You'll get to meet him sometime."

"Yeah . . . sometime." *If the natives ever let us come into town.*

"Of course, you have Tristan. *Major* yummy. I think it's so sweet that you're real soul-mates, a match made by the Angels. I wish they'd do something for me." She sighed wistfully.

I picked up our cake plates and took them over to the sink, debating whether to mention Owen, but I wasn't sure *how* interested he was in Blossom. *Not my business. It'll happen if it's meant to.*

She asked me for some pointers for dealing with Mom and Char, and I told her to be truthful, because Mom would know anyway. Then she chatted about how exciting it was to meet all of us, especially two Amadis daughters . . . and ranted on about several other things, too.

"So where are you going this weekend?" she asked, coming full circle.

"Um . . . I'm not sure. Either Daytona or a bike ride to Lake Okeechobee." I wasn't exactly lying—Tristan still hadn't decided if we would visit the witch coven in Daytona or the Okeechobee wolf pack first—but it wasn't the full truth, either. I *wanted* to trust her, but I didn't know yet. Trust never came easily to me, not since I was a kid and people hurt me one too many times. And right now, I wasn't sure I could trust my own mother, let alone some witch I'd just met. She was probably safer not knowing, anyway.

"Well, I hope you can go," she said. "I'm from Daytona, and it's always a lot of fun. And Okeechobee must mean a Were bike rally, which can be a blast. And you look like you could use some fun."

"I hope we can go, too, but I don't know how much fun it'll be," I muttered.

"Oh, it will be, especially if you go to the bike rally. Wait, maybe not—there's a full moon this weekend. That wouldn't be good. You should go to Daytona."

ʗ

"Ah, dude, I missed Blossom," Owen said, eyeing the cake as soon as he, Tristan and Dorian walked through the door. I shooed Dorian back outside to clean the sand off his feet.

"Sure did, by about fifteen minutes." I retrieved more dessert plates. "I don't think you're her type, though. She seems to prefer the dark and quiet type. You know, dark hair, dark eyes . . . undead."

"Ew. She's a vamp-tramp?"

"A *what*?" I laughed.

"A vamp-tramp . . . someone who's not a vamp but likes to do them. It's disgusting." Owen shuddered, then he shook his head. "What a waste. Ah, well. She's too thin and too . . . uh . . . endowed for my liking, anyway. And then there's that mole on her cheek and how fast she talks and . . ."

I stared at him for a minute as he rattled off a few more of Blossom's "faults" and then shook my head. No wonder he was still single—Owen was incredibly *picky*. And half the things he listed were turn-ons for most guys. I vowed to never set him up with anyone because no one could make him happy. He was on his own.

Dorian came in and went straight to his room. He didn't mind sand on his feet but hated it in his trunks and would change before he returned for his piece of cake.

I lowered my voice, in case he didn't close his bedroom door. "Have you decided where we're going this weekend?"

"Probably Okeechobee," Tristan said. "They're having a bike rally, so lots of people to talk—"

"A *Were* rally?"

"The best kind, from what I've heard," Owen said.

"You realize it's going to be a full moon, right?"

"We're not staying at night," Tristan said. He smiled, his eyes glinting. "Are you afraid, *ma lykita?*"

"Um . . . maybe. Should I be?"

Owen guffawed. "For one last time, will you have some faith, Alexis? You have Tristan, the ultimate warrior, and me, the dreaded warlock. And then there's you and your electric personality. *They* should be the ones afraid."

I laughed. "The dreaded warlock, huh?"

He gave me a sinister look. "Don't mock me. You have no clue about my history."

If he were anyone but Owen, I might have actually been a little frightened.

"They're Amadis, anyway. They won't attack us," Tristan said, dismissing my concern. "Did you—" he twitched his fingers around his temple "—with Blossom?"

"Yes."

He eyed me when I didn't expand my answer. "And?"

I gave him a coy smile. "I'll tell you when you tell me what I want to know."

"You're not being very helpful," he grumbled.

"Ditto," I replied as Dorian entered the room, preventing any further discussion.

As the weekend approached, I dreamt every night about faeries, Vanessa and my pendant, but the night before Mom was to arrive, the dream changed. Vanessa taunted me with her musical laugh, her white-blond hair whipping in the wind as she stood on the edge of a cliff, dangling my necklace over the emptiness beyond. Then suddenly, in her other hand, she held a little girl, about Dorian's age, by her reddish-brown hair. The girl cried and kicked her legs over the nothingness. Vanessa spread her arms wide. She laughed again. And then she let go of them both. I had to choose. I ran for the edge, stopping myself at the lip and watching them both fall in slow motion as I actually considered my choices. My mind screamed for the girl but my heart pulled me toward the pendant. When I finally dove over the edge, I aimed for the necklace. As soon as I grasped it, the girl evaporated into a wisp of smoke.

"NO!" I gasped, waking myself up. I sat up in the bed, pulling gulps of air. *How could I . . . ?*

Tristan pulled me into his arms.

"Just a dream, my love," he murmured.

"Of course. But I can't believe . . ." I couldn't finish. I lay down on my side, my back to him, ashamed of myself.

"You want to talk about it?" He nuzzled his face into my hair and kissed the side of my neck.

"No," I said with a sigh. The pendant was a touchy subject—not something for the middle of the night. "I just feel pulled in so many directions. I guess the stress is creeping into my dreams."

"Hmm . . . let me de-stress you." His mouth moved along my jaw, his lips finding mine.

As he took me far away from my stress, he murmured, "Happy Anniversary, my love."

I glanced at the clock—it was long after midnight, now July 30th—and grinned. Our eighth anniversary, but the first one together. *Tomorrow will be perfect. It has to be. We deserve it.* But since Mom would be in the house tomorrow night, this was our chance to celebrate alone. So we did. Oh, man, did we ever. Tristan brought me to the highest of heights several times, an orgasm for every anniversary we missed.

I hadn't slept so soundly in years, until . . .

"Mom! I thought we told you no jumping on the bed," Dorian reprimanded the next morning when he came into our room and found us on the floor again. "Uncle Owen's going to be so mad at you. He just fixed it!"

Tristan shook with laughter. "Mom's a bad girl. What do you think we should do?"

Dorian crossed his arms over his chest and narrowed his eyes at me. "Maybe she needs a spanking."

"I think you're right," Tristan said. He raised his hand with a gleam in his eye, but Dorian grabbed it.

"No, Dad, her mom's supposed to do it. We'll tell Mimi when she gets here today."

Tristan laughed. "Yeah, you're right. Besides, we're not supposed to hit girls, right?"

"Right. Then you would have to get a spanking, too." Dorian considered Tristan for a long moment. "Who's *your* mom?"

The humor drained out of Tristan's face, and something flickered in his eyes. My stomach formed into a rock. Tristan didn't remember his actual parents. Like me, he never knew his father. He'd been taken from his mother while a tot, and all he knew was that she was evil.

"Um . . . so . . ." I stammered, trying to think of how to get out of this demand. "So, Dorian, why would you say *moms* give spankings? I've never spanked you."

He shrugged. "I know. Naughty Nick's mom spanks him.

And his dad laughs when he's bad and that's all the time."

He chattered on about his favorite cartoon. Tristan thanked me with his eyes for distracting Dorian from the question. We both knew it wouldn't be the last time he'd ask, but at least now we could prepare ourselves for it.

Owen and Dorian were on Captiva later that morning, trying to make peace with the natives—we hoped their sweet faces and engaging personalities could win over the colony residents—when Mom and Charlotte arrived. After I gave them a tour of the house, we sat in the living room and watched Tristan connect a new home entertainment system—a "necessity" by his standards.

"So, are you pregnant yet?" Charlotte asked, direct as always.

I blinked with surprise. "Uh, no. Why?"

"I told you she wasn't," Mom said.

"I hoped you were wrong for once." Charlotte frowned.

"What's going on?" I asked.

Mom sighed. "I didn't want to get into it our first five minutes here, but there's a lot to discuss, honey. The Amadis are getting . . . anxious."

"Yeah, you said they're acting strange. So, is that why you're here? To spy on us? They wouldn't send royalty to investigate a witch, especially right now."

"Actually that was an excuse to come here and see you. They aren't aware you're here yet."

My eyebrows shot up. "Really? Surely someone in the colony—"

"Yes, someone has reported your arrival. But the entire Western Hemisphere reports to me now," Char said with a grin, "and I haven't bothered to tell the council yet. I said I needed your mother because we happened to be in Atlanta anyway, and with her truth-sensing and persuasion abilities, she'd make my investigation easy work."

I resisted the temptation to read their minds and studied their faces instead. Perhaps I really wanted to trust them, wanted them to be on our side, or perhaps they really were sincere, so I decided to give them the benefit of the doubt.

"Okay, so what's going on?" I asked again.

"The council has broken into factions," Mom said, not telling Tristan or me anything new. Until her next statement. "Even the most supportive ones are becoming agitated, up in arms about the next daughter. Rina thinks the sooner you get pregnant, the sooner everyone will settle down and unite again."

"But Rina knows there's already a daughter," I said. "Why doesn't she say so, if that will make everyone happy?"

Mom raised her eyebrows. "Alexis, there is no daughter. You need to let it go."

"There is! I heard it. *You* need to believe *me*."

"You're jumping to conclusions based on snippets of thoughts."

My eyes flew to Charlotte and back to Mom.

"Charlotte knows about your power," Mom said. "I had to tell her so she can help us. Now listen to me. What you heard about Rina, the threat to expose her secret, is not what you think it is. It's not my secret to tell, but just trust me on this."

"Well, if it's not Rina's secret, it *is* somebody's. Julia and her mysterious friend and whoever else are hiding our daughter! If Rina would only listen to me . . ."

"It's nonsense, Alexis. There's no possible way. You need to stop searching for something that doesn't exist."

I narrowed my eyes.

"I know what you're doing," Mom said. "You're going to Daytona this weekend to question a witch coven. I feel the truth of it."

I didn't answer at first. Last I'd heard, we were going to Lake

Okeechobee, but apparently Tristan had changed his mind. I looked at him, and he gave me a shrug.

"Okay, so that's what it is," I conceded. "So what? We need to figure this out. We need to find this girl."

"I also feel the truth that you're searching in vain. You won't find her—there isn't anyone to find." Her mahogany eyes were wide and sincere. *She means it.*

I dropped my head into my hands. Mom was never wrong. *If Mom feels that truth, then what are we doing? What did I hear?* Over a month had already passed since we left the Amadis Island, but the thoughts I heard were still clear. *But the meanings?*

Tristan came over and sat on the arm of my chair. I felt a tug inside my head—his mind signature. He was signaling me, and I opened my mind to him.

"*What do you think,* ma lykita? *I trust you.*"

Time had passed, but the urgency had continued to build. Last night's dream only motivated me more.

"Maybe you're right, Mom," I finally said, "but I'm not taking the chance that you're not. Maybe whoever is blocking Rina's power is messing with yours, too. I can't risk our daughter's life, if she's out there. And as you said, if she *is* out there, finding her will improve things all around."

Mom and Charlotte exchanged a significant look.

"Tell her," Charlotte said.

Mom sighed heavily, closed her eyes and pinched the bridge of her nose. The air in the room thickened even more, making my lungs, my whole body heavy with dread. Whatever she had to say wasn't good.

"What?" I asked to break the silence.

"They gave you six months altogether," Charlotte said when Mom didn't answer. "So, you have two more months."

"Two months for what?" My eyes bounced between her

and Mom, waiting for their answer.

"To become pregnant with a daughter or the council will take it into their own hands," Mom said darkly. "They'll split you and Tristan up."

The air whooshed out of my lungs and tears sprang to my eyes. Tristan took my hand, and I held onto his tightly as if they were already trying to pry us apart.

"Two months?" I finally whispered. "But . . . but that's not enough time."

"I agree, honey, but something—or someone—has them agitated."

"The traitor," I said.

"Probably. But they blame it on the Daemoni attacks . . . and other things. They say there's too much at stake to risk any delays. You conceived Dorian right away, so they think if this is possible between you and Tristan, it'll happen quickly."

"And if it's not possible? Then what?" My tone held an edge as the anger boiled near the surface.

"They want to try Owen."

"*What?*" I flew to my feet and paced the room. "That's ludicrous! What am I—a horse or a dog or something? How does a different stud change anything? *I'm* the one who's gone through the *Ang'dora*. *I'm* the one who wouldn't be able to conceive."

"We can't be certain about that," Mom said. "*I* conceived after the *Ang'dora*."

"Okay, then, why don't *you* and Owen try? That makes more sense than *me* and Owen!" I laughed hysterically, throwing my hands in the air. "Or, better yet, how about you and Tristan? That makes all the sense in the world, according to their thinking. Let's split up the supposed heavenly match, and everyone can fuck each other until we have another daughter!"

Mom pursed her lips, obviously biting back a reprimand. I

thought I heard Tristan and Char chuckle quietly, but I wasn't sure. My head throbbed too loudly with anger.

"This is insane, Mom. We're supposed to serve God and the Angels, but adultery is acceptable, as long as there's another daughter? Does that really make sense to you? Does that end really justify the means?"

"Some people would say yes," Mom said. "In fact, a lot of people would."

"I would," Tristan said quietly.

I spun on him. "*Seriously?*"

He took my hands in his and kissed the knuckles on each one. "Lexi, the future of a whole society relies on *your* daughter. Every possibility needs to be tried until one is successful . . . or until the Amadis die with you. But when the Amadis die, the Daemoni win. And humanity loses."

I stared into his beautiful but dark eyes, tears again filling my own. Put that way, we had no choice. I fell back into my chair and doubled over my knees, crying and blubbering into my thighs. "So we have two months or they'll break us up? We're finally together again, and they'll cut us in two, just like that?"

Tristan stroked my hair as I sobbed. *How could I lose him again?*

"That's not all," Charlotte said. She paused with hesitation, then blurted it out. "If the most extreme faction succeeds, you won't even get two months. They want Tristan removed from the Amadis completely and immediately. They've decided he's the traitor and needs to be eliminated."

Chapter 16

The sobs cut off instantly. Remnants of Psycho Alexis, whom I hadn't felt since before Tristan returned months ago, emerged. The anger didn't bubble under the surface now. The entire volcano exploded. I stood and electricity charged through my veins and crackled around me. I almost expected lightning to shoot out of my eyes as I glared at Mom and Charlotte.

My words came out slow and deliberate. "If they dare, they lose all chances of another daughter. If he goes, I go."

"Alexis." Mom reached out for me. Electricity charged between us, and she flinched.

I stormed out the back door and ran down the empty beach, covering more ground than humanly possible. Tristan grabbed my shoulder from behind and spun me around, ignoring the electricity zapping between us. I fell into his arms.

"They can't separate us, Tristan. They just can't!"

He held me tightly and pressed his cheek against the top of my head, but he didn't reply.

"We're supposed to be *made* for each other. They said it themselves. They *wanted* us together. Why are they doing this?"

"Not everyone believed it then," he said quietly. "Fewer may believe it now, especially after what the Daemoni did to me . . . after what happened in the Keys. Maybe they're right."

I jerked back. "What are you saying? You don't think we belong together?"

My heart hammered in my chest, filling the silence when he didn't answer. Finally, he pulled me back against him. "What *I* think is irrelevant. I love you, and that's what matters."

I leaned my head against his chest. "I knew some of them wanted this, but I didn't seriously think it would happen. I didn't think Rina would let it."

"Lexi, this isn't about what Rina or you or I want. We have an obligation to the Amadis as a whole. An obligation to all of mankind. Without the Amadis, humanity ends."

"But not in the next two months. Not in the next two or twenty *years*. They still have Rina, then Mom and then me. Lots of time." I inhaled deeply, the air rattling in my heaving chest, and exhaled slowly, calming myself. "Why are they being so demanding? How can they put a deadline on something that might be impossible? How can they destroy us for it?"

"Lexi, do you love me? Truly love me?" A ridiculous question, but his voice sounded as though he really needed to hear my answer. As if he weren't sure.

I looked up at him. "Of course."

He blew out a breath, and I couldn't understand why he'd been holding it. "Then they won't destroy us, my love. If we have to leave them for a while until time can prove my loyalty, then that's what we'll do."

"And if Mom is right . . . if this girl . . . this daughter doesn't exist, and I don't get pregnant in two months?" I couldn't say the rest . . . what they expected. So I whispered, "Owen?"

Tristan chuckled, though the sound was void of any joy. "In vitro fertilization, remember?"

Right. That had been my own idea in the past. The reminder calmed me further.

"You'd be okay with raising someone else's kid?"

"I'd *prefer* to be the father of your daughter—" He inhaled a deep breath and let it out. When he finished, his voice came out very quietly. "—but we do what we have to."

I pressed my forehead against his chest, twisting the hem of his shirt around my fingers.

"But if that doesn't work? What if they make us . . . ?" The thought of being with Owen was nauseating. Not only because he was like a brother, but because he *wasn't* Tristan.

He lifted my chin with one hand and looked deeply into my eyes, penetrating my heart. "I pray it'll never come to that, and I'll do everything in my power to prevent it, but if it does . . . well, the pain would be worse than anything I've suffered in my entire long life. It would break my heart. But I would still love you, *ma lykita*. Nothing can change that."

My chest squeezed, and my heart swelled at the same time, feeling both the pain and love he expressed. I threw my arms around his neck and pulled myself up against him. "I love you, my sweet Tristan. Always."

He leaned his forehead against mine. "And I love you."

"Some anniversary, huh?"

"At least we're together."

"Forever?"

"If it's up to me, yes."

I sighed. Unfortunately, not everything was up to us, but I would take what I could get. He kissed me, then took my hand as we walked slowly back to the house. It was farther than I thought—I'd run half a mile in the twenty seconds before he'd stopped me.

We entered the house through the rear door right as Owen walked through the front door.

"That was a mistake," Owen said darkly. "We have a problem."

Mom and Charlotte appeared in the hallway, halfway between Owen and us.

"Where's Dorian?" I asked.

"Come outside and see for yourself. See what he did in front of everyone. Thank God there weren't any Normans around."

We all followed him out the front door and down the steps. When we reached the ground, Owen turned and looked up. I followed his gaze, and my heart jumped in my chest. Dorian stood on the edge of the second-floor roof.

"Dorian! What are you doing?" I yelled.

"Watch, Mom. I can fly. Like Ironman!"

"No, you can't!" The scream tore through my throat as he launched himself off the roof before any of us could flash up there to get him.

Like any other young boy disillusioned by superheroes, his body plummeted toward the ground, my stomach plunging with him. Tristan reached out for him, but when he was just out of reach, Dorian suddenly swooped upward and hovered over the roof for several seconds before slowly descending and landing next to me on his feet, exactly as he'd done on the Amadis Island. By that point, we all stood there, staring at him with our mouths open.

"Yeah, I *can*," he said with an I-just-showed-you tone.

Part of me wanted to scream at him to never do that again, and another part wanted to pull him into my arms, relieved he was safe. But the biggest part of me fought to simply stay upright because the weight of what this meant was enough to crush an elephant.

"Well . . . *bloody hell*," Mom said, and we all turned our heads, mouths still gaping, to stare at her. Mom never cussed. She looked around at us and quickly dismissed it, taking on her normal tone of control. "Get him inside. *Now.*"

Tristan scooped Dorian into one arm, and we all rushed inside.

"Did I do something bad?" Dorian asked, looking up at us as he sat on the couch, all five of us adults standing in front of him, again staring at him as if he were from another planet.

"He did that on Captiva?" Mom asked, her voice tight.

"Yeah, right in the middle of town," Owen said. "Blossom saw. And a couple others, I think."

I closed my eyes, squeezing them tight to hold the tears back. *So not good. Shit, shit,* SHIT.

"What's the matter, Mom?" Dorian asked, but I couldn't answer, knowing my voice would break.

"Dorian, didn't we tell you not to do any tricks in front of other people?" Tristan asked.

"I didn't mean to. The balloon the scary white lady gave to me flew away, and I was trying to catch it."

Dorian didn't frighten easily, which meant he'd sensed the white lady as more than a mere Norman. I peeked into his mind to see the vampire who gave him the balloon. I didn't recognize her, which gave me a slice of relief. For a moment, I was afraid it was Julia or Vanessa.

"I'm sorry, Mom," Dorian said, his voice tiny.

I finally opened my eyes and pulled him into my arms. *Don't cry. Be strong for him.* Sobs stuck in my throat, choking me and making my chest heave. I fell to the floor with him locked in my arms, silently rocking him. All I could think was, *They're going to take him . . . take him away.*

People saw. The Daemoni would find out, and they'd come looking for him. One more reason the Daemoni would come to the quiet colony. One more reason for everyone to think us a danger. Because I certainly wasn't going to simply hand him over, even if doing so meant protecting everyone else. Maybe it was selfish and un-matriarch-like, but he was my son. My *baby*.

After a few minutes, Mom reached for Dorian, and I panicked.

"No," I screamed. "You can't take him!"

Sasha was suddenly at our side, twice as big as normal, a growl in her throat. Tristan knelt beside us, and I felt him tugging in my mind.

"*Lexi, they're not taking him away. You're scaring him.*"

I looked down at Dorian. He trembled in my arms as he looked up at me with wide, haunted eyes. I relaxed my fierce hold, and Mom took him. Tristan picked me up and half-carried me to our room. He sat on our bed with me in his lap, and the tears finally fell.

"I can't take anymore," I blubbered after several minutes. "You two are my life, and everyone wants to take you both away. And this whole daughter thing . . . all this pressure. I feel like I'm losing it again."

"We're not going anywhere," he murmured. "I'm here, Lexi. It's a lot to deal with, but I'm here for you."

I inhaled a jagged breath and nodded. His being here meant a lot. Everything, actually. Which was why I couldn't lose him again.

I eventually calmed down, and Mom must have heard because she popped her head in our doorway to tell us she, Charlotte and Owen were going to Captiva to do some damage control. Dorian came in as she finished, and she slipped away. He climbed onto our bed and into my lap, and wrapped his arms around my neck.

"I'm sorry, Mom," he said. "I'll never do that again."

I wanted to tell him very bad men would take him away otherwise, but such a threat wasn't enough to scare Dorian. So I simply said, "No, you probably shouldn't."

"Are you okay?" he asked quietly. "Because I don't want you to be sad again. I don't want you to be like when Dad was gone."

More tears slid down my cheeks as I kissed the top of his head. "Don't worry. You and Dad are right here, so I'm happy. I'm just having a bad day."

He nodded. "Okay. I love you, Mom."

"I love you too, little man, very, very much."

"I'll never leave you. Me and my wife and our kids will live with you, okay?"

"I would love that," I said with complete sincerity. *If only it were possible.*

"I know what you need," Tristan said, gathering us in his arms and standing up. He placed us on our feet, then took our hands and led us to the kitchen.

He popped open the bottle of wine Charlotte brought, poured us each a glass (well, a glass of juice for Dorian) and turned on some music. Then he started pulling food out of the refrigerator: ingredients for fajitas. And he was right. Cooking dinner together was exactly what I needed and a perfect way to celebrate our anniversary. Our kitchen wasn't fully stocked with all the gadgets and gizmos I couldn't wait to buy one day, but we had the necessities—good knives, pans and food. Listening to 30 Seconds to Mars, feeling the knife move under my hand, tasting the wine, smelling the onions and peppers and joking around with my two guys felt incredibly and necessarily *normal*.

Mom, Owen and Charlotte, along with Blossom, returned just as we started searing the meat. I hadn't expected Blossom, but it turned out she was a bit of a hero. When she saw Dorian spring a little too high for what was normal, she threw a cloak over him, so no one else saw his little flight on Captiva. It wasn't a strong cloak because she wasn't supposed to use magic out in the open, so Owen, a more powerful mage than her, was still able to see through it. He had been too worried at the time to sense the magic. With Mom and Charlotte here, she had been scared to come tell us what she'd done, but they finally tracked her down, and she confessed. When they finished telling me the story, I threw my arms around Blossom with relief. Her actions today laid a huge stretch of foundation for my trust.

℥℥

"If Blossom's from Daytona, that coven is her home coven," Tristan said that night as we lay in bed. "We should take her with us."

"Tristan, I don't think—"

"You trust her, right?"

Because the subject always caused problems and I didn't want to deal with yet another one right now, I'd given up on pressuring him about the stone and divulged all I knew about Blossom. I told him I felt better about her, but I still didn't trust her fully.

"And I really don't want to bring her into the middle of all this. It's too dangerous."

"Unless you can get Sophia to take us to the coven and persuade them to talk, Blossom's our only hope. Owen can cloak the three of us, and Blossom can drive us without raising any suspicion. The Daemoni are looking for us, not her, and it wouldn't be strange for her to be going home for the weekend."

"Can't we flash?"

"And if we run into trouble, they follow our trails. Do you want to deal with that again? Who knows when—or if—we'd be able to get home without leading them straight here. Besides, Blossom can get us *in*."

I sighed. My arguments were useless. He'd already thought everything through and knew the best solution. "I just don't like using her. It's not right, and it's not safe for her."

"We'll keep her safe." He rolled onto his side to face me and pushed my hair away from my face. "How about we let her decide?"

Blossom's decision came quickly and easily. She knew all about the trouble not only in the council, but throughout the Amadis. Like everywhere else, people in the colony were divided, which was why they hadn't been so welcoming to us. She'd known about the traitor, but not, of course, about the girl or my telepathic powers, and her feelings reflected Owen's— she found difficulty in believing any of it, but wanted to find the truth. She wanted to help solve the problem, and she came up with the idea to take us to her home coven before we even mentioned it, although it meant leaving immediately.

So the four of us piled into her car and took off, leaving Dorian with Mom and Char. Owen cloaked himself, Tristan and me, which made Blossom look as though she talked to herself if any drivers looked over at her. She didn't care. She talked non-stop for the five-hour drive, providing us details on the members of the Daytona coven, including her Aunt Sylvie, the leader. She hadn't been home in over a year, because last time, her desire to help some so-called friends back-fired on them all, and the coven, especially Aunt Sylvie, still held it against her.

Once in Daytona, she parked on the side of a street in front of a large, brick home in an older, yet nicely manicured neighborhood. Planters with colorful flowers hung on the window sills, the lawn was beautifully landscaped, and the shady front porch invited you up for tea or lemonade on this hot summer's evening. The house looked as though it belonged to an upper-middle-class family, not twelve witches that made up the coven. I only felt six mind signatures inside at the moment.

"You stay here for now," Blossom said as she opened the car door. "Let me soften up Aunt Sylvie first."

Tension tightened my muscles as Blossom hurried up the front walk. I couldn't help but wonder if she was delivering us right into the Daemoni's hands to protect the colony.

A thin woman who looked about sixty, with silver hair pulled neatly into a bun and wearing a long, tie-dyed skirt, opened the door just as Blossom reached it. Her dark eyes widened when she saw the guest on her front porch, and they silently stared at each other for a long moment. When the woman finally opened her mouth, she spoke quietly, but not too low for *our* ears.

"Blossom! What are you—" She broke off and peered behind her niece, her eyes scanning the neighborhood. "I sense magic. Too powerful to be yours, child."

"Yeah, well . . ." Blossom squirmed and shifted her weight. ". . . because I'm not alone."

The old woman's eyes snapped back to Blossom's face. "What do you mean you're not alone? Who did you bring here?"

"Some friends. They need your help."

"Blossom, we're not going through this again. Last time you brought friends to me, they wanted to raise their dead uncle to dispute a will!"

"I didn't know that's what they really wanted. They told me—" She shook her head. "It doesn't matter. It's not like that this time."

"Good! Because there are no séances or necromancy going on here. We don't do magic for Normans, and we definitely don't use dark magic."

"Of course not, Aunt Sylvie. That's not it at all. They're Amadis. Honestly. They just want information."

Aunt Sylvie narrowed her eyes. "That magic is too powerful for Amadis, even a warlock. It almost feels like a . . . a . . . *sorcerer*. What have you gotten yourself into now, Blossom?"

"I swear, they're Amadis. More Amadis than anyone really." Blossom waved her hand behind her back, her signal for us to join her.

"She won't let us in until she trusts we're not Daemoni," I said after peeking into the older witch's mind. This worry actually made me feel better because it meant Blossom hadn't led us into a trap. "She actually believes a sorcerer has cloaked and shielded us. Are you really that powerful, Owen?"

"No, not quite. But close enough," he said with a grin in his voice as we climbed out of the car.

Owen didn't remove the cloaks on us until we stood behind Blossom on the front porch. Aunt Sylvie gasped when we appeared.

"Oh, no. Blossom! This is almost as bad as Daemoni themselves."

"Aunt Sylvie, your manners," Blossom whispered, as if we couldn't hear anyway. "Don't you know who they are?"

"Of course I do. How could you bring them here?" Fear masked the woman's face, as if she expected us to attack her.

"They need our help."

"We can't help. It's too dangerous!" Aunt Sylvie glanced around the neighborhood again and stepped back into the house, pushing the door nearly closed so we could barely see her drop her head. "I'm sorry, Ms. Alexis, Mr. Tristan. I can't risk my coven. There was a reason I wouldn't respond to Owen's calls. Please, leave now. It's better for all of us."

"But, Aunt Sylvie," Blossom begged, "they just need to ask about a girl. You might know—"

"No, child! I don't—"

Three *pops* behind us cut her off, and we all spun around, hands out.

"That's exactly why I can't help!" The door's slam punctuated Aunt Sylvie's point. I caught enough of her thoughts to realize she knew nothing about a girl and only wanted her coven to be left in peace.

"Who are *they*?" Blossom whispered.

I knew who. I wanted to know how. How did Vanessa and her cronies find us once again? The surprise in Blossom's voice and in her mind meant this wasn't her doing. I felt out for mind signatures, but these three—Vanessa, her brother and another vampire—were the only non-humans around. Besides the witches in the house, of course, who were scrambling around inside and calling to each other about wands and hide-out spots.

"The vampire bitch we told you about," I whispered back. Vanessa giggled, probably pleased to hear we'd been talking about her, regardless of what had been said.

"You're going to attack in daylight, in the middle of a human neighborhood?" Tristan demanded.

"No, we're not here to fight," Vanessa said.

"Really?" Tristan asked, the single word full of doubt.

"We're obviously out-numbered and out-powered. We're not stupid."

"I beg to differ," Owen muttered under his breath.

"I heard that, warlock," Vanessa's brother barked. "You better watch yourself."

"Oh, stop. The warlock has a point about *you*, Victor," Vanessa said with a roll of her ice-blue eyes, which landed back on Tristan. "Let's just say *I'm* not stupid. But I'm beginning to think you are."

Tristan growled. "What are you up to now?"

"I couldn't help but overhear your conversation. Vampire hearing, you know. We've been watching this place, like we have every other coven, nest, pack, den . . . well, you get the picture.

The Amadis refuse to help you. A little discord in paradise, huh?"

"What's your point, Vanessa?" Tristan asked, his voice still a snarl.

"Well, I'm not surprised," she continued, ignoring Tristan's question. "This is what you've planned all along, right, lover? This nonsense search for a girl when you already know what you really need. This."

She whipped her gloved hand out from behind her back, my necklace still wrapped around her wrist, the pendant dangling from it. She couldn't wear the silver on her bare throat, and Vanessa wasn't the type to wear anything high-necked to protect her skin.

I waved my hand and the pendant swung toward me, but the chain was too strong and too tight to easily come off Vanessa's wrist.

"Too bad you'll never get it," Vanessa sang. "It's mine now and soon enough, Seth will be, too."

Without further thought, I jumped from the front porch toward her, but I was yanked back into Tristan's arms.

"I'm waiting for you, darling," Vanessa said, a gleam in her eyes. "Whenever you're ready to call off this charade and return to me. I have the stone now. Just follow your heart."

And with that, she disappeared, followed by her brother and other crony.

"Damn it!" I squirmed in Tristan's arms. When he let me go, I spun on him. "Why did you stop me?"

"Your reaction was exactly what she wanted. She was taunting us. Especially you. The stone's not worth it."

I stared at him, dumbfounded.

"It's just a rock, Lex. Forget about it."

"You think it's a distraction?" Owen asked.

Tristan's jaw muscle twitched. "Yes. She's trying to take advantage of everything going on with the Amadis. She knows we're falling apart. Which means they all know."

If that were true, if the Daemoni knew the Amadis had internal problems, they knew they could easily take us down. Was that what Vanessa had meant about a charade? About Tristan returning to her, because the Amadis would soon be destroyed? But what did she mean about following his heart? And what did she know about the stone?

I couldn't help but think Tristan knew exactly what she meant. His denial didn't ring true in my ears. The stone was a lot more than just a rock. Once again, suspicion crept under my skin and festered, making me question what else he lied about, besides the stone. I was tempted to listen to his thoughts but then shame and anger overcame me. *I can't let Vanessa get to me.* The Amadis were doing enough to split us up. I couldn't allow the Daemoni to do so, too.

Chapter 17

The weeks flew by entirely too fast, as if the world felt compelled to get to October as quickly as possible. Everything went from bad to worse with each passing day. The number of news reports about Normans disappearing from their lives rose sharply. Tristan blamed "natural" disasters, bizarre "accidents" and tense relations among countries on the Daemoni, as well. The Daemoni liked chaos, he said. They liked human suffering and war. Normans became easy pickings during turbulent and violent times, so the Daemoni were wreaking havoc with inciting incidents across the globe. How far would they go? Would they ever stop?

Having their fun in the Norman world and knowing the Amadis were already experiencing our own turbulence, the Daemoni did the opposite from what I expected. Their attacks on Amadis had actually dwindled. They still watched, however, prohibiting anyone from helping us. Tristan, sometimes with me and sometimes with Owen, made a few flash trips to other states in the Southeast, but no one would talk to us. Most worried about attracting attention of the Daemoni, but others said they'd been ordered by their council representative to give us no assistance. Which we knew to be lies, because Char was their council representative. Someone else threatened them, someone within the Amadis. The closer we came to October, the more we were stonewalled.

Mom and Charlotte had returned to the Amadis Island shortly after leaving us in early August, to find things worse than when they had left. If Mom didn't know Amadis daughters just didn't get ill—not physically or mentally—she said she would have thought Rina had dementia or Alzheimer's, often forgetting things, spacing out and even letting others make important decisions for her. Mom's updates became less and less detailed over time, however, and she made more and more references that things had improved, including Rina.

I knew from Blossom's sources that they had not.

The pressure sometimes became too much for us. Tristan and I fought nearly every day. He refused to tell me about the stone and I refused to drop the subject. My dreams had intensified, and I couldn't shake the feeling the stone and our daughter were somehow connected. I tried to convince him to seek out Bree, the person Lisa had spoken about, but he said we had too many other problems right now to be worrying about what a damn faerie said.

I taught myself Ancient Greek and Latin as a distraction. Tristan thought it was a waste of time, saying if I wanted to learn new languages, I should be focused on useful ones—those I would need while traveling in today's world. For me, however, these nearly obsolete languages *were* useful. The first and last few pages of the *Book of Prophecies & Curses*, the only pages I had a close enough look at, were emblazoned in my memory. From

Lisa's words, it sounded as though what Tristan had been told might have been a prophecy, and if he didn't want to, or really couldn't, tell me what it was, I hoped to find out on my own.

The process of translation was painstakingly slow, however. Internet translators didn't do a good enough job for anything to make sense, which was why I had to actually *learn* the languages. At least, enough about them to decipher the prophecies and curses. The fact that they were written in riddles didn't help.

Nothing on the pages in my memory mentioned a stone. I did find the prophecy about Tristan and me, which was fairly simple: "29 February 1736—The one they name for the god of chaos becomes the most powerful warrior for both friend and foe. Likewise, his mate, her soul created for his, shall be the daughter of enemy and ally." I also found, on the first page, what appeared to be a curse about the Amadis sons. Not sure that I translated it correctly, I wrote out what I saw in my memory for Tristan and showed him my translation as he sat at the kitchen table, reviewing stock quotes.

"Is this right?" I asked him, shoving my papers under his nose.

He studied the Ancient Greek and Latin versions and then my translation. "It appears to be. And I have heard of there being a curse before, but—"

"Then we have hope for Dorian!" I bounced on my feet with excitement.

He frowned. "Explain your reasoning."

"If this is right, Eris put a curse on all the Amadis sons. You said it's as if they're *compelled* to go to the Daemoni, right? And this also says the curse can only be broken by the sacrifice of Amadis blood for the greater good of the world, and it must be done by purposefully giving themselves to the Daemoni. But so far, the boys all go for their own benefit, right? But you—"

"*If* it's true, which most doubt it is—"

~ 246 ~

"Would it be in the *Book of Prophecies & Curses* if it wasn't true?"

He lifted an eyebrow. "You read the *Book of Prophecies & Curses?*"

I bit my lip. *Had I not told him? Was there a reason for not telling him?* "Just a few pages. I couldn't actually *read* it at the time, but I remember what I saw, you know, like we can do."

"Well, it doesn't necessarily mean it's true. From what I've heard about the book, everything's recorded, but none of it's completely reliable. Prophecies are always ambiguous and must be interpreted—sometimes incorrectly. A curse depends on the mage who cast it and many other factors, including God's will."

"And you think it's God's will that our son goes to the Daemoni?"

"I don't know God's will, Lex, but Amadis sons converting to the Daemoni does provide a way for balance, and I do believe evil and goodness remain in general balance until God decides otherwise."

"Owen says good always wins. We always win."

"But in order to win, in order to appreciate good, there must be evil in the world."

"Are you *defending* the Daemoni?" I asked, my lip curling with disgust.

He leaned back in his chair and crossed his arms. "I'm defending God's will and His plan."

"And maybe it's His plan that the curse finally be broken." I jabbed my finger at him. "Maybe *you* broke it, when you gave yourself to them to protect me and the rest of the Amadis."

He rolled his eyes. "That's absurd."

"Some people believe Dorian can still lead the Amadis. I heard it myself. Maybe this is why. They believe the curse has been broken."

He severed eye contact with me and stared at the wall in front of him. "I'm not an Amadis son, Alexis."

"You have Amadis blood, though. And you are Amadis now, and you were when you left, when you sacrificed yourself. And maybe that's why we didn't have a daughter, because we don't need one. Because Dorian can lead."

His eyes returned to me and narrowed. "Have you given up on this girl, then? You don't think she exists after all?"

I threw my arms in the air. "Of course not! I'm just considering all the angles and this seems as viable as any of the others. If we don't find the girl or we do and she's not really our daughter . . . if I don't get pregnant again . . . maybe it's all for a reason. Part of God's will."

"It's certainly a nice idea, everything wrapped up so neatly for us, but it's *too* easy. The world doesn't work that way."

"But God and the Angels can."

"Forget it, Alexis. If there's even a real curse, I'm not the one who's broken it. I don't exactly qualify."

"Why not?" I looked into his eyes and found the green dark and muddy and the gold sparks dim. I'd seen that look before. His thoughts came loud and clear through his expression. I didn't have to be a mind reader. "You think you're not good enough."

"I *know* I'm not!" he barked. "I'm not *enough* Amadis to break the curse. I'm not now, and I certainly wasn't then. I'm. Not. Good. *Enough.* Not for you and not for the Amadis."

"Now *that's* absurd. Get over it, Tristan. Get over your past. Get over yourself. You want to put it all behind you, but you don't actually *let it go!*"

In a blur of motion, he suddenly stood on his feet, pushing the table several feet across the floor with a screech.

"I'm done now," he growled, and in an instant, he was gone, leaving me standing there, wondering what was happening to us.

We argued about everything else, as well, and sometimes I wanted to give up on it all. I daydreamed about living a normal life. I fantasized about forgetting my responsibilities and letting everything fall as it may. But then I'd remember what that meant—losing Tristan . . . losing Dorian. Then what would be the point of life anyway?

Besides, I had a duty and a purpose. I had a responsibility to the Amadis, to mankind, to fulfill that duty and purpose. And being responsible meant carrying on even when I didn't want to. Even when I wasn't sure why I should care.

We made love every night, doing what we could to produce a daughter. At least *that* never got old, especially because half the time it was make-up sex.

℥

By the middle of September, panic imprisoned me in its tight vice. I'd bought every store on Captiva and Sanibel out of pregnancy tests. Since the *Ang'dora*, I didn't have periods. A truly awesome thing, unless your entire life—and everyone else's—depended on your getting pregnant. Because Mom had somehow been able to drop an egg, we had to hope I would, too. Hope. It wasn't exactly springing eternal within me, but I held onto as much as I could. Every morning I peed on the stick only to see a negative result, and every night I prayed this would be the time. Even in the midst of a heated argument, I knew I couldn't lose Tristan again.

Although I hated relinquishing them from my sight, afraid it might be the last time I saw either of them, I urged Tristan and Dorian out the door one morning, sending them off to the beach. Blossom had brought me an herbal mix over a week ago, a blend that primed the ovaries and hormones to facilitate fertilization.

She said witches had been using it for centuries without fail, including long after menopause. We didn't know if it would work for me, though, and I'd been too scared of any side effects it might have. But like most people drowning in the waters of desperation, I was willing to grasp at any possible lifeline.

Following her directions, I boiled water and poured it over a tablespoon of the leaves in a coffee mug. I let it steep for the required ten minutes, then stirred it, lifted the cup to my lips and gagged at the smell. *How can this be good for me when it smells like gasoline?*

"Well, Sasha," I said to the puppy at my feet, "here goes nothing."

She cocked her head as I pinched my nose and pulled in a large gulp. And immediately sprayed it everywhere.

Not only because it tasted worse than it smelled. But also because two people had suddenly appeared in my kitchen. Sasha instantly became the size of a Saint Bernard, her stripes, wings and fangs all on display. She growled at the intruders—Mom and Charlotte.

"What the hell?" I sputtered, wiping the tea from my shirt. "You scared the crap out of me!"

"Didn't Owen tell you we were coming?" Char asked as she started purposefully walking around the house, pulling all the window blinds shut.

"No. I haven't seen Owen today."

"He met us at the airport," Mom said. "He must not be back yet."

"What are you doing here?" I demanded, still annoyed at their literally popping in with no notice.

"Where's Tristan?" Char called from the living room.

Something about her tone, about the way she asked the question struck me like a mallet, rattling my bones. Shaking my soul. I knew why they were here. My stomach rolled then fell to my knees. My chest tightened, and I gasped for air. The cup slid from my trembling hands, shattering against the tile floor. *How could Owen do this to us?* He knew they were coming, even retrieved their luggage because they couldn't flash with it.

"You're . . . here . . . to *take* . . . him?" I squeaked out between breaths. "Oh, my God. You're really . . ."

I sank to the floor, unable to finish the sentence, my hand over my gaping mouth.

"You can't have him," I whispered, shaking my head violently. "You can't do this to us. Our time isn't up."

The image of Owen coming to the safe house and announcing Tristan's disappearance nearly eight years ago wavered in my mind, and now I felt the loss, the emptiness, the half-existence all over again. My body began to quake. Mom took a step toward me. Sasha growled again, louder this time.

"It's okay, Sasha. You know my intentions," Mom said to the Lykora. Sasha snuffed and stepped out of Mom's way. Mom dropped to her knees next to me. "Alexis, honey, no. Shh. Calm down. That's not why we're here."

She wrapped her arms around me and stroked my hair as I inhaled jagged breaths.

"Then why are you? Why the big ambush?"

Char, now back in the kitchen, chuckled. "Sorry about that. We didn't mean to make it look like an ambush. Owen was supposed to warn you last night that we were on our way."

"What's going on? Are you here for another investigation? More ultimatums to give us?"

"No, honey," Mom said softly. "We're here because . . . well, I guess you could say I ran away."

"More like we escaped," Char said. "Escaped the crazies."

"The who?" I asked.

"The crazies. More than half the council have lost their minds. Martin and Solomon are trying to hold everything together, but even Rina's messed up. We're hoping Tristan can help us with a plan because the whole council is going down fast and ugly."

I wiped the tears that had gathered in my eyes. Sasha shrank to her normal, toy-dog size and nudged her nose against my hand. I let her on my lap and dug my fingers into her silky fur.

"I don't understand," I said.

"When we came here in July," Mom said, "I told Char about how different I felt after leaving the island, but we'd forgotten about it when we returned. We'd been back a few weeks when I started feeling . . . *off* again."

"She was saying and doing things completely unlike her," Char said. "Martin had often talked about how the Daemoni found ways to mess with people's minds, and it seems that someone on the island is doing the same. Martin hasn't left there in weeks, working with Solomon to try to figure it out. It took some doing, but I convinced Sophia to get off the island. She's finally starting to get back to herself."

I hugged Mom. "Are you okay now?"

"Yes, I think so. I'm not so sure about Rina, though . . . ."

"You think someone's messing with everyone's minds? Is that why they're all crazy?"

Mom shrugged. Char shook her head. "There aren't any mages powerful enough to affect everyone at once. But someone does seem to be messing with a few of the key people—Sophia, Rina, Julia . . . ."

I snorted. "Julia's in on it. If she's acting crazy, she's just *acting*."

Mom opened her mouth to say something, but then she stopped and sniffed the air. "What is that smell?"

My face heated. "Sorry. It smells horrible. It's an herbal tea I thought I'd—"

"No, I mean it's familiar." She sniffed again. Then she noticed the pool of greenish liquid on the floor with shards of my coffee mug in it. She swirled her fingers in the tea and lifted her fingertips to her nose. "I've had this before. A long time ago." She paused, trying to remember, but I knew she was wrong. Mistaking it for something else. If she knew what it really was . . . "Yes. London. I'd visited a witch . . . we'd had tea. This tea. It's when . . . when I was with Tristan and Lucas, actually."

If I'd had the tea in my mouth, I would have sprayed it out all over again. "*Seriously?*"

"Yes. It tasted like gasoline but the witch said it would strengthen me, which I needed, to be able to handle Lucas."

"Mom . . ." I hesitated, knowing she'd probably freak out that I'd even considered taking a concoction on purpose. But I didn't have to make a decision.

Char blurted it out for me. "That's a pregnancy potion, Sophia. No doubt, by the smell of it."

The realization hit Mom and me at the same time, and we both sprang to our feet.

"Mom, it worked for you. That's what did it!" My hope soared beyond the ceiling, beyond the trees, all the way to the sky. "If it worked for you . . . maybe . . ."

Mom looked at Charlotte. "Is it safe?"

"You're still alive, aren't you?"

Mom turned to me again and her face reminded me of Dorian's on Christmas morning—full of excitement and hope. "Did you drink it? All of it?"

"No, none of it. I spit out the first gulp and dropped the rest, remember?"

She grabbed the teapot, filled it with water and set it on

the stove. "I can't believe I didn't remember this . . . that I didn't realize . . ."

I noticed what Char must have on the island—a difference in Mom. I'd never seen her so hesitant, almost unsure of herself, as if she doubted her own memories or thoughts.

"It doesn't sound like you knew exactly what you'd been drinking at the time," Charlotte said.

"No, but . . . we never even thought about it. Alexis could have tried this months ago."

"Actually, Minh and Galina had brought it up one time, but no one thought it would work on an Amadis daughter, and Rina didn't want to take the chance," Charlotte said. "No one knew it had been done before. Makes me wonder who this witch was who gave it to you. Why she hasn't piped up about it, with everything going on."

"Actually . . ." Mom paused again, and her face screwed up in a way I'd never seen before, as if she had to physically concentrate on making her brain work. "I think . . ."

She stopped, and Char and I both waited to hear what she thought. The teapot started whistling, steam rising from its spout. Mom picked it up and began fixing my tea and seemed as though she forgot what she'd been thinking. I looked at Charlotte who gave me a see-what-I-mean look. I hated seeing Mom like this. What had they done to her? Who? Why?

"Uh . . . Mom? The witch?"

She looked at me as if confused.

"The witch who gave you the tea?" I prompted.

"Oh. Right." Her brows pushed together with deep concentration. "There was something about her . . . it bothered me at the time. I couldn't feel the full truth in her intentions. I felt she intended to do more for me . . . or for the Amadis . . . than I asked of her, which she had. Because of her, we have you. There

~ 254 ~

was something else, though . . . I felt she wasn't really a witch."
She paused for another long moment and cocked her head. "I
think . . . I think she was really a *faerie*."

"Well, that explains a lot," Char muttered. "But not
everything. The faeries had an interest in you and Lucas having
a child. Why?"

"Maybe they thought it would be fun to see what happened
with a crossbreed," I said. "It's definitely created all kinds of
chaos."

"Maybe," Char said, but she didn't sound convinced.

Mom shook her head. "I don't think so. I don't think she
was really part of the Otherworld anymore."

"What do you mean you don't *think*? Don't you know the
truth?" I demanded.

"That's part of my problem. I haven't felt the real truth in
things for a while. It's so . . . disorienting. And my memories
aren't quite as clear as they usually are. Yes . . . I *think* she had
lost some of her Otherworldliness."

"You think she was ousted?" Char asked.

"Not exactly. I felt then she was helping the Amadis, and
faeries, as a group, don't get involved in our affairs. Not to this
extent. She'd gone through such lengths to disguise herself and
make sure I drank that potion. I thought her intent was about
converting Lucas, so I didn't think much of it at the time."

Mom stopped again, and her expression bothered me. She
looked so lost, not like herself at all. I was about to ask if she
really was okay, but both the front and back doors burst open at
the same time. Owen dropped Mom and Char's luggage in the
foyer and rushed into the kitchen just as Tristan pulled Dorian
through the rear door.

"Mimi," Dorian squealed, and he ran into Mom's arms. "I
missed you!"

"Did you get my text?" Owen asked Tristan.

"Sure did," Tristan said, holding his phone up. "Let's move."

"What's going on?" I asked.

"I finally got word about the Okeechobee wolf pack," Owen said. "They're gathering tonight, and I know exactly where."

"We're going for a bike ride," Tristan said. "Get dressed."

I moved for the doorway but Char grabbed my wrist. She held the mug out to me. "Drink up. Then Sophia and I have something for you."

I pinched my nose and swallowed the foul tea in three large gulps. A shudder ran up my spine, and I fought my stomach's desire to expel the liquid back the way it came.

"A little early to be drinking hard stuff, don't you think?" Owen asked.

"Come on," Char said, ignoring her son. She took my wrist again and pulled me toward their luggage in the foyer.

"Can't this wait?" Tristan asked. "It's not exactly a short ride."

"I don't like this idea one bit, Tristan," Mom said, sounding like my mother again, at least for a moment, "but . . . you will at least have as much protection as possible. Especially Alexis."

Tristan threw me a questioning look. He saw the changes in Mom, too. Before, she would have been adamant about trying to stop us, saying it was an absurd idea. I returned his gaze with one that said, "I'll tell you later."

Char opened one of the suitcases, grabbed something black, examined it and tossed it to Owen. She picked up something else and tossed it to Tristan. She continued throwing things at them and finally started tossing stuff to me. First, a black leather jacket. It wasn't heavy; in fact, the leather was thin and supple, and it reminded me of the one Char herself wore. Second, a bustier made of black leather and adorned with purple-dyed suede and silver embellishments. Third, pants made of the same kind of leather as the jacket and a belt with several loops hanging from it, and, finally, a pair of combat boots.

"Are we going to a bike rally? Is this supposed to make me fit in?" I asked, not quite understanding why Char and Mom brought me leathers. Not that I had any—we weren't the rally kind of bikers, and I didn't need them to protect my skin from road burn.

"These are warrior clothes," Char said. "What we all wear out in the field. The leather's enchanted for maximum protection."

Warrior clothes. Of course. We could no longer leave home without being prepared for a fight.

"And your weapons," Char said, waving her hand over the suitcase. She lifted what had appeared to be the bottom of it, exposing a hidden section. She handed me a small knife that flipped in and out of its own hilt, much like a pocket knife, but bigger. "This is your back-up weapon."

I took it and examined it, flipping it a few times to get used to it. Then she pulled out something longer, nearly as long as my forearm. A silver vine with leaves wound around the gold hilt, circling to the center, where it ended with an amethyst the size of a nickel. The blade hid in a black and purple sheath that matched my bustier.

"Your dagger, Ms. Alexis," Char said with a bow of her head as she held the hilt toward me.

I took the dagger and pulled it out of its sheath. The sun coming through the window shone through an intricate design of vines and leaves that was cut out of the center of the blade.

"It's a hand-me-down," Mom said. "The same dagger Andrew gave to Cassandra."

Wow. I actually held Cassandra's dagger. *Andrew's* dagger.

Specially made in the Otherworld. My earliest ancestors had once wielded this same weapon.

"Of course, Ferrer enchanted it to take your powers," Char said.

"You remember how to use it?" Tristan asked.

I stepped back and made a few moves. Then Char showed me how swiping my thumb over the amethyst could make the dagger disappear and appear again.

"Not even metal detectors will sense it," she said.

"It would have been nice to have this all before," I said. "Like when we first left and had to fight Vanessa all the time."

"It wasn't ready yet," Char said.

"Then they wouldn't let us bring it to you the first time we came," Mom added.

"They didn't exactly *let* us bring it this time either," Char said.

"We were always good at covert operations," Mom said with a smile.

"Thanks to Martin and his help, too," Char added and Mom nodded.

Owen looked at his phone. "We need to get out of here, big guy. I'll be back in a few."

He disappeared with a *pop*. Tristan and I quickly changed into our new gear. I expected the leather to be difficult to pull on and uncomfortable to wear, but it came on easily and molded itself to my body, like a second skin. I moved around in it, and after a few minutes, I felt both naked, as if nothing impeded me, yet protected at the same time. I thought I might have found clothes I liked almost as much as shorts and T-shirts.

I was never one who found guys in leather pants sexy, but Tristan changed my mind. At least, for him. The leather didn't cling to him as it did me, but fit him like jeans, accentuating the curve of his perfect ass, but not in a porn-star kind of way. He showed me how to secure my weapons in my belt loops for easiest retrieval, and he filled his with his own dagger, knives and discs. Out of the corner of my eye, I caught our reflections as we strode past the bedroom mirror for the door. We looked as though we belonged on the set of some post-apocalyptic movie where the characters were armed up to fight zombies. Of course, we fought vampires, mages and shape-shifters, not zombies. I didn't think.

"Do zombies exist?" I asked Tristan.

"Only if the Daemoni want to create them. Which they might, if we really do go to war."

"I wish you wouldn't do this," Mom said standing in front of the back door, blocking our way, and I thought maybe she'd returned to herself. But then she moved to the side. "But I realize you're going to anyway. Who am I to stop you now? I don't even know the truth anymore."

"That's what we're looking for, Mom. The truth."

She nodded. "I know."

Char took my hand and rubbed my thumb over the dagger's hilt, making the weapon disappear. "No need for that hanging off your waist as you're driving down the highway."

That's when I realized how dangerous this trip really was. The Weres didn't pose the real threat. Although they'd been avoiding us, they would fight for us if they had to. The true danger came from the exposure. Owen couldn't cloak us, otherwise other drivers wouldn't see us on the road.

"Why are we taking the bikes?" I asked as Tristan and I headed out to the garage.

"We're going to a *bike* rally."

I ignored his obvious point. "I mean, a car's safer, isn't it? We could do it how we did when we went to Daytona."

"Owen can't get a hold of Blossom, who probably can't drop everything for us anyway. Sophia's in no shape to go, Char has to stay with her and they both have to stay with Dorian. Besides, if we're going to put our lives in danger, we may as well have fun doing it." He grinned and winked at me, and I forgot my concerns.

At least until we merged onto I-75 and the lights of magic spells and curses bombarded us.

Chapter 18

Although he couldn't cloak us for our own driving safety, Owen had shielded us before we left, so the red and blue lights coming from the truck behind us bounced off the invisible bubbles protecting us. One collided with a car, sending it careening into another lane and causing an accident.

"This isn't good," I cried out to Tristan over the screech of scraping metal and the roar of the bike.

"No shit," he muttered.

"*Alexis!*" Owen called to my mind. "*I have to cloak us, or they won't stop.*"

I still couldn't open my mind between two other people, not even Tristan and Owen, so I had to relay between them. Owen pulled up next to us, lifted both hands from the handlebars and thrust them out at us several times, then did the same to himself and he disappeared. I could no longer see Owen or his motorcycle, or Tristan or ours, for that matter. Without any kind of structure enclosing us, he had to cloak the bikes and each of us individually. I clung to Tristan, though, and felt the rumble underneath me. Brakes squealed and the acrid smell of hot rubber burned my nose as drivers around us panicked at our disappearance.

The truck full of mages sped up behind us. Not able to see their targets anymore, they didn't throw magic. Apparently, they decided to run us over instead.

"*Hang on,* ma lykita. *This is about to get ugly!*"

I clutched him tighter.

"*Stay connected to Owen so he can see through your eyes and know what we're doing.*"

I'm no good at that, Tristan!

"*It's just him. You don't have a choice!*"

The sound of the truck's engine closed in on us, and a car in front of us blocked our way. Tristan swerved around it, onto the shoulder, and back up onto the road in front of the car. I felt Owen's mind signature and sensed him do the same, but he narrowly missed crashing into us. The shields would have kept us from colliding, but the bounce of the protective bubbles could have sent us all out of control and skidding across asphalt. I really didn't have a choice.

Owen, see what I'm seeing.

I opened my mind to Owen and wished I could open it to Tristan, too, so that his thoughts could go straight through me to Owen. But as hard as I tried, my shield wouldn't budge. There were too many people around, and it remained solid, protecting my own thoughts from broadcasting to everyone on the highway. So Owen followed us as best he could, trying to keep his eyes on the road and watch through my mind at the same time.

A car started moving into our lane right next to us, and I shrieked. Tristan and Owen both accelerated to avoid it. We weaved in and around vehicles, narrowly missing cars and semis. I stopped shrieking with every close call, but my breath caught each time until I simply held it indefinitely. My heart raced faster than we drove. I wanted to squeeze my eyes tightly shut and hide my face against Tristan's back until it was over, but then Owen would lose us.

"*Relax, Alexis, or you'll block me out,*" Owen said. "*Trust Tristan. You're in very capable hands. Besides, I thought you liked to go fast now.*"

He was right. Since the *Ang'dora* had started coming on, speed had become an addiction. The speed didn't scare me, though. The darting in and out of people's ways did. But Owen was right in that regard, as well. Tristan reacted expertly each time. I tried to relax and trust him and, once I did, the ride became exhilarating. Still, relief washed over me when we pulled off the highway onto a deserted road.

We rode for another hour, still cloaked in case any Daemoni watched us. In fact, the closer we came to the Weres' location, the more likely they'd be around. Tristan took us right past a guard station "manned" with three wolves—they sniffed our way, but didn't catch our scents through Owen's shields—and into an encampment. A few motor homes and many tents encircled a wide area that bordered Lake Okeechobee's shore.

A rough-looking crowd milled around the open space, everyone dressed in leather and denim, their exposed skin displaying piercings and tattoos. Some whooped, hollered and even growled or laughed and clapped each other on the shoulders, as if they hadn't seen their pack-mates in a while. Others strode around, their eyes constantly surveying and their bodies tense, as if on guard. We parked at the head of a long line of bikes, the engines still rumbling, when they all suddenly turned and stared at us. Owen had lifted the cloaks and shields.

Tristan gave my thigh a squeeze. I self-consciously swung my leg over to dismount, everyone still watching us, some of their eyes piercing us like laser beams, others full of curiosity. When he and Owen cut the engines, I didn't think I'd ever heard such dead silence. Then they all dropped to a knee and lowered their heads. Thinking it was some kind of Were greeting and wanting to show them respect, I began to sink down, too. Tristan grabbed my upper arm.

"They're bowing to you," he said under his breath.

Oh. Right. Royalty and all that crap. Since they hadn't responded to Owen's calls . . . and just looking at them . . . I hadn't expected all the formalities. In fact, I thought they'd be more hostile than Blossom's Aunt Sylvie. Instead, this big biker gang was honoring *me*.

"What do I do?" I whispered when no one made a move to rise. Nobody had bothered to teach me how to act in such situations. Was I supposed to say something? Give some kind of salute? *Blow kisses?*

"Follow me." Tristan took my hand, and we walked toward them, his stride full of confidence. As we reached the outer edge of the crowd, a big, burly man barged out of one of the RVs.

"What the hell's going on?" he barked. He took in the crowd, and his dark eyes followed their attention to Tristan, Owen and me. His strides covered several yards at a time as he came toward us, a beer bottle in one hand and a cigar in the other. His black leather vest strained against his barrel chest and exposed bulging, tanned arms decorated with multiple tattoos. He went down on one knee in front of us, and his shoulder-length salt-and-pepper hair, which matched his goatee, fell forward as he quickly bowed. Unlike the others, he didn't stay down and as soon as he rose, so did everyone else. He must have been the pack's leader.

"What the fuck do you want?" he growled at us.

Tristan looked at me, back at him and raised an eyebrow.

"This is *my* house. If she can't handle it, she shouldn't be here." He looked me over, from head to toe and back up again. "But something tells me she can. So. What the fuck do you want?"

"Just a moment of your time," Tristan said. He sounded polite, but his jaw muscle twitched, and his voice was steel-hard.

The pack leader narrowed his eyes and lifted his finger, which he shook in Tristan's face. "I ain't talkin' to you. I ain't stupid. You got no business comin' here and ruinin' our party. Get the hell out before you regret comin'."

Tristan grabbed the Were's hand and leaned forward so their faces were only inches apart. His voice came out low, almost a growl. "Get your finger out of my face before *you* regret me coming. I don't think you want me to embarrass you in front of your pack. I might accidentally kill you, and I really don't want to take over as their lead. So back off and take us somewhere we can talk."

The leader's huge arm muscles bulged as he tried to pull out of Tristan's grip, but he wasn't strong enough. Tristan kept hold of him until he finally relaxed and nodded his head.

"And show some respect for my wife," Tristan added as the Were jerked his hand free. "*She* leads *you*."

"Not yet. And not ever, from what I gather," the Were mumbled under his breath. He strode past us, headed for a clump of trees and brush. He threw a jerk of a wave at his pack, who pretended as though nothing had happened and returned to their party.

Tristan, Owen and I followed the leader into the trees. When the party became a distant hum of noise, he finally stopped and spun on us.

"I ain't got nothin' to say to you," he said.

"Do you even know why we're here?" Tristan asked.

"No. And I don't want to. I ain't gettin' in the middle of things. My pack don't bother no one, and we don't want no one botherin' us."

"We only want to know if you've heard anything about a young girl, about seven years old, probably brown or red hair. We have no idea who she's with, but my guess would be a witch."

"I don't know nothin'."

Tristan looked at me. I followed the Were's mind signature, and something flickered in his thoughts. Some kind of familiarity. Right as I was about to grasp the full thought, screams pierced the air overhead. Shadows passed over us, and we all looked up. Two gigantic, black birds tucked their wings close to their bodies and dive-bombed toward us.

I flattened myself to the ground, and Owen was instantly on top of me. Tristan and the pack leader stood on either side of us, both in protective stances. The birds dove at us again and Tristan hit them with his power. Black feathers exploded.

"Just birds, but under someone's control," he said.

Chaos erupted from the party. The screams and yells weren't playful anymore, and feral growls and bays joined the racket.

The next thing I knew, I was lifted from the ground, and air rushed past me.

"Get her in that one!" the pack leader growled, jerking his head toward the RV he had come out of earlier. He exploded into a giant silver wolf as he ran for his pack.

Owen dropped me to my feet inside the little living room of a decked-out RV.

"You okay?" Tristan asked me, surveying my head and body.

"I'm fine." I rushed to the window that looked out to the clearing full of the wolf pack. "But they won't be."

People disappeared, replaced by wolves of various colors and sizes, their were-pulp splattering everywhere—a chunk hit the RV just below the window. Daemoni vampires swarmed in from all sides. The party became a battle. Wolves and vampires lunged and knocked each other to the ground. Wolves' muzzles latched onto their enemies' limbs while vamps' fangs sunk into their necks. Blood spurted and bones snapped. Fighting duos became blurs of motion.

"They'll kill each other," I whispered with horror. "Not for us. Not again."

I placed my hand on the hilt of my dagger and flashed into the middle of the battle.

"Stop!" I bellowed over the ruckus as I drew out my weapon.

To my amazement, everyone actually stopped. And stared at me. My eyes scanned the crowd. Wolves panted, but otherwise remained still. Vampires looked as though they'd turned to stone, their red eyes watching me.

"It's me you want, right? Us? Leave them out of this!"

"Damn it, Alexis," Tristan muttered after he and Owen popped in right next to me.

"I stopped them," I whispered.

"Fine! Have it your way," one of the vamps yelled, and they slowly closed in on us.

"They're not exactly stopped," Owen said. He, Tristan and I stood shoulder-to-shoulder, facing the vampires encircling us. Owen held his hands out, ready to fight with magic. Tristan, always strategic, seemed to just stand there, but I knew he was calculating, planning his attack and how he would defend both of us at the same time.

"Well . . . at least they're distracted," I said.

"*Use your mind*," Tristan told me as the vamps came closer.

Of course. I made the thought sound confident for his benefit, but I didn't feel it. I didn't know if I could use my one major advantage in this large group of people. Especially without alerting anyone I even had the power.

"Let's do this," Tristan growled, and faster than a blur, he'd pulled a razor-sharp disc from his belt and sent it flying at a random bloodsucker, severing its ear before even the vampires could react.

That did it. The vamps put on their speed and charged us. Tristan hit the closest ones with his power, and they dropped to the ground. He continued hitting more, and Owen and I helped with our own powers until they swarmed on top of us, and it became mano-a-mano. Well, sort of. They vastly outnumbered us.

I swung my dagger in an arc at the two leeches rushing at me, and they jumped out of reach, afraid of the silver. They separated enough to take me from both sides. I used my left hand to shoot lightning at the male vamp and used my right to wield the knife at the female. She dodged my swipes, and he tried to out-move me, but the electric current zapped him until his skin turned purple and smoke rose. He disappeared with a *pop*.

The female, with black hair that made her skin look whiter than white, moved fast—faster than the human eye could see—but so did I. Just one-on-one, I could focus on her mind and knew her plan before she charged me. I jumped out of her way and swung my dagger in a perfect, smooth move that sliced across her stomach. The slash wasn't deep—not deep enough to kill her—but she screeched with pain from the enchanted metal.

"You bitch," she shrieked, flying at me again.

I jumped and cartwheeled in the air, getting another swipe across her back before I landed on my feet. Another male blurred toward my left as the female, weaker now, charged me again. Remembering everything Charlotte and Tristan taught me, I did a roundhouse on the woman, kicking her in the jaw and sending her backwards several yards. At the same time, I jabbed my dagger at the male, and it sunk three inches into his ribs. Hearing his thought about flashing, I jerked it out before he disappeared with it still in him. The female took advantage of this moment and jumped on my back. Her height and my lack of it made her feet drag, bringing us down. My dagger flew out of my hand and skidded across the ground, out of reach, as I sprawled on my stomach, the vampire on top of me.

I wiggled under her, trying to reach for my other knife on my left side. She pinned my hips down with her full weight. Her hand pushed between my shoulder blades, pressing me into the ground with all of her vampire strength. Then she grabbed my hair and yanked my head backwards so hard, I was surprised my neck didn't snap. Tristan and Owen both caught sight of my struggle, but neither could do anything, occupied with their own fights. I writhed again, but it was no use. The vampire weighed me down like a boulder on a sheet of paper.

"Vanessa and Lucas will be pissed," she said, her voice hoarse and gravelly, "but . . . oh, well. Your blood in my veins will be worth it."

She leaned down for my throat. I reached back, grabbed her thigh with my right hand, and forced my Amadis power into her. She wailed a toe-curling scream. I gathered the power in my body and, as I had once done with Tristan, I pushed the bubble outward. She exploded off of me. I rolled, grabbed my back-up knife and sprang to my feet in time to see a silver werewolf jump at the vamp flying in the air. He knocked her to the ground and tore into her limbs. His actions signaled the other wolves to rejoin the fight.

Tristan, Owen and I had already taken out several of the Daemoni, evening our numbers. I fought with just the knife until Owen finally had a chance to toss my dagger to me. No one could beat me one-on-one. A weapon in each hand, I read my enemies' minds and danced out of their way, taking my own swipes as I spun, twirled and flipped around them. My silver blades dug mercilessly into their skin until they could stand no more and disappeared. As soon as Tristan had the chance, he swung his arm around and hit the remaining vamps with his power. They all disappeared with a resonance of *pops*.

Tristan and Owen instantly stood by my side, and we quickly assessed each other for injuries. Owen had a cut over his eyebrow, but that was all.

"Let's get out of here," Tristan said, taking my hand. We headed for the bikes.

"Wait," snarled the pack leader from behind us, his voice not quite human.

We turned and waited for him to finish transforming. Avoiding his nakedness, I averted my eyes, but all the wolves were shifting, as well. So I stared at the ground.

"Come with me," he said, and he started for his RV.

We hesitated and then, without a word, followed the pack leader.

"The name's Trevor," he said once we were inside. He went into the back room and came out with fresh clothes on. "I do have somethin' for ya."

Tristan crossed his arms over his chest.

"'I don't know nothin',"" Owen quoted, his voice perfectly mocking Trevor's. The Were narrowed his eyes at Owen for a moment, but then he looked at me, and they softened.

"I was ordered not to talk to ya," Trevor said. "Told we couldn't trust ya for nothin'. Didn't know what was goin' on, but like I said, I don't want to get in the middle of your polytics. But when Ms. Alexis here came out to protect us, willin' to give her life for us, I knew they was wrong. You can be trusted."

"So you do know something?" I asked. "About a little girl?"

"I got a message just yesterday, from another Were. He's ain't a wolf, but not from 'round here neither, and I was closest. Location-wise, you know? He said you was lookin' for a girl, and he thinks he found her. He wanted me to get the message to ya." He knelt on a knee in front of me and dropped his head. "I'm sorry I didn't trust ya, Ms. Alexis."

I barely heard the apology as I tried to squelch the excitement pulsing like lightning through my veins. How did we know he was telling the truth? Or that this other Were was?

"Who is it?" Tristan demanded, also skeptical. "How do you know you can trust this stranger?"

"I got curious and sent a couple of my wolves out. He's awright. Amadis, for sure."

"And you said he's close?"

"In the Everglades. I'd go with ya, even bring some of my pack after what ya just did, but I don't need no shit from no one."

"We understand," I said. "Can you tell us where, exactly, in the Everglades?"

I latched onto his thoughts and saw the location in his mind.

He pulled a paper towel off the roll sitting on the counter that separated the living room and little kitchen, and fished a pen out of a drawer. "I'll draw ya a map."

I almost stopped him, saying we'd figure it out ourselves because I didn't want to delay one second longer. But then I realized it could be a test—if the map he drew was the same as what I saw in his mind, we could trust him and his story. We took his map, and once again headed for the bikes. We didn't need to bring them anymore trouble.

"He's telling the truth," I said, keeping my voice low as Tristan and Owen mounted the motorcycles. "We're going right away, right? Now?"

Tristan shook his head. "We need to go home first."

"What? *Why?*"

"Many reasons, which I'll tell you later. Right now, we need to get out of here." He fired up the loud engine, then stood so I could get on.

I stuffed the map into my pocket, swiped my dagger's hilt to make it disappear and swung myself onto the bike. Owen cloaked and shielded us before we took off into the darkening evening. By the time we whipped onto I-75, full night had come on, and the highway was much less crowded than it had been earlier. I didn't feel the fear at all now, so my mind kept drifting, wanting to search for the girl right away, and Owen had to keep mentally yelling at me to stay focused so he could see through my thoughts.

"Why couldn't we go right away?" I asked Tristan as soon as we stood in our own garage. After removing our cloaks, Owen had gone on home. "We were halfway there already."

"Because we don't know what we're going up against," he said. "If it's Amadis, they must have had help over the years, so it's probably more than one person, and we have to be careful how we handle it. If it is, by chance, Daemoni, then you're looking at a battle much bigger than what we just finished. I need a chance to regroup and make a plan."

I crossed my arms and stared at him. He stared back at me.

"Are you making a plan?" I asked impatiently.

The corners of his mouth twitched and eventually tugged up into a smile.

"You've certainly become all full of yourself today." He pulled me into his embrace and held me tightly against him. "Please give me a moment to feel you safely in my arms before we throw ourselves into the pits again."

I wrapped my arms around his waist and leaned my head against his chest. "I suppose we can spare a moment."

"How about a night?"

"The whole *night?*"

"You really don't want to be out there in the middle of the night."

I snorted. "After what we just went through, you think I'm afraid of the dark?"

"Not the dark. The swamps. The homes of gators, anacondas . . ."

"As in big snakes?"

"As in ginormous snakes."

I shuddered, but said, "I can handle it."

He heard the hesitation in my voice and knew he almost had me convinced. "A few hours sleep will give our bodies time to completely heal, and Owen especially needs it."

Ugh. He knew how to get to me.

"Okay, fine. We leave first thing in the morning."

"Perfect." He took my hand and we headed into the house. To find Dorian in bed and Mom and Charlotte at the kitchen table. And they weren't alone.

Chapter 19

Wearing a charcoal gray pants suit and her dark hair pulled into a twist at the nape of her neck, Julia looked almost like a Norman visiting friends during a business trip. But the vampire's only business here would be to take Tristan. My hackles rose. I stepped in front of Tristan.

"What the hell are you doing in my house?" I demanded, though I already knew the answer.

"Rina was worried. I told her I'd check on you and Sophia," Julia answered smoothly.

"And we're supposed to believe that? Believe *you?*"

"*Alexis!*" Mom thought. "*Calm down. She's not here for Tristan. Rina seems to think we need a babysitter.*"

She followed you? I asked. Mom barely moved her head in a nod.

"That's my official business," Julia said. "But while I'm here, it's only prudent of me to tell you that your actions are making your situation worse."

"What's that supposed to mean?" Tristan asked.

"Today's events mean nothing to you? The Amadis who fought for you—their lives mean nothing?" So she had already received word of the battle at the Were encampment.

"Of course they do! And if you knew as much as you think you do, you'd know that *we* protected *them*," I seethed through clenched teeth.

"Which is no better. You risk their lives by going there in the first place. Then you risk your own—their only hope for a future—because of the danger you brought down on them. Either way you look at it, your actions can't be trusted."

"Well, our *actions*," I said, "led us to what we're looking for. A girl who everyone says doesn't exist. Don't talk to *me* about trust!"

Mom, Charlotte and Julia stared at us for a long moment. Then the questions started flying, and Tristan and I shared what little information we gleaned, before discussing our plans for tomorrow. I absolutely insisted on going, and everyone except Tristan protested, but I shut them down by pointing out what I had done today. Mom couldn't risk going, and Char was sworn to protect her. They would stay with Dorian. So it came down to only Tristan, Owen and me again. Perfect.

As the three of us prepared to leave the next morning, Julia *popped* into our living room, dressed in leathers like us.

"I'm going with you," she announced.

"What?" I demanded. *The hell she is!*

"I did a little of my own investigating last night and confirmed what I suspected. Nobody knows anything about this witch or this girl," Julia said. "We have no idea what kind of danger you're headed for. You're risking your lives again, and since I can't stop you, I can protect you."

I had all kinds of things to say about that, but Tristan squeezed my hand, keeping them from flying out of my mouth.

I don't trust her, Tristan.

"*Me neither. But she won't leave and it's the best solution. Do you want her here with your mother and Dorian? At least she'll be with us, where we can watch her.*"

"Charlotte is here," Julia continued. "Your mother and son have a warlock and a Lykora, and they'll be safe in this house. Rina said you need me more. I can't break her orders, regardless of what you think or want."

Regardless of the fact Rina's out of her mind and has no clue what orders she's giving. I wanted to say it aloud, but didn't. Tristan made a good point. I'd rather Julia be with us than here. Who knew what she could pull while we were gone? Who knew what we might come back to if we left her here?

"Fine," I muttered. "Let's just go."

Tristan had explained to me that if you had a place on a map to concentrate on, you could flash there, even if you'd never been there before. However, without street names or landmarks, such as in the wilderness, and no coordinates, you might not appear in the exact spot you wanted, possibly as much as a few miles off. So flashing into the middle of the Everglades? Risky, even without considering that we could appear in a snake or alligator pit.

To avoid the chance of us appearing several miles apart, one of us would have to take the lead for the others to follow. I should have been the lead, since I'd seen the place more specifically in Trevor's mind than a map provided, but none of us, especially me, felt confident in my abilities to lead a flash. So we all lay a hand on Tristan, and without Julia knowing, I shared Trevor's image with Tristan, and we flashed.

We appeared hip-deep in the middle of a swamp. Well, I was hip-deep. Everyone else was more like thigh-deep. The muck at the bottom sucked at my boots as we waded through the reeds to the bank, watching for gators and snakes. As I neared the grassy bank, I saw something out of the corner of my eye. Something big and white disappearing into the water about forty yards away. I shivered as my imagination ran wild with visions of enormous anacondas and alligators. Standing on solid ground, I lamented the desecration of my new leather gear, but, to my amazement, it had already dried and returned to perfect condition.

"I've been waiting for you, princess," said a familiar voice with an Australian accent coming through the brush. A bulky figure topped by a bald head emerged from a clump of trees.

"Jax?" I asked, though the answer was obvious. That must have been him, in crocodile form, I'd seen slithering off a few moments ago. He apparently had clothes nearby this time, because now, thank God, he was dressed. "What are you doing here?"

"I think I found the girl you're looking for."

"You? Here? But how—?" I paused. "Oh, wait. Let me guess. A little birdie told you?"

He grinned, and the scar over his eye crinkled. "She'd spent some time here, and when she flew home, she told me all about it. Including a witch and a little girl she'd met hiding in the middle of the bloody bush—or whatever you call this place."

"So you *came* here? I thought you never leave—"

"I couldn't help it. You struck something in me, princess, and I had to do what I could to help." He shrugged. "It's been a ripper of a trip, actually. This place is a lot like Oz, but . . . different. An all right change. Especially these gators. They're nothing like the crocs at home."

"Glad you've been enjoying your vacay," Owen said, "but let's get back to this witch and girl."

"Sure, mate," Jax said, and he told us about how he'd been here for a couple of months, learning his way around the

Everglades and searching for what his were-bird friend had told him about—the girl and the witch. He hadn't found them until his friend arrived and led him to their hideout, then he had her fly to the nearest Amadis Were to deliver a message to us. The visit from Trevor's wolves surprised him when they came to check him out and make sure the message was real. He didn't like them much, but he was friendly enough to build their trust in him.

"Well . . . where are they?" I demanded when he finished his story. My patience ran thin. After months of searching, we were So. Close. The girl hid somewhere in the vicinity. The girl who could be our daughter.

Jax led us through the woods, swamps and brush, Tristan and I behind him, and Owen and Julia covering our backs. Although our summer had seen less rainfall than normal, much of the ground was mushy under our feet. We waded through water and reeds, squelched and squished through mucky marshes, avoiding the sharp edges of waist-high saw grass, and crossed broad areas of solid ground with forests of cypress, pine and palm trees. Birds floated lazily overhead when we were out in the open, their shadows often making me duck after yesterday's attack. The noises of the subtropical wild—birds' squawks, the plop of something dropping into the water, whispers of waving grass—filled me with both awe and anxiety. After all, those movements were made by wild animals, including panthers, snakes and alligators.

I tried to suppress the excitement I felt by staying alert and focusing on my surroundings, but the butterflies in my stomach wouldn't go away. I'd been thinking of this day for months, visualizing what this girl would look like—a lot like Mom, Rina and me, I assumed. Imagining how it would feel to be certain I had a daughter, a daughter I hadn't been able to raise myself, a daughter who might know nothing about us. And envisioning the consequences—how it would release the pressure off Tristan and me to produce a daughter, how the council would settle down and the Amadis unity could be restored, how everyone's trust in us and each other could be regained so we could do what we're meant to do: fight the Daemoni, not each other. Of course, there was still a traitor trying to take things over, but this girl seemed to be tied to her in some way, and when everything came out, surely we'd be able to identify the traitor, too.

Speaking of traitors, I wondered what Julia thought right now, knowing secrets were about to be exposed. She knew Rina kept a secret about the next daughter, and this was probably it. Was this why she didn't trust Tristan and me? Because she knew we'd discover Rina's secret before Rina wanted us to? Or did she expect to find us somehow betraying the Amadis with this trip? Was that why she really came, to prove herself right? Did she really think we'd take her along with us to have a powwow with the Daemoni? Or . . .

Shit! Why hadn't we thought of this sooner? She could have been setting us up! Perhaps this was all her doing. Now that I thought about it, it was rather convenient that she showed up just as we received the information we'd been seeking all this time. *Only one way to find out.*

I felt out for her mind signature but before I latched onto her thoughts, three extra signatures floating around distracted me from Julia. Three more than our expedition accounted for, and two were relatively close by. And very different than I expected. The childlike one was vivid, like Dorian's, but not quite the same. It had a rougher and darker edge to it. The other one felt more human than anything, but that wasn't quite right. Something . . . different . . . layered it, a suppressed undertone. Tristan had expected a witch, and Jax had confirmed it, but this signature didn't feel like a mage's. Perhaps the witch worked with a Norman who helped care for the child. Perhaps that third signature belonged to the witch, but now I couldn't find it. The third one had disappeared from my range.

I tried to focus in on the second signature, the strange one, to find the thoughts that followed it, but there was nothing there. No thoughts at all. Completely blank. Perhaps she was a witch after all and was somehow able to block me. Did she know we were coming? Did she know about my telepathy? Or perhaps she was extremely cautious, which made sense considering she'd purposefully been hiding for all these years.

The trees began to thin, and beyond the edge of this wooded area was a clearing with a small pond and a little shack jutting out of its center. Jax held his hand up, and we all stopped short and fell silent.

"Nona, someone's here," a young child's voice said.

"It's okay, Lilith," said a scratchier voice, one that sounded as though it belonged to someone elderly. The second mind signature with the blank thoughts must have belonged to her. "They are friends."

At this, we took several steps closer and emerged into the clearing, seeing the faces of the voices for the first time. *Oh!* My breath caught, and my hand flew to my mouth. Partly to keep my heart from flying out because it had jumped into my throat.

They crouched on the other side of the pond, and now they both stood. The elderly woman's dull gray hair sprouted everywhere in a wild nest, seeming to have a life of its own as she lifted her head up to us. Her light gray eyes looked our way, but I had no idea if she actually saw us through their milky lenses. She hunched over in a stoop, her hand resting on the child's shoulder.

The child. The child took my breath away.

"*Tristan,*" I whispered, grabbing his arm. We both stood frozen in complete shock.

This girl, this Lilith, looked nothing like I'd expected, how I'd envisioned her for the last several months. I looked so much like Mom, who appeared to be Rina's twin. Tristan had once mentioned my features—brown eyes, dark auburn hair and light olive skin—gave me away as an Amadis daughter. I assumed our genes dominated in our daughters, giving us all a similar, distinct appearance. But this girl . . .

She stood a couple inches shorter than Dorian, but since he was taller than average, I guessed them to be the same age. And her hair was a darker blond than his, but otherwise . . . she was a spitting image of my son.

"Friends and . . . ," the old woman paused for a moment, ". . . some are even closer. Family."

Holy shit! Can it be? Is she for real? I waited for something in my heart to pull toward her, some kind of mother-daughter connection we surely had to have. I'd been looking forward to this moment for so long, but the emotions I'd expected didn't surge through me. I felt nothing but a shocked numbness. She apparently felt nothing for me either, because her eyes skimmed over me and dismissed me. But when she looked at Tristan, they stopped, and something flickered in them. *Recognition? But how?*

"Family?" Lilith echoed. "Family like . . . like my brother?"

The woman never had a chance to answer. The last few minutes had passed as if in slow motion as we took in the scene, Nona and Lilith, and their conversation. Now someone pushed the fast-forward button, and everything sped in a blur.

The third mind signature appeared back in my range—a very familiar one. One I hadn't felt since we'd been on the Amadis Island. In the Council Hall, waiting for the coronation ceremony to begin. When Julia had threatened Rina.

"*Alexis and Tristan,*" she thought. The other voice, the other person no one else had sensed then, and no one seemed to now. "*Finally, they found her. And now it is time . . .*"

At exactly the same moment, Julia's face twitched in my peripheral vision, and then she was suddenly on the other side of the pond, gripping the old woman in a chokehold.

"Explain this," Julia demanded. "Explain this girl!"

The woman choked and gasped for breath. Lilith's eyes grew wide at the threat to her caregiver, and her sweet face, so much like my Dorian's, immediately changed. Her hazel eyes narrowed to slits. She bared sharp, pointy teeth. Her features twisted into those of a monster. Then she flew our way in a blur. She hit Jax first, and he dropped like a stone. Then she whizzed by Owen, and he, too, fell to the ground.

"Owen," I cried out, springing toward his still body.

But the girl already zoomed at me now, a noise like a siren escaping her throat.

"No, Lilith," Nona yelled. "Stop!"

Lilith halted in mid-motion. But not out of obedience. Tristan's hand was up, palm facing her, paralyzing her with his power.

I dropped to Owen's side and took his limp hand into mine.

"*Why?*" I cried, heartbreak ripping through my throat and causing my voice to crack.

But I knew why. I knew why Rina had taken her, why our daughter had been kept from us, away from everyone, why I didn't feel as I should about her. Why she needed to be kept a secret.

Her Daemoni blood was too strong.

It overpowered her Amadis blood and humanity. Evil dominated her. She'd never be able to lead the Amadis, so her existence failed them. Rina had told me they would have killed me when I was an infant, if the Daemoni power was too strong

~ 282 ~

in my blood and there had been no hope.

But . . . they hadn't killed this girl, which meant . . .

"Lilith, you don't need to do this," I said, conviction now strong in my voice as I slowly rose to my feet. "There's no reason for it. You don't *have* to be this way. We can help you."

The hatred in her eyes flickered, then dissipated. Tears welled up and spilled over her cheeks. "I'm sorry! I'm so sorry. But I can't help it."

"Alexis—" both Nona and Julia warned at the same time. I waved them off.

"I understand, Lilith," I said. "Sometimes we can't control our feelings. But we can help you. You can learn to be different."

I lifted my right hand and pushed Amadis power her way. She yelped, but she didn't writhe in pain as the vampire yesterday did or Sheree had when I'd tried to help her change over. Maybe Lilith wasn't as bad as everyone thought. Maybe she simply needed Amadis power and real love—love only her parents could give her—to overcome the Daemoni blood.

"Do you know what love is?" I asked her.

"Nona loves me," she said in a small voice. "I love her."

I nodded. "Good. Think about that love."

I delivered more Amadis power at her for several moments. Her body stiffened at first and trembled in mid-air, but it eventually slackened, even under Tristan's power. He slowly lowered his hand, and she dropped to the ground in a heap. Nona struggled in Julia's arms, wanting to comfort her charge, but Julia refused to let her go. Lilith lifted her face, streaked with tears and dirt, but so much like Dorian's. My heart finally responded.

I looked at Tristan, a small smile tugging at the corners of my mouth as I started toward Lilith to give her more direct Amadis power. Everything would be okay, just as I'd hoped. We already had the next daughter, and she would eventually be fit to lead. She had at least a hundred years, after all, to learn the Amadis ways, to overcome the Daemoni within her and become a true Amadis. She only needed our help.

Tristan's face twisted in horror. *It's okay*, I told him. *She'll be okay. We'll all be okay now.*

"Alexis," he shouted, looking past me. "Focus!"

Uh-oh. I spun back toward Lilith in time to see her springing to her feet. She crouched, one hand on the ground. She reared her head and curled her lip to bare her teeth. Her eyes glowed red. She became a monster once again.

Then she lunged at me.

Julia shouted something incomprehensible and flew our way, a murderous look in her eye.

"NOOO!" I screamed.

I threw myself in front of Lilith. Julia's stone body collided with mine, knocking me to the ground. My head slammed against a rock with a deafening crack, and stars shot across my vision. My eyes rolled up to see Julia's arms wrapped tightly around Lilith, both of them still as statues. Tristan stood over me, his hand facing them.

"You threaten a council member?" Julia seethed.

"You harmed an Amadis daughter and are about to kill another?" Tristan shot back.

"This is not—"

I didn't hear the end of her statement, distracted by the voice in my head.

"*Perfect*," thought the traitor. "*This ended perfectly.*"

A tree branch snapped in the woods behind us. I rolled over and peered into the trees, catching a glimpse of movement. I pushed myself to my knees. The world tilted, then settled. Forcing myself to focus, I finally made out a cloaked figure half-hidden behind a palmetto tree. I tried to stand up. I lifted my left hand in defense. But as I struggled to my feet, before I could shoot electricity, a flash of blue light flew at me and drove into my chest like a double-edged sword.

My heart exploded.

Ice shot through my veins.

All I could think about was the *Ang'dora* and how that pain felt nothing like this.

I screamed.

Then all went silent and dark.

Chapter 20

I came to with a gasp and bright light blinded me. When my gaze focused, it rested on Dorian and Sasha sitting on a bed next to me. Dorian's eyes grew huge.

"Mimi," he called as he bounced on the bed. "Mimi, she's awake! Mom's awake!"

I tried to sit up, to get my bearings, but I didn't have a chance.

"Oh, thank God," Mom breathed, gathering me in her arms and holding me tightly. "I was so worried."

As she held me, my eyes drank in the familiar surroundings. We sat on the bed in my suite. But not in Tristan's and my bedroom on Sanibel Island. This bed had stone pillars at the corners and a gossamer canopy. Somehow, I'd been brought to our suite in the Amadis mansion.

Mom pulled away, and her eyes scanned my face from forehead to chin. "Are you okay?"

I blinked in confusion, then remembered the explosive pain before I blacked out. I felt no discomfort at all now, though.

"Yeah. Fine. But why am I here? How'd I even get here?"

"You were really sick," Dorian said before Mom could answer. "You've been sleeping for three whole days!"

"Three *days*?" I echoed with disbelief. Then I looked around the room again and felt out with my mind for Tristan, but didn't find his signature. Why wasn't he here? Of course I hadn't actually been sick, but whatever was wrong, if I'd been out of it for three days, he should have been here, waiting for me to wake up. *Healing* me, if anything.

But he wasn't, and we were on the Amadis Island. Which meant only one thing.

"Where's Tristan?" I asked, my voice lilting with panic.

Mom frowned. So did Dorian. His eyes filled with tears. *Oh, no. They really took him!*

"He's even sicker, Mom," Dorian said, his lip trembling. "He's in the hospital and they won't let me see him. Uncle Owen, too."

My stomach knotted with the lies they'd told Dorian. "Mom? What's going on?"

Mom looked at Dorian and back at me. She couldn't talk with him around. I pulled him into my arms.

"Little man, I need to talk to Mimi for a minute, and then I need to take a bath. You and Sasha go to your room and play, okay?"

He sighed and his shoulders sank, making it obvious he didn't want to leave my side. I couldn't blame him, not when Tristan, Owen and I, the three people closest to him besides Mom, had been out of commission for several days.

"Actually, Dorian," Mom said, "Ophelia probably has lunch ready for you, and then she's taking you out to the beach."

"Okay," Dorian said with no enthusiasm at all. He skulked out of the room with Sasha at his side. My heart squeezed painfully, and I wanted to tell him to stay with me. Because that's what I wanted more than anything—for him to stay with me forever. But something was really wrong.

"What's going on?" I asked Mom again when I sensed Dorian had moved out of earshot.

Mom closed her eyes and rubbed her temples. She exhaled a sigh. "Everything. So many things, I don't know where to start and I don't know it all. I've kept myself sequestered in here with you to keep out of the influence of the council again. I didn't want to forget anything so I could tell you."

"Okay," I said, the knot in my stomach pulling tighter. "Let's start with Tristan. Where the hell is he? They have him, don't they?"

Mom dropped her hands into her lap and opened her eyes. They filled with a deep sadness. "Honey, he's . . . yes . . . they're holding him prisoner."

I sprang to my feet, looking around wildly for . . . something. Answers, I supposed. Or Tristan himself. "*Why?* Because we don't have a daughter yet? Don't they—"

An image of Lilith in Julia's arms and Tristan holding them under his power flashed across my vision. The vampire's words echoed in my mind: "You threaten a *council* member?" But after that . . . my mind drew a big blank.

"What happened out there? Do you know? All I remem—"

Mom jumped up and grabbed my hands. "What? What do you remember, Alexis? There are so many different versions about it. My sense is still blocked, so I can't feel the truth at all."

I stared past her, at the wall, as the memories flooded my mind. "I remember . . . chaos. The girl attacked us, but . . . I thought there was hope for her and tried to help her. Then Julia flew at us, nearly knocking me unconscious, and Tristan stopped her, but she already had Lilith in her arms, ready to kill her. Then there was the traitor—the one I'd heard here on the island. Only her mind, though. I never saw her. I did see someone hiding in the woods, but couldn't see their face. And . . . that's it. That's all I remember." I returned my gaze to Mom, and an array of emotions played across her face. "Why? What's everyone else saying?"

"Julia's accusing Tristan of attacking her, a council member, and attempting to kill the next Amadis daughter. If the girl doesn't make it . . ."

My breath caught. "What do you mean? What happened to her?"

"She's been unconscious this whole time, like you, but she's much weaker. It doesn't look good."

"My daughter . . . ," I breathed, my eyes stinging and my throat tightening. I hadn't known her as a daughter, and now I might not ever have that chance.

Mom squeezed my hands. "Honey, we're not sure she's your daughter. It's practically impossible. Rina and I were at the birth."

"But Rina *does* know! She had a secret and this is it. She kept her from us because of her powerful Daemoni blood."

Mom frowned. "I understand that makes sense. But there are so many things that *don't* make sense. They're testing the girl's physical and magical qualities right now, to determine lineage."

A hundred-thousand thoughts and emotions swirled through me. The grief, however, didn't consume me. Not like it would if Dorian had been unconscious for this long. The worry encompassed the feeling of sadness when a young child, any young child, was in grave danger combined with the loss of hope—hope for the Amadis. Regardless of the test results, Lilith would never be able to lead the Amadis. Tristan and I had failed them again. He'd been—

"Tristan didn't do it, Mom! He *protected* her. Julia was the one . . . Wait. If they don't know yet that she's ours, how can Julia accuse Tristan of doing anything to the next daughter?"

"She argues that it seemed a strong enough possibility so whether or not it's true, he intended to kill the next daughter. She's claiming he's the traitor."

"This is absolutely ridiculous! It's Julia. Julia and her creepy sidekick who's too afraid to show her face. Let me guess. No one has a clue about this other person, right?"

Mom shook her head. "No. There's no proof Julia is working with anyone and no proof Julia did anything wrong."

"But she attacked *me*. And her argument about the next daughter can be turned around against her. She had the girl trapped in her arms! And explain who the hell knocked me out."

Mom blew out a heavy breath. "Here's the story as I've pieced it together. Julia had called Martin the night before and told him about your plans. He agreed with Rina that Julia should accompany you and told her he would try to get out there in time, if he could. It took him a while to find you, and when he finally did, he said Daemoni were encroaching. You—" Her breath hitched, and she swallowed before continuing, sounding as though tears filled her voice. "You were hit by dark magic— that's why you were out for so long. A Daemoni warlock's spell. I . . . I was so worried."

"Mom." I tightened my grip on her hands. "I'm okay now. It's okay."

She sniffed and then nodded, but still not behaving like herself, she threw her arms around me and cried. "What would I do if I lost you, Alexis? Nothing else—"

"I love you, too, Mom." I patted her back, feeling at a loss of what to do. Even at her worst moments of distress, Mom had never acted like this. "But can you please tell me the rest?"

She sat up, wiped her eyes and cleared her throat. "Right. Well, Martin fought the Daemoni off until they disappeared. By the time he got to the clearing, you—" She sniffled again and took a deep breath, blowing it out slowly as if releasing the concern once and for all. "You, Owen, the were-croc and the little girl were on the ground, and Julia and Tristan were in a stand-off. Martin diffused the situation, and then Owen came to. They were able to get you all to the airport, where Char and I met them with Dorian, and we took the Amadis jet here." She flipped her hand in the air. "By then, Julia had enough of the council convinced about Tristan, and they took him into custody as soon as we landed on the island. I've been in here with you ever since, and Char's been bringing me updates."

I exhaled a sharp breath I hadn't realized I'd been holding and sat hard on the edge of the bed. "What about the old woman?"

"She tells the same story as Tristan—and now you—but no one will listen to her. Nobody feels she's Amadis. It's strange, actually, as if she's a witch with no allegiance to either side."

"I don't know that she's a witch," I muttered. "She doesn't have a mage's mind signature. Not exactly, anyway."

"Then you see what I mean. She's not quite right . . . so no one trusts her. She's being held, too."

"Did she say anything about Lilith? Explain her?"

"Like I said, no one trusts her to listen to her, but she won't talk right now anyway. I think she's just an old, confused woman who doesn't really understand what's going on, what she's been put into the middle of. She's grieving, too. They won't let her near the girl."

"And Jax? The were-croc?"

"I think Martin let him go. He didn't witness anything useful, and Rina didn't find anything suspicious in his thoughts.

~ 291 ~

They had no reason to believe he was a part of any conspiracy. He only wanted to help you."

Whew. I liked Jax and would have hated hearing he'd been part of setting us up, which, obviously, we had been. He didn't deserve to be dragged into this farce.

Convinced I had enough grasp of the situation, I stood up and pulled on my leather gear, which lay clean and folded neatly at the foot of my bed, the only clothes in sight.

"What are you doing?" Mom asked.

"Going to see Tristan, of course, and getting him out of there. He doesn't belong in jail. If anything, Julia does."

Mom's eyes flew to the door and back to me. "You'll see him soon. His trial's this afternoon."

"*What?* Already? Then I definitely need to see him first." I moved for the front room of the suite.

Mom shook her head and looked again at the door. Her eyes tightened, and I could tell she tried to communicate with me. I opened my mind to her. "*They're guarding us.*"

Then I'll flash. Where is he?

A vision of the corridor under the Council Hall popped into her mind. "*Third on the right. But wait.*"

"You need to rest, honey, before the trial," she said aloud as she leaned over and appeared to pick something up off the floor. Her thumb moved and my dagger appeared in her hand. I tucked it into my belt and made it invisible again, thought *thank you* and flashed.

Someone apparently had shielded the Council Hall because I didn't appear inside the dark cellar as expected. Instead, I showed up right outside the door at the top of the stairs, at the rear of the building. A guard—a Were in human form—blocked the doorway. He didn't bow.

"No visitors," he said curtly as I stepped toward the door.

"Do you forget my authority?" I demanded as haughtily as I could muster.

"Until I have further orders, you have no authority. Sorry, Ms. Alexis, but I can't let you down."

I flexed my left hand, preparing to show him I *did* have authority, but then Mom popped by my side, and we both looked at her with surprise.

She shrugged. "Thought I could help out."

The guard and I both smiled, each of us under a different impression of whom she planned to help. Mom placed her hand on the guard's arm while talking to him in hushed tones. She nodded her head slowly a few times, and he started nodding his, too.

"Yes, Ms. Sophia, a nap's a good idea," he said. "I didn't get any sleep last night."

He slid down the wall until he landed on his rump. His eyes began to droop close. Mom jerked her head at the door.

"*More will be here soon for the trial,*" she thought. "*Make it quick.*"

I rushed through the door and hurdled the entire flight of steps, landing at the bottom with a jolt. I ran to the third cell on the right, surprised to see the heavy wooden door wide open. But metal bars still kept me out. Tristan stood on the other side, his hands pressing at the space between the bars, but unable to go through it. Something blocked him from reaching out. I leaned against the bars and pushed my own arms through the openings—nothing stopped me from going in.

"Tristan," I half-breathed, half-cried as I caressed his beautiful, but tired looking face.

"*Ma lykita,*" he said, his voice full of relief. "You're okay."

"We have to get you out of here."

He shook his head. "Magic blocks me from even passing my hands through, so I can't use my powers. But it's fine. We'll deal with this their way."

"But their way is *wrong*. They're all screwed up. You know what will happen."

"I do." His jaw tightened, making the muscle jump. "But there's a reason for it all, my love. Whatever happens, it's meant to be."

"Not if they're doing it on their own or . . . with the wrong influence."

"There's nothing we can do, Lex. We have to trust them. In the end, they'll do what's right."

Trust them? *Ha!* "You mean trust them to split us up? Because you know that's what they'll do. They want to get rid of you. This is all the traitor's doing, Tristan. There's nothing *right* about it."

"Lexi," he said, his voice lower yet still firm. He took my hands in his and pulled them to his soft lips. "Lexi, my love, none of it matters. We have to remain loyal. We have to do what's best for the Amadis. This is the best—"

"*What?* Separating us is *not* what's best. It's the absolute worst! I can't do that again, Tristan."

He pursed his lips together. "You *have* to, Lex. It's your responsibility and if you do it—and you *are* strong enough— you can bring the Amadis back together. You have to live your duty and your purpose. Even without me." He paused for a long moment. When he spoke again, his voice came out bleaker than I'd ever heard it before. "What we have . . ." He stopped again and swallowed hard. "What we have, Alexis . . . it's not real."

My eyes bugged with incredulity. Had the crazies overtaken him, too? "What the hell are you talking about? How can you *say* that?"

"Listen to me," he said. His eyes looked deeply into mine, his dark with no gold flecks, the green a murky swirl of pain and turmoil. "I need to tell you something. As soon as Lisa mentioned the stone, I remembered it all. I said I didn't because I didn't want to believe what it meant, and your knowing would only make things worse. I thought . . ." He shook his head. "It doesn't matter what I thought. What I wanted. It's obviously true."

"What?" His defeated tone frightened me. *How bad could it be?*

"The stone, Lex, in the pendant. You and me—it only happened because of it. It's always been the stone. It had been given to me as a young child." His vision of a beautiful, golden-haired and golden-eyed woman showed in my mind, standing before us. From the perspective, I guessed Tristan to be very small. The golden woman held the triangular stone in her hand and pressed it against his chest, until it sank below his skin and disappeared. "She told me I would know when the right one came—my true love—the stone would tell me. I was to remove the stone and give it to this person, my soul mate. *Only* her, the woman stressed. Anyone else would be dangerous, perhaps fatal. But my soul mate would love me forever. For hundreds of years, the right one never came along. Not until I met you. Only then did the stone warm, whenever I was with you."

I saw the vision of him taking a scalpel to the skin over his heart, reaching in and removing the stone, then creating the pendant for me.

"Ooo-kaaay," I said, trying not to be creeped-out with where the stone came from. "You gave it to me. I *am* your soul mate. I do love you forever."

He shook his head. "Only because of the stone."

I couldn't help it. I laughed. After all, he had to have been kidding. This had to be a joke. But what awful timing for such a joke, and looking at his face, I knew he was completely serious. My jaw dropped, and I sobered. "Have you lost your *mind?* My love has nothing to do with a stupid stone."

He pressed his lips against my knuckles. "I wish I could believe that. I really do. But ever since we lost the pendant . . . we argue all the time."

"We've been under a lot of pressure."

"We've always been under a lot of pressure, and we never argued before. We always stood together. The stone united us."

"Bullshit," I spat. "Why are you doing this? You don't even sound like yourself. What's *wrong* with you?"

"Alexis, please don't make this more difficult for me. I *do* love you, regardless of your real feelings. And I love the Amadis. You need to do what's right for them, and *I'm* not right for them. I can't give you a daughter. I can't give you—or them—what they need."

"Tristan—"

"Listen to me. The ones who thought we were meant for each other were wrong. Rina must have interpreted the Angels' message incorrectly. I'm obviously not meant for you. I'm not the right one. We only believed it because of the stone."

"Stop talking about the fucking stone!" I yelled. "My love for you has nothing to do with it. And I will not let them separate us!"

"Don't you get it?" he growled. His eyes flashed as he lost all patience. "She only gave the stone to me so I could *trick* you into loving me."

"You didn't trick me. You can't do that to someone's feelings. You can't do that to *my* heart. I know what I feel!"

"And it can't be love, Alexis. Not true love. I. Can't. Be. Loved."

"Oh, no! No, no, no. You're *not* doing this. You're not destroying us because of your guilt." I jabbed my finger into his chest. "Stop it now, Tristan. Because I love you whether you like it or not. I love *you*. No matter what you or some stupid woman says! Besides, there's a prophecy. I've read it myself."

"Prophecies aren't specific enough. You can't be certain it means you and me."

"Then so what? Screw the prophecy. Screw the stone. There's still you and me, and I feel what I feel. I *won't* deny it. But are you? Are you denying our love? Do you love *me?*"

He growled again. "Of course, Alexis. More than anything and everything combined. Which is why I've been so selfish. It's wrong. I have to let you go, to do what's best for everyone." He pulled my arms to his chest and stepped forward so we both pressed against the bars. But our faces—our lips—couldn't touch. "Do what's right, Lex. In the end, it will be good. It's what's *supposed* to happen."

Two hands grabbed my waist from behind and tugged. "No! Tristan, no! I don't believe this! I'm not giving up on us!"

"Go, my love. Just go." He lifted my hands to his lips again, but the guard jerked me out of Tristan's grasp. "*I love you, ma lykita.*"

I love you, too, my sweet Tristan, I called back. *Whether you believe it or not. I love you. Forever!*

I didn't know if he heard my last words. The guard had me outside by then, beyond the shield, which might have severed our mental connection. Without a word, Mom took my hand and pulled me around the side of the building. She stopped and wiped the tears from my cheeks.

"Are you okay?" she asked.

I shook my head and more tears flowed. "He's giving up, Mom. He thinks it's best for the Amadis."

Mom sighed and wrapped her arms around me. I cried into her shoulder for several minutes. Then she gently pushed me back and looked into my eyes. "The trial will start soon. I assume you want to be there?"

I nodded.

"Then you need to straighten up. You can't be a mess, especially if they call on you as a witness. You need to look and act confident, not like a blubbering idiot."

I nodded again and inhaled a deep, jagged breath. Mom cleaned my face off once more and ran her hands over my hair to straighten it. Once I could breathe without hitches, she led me to the front of the Council Hall and inside. The low thrum of many muted conversations carried out from the meeting room, but Mom turned the opposite way. We entered the smaller holding room where we'd come six months ago when I attended my first council meeting.

The atmosphere then had been tense, but had also held a bit of a homecoming buzz, making the room feel bright and inviting. Now, with only Rina there and no light flooding the room or conversation filling it, the room felt dark and cold, and I almost expected to see Rina shivering in her sleeveless silk gown. She leaned against the wall, peering out the same window I had looked out that day, seeing the same village that had awed me at the time—her village, her people. I could only see her profile silhouetted against the window, but the slump of her bare shoulders was expression enough. Her sadness felt almost palpable, hanging in the air as if a dark cloud had settled in the room.

She finally turned to us, and I'd never seen anyone look so haggard. Dark half-moons shaded the skin under her tired eyes, and her bottom lip looked swollen, as if she'd been chewing on it nonstop. Considering we regenerated every night while we slept, returning to near perfection each morning, her appearance was a result of only this morning's stress. Either that or she hadn't slept. Seeing us, though, her mouth pulled into a small smile, and her eyes brightened a tad.

I should have felt sorry for her, but when she said, "Alexis, darling," and spread her arms out to welcome me with an embrace, something in me snapped. I took a step backward, pulling away from her.

"Don't 'Alexis, darling' me," I sneered. "I want nothing to do with you right now."

Her arms fell to her sides, and her eyes opened wide. "Alexis . . ."

"You knew about this little girl—*my daughter*—all along. You *knew!* And you called *me* absurd for even thinking it possible."

Rina shook her head. "No. I did not know at all."

"I don't believe you! You're still lying to me, after all this. I get it, Rina. She's evil. Her Daemoni blood's too strong. I understand that you—or someone—decided she needed to be taken away. I get it. But why do you stand here and lie to me now? Why did you lie to me before, when I first heard about her? Why would you make me feel like . . . like such a *failure?*"

"Alexis, darling, no. That is not how it is."

"Stop lying to me! You had a secret about my daughter. Tell me the truth for once. Please, Rina, just tell me the damn truth."

She looked at her hands clasped in front of her, then up at me. Her answer came in my head, keeping her confession from powerful ears. "*Alexis, I do have a secret. A secret about your daughter. But it has nothing to do with this girl you found.*" Rina paused and I almost went off on her again. "*My secret is actually very simple compared. Alexis . . . I never received a message from the Angels that you would have a daughter. That is my secret.*"

My mouth fell open. *That's all? If that's it, why wouldn't you tell me sooner? All this time . . . I thought . . .*

"*I wanted to give you hope. So you would keep trying. I wanted to give the council hope so they would not give up on you and Tristan. I tried to make them believe for as long as I could.*" Rina shook her head as she stared at the floor, then she spoke aloud, in barely more than a whisper. "But it only—how do you say—backfired? I have failed. I have failed you and Tristan. I have failed the Amadis. And now—"

"And now you're still a liar."

The door opened before she could respond, and Solomon stepped inside.

"The meeting hall is standing room only," he said. "The council would like to meet here, in private, before the trial."

"It matters little what I would like, no?" Rina asked with a sigh. Then she nodded, and Solomon opened the door wider. The council, all dressed in black robes, filed in.

Everyone stood in silence for a long moment, tension heavier and colder than a three-foot blanket of snow. The village clock tolled a single note, muffled through the window and stone walls. Rina looked at them all expectantly, but they remained silent.

"Armand, I believe you have something to say," Solomon finally said, his baritone voice sounding tired, as if he, too, had been beaten down by the council.

"Yes, I do," the short and stocky vampire said, taking two steps forward and turning to face the council who stood in a half-circle. As the chief of the Amadis police force, Armand had probably been the one who'd taken Tristan into custody. My mouth soured with hatred as he straightened his spine and cleared his throat before making his announcement. "I believe we need to temporarily remove Katerina Camilla Ames from the role of matriarch."

Chapter 21

Mom and I both gasped, along with a few others. Rina's face, however, remained emotionless.

"Don't be absurd, Armand," Charlotte said. "We *can't* remove her from our rule. We're ordained."

"It is temporary only," Armand said.

"Only for the trial?" asked Robin, the were-falcon. "There *is* a . . . conflict of interest."

"Until further notice. Until she has returned to herself," Armand said. "There has obviously been a lapse of judgment with the handling of Tristan and Alexis and this whole situation."

Several conversations broke out among the council members, and I took the moment to silently ask Mom if they could actually get away with this. But she didn't answer me. *Mom?* She ignored me, her full attention engrossed in one of the debates. *Mom!* I screamed to no avail. *What the hell?* Even if Rina had sourced that last conversation, I'd used my power with Tristan only ten minutes ago. How could Mom not hear me?

"Sophia will take her place, right?" someone asked.

"Of course she will," Solomon answered. I couldn't believe he actually went along with this and tried to listen to his thoughts for an explanation but I heard nothing. In fact, with all the mind signatures floating around, I couldn't focus on a single one. I couldn't hear anyone. The traitor must have learned about my gift and now blocked me, too. *Shit.*

"No one else—" someone started but was interrupted.

"Sophia can *not* take the seat!" Adolf, the German werewolf, declared. "Her actions do not prove her trustworthy."

Mom spun on him. "You can't name anyone else leader of the Amadis. It is against the Angels. Against *God!*"

Adolf stumbled over his English. "The Angels are apparently not caring about us with the moment. Neither of you are worth the position."

Anger flared within me, but I bit back my temper.

"Then who?" someone demanded as I watched Rina exchange a look with Julia.

"Solomon," someone else suggested.

"He's no better than Sophia," Armand said. "He'll just be Rina's puppet."

Solomon hissed but otherwise didn't respond. Rina and Julia shared another significant look.

"I propose Martin," Julia said. I was surprised she didn't say herself.

Mom freed Adolf from her glare and returned to my side. Apparently, she and I agreed with Julia, for once: if not Rina, Mom or Solomon, Martin was the next best leader. Temporarily, of course. He had enough distance from our family that the council might accept him, but he and his family were close enough to us that he'd defend our wishes. I wondered if Rina had actually told Julia to suggest Martin.

If so, it meant Rina's powers weren't completely blocked like mine were. The traitor had made a point to silence me from everyone, both ways, allowing no communication at all. Who knew about my power? Who had Rina told? And how the hell did they get into my head to do this without my knowing?

"I second the motion," Adolf said, "but not for the trial only. I move we appoint Martin to rule the council and the Amadis."

With raised brows, Martin's eyes bounced between Julia and Adolf as if he waited for them to say, "just kidding."

"I doubt it possible," he finally said when he realized they were serious. "Think about what you're saying. Our leadership is not up for election, even if we did agree in a vote."

They all spoke at once, challenging each other's statements and talking over one another.

"Enough!" Rina said, actually sounding firm, like her old self. Everyone fell silent. "There will be no vote."

I wondered, if she was able to quiet them like that, why she hadn't stopped this sooner. She displayed complete control over herself and them, so why let the discussion go on? Apparently, it wasn't lasting. She sighed wearily, and her voice came out heavy and tired.

"Martin is right. Only I can make the decision." She held her hand up when others started to speak again. "I temporarily relinquish my rule to Martin Allbright. That is an order, Martin."

With an exhalation of his breath, as if in resignation, he nodded, bowed his head to Rina and walked to the door. Without a word from anyone, he led the council, with Rina, Mom and I at the end of their procession, down a long corridor, toward the rear of the Council Hall, not to the front of the grand meeting room as we'd gone before. A thick and heavy silence weighed down on us, as if trying to press us into the stone floor.

I couldn't make sense of what happened—the council trying to oust Rina and Rina giving up her authority voluntarily. I half-expected lightning bolts to shoot from the sky and strike down the traitor and her sheep for taking this too far, beyond their boundaries. Surely the Angels didn't want this. How could they even allow it? My understanding of the Amadis, the council and the Angels' role and rule in our society had flipped over, whirled and twisted into a senseless pretzel. How could I be devoted to these . . . these *politicians* . . . whose values and beliefs obviously meant so little? They didn't seem so loyal to God and the Angels now. Why should I be loyal to them? How could Tristan be so adamant about it?

My heart felt nothing but a burning rage toward them now. If it weren't Tristan on trial, I would have left with Dorian right then, not caring what they did anymore. I wanted to forget my position and leave the Amadis forever. They weren't worthy of my allegiance.

But it *was* Tristan on trial.

We stopped in the dark hall as Martin, up ahead, paused in a doorway. The room beyond, which had been buzzing with voices, fell silent. As we filed into the back of the grand meeting hall, I thought at first we had come to a completely different room. But, no, it was the same one; only the arrangements had changed.

The King Arthur's table had been removed and the throne-like chairs moved to this end, placed behind a long table on a raised platform. Rows of chairs, a center aisle splitting them in two, faced the dais, all of them filled—well, they would be, once everyone sat down. More Amadis lined the walls and the crowd seemed to flow out the doors. The warrior angel statues—one above the doors and one above the head table—looked fiercer than ever, their anger directed at us.

The council members paraded behind the table to their chairs. Solomon, who preceded Rina, took the last one at the table, meaning Rina, Mom and I would not be joining the council at the head of the room. Instead, Martin motioned toward a line of three chairs against the wall, perpendicular to the dais, between the council and the crowd, as if we were the jury. But I already knew we'd have no say in the outcome of this trial.

Once Rina, Mom and I sat down, everyone else sat, too, showing at least some kind of respect. Then Armand raised his hand and flicked it, as if hailing a waiter. Everyone turned toward the doors, and I did, too. I held back a gasp as two guards sandwiched Tristan between them and brought him down the center aisle. The urge to run to him, to throw my arms around him, to blast the guards and the council with electricity and then run away with him, nearly overcame me. But the look on Tristan's face stopped that thought.

He barely glanced at me, his eyes hard, and quickly looked away. His face remained stony and indifferent as the guards led him to stand before the council. *I love you*, I thought as he took his place. But he didn't respond. Of course, he couldn't hear me. No one could.

Nothing bound him, at least, nothing I could see, but his hands were gloved in some strange, metallic material that must have blocked his powers. But the extra precautions weren't necessary. Although he stood straight and confident and kept all emotions from his face, he would never fight them. Like Rina, he would submit to them. As a true Amadis should do, he'd go along with whatever they decided. He really had given up.

The anger within me flared hotter. *This is not my Tristan! Who is doing this? What have they done to him?* They were breaking the ultimate warrior. Shattering his spirit. And for that, I hated every single council member up there except Char and Martin.

Martin stared at Tristan for a long time as the crowd settled and quieted, then he frowned, as if he didn't want to proceed.

"Tristan Knight," he said, "you are brought here before us in response to charges of treason against the Amadis. According to council member Julia Acerbi, you attacked her and threatened her. She also claims you attempted to kill what may be the youngest Amadis daughter. Based on your background with the Daemoni and many other actions, it is believed you are working on behalf of the Daemoni to infiltrate and destroy the Amadis. If found guilty, you will be banished from the Amadis or . . . executed."

I inhaled sharply, the breath catching in my throat. My hand flew to my mouth to muffle the cry.

"Do you have anything to say to these charges?" Martin asked.

"Only that they're absolutely ridiculous," Tristan said, the familiar steeliness in his voice. He paused as a wave of gasps and murmurs flowed through the crowd. I let out my breath—he wasn't just going to bow down after all. "I am loyal and devoted only to the Amadis. I did not attack or threaten Julia. I simply defended my wife, an Amadis daughter, as well as the girl you accuse me of harming. As far as any other actions, I do not know what they are, so I cannot possibly respond to them."

"Are you denying that you threatened to use your killing power on Julia?" Martin asked.

"Yes."

"Liar!" Julia said. Always quiet, mostly communicating only with Rina, especially in large groups, Julia shed any pretense of being submissive and became the monster she was. An arrogant, aggressive and threatening vampire. "You had your hand out, ready. That's no different than pointing a loaded and cocked gun. You saw it yourself, Martin, when you arrived."

"While fighting the Daemoni, I saw you holding the girl

in a death grip, and the next time I looked, the girl lay on the ground. And, yes, I saw Tristan facing you, his hand lifted toward you the whole time."

"I was holding Julia in place," Tristan said. "Before she killed the girl or Alexis."

"Are you accusing *me* of threatening an Amadis daughter?" Julia demanded.

Tristan didn't answer at first. His jaw muscle twitched. "The situation escalated out of control. The girl attacked, and Julia tried to stop her. In the chaos, she knocked Alexis to the ground. Whether Julia intended to hurt her or not, I cannot say."

Another round of whispers and murmurs ran through the crowd. Martin signaled to them for silence.

"Yet you still threatened to kill Julia?" Adolf said. "Even though you weren't certain if she'd intentionally hurt Alexis."

"No. I paralyzed her and the girl to stop the violence. Jax, Owen and Alexis were already down. I didn't want anyone else getting hurt . . . or killed."

"You lie," Julia seethed. "If you didn't want anyone else to be hurt, explain what happened to the girl."

Tristan dropped his head for a moment, then looked up. "I cannot explain it. When Alexis fell from the Daemoni magic, I turned toward my wife. When I turned back, the girl lay still on the ground. How do *you* explain it, Julia?"

"You hit her with your power, of course."

"It might have been Daemoni," Martin said. "They might have hit the girl just as they hit Alexis, but harder. We can't prove who harmed the girl."

Or it could have been the traitor, working with Julia. Tristan had to suspect Julia, too, but he pursed his lips tightly closed. He didn't exactly defend the vamp, but he was very careful about accusing her.

"If Tristan wanted to kill Julia, he would have. Nothing could have stopped him," said Chandra, the exotically beautiful were-leopard who thought Dorian could lead the Amadis. "We cannot prove he did anything to the girl and there is much doubt that he did. So what are the other charges against him?"

"After tying yourself to Amadis royalty, gaining your way in, you returned to the Daemoni," Savio, the Italian shark, said to Tristan. "Is that correct?"

"Not intentionally," Tristan said. "I was defending the Amadis and protecting Alexis."

"And before doing so," Savio continued, ignoring Tristan's defense, "you impregnated the Amadis daughter with only a son, who you knew would eventually convert to the Daemoni, leaving the Amadis with nothing."

"What are you saying, Savio?" Charlotte asked. "That he purposefully shot only male sperm?"

A chuckle ran through the audience.

"You must not really know the Daemoni if you can't believe they're capable of anything," Savio countered.

A murmur of agreement came from the crowd. I bit my lip, suppressing the urge to shout at them about how absurd they sounded. How they grasped at straws. At one moment, they talked about Lilith as an Amadis daughter, and in the next, when convenient for them, they spoke as if we didn't have a daughter at all.

"If you're asking if I married Alexis and she conceived a son, yes, that is true," Tristan said. "If you're asking if I gave myself to the Daemoni, yes, that is true, as well, but not to return to them. Only to protect Alexis and the Amadis. To protect you."

"That's what you say," someone nearby muttered. I leaned forward and twisted toward the source, wishing I could shoot daggers with my eyes. Many faces met my glare, some with pity and empathy, others hard and accusing. I narrowed my eyes, then turned back to Tristan and the council.

"Did you or did you not spend over seven years with the Daemoni and upon your return, attempt to murder your wife, an Amadis daughter, last March?" Armand the vampire asked.

The crowd became louder this time, with both defensive and accusing tones. I jumped to my feet, unable to keep quiet a moment longer. Especially because Tristan would never defend himself against this accusation. "No! That wasn't him. You know how the Daemoni are. You can't blame him for that!"

Several council members threw me a dirty look, while a couple looked at me with pride. Martin ignored my outburst, distracted by a piece of paper that appeared in mid-air and fluttered in front of him. He snatched it out of the air, unfolded it and studied the contents.

"Yes," Tristan said, also ignoring me. "I am sorry for not maintaining control of myself. That is a regret I have to live with for the rest of my life."

"Which may not be much longer," a voice from the crowd said.

Martin's eyes shot daggers this time. "Silence," he hissed.

"We all know Ms. Alexis is right," said Galina, one of Rina's favorite mages. "Tristan would never purposefully harm her. He was not under his own control."

"I believe it," spoke up Minh, her silly green hat now gone. "They are meant for each other, are they not? We agreed years ago they are to produce the next Amadis daughter. Why do we contradict ourselves now?"

I sat down, my arms across my chest, finally understanding why Rina had trusted those two mages so much. They were utterly loyal; you could feel it emanating off their bodies.

"*Have* you produced a daughter, as you agreed to do

twenty-eight years ago?" asked one of the Middle Eastern mages—whether Attair or Shihab, I couldn't remember.

"You tell me," Tristan said. "You've tested the girl's qualities. Since you accuse me of attempting to murder the youngest Amadis daughter, you tell me if she's even been born yet."

The mage pressed his lips together, having no answer.

"As to how you convinced Alexis to marry you in the first place . . . is it true you deceived her with a faerie stone?" Julia asked. *How did she know about it?*

Tristan's eyes flicked to me, and I shook my head before his glare returned to Julia.

"I didn't remember the meaning of the stone at the time," he said.

"But you did give her a faerie stone? And it did make her believe she loved you?"

Tristan's Adam's apple bobbed as he swallowed. "Yes. It is true."

I flew to my feet again. "No, it's not! You've gone too far! He didn't make me do anything. My love for him is real. More authentic than any of you!"

Mom tugged on my arm, pulling me back to my seat. Rina opened her mouth as if to say something—finally—but then snapped it closed, as if she couldn't bring herself to voice her own thoughts.

"A faerie stone does not work in that way," Chandra said dismissively. "We are fully aware that no magic, no powers, not even faerie powers can force or create love."

Exactly.

"If you're going to accuse Tristan of treason, your grounds must be better than what you've put forth so far," Galina said.

"Is it true you can flash while holding another living being?" Armand asked, and everyone looked at him with confusion, the question seeming to have no grounds for treason. He ignored them, staring at Tristan expectantly.

"Yes. I've flashed with Alexis a few times."

"You do realize no one has ever heard of that being done?" Armand pressed.

"Of course I'm aware. There are many things I can do that no one else can."

"So if a baby—a baby girl, in this case—were taken at birth, the kidnapper would have to flash in and out . . . leaving *with* the baby. And no one but you can accomplish such a feat."

The crowd broke out in a quiet roar. Mom, Rina and I exchanged glances. So many holes peppered that insinuation . . . .

"Let me get this straight," Tristan said, rocking back on his heels. "You're accusing me of *pretending* to become Amadis; somehow convincing the council and the matriarch *and* the youngest daughter that I should have a child with the next daughter who hadn't been born yet at the time; purposefully giving her only a son and no daughter . . . except, no, now you're saying something different. I did actually give her a daughter, but right after conception, I went back to the Daemoni for nearly eight years; and at the birth, I somehow flashed into the room, delivered a baby, cut the cord and flashed away without Rina, Sophia or one of your most powerful warlocks noticing and took the girl with me, leaving the boy. Years later, I returned to kill my wife, but since that didn't work, I took her on a wild goose chase around the globe, although I would know exactly where to find our daughter, only to try to kill her and attack a council member. Is that what you're accusing me of?"

Everyone stared at Tristan for a long moment, probably still weaving through the tangled web he'd thrown.

"Something like that," Adolf finally said.

"Except you're not even sure the girl *is* an Amadis daughter, in which case your stories and allegations change. Again."

The crowd sat silently as the accusing council members

averted their eyes and squirmed uncomfortably. Martin, who'd been studying the piece of paper he'd been delivered a few minutes ago, lifted the page and waved it in the air.

"We do have an answer to that now," he said. He looked at Tristan, then glanced at me, his expression wary. "I believe, however, we should discuss this in private. It's very personal in nature."

"Nonsense!" Julia said. "The results are pertinent to the case. They will be disclosed publicly."

"I agree," Armand said.

Martin sighed and gave a shake of his head as he glanced down at the results. I sat on the edge of my seat, my knuckles white from the tight fists I held in my lap, and waited to hear if Lilith really belonged to me. My heart pounded louder with each passing moment as Martin took his time to form his thoughts. Unable to read his mind, I wanted to physically reach in and grab the words out of his throat. Finally, he spoke. "The results show a trace of Amadis blood, but not enough to be an Amadis daughter. She is not Alexis's child, not the youngest daughter."

I sat frozen for several beats as the news set in, then finally blew out the air I'd been holding. My mind spun, swirling the crowd's loud reaction into a background cacophony. I wasn't sure what I felt. Relief, disappointment and several other emotions roiled together, fighting for dominance. *She's not my daughter. I don't* have *a daughter.* What did this mean for us? For Tristan and me? For the Amadis?

Was there still a chance I could have a girl? Although Rina never had a message from the Angels, Mom had felt the truth that I would. So perhaps all was not lost. If we could move beyond this stupid trial, if they would only give us a chance, Tristan and I might possibly still be able to give them a daughter. They had to see that now. They had to see that the girl we found, whoever she was, didn't change anything. They *had* to give us another chance.

Lost in thought, I almost missed what Martin had to add. He banged his fist on the table, silencing the crowd and catching my attention.

"However," he said, "there is a very close match to Tristan, leaving no trace of doubt of relation."

Chapter 22

A deafening silence filled the room. No one seemed to understand the meaning behind Martin's words, including me. My brain slowly processed them, and it eventually understood. The girl was not mine . . . but she *was* Tristan's.

"Tristan?" I whispered, unable to speak clearly around my heart lodged in my throat. He turned toward me and our eyes locked.

"No," he mouthed, shaking his head, truly acknowledging me for the first time since entering the room. He turned back to the council table and bellowed, "Impossible!"

The crowd finally reacted, just now figuring it out. They gasped and clicked their tongues, and at least one man chuckled. Hatred boiled within me. I hated the council, particularly Julia, for insisting this shame be exposed to everyone. Especially because it couldn't possibly be true. *It's a set-up. It has to be.* My brain, my heart, my soul couldn't accept anything else.

Julia's eyes narrowed as they scanned the paper Martin held in front of her, then she looked up at Tristan, the corners of her mouth twitching as if she fought a triumphant grin. She kept the smile to herself and maintained a ruthless glare. "The results are right here. Further proof of your betrayal. Not only did you fail—or refuse—to produce a girl for the Amadis, but you *did* produce a daughter with someone else and tried to make it appear as if she were ours."

"And what would be my reasoning?" Tristan demanded.

"It's obvious," Armand said. "Look at the disruption you've caused in the Amadis. Look how close we are to collapse. All at your doing."

"You're setting me up."

"It explains your defense of the girl," Julia pointed out.

"You contradict yourself. You said *I* attacked the girl. Are you admitting it was you?"

Julia stood and leaned over the table, baring her teeth, fangs and all. "You've betrayed us. *You* are the traitor. The proof is right here."

"Bullshit!" I shouted, jumping to my feet again and ignoring the reaction to my language. I looked Julia directly in the eye. "You're making it up to frame him. You've been trying to set us up for months, for some reason trying to get rid of us. It won't work!"

"You have no idea what you're talking about, girl," Julia said through clenched teeth.

"I agree we've found the traitor," Adolf said, and he sneered at me as he continued, as if to prove Julia's plan *would* work. "I move for a conviction of Tristan Knight for treason against the Amadis. I also move we annul his marriage to Alexis Ames and she marry Owen Allbright."

"*What?*" I shrieked. "You can't do this! You can't force me to marry anyone!"

Mom grabbed me by the waist, but I struggled against her.

"You are an Amadis daughter. If you are loyal to us, you will do what's best for the Amadis," Armand warned. "I second the motion."

"No! You can't do this!" I yelled louder, fighting against Mom's tight grip.

"All in favor?" Martin asked unenthusiastically, his voice loaded with defeat. I thrashed against Mom as I watched seven hands rise . . . against six that didn't.

Mass confusion broke out in the crowd, drowning out my cries of refusal.

"Martin didn't vote," someone called out above all the other voices and the crowd quieted.

"What's your vote, Martin?" someone else asked.

"What does it matter?" a vaguely familiar, gravelly voice said. I thought it belonged to Ferrer, the blacksmith, but I couldn't see his stooped frame in the crowd. "This is not a democracy. It's up to the matriarch. She must make the final decision."

"What say you, Ms. Katerina?" an old, small witch at the front of the crowd asked.

Rina didn't answer, but only stared at the dais. Martin pressed his lips together.

"I did not vote because I will make the final decision," he finally said. "I have been asked to take the rule for the time being. Katerina Camilla Ames has removed herself as matriarch."

And all hell broke loose.

People yelled at the council, at Martin, at Rina and at each other. The rise of emotions literally heated the room. The crowd began pushing their way toward the dais, demanding answers.

"Silence!" Solomon's voice boomed over the chaos and everyone obeyed, more out of being startled than anything. He looked every bit vampire at this moment. "We are taking a recess. Everyone out!"

When nobody moved and the protests broke out again, the council left the room themselves. The two warlock-guards led Tristan out the back, too, and Rina, Mom and I headed for the same door we came through, Mom half-carrying me.

"Rina, you have to do something!" I said as soon as the three of us were alone in the holding room. "They're obviously framing him. *You* can stop this."

When she looked at me, her mahogany eyes wide and moist, I could tell the fight had completely left her. "There is nothing I can do, Alexis dear. They will not listen to me. Let Martin handle this. He will do the right thing."

I whirled on Mom, and she held up her hand.

"Martin will take them in private quarters and talk sense into them," she said. "They've put their trust in him, honey. He'll take care of this and they'll have to go along with him now."

"You have listened to his thoughts, no?" Rina asked. "You know what he will do."

"I'm blocked," I said. "I can't hear anyone and no one can hear me."

"Then the traitor is here, in the crowd," Rina said.

"Obviously. No doubt creating all this mayhem to distract everyone from what's really going on. Probably influencing everyone in that room, especially with those bogus test results. And if destroying the Amadis is her goal, she's doing a damn good job of it."

Mom sat in a wingback chair in the seating area. "As soon as Martin takes care of this, we can move on and address the issue of the real traitor. We just have to wait now."

I sank onto one end of the couch across from her. "For how long?"

Mom shrugged. "For as long as it takes for him to feel he can overrule their vote without causing too many problems among them. He has to do it diplomatically, or we'll have even more trouble on our hands."

"You're sure he's with us?" I asked. "I mean, they want me to marry Owen. He might want— Wait. Where is Owen? He's not really in the hospital is he?"

"I sent him on an errand," Rina murmured.

"Oh." I snorted. "I thought maybe he ran away, before they forced him to marry me." The idea sounded appealing, much better than annulling my marriage and being forced together with Owen. If only I could talk Tristan into it. He, Dorian and I could get away from here for good, escape the crazies, as Charlotte had called them. Now I understood fully. But I didn't understand why Rina would send Owen away now, during such an important trial. His future was at stake, too, after all.

"Alexis," Rina said, and I looked over my shoulder at her. She stood where she had earlier, leaning against the wall and watching out the window, still looking just as forlorn. "Have you been able to lower your shield yet?"

"No. Why does it matter, though? I can't communicate with one person, let alone more."

She turned her head toward me and pierced me with fierce eyes. "You are powerful enough to break the block. You can do this. You *must* do it."

Then she turned back to the window and fell silent again. The woman was as crazy as the rest of them, and I no longer knew what to think of her. One moment, she acted like my grandmother, caring and protective. And the next, she appeared to have given up and acceded to everyone against us.

Someone knocked on the door, but didn't wait for an answer. Charlotte strode in, closed the door behind her and handed a sheet of paper to Rina.

"We'll be reconvening soon," Char said.

"Already?" Mom asked.

"We have to. We have to wrap this up, settle everything else and get out of here. We're needed in the field. The Daemoni have increased their attacks."

Rina gasped. I thought she reacted to Char's statement, but when I looked at her, her face looked white as snow, and she held the paper out. "It cannot be true," she whispered.

Mom made a move, but I was closer. I snatched the paper out of Rina's hands, and my eyes fell upon the test results. I'd never seen a normal DNA report, but this surely wasn't anything like it. Not when phrases such as "dark magic levels," "total magical quotient" and "individualized abilities" plastered it. There were also what I assumed traditional phrases: "alleged father," "child," "alleged mother," "genetic markers" and "probability percentage." I ignored the interpretation and studied the details for myself—numbers on a page. The child's numbers were nowhere near the alleged mother's. Lilith and I were remotely related, if at all.

But . . . the breath caught in my lungs, and my heart stilled. The paper rattled in my trembling hands.

"Is this . . . is this right?" I choked, hoping against everything that it wasn't. Tears blurred my vision as I stared at the results.

"I'm sorry, Alexis," Char said.

I shook my head violently. "No. It's not possible. They're only numbers. Just numbers. Anyone could fill those in however they want to!"

"I checked with my friend, the wizard-doctor who ran the tests. He said there's no doubt. The girl's genetic markers are very similar to Tristan's."

I blinked away the tears and glared at her. "Then your friend must be working for them. For the traitor. He's part of the set-up."

Of course that was it. He had to be part of it all. Because otherwise . . .

"I'm sorry," Char said again, pity written all over her face.

"I don't want your apologies!" I nearly yelled. "I don't want your pity. I want the truth!"

Charlotte held out a white envelope I hadn't noticed in her hand before. "Tristan expected the same thing, so he had Owen take samples to his own guy in London. This just came in, after Martin called for the recess. Tristan said to deliver it straight to you, and you would know what to do with the truth. No one else has seen what it says."

I stared at the envelope held between us. Such an innocuous object, paper with markings on it. An object that could be destroyed so easily—torn to bits, held to a flame, disintegrated with water and flushed down a drain—yet could hold enough power to decimate a kingdom, start or end a war, free the imprisoned innocent, lift the souls of the downtrodden . . . and break the hearts of lovers. For the paper and the ink didn't hold the real power. They were simply tools used by people. No, the power lay in the message contained within.

I suddenly didn't want to see the message on this particular piece of paper. I forced myself to lift my hand, to close my fingers on the envelope's edges, to take it from Charlotte and tear it open. I commanded my eyes to look at the paper, my brain to interpret the message.

Unlike the wizard's results page, this one only showed a DNA chart. It was purely scientific—the test performed and the results recorded by a doctor on stationery from a medical research lab in London. Like the false-ID creator, the doctor must have been one of "Tristan's guys" located around the world whom he could rely on for help. One of the many Normans who knew Tristan as someone who occasionally needed to circumvent authorities or cut through red tape and had the money to pay for it. They would be unaware of the Amadis and our politics just as the Amadis were likely unaware of them. Knowing Tristan, who put the Amadis above all, including himself, he would only hire someone who'd provide accurate results, even if they incriminated him. Tristan trusted this doctor to deliver only the truth.

And the results were the same.

"It . . . it wasn't a set-up," I said, the whisper sounding distant to my own ears.

The paper fluttered toward the floor as my body went numb. My hands fell limp in my lap, and I simply stared at them. My mind tried to grasp the true meaning of this, but some part of me kept it from doing so, still trying to deny it. I squeezed my eyes shut to block out this place, wanting to leave and go to another world where Tristan and I lived happily ever after. But Lilith's face—the sweet one, before she went all monster on us—showed on the back of my eyelids. Just like Dorian's face . . . which was just like his father's.

And then the thoughts I wanted to avoid bombarded me. Questions. So many questions. How could this happen? When did it happen? I'd become pregnant with Dorian on our honeymoon right before Tristan disappeared. There was no doubt because I'd been a virgin before our wedding. Had the wait been too long for him? Had he been with someone else, unable to hold out for me? Or did it happen after he left? He'd said he'd been completely faithful during his absence, but . . . what was I to believe now?

Then the worst images of all battered my mind and assaulted my soul. Tristan actually with another woman. Someone else embraced in his powerful arms. Limbs entangled, eyes locked on each other's with that shared look of love and lust. Strange fingers touching his naked flesh, lips kissing his full ones, hands that weren't mine on his face, on his biceps and chest, stroking him . . . another woman's body making him respond in a way I thought only I could do. And him caressing her, kissing her, holding her . . . making love to her. Doing everything he did to me to her.

Giving her a baby. A piece of him to hold onto when he wasn't with her.

I pulled my knees to my chest and bent my head to curl into a ball, trying to protect my heart and soul from the pain. But no one attacked me from the outside. The agony already burgeoned within, tightening its hold, knifing its way across my heart.

"How could he do this to me?" I whispered against my thighs. Nobody answered. "To all of us?"

He hadn't betrayed only me. I envisioned him in the meeting hall, denying it. Denying everything. If he could do this . . . get away with it all these years . . . what else had he done? What else had he lied about? Was *anything* he said true? The horrible idea that Julia and the others were right about him crept into my mind like a dark mist seeping in and blacking out everything I'd ever believed. He'd summarized it all himself, and now I could almost believe it, either way the story went. Not everything—some of it was outright ludicrous—but the general idea that he made all this happen to bring down the Amadis . . . *No! Not my Tristan. Impossible!*

Right?

More and more, the council's accusations began to make sense. Rina and Mom had believed in Tristan all along, before I was even born, based on feelings and messages from the Angels. The traitor had thought them foolish leaders, relying so much on their senses and directives that truly didn't exist. With his ability to identify possible options and solutions, could Tristan figure that out, realize there'd never been a message about our daughter? Had he told the traitor about Rina's lie? *Oh, my God. Every time I'd heard the traitor's voice, Tristan had been there!* Had his mistress been around, too? Was that her voice I'd heard? Did she stop us from making love that one night in the woods? Is that how Tristan dealt with my inability to have sex—by going to her?

Their faces overcome with bliss. Cries of pleasure escaping their lips.

The image made my stomach heave. I had nothing to vomit, though. Acid burned the back of my throat.

I clutched at my hair with my hands, my fingernails digging into my scalp. *No. It can't be. I can't believe this!*

Charlotte cleared her throat, a reminder she still stood before me.

"He wants to see you," she said, her voice uncharacteristically soft and quiet. "Martin says he can come in."

I tried to imagine what I would do when I saw him face-to-face. When I looked into his eyes. What I would say. But the image eluded me. As if Foggy Alexis tried to ooze her way in to protect me.

"I don't think I can," I said, my forehead still pressed against my knees.

Charlotte sighed. "I want to say I know what Martin will do, but I can't guarantee it. He's having a hard time with the others." A beat passed before she added, very quietly, "Alexis, this might be your last chance to see Tristan alone. Ever."

And that finally got to me. The fog disappeared as the idea of never seeing Tristan—the only man I'd ever loved—squeezed my heart with panic. I couldn't let it end like this.

"Okay," I mumbled. I remained in my protective ball as hands touched my shoulder and hair, followed by the noises of people coming and going. Then the room fell silent, and a heavy weight sat on my couch, at the other end.

"*Ma lykita.*" The loveliest voice in the world carved a gash into my soul.

Chapter 23

Tears stung my eyes just to hear Tristan's voice. I didn't move, didn't respond, afraid of him. Of myself. His weight shifted, and I knew he reached out to touch me. I pulled my ball tighter. He let out a heavy sigh. "You don't believe me."

"Believe what?" I asked. "You haven't even tried to defend yourself. Not to me."

"What? Do you think it was Rina who I tried so hard to convince that it's not true? That it's absolutely impossible? I was telling you, Lexi. You're the only one who matters."

I finally lifted my head and rested my chin on my knees, staring straight forward at the wall. Not allowing myself to look his way. "If you mean with your thoughts, I can't hear anyone. I'm blocked. But I've seen the results myself. There really is no doubt." My voice cracked on the last word as my eyes flicked to the paper from Tristan's guy on the floor.

He leaned over to retrieve it, and several moments of silence passed as he studied the results. He let it fall to the floor again as he leaned his elbows on his knees and rested his head in his hands, still not saying a word. Then he moved closer to me. His large hand landed softly on my head, smoothed down my hair and rested on my back. I began to shake uncontrollably. He wrapped his other arm around me and pulled me to his chest. I couldn't bring myself to stop him. *Just one last time. Feel him one more time.* The dam finally broke, and I could no longer stop the sobs.

"Lexi," he murmured as he tightened his arms around me. "My Lexi. Please listen to me. Everything has changed now, I understand, but not my love for you. Whatever happens, I need you to know I've always been faithful to you. Only you, Lex. It's always been only you, my love."

"Then—" My breath hitched with the sobs. "Then how can it be?"

"I honestly have no idea. The traitor must be blocking me, too, because I see no options, no possible answers except the obvious. But it's *not* true. I promise you that. Please, Lexi, believe me."

Each pleading word, pointed with his despair, pierced my heart. I finally forced myself to look up at his beautiful face, and as soon as I did, as soon as I looked into those hazel eyes begging for my trust, I *wanted* to have faith in him. But . . .

"I don't know what to believe anymore," I said.

The pain in his eyes nearly killed me. He took my face in his hands, and I didn't pull away, unable to hurt him anymore. He leaned his forehead against mine.

"I understand. You need to shield your heart." His thumb stroked my face, and I wanted so badly to lean into his palm. "But open your mind, Lex, and use it. Find out the truth. Promise me you'll try. I understand that you can't love me, but I can't bear the thought of leaving you like this, believing their lies."

So I should believe yours? I couldn't bring myself to say it. Especially because I *wanted* to believe him. I'd made the decision years ago to take his word over everyone else's, but that was when his word meant something. When I thought he and I were on the same side, together, as one.

The door opened and Charlotte stepped inside. "It's time."

"*No*," we said at once, desperation filling both of our voices. Desperation to believe. To be believed.

"I'm sorry, but they're ready."

The two warlock-guards pushed past Charlotte and each grabbed one of Tristan's arms. Before he stood on his own, he leaned forward and brushed his lips across my forehead, leaving a trail of electricity under my skin.

"Use your head. If not for me, Lex, do it for our son. For the Amadis. You have the advantage, *ma lykita*. Use it." He didn't fight the guards as they pushed him toward the door and out of the room.

Away from me.

Perhaps forever.

I didn't remember moving, but I suddenly found myself standing. Standing in an empty, gloomy room alone. All alone. A feeling I'd lived with for over seven years. Something I thought I'd never have to do again, yet here I was. But I wanted to be alone. *Needed* it. Distant noises thrummed from the hall and the meeting room, setting my teeth on edge. I couldn't deal with being in that noisy crowd again. I couldn't stand seeing the smug faces of the council.

I'd trusted them easier than I'd ever trusted anyone. I'd been convinced years ago, when I first learned of the Amadis, they were the good guys. The Daemoni were evil. The Amadis were good. If you were Amadis, I could trust you. Black and white. I'd never been so wrong. Like anything in life, this covert world was colored with grays. Nothing—nobody—could be trusted for how they appeared on the surface. How could I ever be loyal to those I couldn't trust? I wanted nothing to do with them, with my position, with the Amadis at all. I wanted out.

"Alexis, they're about to start," Mom said from the doorway.

"I'm not going back in there. I've heard enough."

"You don't want to hear Martin's final decision?"

I shook my head. "What does it matter? What do I care what happens?"

Mom moved into the room, and I took a step backward. She sighed. "You don't believe that. You know it matters to you. Whatever has happened in the past, you love him. You care what happens to him."

I shook my head again, but my eyes stung. She pursed her lips together and stared at me for a long moment. Then she left. And my eyes burned hotter. *I do care. I do love him. No matter what.* Besides, he was the father of my son. Even if I no longer cared about the Amadis or their future, I did need to hear Martin's decision about Tristan.

I hurried down the corridor to the grand room, which sounded as though an angry mob filled it. Rina and Mom were just entering, and I slid into step behind Mom. People shouted accusations and questions, not noticing as the three of us came inside and took our seats.

"The Ames women must lead us!"

"We're nothing without them! We'll collapse!"

"Ms. Katerina, why did you step down? How could you abandon us?"

"How can you rule, Martin? You aren't of Amadis blood! You're not ordained to rule!"

"We are here for the trial of Tristan Knight, not Katerina Ames or this council," Solomon said over the crowd, somewhat quieting them. "We will finish this trial, then we will discuss the future of the Amadis."

"Get this over with! We should be out there fighting!"

"Yeah! We should be fighting Daemoni, not each other!"

"But we have no future without a matriarch!"

I didn't know where to take my gaze. I avoided the front of the room, definitely not wanting to see the council. I didn't want to look into the faces of the angry crowd either. My eyes kept pulling toward Tristan, but I knew looking at him would only bring more tears. So I looked up, over the crowd's heads to stare at a point on the wall. Across the room from us, a little higher than the rest of the heads, bobbed a familiar blond one.

Owen's eyes caught mine for a second, then he looked away, as if unable to bear the sight of me. He stood against the wall with a woman on each side of him, one blue-haired and the other purple—Jessica and Lisa, the faeries. *Is this his defense? Trying to show he's already in love with someone else—two somebody elses?* He couldn't believe that would work. It would only be infatuation, faeries creating lust, not love. Everyone would see that.

Not that he looked in love. The crowd must have diluted the faeries' influence because he didn't have the same expression as he'd had at their cottage in the Tennessee woods. Instead, he looked composed and . . . calculating. As if he had something up his sleeve and simply waited for the right time to reveal it. *Did Rina send him after the faeries? But why?*

I followed Owen's gaze to the old woman who'd cared for Lilith, sitting not too far from Owen and the faeries. Her face was drawn tight, making her look older. I didn't remember her presence earlier and wondered why they'd brought her in. I could only figure that after Tristan's trial, they planned to question her about Lilith—their relationship, why she was raising her, what she might know about Lilith's mother. That thought made me physically cringe. Did I want to stay for that? I might learn something that would help me to believe Tristan . . . or I might not and instead subject myself to even more agony.

Nona, as Lilith had called her, was the only person sitting in the room, besides the council members and us. Everyone else stood, and as I finally looked at the crowd, I found a variety of expressions, but all of them full of passion. Their spirits animated with the desire to fight or to protect, with rage or with worry, with hate or with love. Some had pointy ears and extra facial hair, as if they were about to lose control over their human forms. Others' fangs showed, brought out by the anger and fear in the room.

"What about the Daemoni?" someone called out, the voice spiked with terror.

"Yeah! They're attacking right now and we're doing nothing. They'll win!" A voice agitated with the desire to fight.

"What about our children?"

"They have no future now," a woman wailed. "What will happen to them?"

"What about the unprotected humans? The innocents?" Owen yelled louder than anyone, and many shouts rallied with him.

I saw then what Mom must have seen years ago, what council members now realized. Owen could become a great leader. He might try to push things a little too far, as Rina had once pointed out, but that was a sign of courage. He never overreacted to anything, but was passionate about his beliefs. And as seen now, he could control a crowd, keep them focused on the right things. He was definitely strong and powerful enough. No wonder he was their next choice as the father of my daughter.

But I could never be with him, even after what Tristan had apparently done. It'd still have to be by in vitro . . .

Oh! Oh, my god.

That's it!

My breath caught as the obvious slammed into me twofold. Solomon's words echoed in my mind: *The best stories—and the best lies—are woven around the truth. It is up to us to discover which is which.* The traitor knew about this girl with Tristan's DNA and had intertwined that thread of truth into her lies to authenticate her claims. This wasn't Tristan's doing. He hadn't orchestrated the Amadis' downfall.

"Quiet!" Solomon bellowed once again.

"Martin, do you have a decision?" Armand asked, seizing the opportunity of silence.

Before Martin could answer, I jumped to my feet.

"Wait! You can't prove Tristan's betrayal with those results," I said. Everyone stared at me with raised eyebrows, including Tristan. I took two steps forward. "In vitro fertilization. The Daemoni could have taken—" I swallowed my embarrassment and pushed forward, holding Tristan's gaze as I spoke. "They could have taken Tristan's semen and created this girl without his knowledge."

Tristan's face showed a flicker of relief . . . or affirmation . . . or something. *Could I be right?* If he'd told me the truth—that he had no idea how Lilith could be his daughter—then this was the only solution. The one he hadn't been able to see. The Daemoni could have taken anything from him as soon as they captured him. They'd knocked him out with black magic, and he would have never known. *He'd been telling me the truth!*

This meant Lilith really was his daughter. And I'd have a decision to make. Which explained Tristan's expression. He felt relieved to see I believed him about being faithful . . . but worried about what this would do to us, if we made it out of here together. He'd said he'd raise someone else's daughter if he had to. *Could I do the same?*

My decision would have to wait. The crowd's noisy response drowned out my own thoughts.

Martin banged his fist on the table. "Enough."

"Is there a way to prove this?" Chandra asked.

"Of course not," Armand said. "And as such, we must proceed. We cannot take the risk this is another lie."

"You can't prove it's not true either," Mom challenged.

"You can't be certain either way," I added. "What happened to innocent until proven guilty?"

"This is not America," one of the Middle Eastern mages said. "Nor a democracy. Martin, what is your decision?"

"But she might be right!" someone said from the crowd.

"Which means the Daemoni are part of this," someone else said.

The audience let loose with another outburst, some members supporting me, others backing Armand, saying the risk wasn't worth their lives.

"Even if it's true, he could be working with them," Savio said. "They can produce all kinds of his offspring, *and* they get the boy."

"That's all we need to remember," Armand said. "More proof that Tristan is the traitor."

"Does your vote remain then?" Martin asked, looking up and down the table. Everyone nodded.

"We agreed at recess that he ought to be banished," Savio said. "We move forward with Owen and Alexis."

Martin rubbed his forehead with this thumb and forefinger. He opened his mouth to speak, closed it again. He looked at Tristan and then at me with blue eyes that darkened and softened with each heartbeat. As if to say he was sorry.

Tears sprang to my eyes.

"No. You can't," I whispered, holding Martin's eyes as I shook my head slowly. And when he didn't respond, I nearly shouted, "No! You banish Tristan, you banish me, too. You won't control me like this!"

I pushed one of the warlocks to the side and latched onto Tristan's arm.

"Get her out of here," Armand barked. "Get them both out of here."

Someone grabbed me from behind—another guard. I gripped Tristan's arm, holding on tightly. The guard yanked at me. My fingers slipped. The warlocks pulled on Tristan from the other side, and Tristan easily went with them toward the door.

"No!" I screamed, my hands held out toward him. "Tristan! No!"

I fought against the guard who carried me toward the opposite door, but he held me with all his strength. I yelled out a variety of profanities, letting the anger consume me before the pain did as I watched them take Tristan away from me. The current reality blended with the past, when he left me crying and begging for him to stay at the safe house. When he left me, left us, both Dorian and me. My heart cracked, and I knew when it broke into a million pieces again, it couldn't possibly be put back together a second time. Tears flowed down my cheeks. *Please. No. Not again.*

"Bree, you must say your piece *now*," Lisa the faerie whispered as the guard dragged me by. "This is the time!"

"Now or never, Bree," Jessica said. "Or everything will be for naught."

My eyes went wild. *Bree? She's here?!*

"Wait!" Lilith's witch stood up so fast, her chair fell over behind her. Everyone stopped and stared at her, including the guards holding Tristan and me, surprised by her clear and strong voice. "You are mistaken."

"Excuse me, old witch?" Savio drawled.

The woman's upper lip curled in a snarl at the insult. "There was no outside fertilization. The Daemoni didn't take Tristan's seed."

My stomach tilted as she looked at me. *I'm wrong?! But . . . that could only mean . . .* The old woman's milky eyes began to clear and change color. Her body straightened and lengthened several inches until she stood to nearly six feet tall. The wrinkles smoothed and the blotchy skin cleared to a golden tan. Her gray hair transformed into thick, wavy golden strands, and her eyes finally settled on a matching golden color. And my stomach more than tilted—it dropped. *Is this Tristan's mistress?*

"In fact," she said, her sparkling gaze still directly on me, "no one can take Tristan's seed except Alexis. The faerie stone is a fertility stone."

Her mouth turned up in a soft smile toward me. Of course she wasn't Tristan's mistress. She was the golden lady from his memories.

"You're a *faerie?*" Robin asked with shock.

The golden lady's lips pulled up in a smile. "Yes. I am Bree. And I must stop you from making this horrible mistake."

"What do you know about it?" Savio demanded.

"I know quite a bit about it," Bree said. "Much more than any of you. Did you not hear? I am a faerie! I may not be part of the Otherworld anymore, but I know exactly what is going on here, and you are about to destroy the Amadis."

"Explain yourself!" Julia demanded.

Bree's golden eyes sparked with anger at Julia's tone. "Just as you demanded in the Everglades, but you never gave me a chance. I will start with the girl, whom you also told me to explain. And I will tell you, and you will finally listen to me."

Her expression toward me softened and then, when she looked at Tristan, she smiled. She sauntered to the front of the room, all eyes following her.

Bree peered at each of the council members as she strode the length of the dais. "The girl has a name. Lilith. And she is my daughter." She turned to me again, her stunning gold eyes capturing mine, and I could do nothing but stare back, mesmerized. "But she is not Tristan's daughter. She is his sister."

My breath caught in my throat. I blinked. Then, as if we were all controlled by the same puppet string, everyone's heads jerked toward Tristan. I knew his face well enough to see the range of emotions play out—shock, confusion, anger and then rage.

"*LIAR!*" he bellowed. Then he disappeared.

Chapter 24

Tristan moved so fast at the faerie even my eyes couldn't see him. The next thing I knew, the faerie held up her hand, and Tristan appeared, bouncing off an invisible wall she'd thrown up. He landed on his feet a yard away from her, and his eyes sparked so brightly with anger, I expected them to burst into flames.

I broke free from the guard's slackened hold on me, and rushed to Tristan's side.

"Tristan," I said softly, placing my hands on his bulging forearm, "relax. She's not hurting anyone. Please calm down."

He glanced down at me, and his eyes softened . . . slightly. Then he lifted his eyes to Bree, and a low growl rumbled in his chest.

"I won't stand for your lies," he said. "We don't need your faerie bullshit!"

"I tell the truth, Tristan," Bree said, her gold eyes wide and sincere. "I *am* your mother."

Tristan leaned in toward her, and his voice came out low, each word distinct. "I don't have a mother. The woman who gave birth to me was an abhorrent Daemoni witch who died over two centuries ago. So drop the faerie antics. They're not helping anyone."

Bree shook her head and the light sparked off her Otherworldly hair. "That's what they told you, Tristan. They wanted you to believe I cared nothing about you so you would hate me. They wanted you to themselves, to raise you *their* way, not mine."

"They said you tried to kill me! You wanted me dead."

"No, my son. All part of their lies. The truth is . . . I loved—*love*—you. I always have."

"Faeries don't love! You don't care about anything in this world!"

"But *I* did. I still do. It's why they took you from me. You couldn't experience love, not for their purposes. When they saw how much I cared for you . . . they didn't expect that at all. They didn't know I was a faerie. They saw the witch you saw just a bit ago—a couple hundred years younger, but the same witch. They thought I served them. They would have never allowed me to be your birth mother if they knew."

Tristan's hands flew to the sides of his head, grabbing at his hair. He blew out a rumbling breath—a growl of anger or exasperation, I wasn't sure. I placed my hand on the small of his back and felt his muscles pulled taut under my touch.

"Why then?" he demanded of Bree. "Why would the faeries get involved? Why did they care?"

Bree tilted her head. "It wasn't the faeries. It was the Angels. Do you really think they'd let the Daemoni get away with creating a warrior . . . someone like *you* . . . without a plan? They played a part in it all along, planning how you would eventually come to their side. They came to the faeries, asking for our help. I've always favored the Angels, favored Heaven's ways, so I volunteered."

Martin shifted, the movement catching my eye. His eyes narrowed. "That would mean you'd have to give up the Otherworld and live in the physical realm for eternity. No faerie would do such a thing."

"I did," Bree said, turning toward him and the council. "I saw their need and if I didn't do it, if none of us did, the Daemoni would have created something much worse than Tristan. A beast with no goodness at all, no conscience, a killing machine."

"And they *trusted* you?" Julia demanded. "Knew you wouldn't turn on them?"

"Not at first, but *they* requested this favor, so they'd already devised a variety of challenges to test my goodness, to be certain I served them and God. When they were satisfied, they sent me into this world as a witch, someone who would meet the Daemoni's criteria for their warrior's biological mother. They *planted* me so I could give Tristan their goodness and my faerie blood." Bree took several steps toward the dais. "Don't you see? The Angels wanted Tristan to be *here*, serving you, not the Daemoni. They planned this all along."

"How can we trust *you*?" Martin demanded. His eyes had gone from pale blue to so dark, they almost looked purple. He leaned forward, his knuckles white as he gripped the edge of the table, his body tense as if he used every bit of control he had to keep himself from attacking Bree. His voice came out as a growl that rivaled Tristan's. "You're a faerie!"

Jessica, who'd been standing with Lisa in the shadows, stepped forward. "We'll just have to show ya'll."

She and Lisa went over to Bree and grasped her hands in theirs. Then they all lifted their hands together into a peak over their heads, which they leaned together. The light in the room darkened and colorful sparks rained down on them. Then I lost them as the whole room disappeared in darkness.

I found myself in a different place and time. I stood on the side of a mountain covered in green grass and gray boulders, reminding me of pictures I'd seen of Ireland. Bree floated in the air above me with a blinding light surrounding her. She appeared to be alone, but a clear voice with an unearthly quality spoke.

"Thank you, Bree, for aiding us," the voice said. "We understand this changes your existence, and we celebrate your commitment."

"I do it for you, my Angel. And for God," Bree said.

"And we, the Angels, will be with you forever. You may feel outcast, but know you are not. You will rejoin us all in the Otherworld when your time comes. Now go. Do your duty. Create the most powerful warrior for the Amadis."

The light disappeared, and Bree dropped to the ground. Then the scene changed. Bree sat in a hut made of sticks, looking quite different. The light glinted off a few golden streaks, but her hair was now a dull, dishwater blond, and her eyes were no longer shining, but a muddy yellowish-brown. She wasn't exactly ugly, but not as vibrant and striking as she was as a faerie. She sat on a wooden stool, drinking from a mug.

"Drink it all," croaked an old woman, obviously a witch, who stood by the fireplace, eyeing Bree. "Every day, morning and night. Jordan's potion might cause changes in you, but it is mostly for the baby."

"But I am not with child yet," Bree said.

"We are still preparing you," the witch said. "Just as we are preparing the chosen father. He is very handsome, with enough Amadis blood. Soon, you will meet."

The air around us wavered, and the scene wasn't much different, but time had passed. We were still in the hut, but Bree no longer sat on the stool. Her hand pressed against her swollen belly as she waddled toward the bed.

"I am certain it's time," she said, and her face tightened in pain.

"One more dose, then," the witch said, handing Bree a mug.

The scene changed again, and we were now outside what appeared to be the same hut. Bree chased after a small, tow-headed child, both of them laughing. When he turned to look at her, my breath caught. *Dorian*, I thought at first. But of course not . . . it was Tristan as a little tot, no more than two or three years old. She scooped him up in her arms and held him closely to her in a loving embrace. Then she gave him the stone, showing her viewpoint of what Tristan had shown me earlier, when my telepathy still worked.

The air wavered again, and Tristan now looked more like six or seven years old, again running around outside the hut. Bree apparently had been watching him from her perch on a fallen tree trunk, but now she glanced around, alarm all over her face. She stood, placed one hand over her enlarged belly and called out, panic lilting her voice. But Tristan never made it back to her. Two men—vampires—shot out of the nearby woods, grabbed Tristan and blurred away, too fast for a pregnant Bree to catch. She fell to the ground sobbing and screaming, "My son! My son!"

Our surroundings changed, and we appeared to be in modern day London. Bree, looking much older and more like the witch we'd found in the Everglades, sat at a small table at a sidewalk café. Based on the fashion people wore, I guessed the time to be the late 1970s or early '80s. When Mom joined her at the table, I knew I guessed right. They spoke briefly until the waiter brought them two mugs of tea. Bree dumped herbs into Mom's mug—the same herbs Blossom had given me last week.

"This will keep me strong so I can handle Lucas?" Mom asked, lifting the cup to her face. She grimaced as the steam rose into her nostrils.

"Yes. It is often used to foster pregnancy, but also fortifies the body."

"Well, I don't have to worry about getting pregnant," Mom said. Then she tipped the cup to her lips and downed the tea. Her eyes watered as she swallowed, which was probably how she missed the golden glint in Bree's eyes—a gleam that said, "let's hope you're wrong."

The scene disappeared, and it took me a moment to realize we were in the Council Hall. The room lightened and everyone looked around, blinking, somewhat disoriented, reminding me of when they showed films in school and the students fell asleep until the teacher flipped the light back on.

"How do we know it's not faerie tricks?" Robin finally asked.

"Of course it's faerie tricks!" Martin bellowed.

"It's not," Tristan said. He stared at Bree, who stood between Lisa and Jessica, but not with hard, glaring eyes sparking with anger. Grief filled them now. His voice came low, full of shock. "I remember now. I remember them taking me and brainwashing me. And . . . I remember Bree . . . my mother."

His voice cracked on the last word. I wrapped my arms around him and held him tightly.

"How do you explain the girl?" Martin asked, his voice heavy with a challenge.

"Yes," Julia said. "You looked to be pregnant again when they took Tristan, but that was two-hundred-sixty-years ago."

Bree nodded. "Yes, it was. Lilith is only six years younger than Tristan. The Daemoni were pleased with Tristan when he was young, and they wanted more just like him. However, they didn't get the same results with Lilith. She came into her powers like a boy does, but at seven years old. She stopped aging then, too. She is powerful, but they couldn't train her. She didn't have the same Angels' blessing as Tristan did. She doesn't have enough goodness in her, making her worse than even a vampire when it comes to self-control." Bree said this last statement with hard eyes on Julia and Armand.

"One of their experiments gone wrong," I muttered.

"Yes," Bree said. "And all of their experiments will continue to go wrong. Tristan is only right because of the Angels' involvement."

"So they allowed you to raise the girl?" Martin asked, his tone still accusing.

"Not exactly. They left her to me, but ordered me to kill her. I should have done it and not let her live so long in the body of a child. I understand it wasn't fair, and sometimes she hates me for it. But I couldn't kill her. She's my *daughter*. For over two hundred years, we lived our outcast lives together. And then we were found, captured and planted in the Everglades, waiting for Tristan and Alexis to find us."

Bree's eyes rested on Martin, and she went silent. He glared at her with measuring eyes.

"It's all faerie antics," Armand said, leaning back in his chair and crossing his arms over his chest. "Tristan said it himself."

"Before she proved herself," Chandra said. "What more do you want? Tristan is obviously innocent."

"Tristan hasn't betrayed us," someone said from the audience.

"He's not the traitor," Minh agreed. "So who is? Who planted you?"

Adolph cut off any answer Bree might have given.

"You hold belief in her? A *faerie*?" he demanded as he and Armand looked down the table at Minh, their expressions incredulous.

"I do!" The gravelly voice came from the crowd, and this time I felt sure it belonged to Ferrer. Many chants of support followed his.

"Let's get this over with!" someone said. "We need to be out there fighting!"

"Yeah! Call this meeting to a close!" someone else yelled.

"The Normans need us!"

"Our children need us!"

But the same people up on that dais who had voted against Tristan earlier shook their heads, their faces set with determination. They weren't going to change their votes. Everything Bree had said and Tristan confirmed meant nothing to them. They didn't care about any evidence. They didn't care about witnesses or what anyone else believed. Their minds had been made up before the trial even started. They only had one goal: oust Tristan from the Amadis.

But I *did* see the evidence: This was all the traitor's doing. She controlled them.

Much of the crowd knew the truth, as well. Their cries for righteousness slammed into my chest with the force of a semi. *These are my people.* With no coronation ceremony, I had never sworn myself to anyone except Tristan, but my heart had been pledged to God, to the Angels and to the Amadis. *This* Amadis. Not the council, but the people—the people here, the Amadis in the villages, colonies, packs, covens and dens around the world, as well as the Normans. *They* deserved my allegiance and my devotion. If I gave up and walked away, I'd be no better than the council, than the traitor trying to destroy us all. These were the people I must sacrifice for. The people I served. *My* people.

But I had no idea what to do to help them. How to protect them against the traitor.

"*You serve the least of these, you serve Me, and I will return it to you sevenfold,*" a voice whispered in my mind. I had no idea where it came from. A memory from Mom's teachings of the bible? Or, perhaps, God Himself had spoken. It wouldn't have been the first time He'd helped me when I needed Him. Then Tristan's words echoed in my mind, "*You have the advantage.*"

Dear God, I thought, *I know I haven't appreciated the gift You've given me, but I could really use it back. All of it. The way I'm supposed to use it. The way You intended.*

If He answered, I didn't hear.

"Your vote stands?" Martin asked the council. Everyone nodded. Martin blew out a breath and his words came out heavy. "The council has decided. I must go with their decision."

What?

"No!" I shouted, striding to face the center of the table, between Tristan and the council. I stared at Martin—Owen's dad, Char's husband, our *friend*—with disbelief. "How can you do this?"

"Sit down, Alexis," Martin said, his voice full of warning.

"Not until you explain yourself. All of you! These people—" I swept my arm out at the crowd. "—they *trust* you to do the right thing. How can you betray them like this? You overstep your boundaries and make false accusations, trying to destroy us all instead of supporting and leading us!"

"Apprehend her," Armand ordered.

"Martin, you must deal the sentencing," Julia said, ignoring me. "Banishment or death?"

The guard tried to grab me again. I twisted and flipped out of his grasp, pulling my dagger at the same time. The crowd fell deathly silent except for a few gasps.

"You *can't* do this," I said. "You're tearing us apart, not building us up! You're destroying the entire Amadis."

"Tristan has torn us apart," Julia seethed. "It's all his doing.

And this faerie's. And yours, too. Perhaps you'd like to go with your traitor husband?"

I'd had enough of her. I'd known the truth all along and had let her and her posse nearly convince me otherwise. I pointed the tip of my dagger at her. "*You're* the traitor, you lying bitch!" Julia's eyes widened and her fangs slid below her upper lip. My left hand twitched as electricity sparked between my fingers. I slowly lifted my arm.

"*Alexis, no!*" Tristan's voice bellowed in my head. I froze.

I heard you, I told him.

"*Then listen to me. Don't do this. You have to do what's right.*"

I am doing what's right! The Amadis deserve to be protected.

"*But getting yourself banished or killed along with me won't do them any good. You need to calm down and do what they want. Do what they need you to do.*" His thoughts fell silent for a beat, and when they returned, they were quiet, somber. "*They need a daughter, and I can't give you one without the stone. We've lost, Lex. You have to be with Owen. It's what's right for the Amadis.*"

And here we were again. Tristan telling me to do the right thing for the Amadis, even if it meant being with Owen. He'd said before it would break his heart . . . as in, I wouldn't have it anymore. He'd given his heart to me, and I had protected it from the Daemoni while they held him captive. If I did this to him— left him for Owen and the Amadis—and let Martin sentence him to banishment, he would be out there, vulnerable to the enemy. Possibly vulnerable to death. Tristan with the Daemoni or dead . . . what his creators wanted more than anything. Either way, they would win. It had been them all along.

Which meant they'd infiltrated the council.

I won't let them do this, Tristan. They're not going to win. Not this time.

"Your sentence, Martin?" Adolph asked.

"*Banish him. We can't be certain we can kill him.*" The thought startled me. The voice certainly didn't belong to Tristan, but I knew it well enough. The traitor. "*Banish the faerie and Alexis, too.*"

"Banish him," Martin said. "The faerie and Alexis, too."

My arm holding the dagger fell to my side with astonishment. *How did Martin hear the traitor's thoughts? And why did he repeat them?* I felt for the mind signatures, now finding hundreds of them floating around the room, and focused on the one straight ahead of me. It wasn't normal, but thick and heavy, as if weighed down. Because it wasn't only one signature. Two signatures floated where Martin sat, almost as if bound together. One much more powerful than the other. And that one belonged to the traitor. *But how? How could she be doing this?*

Only Rina would know, but the traitor blocked her. I had to make her hear. I had to figure out how to share this with her. But my shield would certainly hold strong now, with all these people around, protecting my own vulnerability.

But I have to do this! It's the only way.

"*You* can *do this*," Rina's thoughts echoed in my mind. Not her current ones. A memory from earlier.

The only way I knew how was to let go of my control and broadcast my thoughts to everyone. Let the entire crowd hear and feel it all. Expose myself to them completely, my innermost thoughts, everything. I had no choice. Too much was at stake.

I focused all my energy on my power and imagined blowing my shield away as I blew out the breath I'd been holding. I mentally returned to the last time I'd been able to broadcast— during a beautiful orgasm six months ago—and tried to recapture that feeling of a completely open mind, an open heart and soul. *Let it go*, I told myself. *Relax.* And somehow I did. A feeling of peace overcame me as the shield, which had once felt solid as steel, simply disappeared. I visualized my own mind as an open door and followed the strange mind signature to the traitor's thoughts, letting them flow through me and out to everyone else.

"With Tristan and Alexis out of the way, Sophia and Rina will be easily disposed of," the traitor's voice said in my mind . . . and in the minds of everyone else. I knew it worked because shocked sounds filled the room, and Mom and Rina suddenly stood on each side of me. *"And then I will rule."*

Martin looked at the three Ames women standing united, and his brows furrowed. Did he not understand what just happened? Was he the only one who didn't hear the traitor's thoughts, although he'd heard them only a few moments ago? But his befuddled expression quickly disappeared, and he stood, lifting his arms as if wanting to embrace us all.

"Now," he said, his eyes bright and excited as he looked over the crowd, "we may discuss the future of the Amadis. It is time to end the reign of the Ames women and declare a new leader."

"And I'll lead them right into Hell."

Chapter 25

"Martin!" several people exclaimed, Rina and Charlotte the loudest.

"Yes, I would be honored," he said instantly. "It would be my pleasure to rule—"

Cries and yells from the crowd cut him off. Confusion clouded his face.

"*They know*," the traitor thought. "*Katerina!*"

Martin snarled as his hand flicked, and a blue light streaked through the air. My grandmother dropped to the floor next to me. Several people cried out as Mom fell to her knees, and Julia blurred to Rina's still form.

"*Ignorant vamp tramp. The first of many to—*" The traitor stopped, realizing her thoughts were still being broadcast although Rina lay unconscious on the floor. Then the voice changed, dropping several octaves from female to male, and went from a thought to spoken words. "*The first of . . .* many to die." Martin smirked. "Ah, Alexis. You broke my block."

"But how—?" I wondered as the crowd murmured with the realization of what I'd done—that I shared Rina's gift.

"Charlotte!" Mom cried out. "How could you tell him? I *trusted* you!"

"No, not me," Charlotte said, shaking her head, her blue eyes wide and her face paler than her blond hair.

"No, not Charlotte," Martin said. "And not Owen, either. They're more loyal to the Amadis than to their own husband and father. I have my own way of discovering things."

Martin hurdled the table and jumped toward us, but before he landed, my hand flew up, and lightning shot out of it. The electricity didn't stop him, though, didn't even slow him down as he dropped to his feet. In fact, he began *pulling* on it, drawing it out of me harder than I could push it at him.

"Foolish girl!" Martin threw his head back and laughed—an eerie sound synthesizing a man's low guffaw with a woman's higher pitched giggle—as he pulled the power out of my body and into his own. His physical form wavered. A ghostly image emerged from it like smoke from a fire. A dark-haired woman, her body transparent, stood with Martin, half of her still a part of him. Several people cried out—vampires, Weres and mages afraid of this strange apparition. Martin's voice changed to the traitor's as both of their lips moved. "I *feed* off your energy!"

He continued pulling on my power, draining me, and I couldn't stop him, couldn't break his hold. My body began to tremble, weakening, but he kept drawing on me, sucking all the force out of me. And as he did, the image of the woman became clearer and more defined. Just as my head began to swim with darkness and my knees began to buckle, a massive figure blurred in front of me, severing the connection. I fell to the floor, next to Rina and Mom, behind Tristan. The woman's image dissolved back into Martin's body.

"Your life force is nearly as good, Tristan." Martin's mouth moved, but the traitor's voice came out of it. "Or should I call you Seth? That is more appropriate."

"Daemoni!" someone from the crowd shouted.

"A sorceress!" someone else yelled.

Commotion broke out behind us—the sounds of Weres trying to control their inner animals and not quite succeeding, and hisses and growls coming from others.

The traitor pulled Martin's mouth into a wicked grin. "Correct. A sorceress. Took you long enough to figure it out."

"But how?" Galina demanded from the dais. All the council members stood now, looking down at the person they'd trusted to be their leader. This person who was . . . *possessed?*

Martin's grin became a proud beam. "I am Kali, a sorceress. And it was quite easy. I simply overpowered Martin's spirit with my own and took control of his physicality."

Charlotte jumped down from the dais and stood in Martin's face. "What have you done to my husband?"

He lifted his hand toward her cheek, and she recoiled. His hand fell to his side. "Charlotte, my dear Charlotte. Your husband hasn't been around since . . . 1939, I believe."

Char's hand flew to her mouth, and her body jerked, as if she'd been punched in the gut. "You lie! It can't be!"

"Oh, yes, it can be. It has been done. How kind of you to be so busy protecting Sophia and the Amadis that you didn't even notice. Such a great wife you have been."

Char raised her hand and whipped it out to slap Martin, but he caught her hand in mid-air and twisted her arm. I sprang back to my feet as Char—brave, strong Char—cried out when the bone snapped. Martin pushed her toward us, and I caught her in my arms. I gently lowered her to the ground next to Mom.

"All I wanted was my bloodline carried on," Kali said through Martin's mouth, his eyes tinted red as he stared at Charlotte, who returned his glare. "I chose Martin because his parents were such powerful warlocks and both physically stronger than any sorcerer—he'd be the best father to my child. I killed his parents, took him and planted him in the Amadis over a century ago. But he wouldn't give in to my desires, always loyal to *you*." Martin's eyes flared brighter red as he jabbed his finger at Char. "Since you're such a strong warlock, too, though, I decided it was worth it. So I gave up *everything*. I gave up my life as a sorceress, even gave up my corporeal body, which had aged and weakened, anyway. But my powers remained strong, and I took Martin's body. Whether he liked it or not, you both still gave me a child—a boy with Martin's physical DNA and my magic. The most powerful warlock the Amadis has ever seen!"

Everyone's heads snapped toward Owen, who stood frozen, his face a white mask of shock.

"I lived Martin's life, pretending to be one of you, waiting for my opportunity," Kali continued, her voice cold yet mesmerizing. "The Daemoni grew restless. They have no patience, no self-control, but I have mastered it. Killing Stefan was their way of getting me on the council, but it wasn't until Seth's return that the opportunity really arose. I knew about you then, Alexis, about your power, and purposely planted those ideas in your head. Ideas about a daughter. It took you and Tristan away from here, letting me execute my plan while at the same time, knowing what would happen when you found the girl. It all played out beautifully. Until now. You're better than I realized."

Martin's wrist flicked again, but no blue light shot out of his palm. Instead, a staff, taller than him with a blue, crystal-like ball on its top, appeared in his hand. He lifted the staff and banged the end on the floor. My body jerked as the electricity shot out of me and to the shimmering ball. But not only from me. Energy from the atmosphere created an electric flow to the staff, like lightning being pulled from the sky, and the ball's interior glowed and swirled. People started crying out, even whimpering, as the sorceress pulled on our life forces.

Owen yelled something over the noise, and the air around Martin trembled—Owen must have shot some kind of magic at the sorceress, but she had herself shielded.

"Use your power, Alexis," Tristan said.

"She's already taking it!"

"Your Amadis power. She's Daemoni!"

"Alexis, I think I can break the shield," Owen thought. *"Be ready. She's weakening me, so we only have one chance."*

Resisting the desire to sag to the ground, my energy all but gone, I dragged my right arm up. Owen yelled out again, and the air around Martin wavered once more. I seized the opportunity and pushed the Amadis power at the sorceress. She shrieked. Martin's body convulsed. But the sorceress fought it. She pointed the top of the staff my way, and a blue light streaked out of it. With a writhing body, though, her aim jerked to the right, and the blast missed me. A thud sounded from behind.

"Ferrer!" someone cried out. The spell must have hit the blacksmith.

Before I could react, another streak blasted out of Martin's hand. My arm shot up with my dagger out to parry it. The spell bounced off the blade, soared over the council members' heads and hit the wall above them. The angel's stone sword shattered and debris rained down on the dais. I gathered all my Amadis power within me and pushed it out at Martin. But it wasn't enough to bring the sorceress down.

"Mom!" I shouted. "Help!"

She sprang to her feet, grasped my shoulder and lifted her own right hand toward Martin. Our powers more than doubled—they grew exponentially. Then Tristan stood behind us, placed his hands on us and gave us what he had. No one else could project Amadis power and none were as strong as Mom and me, but the rest of the Amadis in the room did what they could. Council members jumped down from the dais and formed a human chain, ending with Minh's hand on my wrist. Others from the crowd joined us, too. Their hands—some bone white, others looking more like claws—grabbed our arms and legs, held on wherever they could and shared their power with us. The Amadis came together as one, the power of all that's good streaming through them, into me and out my hand. The sorceress couldn't fight the goodness. A siren of a scream escaped Martin's mouth as he collapsed to the floor. Our energy sapped, the rest of us fell, too.

An eerie stillness blanketed the room as we all processed what happened. But before anyone could move, motion from the center of the floor caught our attention. Martin flinched. His arm jerked upwards. His hand waved weakly, and the air around us trembled.

"The shield!" Charlotte shouted. "She's trying to take it down!"

"Owen! Stop her!" Mom said.

"Kill her!" Charlotte yelled.

But Owen didn't move. He only stared at Martin's upraised arm. And I knew he couldn't do it. He didn't see the sorceress anymore. He saw his father. And stopping the sorceress from hurting us was much different than killing his own father.

Martin's hand moved again, and the air shook harder. We had to do something. I switched the dagger to my right hand and pulled it up, behind my shoulder. Tristan's palm rose, and he paralyzed Martin just as I swung up and let go. The knife arced up and over, the light flashing off the silver blade as it flew end over end and stabbed Martin right where I intended. The dagger pierced through his hand and pulled it down, nailing him to the stone floor. The sorceress was too weak to withstand the silver. Her ghostly image rose from Martin's body, swirled and disintegrated. Her spirit became smoke in the wind.

I dropped my arm to my side and stared at Martin's lifeless body. Unable to move. Unable to *breathe*. As others began to stir, I remained on my knees. *What have I done?* A huge lump formed in my throat. My chest tightened. My stomach felt like a small stone. *I . . . killed . . . someone.* That was what I'd done. I'd ended a life. Martin's life.

But had I? Had there been anything of the real Martin left? Or had he already been dead, killed by the sorceress when she overtook his body decades ago? Who *did* I kill? Char's husband? Owen's dad? Or an evil and powerful sorceress? Or was she even dead?

I vaguely noticed people rising around me or the change in the air—relief that the real traitor had been identified and the situation managed. Mom, sounding distant to my ears, asked Tristan to flash Rina to the mansion. I finally tore my eyes away from the heap of robes and flesh that had been Martin and looked at Rina, who appeared to be just as dead.

My stomach clenched. "Is she . . . ?"

"No," Mom said, "but she's not well."

"How bad?"

"I don't know, honey. She got the same dark magic you did."

Tristan bent down to lift Rina into his arms.

"Don't you dare touch her!" Julia hissed at him, her body protecting Rina's.

Chandra placed a hand on Julia's arm. "Julia, it's over. Tristan is obviously not the traitor."

"Yes, we have been made fools of," Armand said, his tone mixed with exhaustion and anger. "Martin was the traitor. He—or *she*, I should say—had all of our thoughts twisted up."

"Then are you done accusing my husband?" I asked.

Savio, Robin and several others averted their eyes and fidgeted nervously.

"I believe it is obvious," Solomon said, "that not only is Tristan not a traitor, but that he is meant to be with us. The Angels have given him to the Amadis, and we shall not disregard their gift."

Several council members murmured their assent, and the crowd cheered.

"Allow me to apologize on behalf of all of us who doubted," Savio said without raising his head.

"We'll deal with the consequences later," Mom said, and she turned toward Rina. "Tristan, you probably want to spend some time with Bree . . ."

Tristan looked at Bree and then at me. "I'd rather spend time with my wife and son first. I have much to think about."

"Then can you please take Rina to the mansion?"

"No, I will take her," Julia said, no longer defensive or protective, but more like she didn't want to let Rina go. Her eyes looked pained and grief-stricken as she looked down at Rina's still body.

"You can't flash with her," Mom said. "You have to see the logic in getting her to her bed as soon as possible."

Julia didn't respond at first, but finally nodded. Tristan bent down and lifted Rina into his arms. Her body fell limply against him as he turned to Bree.

"Go," Bree said before he could say anything. "I understand. I'll be here when you're ready."

Tristan disappeared, and Mom followed. The crowd noisily

filtered through the doors. I was about to leave, too, but not before checking on Owen. He was nowhere around. Lisa and Jessica caught my eye, and I hurried over to them.

"Do you know where Owen went?" I asked them.

"No, but he left this for you." Lisa held out my dagger.

"We can probably find him," Jessica said with a mischievous smile.

I narrowed my eyes as I slid my dagger into my belt. "Can I trust you?"

"Probably not." Lisa's smile matched her sister's. "But we promise not to hurt him."

"Unless he wants us to," Jessica added. "Some males like that."

I cringed, not wanting to think about Owen's bedroom preferences. I probably shouldn't have trusted them, but my heart hurt for Owen. He couldn't have been in a good frame of mind. I thought he could use the distraction the faeries would provide.

"Please find him," I said. "And bring him back. He needs his family. His *real* family."

Lisa and Jessica grinned excitedly. "We are more than happy to do this favor for you."

They disappeared before I could say anything. I hit my forehead with my palm. *Crap. Now we owe the faeries even more.* I didn't know what that meant—how bad it would be—but since they'd come here in support of Bree, I hoped it wouldn't be too awfully bad. But if it was, Owen was worth it.

I'd go looking for him myself, but I had too much to deal with . . . and I was probably the last person he wanted to see anyway, since I'd played a key role in his father's death. *No, not his father's. That wasn't really Martin.* Perhaps that was true, but that meant this Martin—the one we all knew—was the one who raised Owen. The only one Owen knew as a father.

With a heavy heart, I glanced around the room, expecting to find it cleared out. Guards stood right outside the door waiting to take care of Martin's body once everyone left. But the room wasn't empty. Charlotte still stood there, holding her broken arm and staring at the lump of robes on the floor. Tears streamed down her cheeks.

"Char . . . ?" I said quietly, taking a step toward her.

Faster than a vampire, she yanked the dagger out of her corset and sprang at Martin's body.

"You son of a bitch!" she screeched, slamming the dagger down. Making sure he was truly dead. But instead of the sound of the blade sliding through flesh and bones, we only heard the sharp twang of metal hitting stone. The robes billowed around her as she fell on her knees, nothing padding her landing. "What the *hell*?"

Charlotte pawed through the robes, shoving and swirling and lifting them in the air. Her movements became frenzied and her sobs desperate. I rushed to her side, knelt beside her and pulled her into my arms.

"He's gone," she sobbed against my shoulder. "The damn coward is *gone*."

I held her and rocked her. "I'm sorry, Char. I'm so sorry."

And I was—the last seventy-something years of her life had been a lie and now she couldn't even have her revenge—but part of me felt relieved. Because if Martin's body was gone, that meant *I* hadn't killed him.

Charlotte pulled in a raggedy breath and straightened in my arms. She gave a sharp nod. Her voice came out hard and cold. "Don't worry. I'll get the bastard."

With that, she disappeared. And I had no doubt she'd keep her word.

I flashed, too, to the mansion, anxious to hold my two men, but I needed to see Rina first. Julia stood in the hallway of Rina's wing, all alone. I bristled and prepared to push past her to see Rina. But looking at her more closely, I realized she wasn't guarding Rina's door. Her shoulders were slumped as she leaned against the wall, and she didn't glance up at me, although I knew her vampire ears had heard me minutes ago.

"Tristan and Sophia are assessing her," Julia murmured as she continued staring at the floor. "They would only allow Solomon in."

I leaned against the opposite wall and waited, not wanting to bother them.

"Alexis," Julia said after several long moments, "I am sorry for my behavior. Part of it, I am sure, was Martin's influence, but part of it, I admit, was my own obstinacy. I was very frightened for Rina. My feelings for her . . . they make me very distrusting of anyone. I only wanted what was best for her, even if it meant removing her as matriarch. It would have kept her safe." She sighed. "That's what I thought at the time. Now look at her."

Perhaps I should have told Julia it wasn't her fault because that was probably the right thing to do. After all, she'd just apologized and explained her reasoning. And no one had been themselves with Kali controlling them. But I didn't feel so forgiving at the moment, at least, not toward this vampire who'd been at the heart of everything wrong. Including Rina's condition. So I didn't say anything.

Luckily, I didn't have to. Rina's suite door opened, and Solomon came out. Julia straightened and searched his face for answers.

"How is she?" we both asked at the same time.

Solomon shook his head. "She has a pulse—it is faint but it is there—and she breathes normally, but her eyes do not respond to light and she does not respond to pain at all. We will have to wait to see if her body can regenerate from the damage done. Tristan is trying to help her heal."

"He's giving her his blood?" I asked with mild surprise.

Both Solomon and Julia wrinkled their noses.

"Yes," Solomon said, his voice thick, full of revulsion.

I couldn't help the chuckle that escaped my throat. "You're *disgusted* by that? You're vampires!"

"It is not the blood transfusion," Solomon said, "which *is* rather repugnant, but it will change her scent."

I thought about what it would be like if Tristan's scent changed and he smelled more like Solomon or Mom, and I understood the vamps' revulsion. I loved his scent, found it quite mouthwatering actually, but it was *his* scent. Not anyone else's. And for Solomon to have his mate smelling like another guy?

"At least it is only temporary," Julia said. "Can I see her now?"

"Not yet," Solomon said. "But Sophia is asking for you, Alexis."

Julia scowled.

"She needs Amadis power, Julia," Solomon said as I entered Rina's suite and closed the door behind me. "Be patient."

I thought our suite was grand and luxurious, but it looked like a shabby motel room compared to Rina's. The front sitting room was larger than our entire suite and elaborately decorated in warm, neutral browns and beiges, with the obligatory antique furniture. I entered the bedroom and found Rina laid out on what Dorian would call a ginormous bed—like ours, it consisted of a stone platform and pillars, topped with a two-foot-thick pad. With Rina's dark auburn hair spread out on the pillows and her eyes closed, she looked like Sleeping Beauty. Except for the tube snaking out of her arm.

Mom and Tristan had set up a transfusion system, removing Tristan's blood through a tube and sending it into Rina's body.

"We can't give her too much," Tristan said, pulling the tube out of Rina's arm. "Her body can't hold it."

Mom sat on the bed on Rina's other side, holding her mother's hand. As soon as Tristan had removed the almost normal looking medical equipment, Mom motioned me to sit down. I took Rina's other hand into both of mine and pushed my Amadis power into her.

"How long do we have to wait?" I whispered, as if afraid to wake her up, which was actually what we wanted.

"It took you three days, but you only had me for Amadis power, and Tristan couldn't help you," Mom said.

"But the hit she took was at a much closer range than yours," Tristan said.

"You think it was the same thing?" I asked.

"Yes, I think Martin hit you in the Everglades," Tristan said. "There was a lot of commotion, but I never felt Daemoni. Did you?"

I shook my head. "No. He probably made that part up, huh?"

"He did a fine job of framing both Julia and me."

"Julia really loves Rina, doesn't she?" I asked. "I mean, more than only a friend or as her leader."

Mom raised her eyebrows. "You noticed, did you?"

"She pretty much just told me."

"Yes, Julia loves Rina very much."

"But she realizes Rina's not that way, right? I mean, she's with Solomon. Does she hold out for some kind of hope or something?"

Mom shook her head. "No. Rina is aware of how Julia feels, and Julia understands Rina doesn't return her feelings."

Tristan sat next to me and put his arm around my shoulder. "We can't help who we fall in love with, even if the other person doesn't share those feelings."

I gave him a pointed look. "Which doesn't apply in our situation."

"I know," he said quietly.

I turned back to Mom. "Well, I'd think Julia would at least make some kind of effort to find another mate. Has she? Does she even try to love anyone else?"

Mom sighed. "What Julia does is her own choice. Her free will. She has reasons for her actions, and it is not my place to share them."

I nodded, understanding.

We sat in silence for a while, holding Rina's warm but lifeless hands.

"Do you think Rina knew about Martin?" I asked. "I'm sure she told Julia to recommend him as her replacement. She apparently sent Owen to find the faeries and bring them here. It seems she knew something, doesn't it?"

Tristan looked up at me, the corners of his mouth twitching with a smile. "You think she set Martin up?"

We both looked at Mom.

"My feelings aren't all back to normal," she said, and then she smiled. "But I do detect some truth in that."

I shook my head and snorted. Tristan and Mom chuckled. Martin wasn't the only one who had underestimated the matriarch.

I studied my grandmother's face with renewed respect. The dark circles remained under her eyes, but other than that, she looked more peaceful than I'd seen her in a long time. Perhaps ever. Remorse squeezed my heart. Guilt for adding more to her stress when all along she'd been trying to protect us. All of us. The power of her blood may have been more diluted than mine with the generations who had mated with Normans before Mom joined with Lucas, but I wondered how I would ever be able to rule as well as she did.

I didn't always like Rina's actions, but difficult decisions were part of being a great leader. I wouldn't be able to rule off my emotions and feelings as I did so much now. I knew that was a fault of mine. A fault I would have to overcome.

Rina's hand barely returned my pressure, and my heart leapt. It was a brief, probably involuntary action, but at least I knew she wasn't completely gone. She would return to us, and she would be a great leader once again. And with Mom between us, I had plenty of time to learn and earn the right to walk in her shoes. Good thing. I would need all the time I could get.

Tristan gave my shoulder a squeeze. "I haven't seen my son in over three days. Ready to get Dorian?"

I looked at Mom, and she nodded. "I'll sit here for a while. You can come back later."

I felt out for Dorian's mind signature and found him in his room, so Tristan and I headed toward our wing. Before we came to his door, however, I stepped in front of Tristan, put my hands on his shoulders and pushed him against the wall. He gave me a questioning look, although a smile played on his full lips.

"You do know I love you, right?" I asked. He nodded. "You won't give me anymore of that crap about how you can't be loved, that I don't really feel it, blah blah blah, right?"

"I promise, *ma lykita*. I'm sorry I doubted you."

"And I'm sorry I doubted your faithfulness."

"Only you, my love. Always."

"And forever," I said. "Don't forget forever."

I lifted up on my toes and leaned forward. The kiss we shared sent electricity charging throughout my body, a pleasant charge that I shared with him.

He smiled against my lips. "I'll never forget forever."

Epilogue

I emerged from Rina's suite two days later to find Tristan waiting for me in the hallway. It had been my shift to sit with Rina while Mom took a much-needed break, but she had returned to relieve me. Between the two of us, we sat with her around the clock to share our Amadis power.

"Any change?" Tristan asked. He'd spent the morning with Dorian and then with Bree and Lilith. The girl still remained unconscious, and we'd come to the conclusion that Martin had hit her, too.

I shook my head. "Not really. She kind of pulls away from pain, but not all the time. And her eyelids fluttered a couple times, but then she left us again. She pretty much just lies there, as if stuck between death and unconsciousness. It makes me wonder what's going on in her head. Does she dream? Is she talking to the Angels? Does she hear us but can't respond? Or is it just a black emptiness, nothing going on at all in that head of hers?"

"Have you tried finding out?"

"Actually, yeah. But I get nothing. I'm not sure what that means. I hope it's not because there's nothing to get." My brows pushed together. "I wonder if the dark magic can create a block."

"Or maybe the Angels have." Tristan gave my hand a squeeze.

I looked up at him and smiled. "I like that idea better. Hopefully she's talking to the Angels about a future daughter or about Dorian or, at least, about how to fight the Daemoni, since they keep attacking more. And it makes sense. Only she's allowed to hear their messages."

We started down the stone stairs, and I had no idea where we were going, but Tristan moved with purpose.

"Have you heard anything from Owen?" I asked as we descended.

Tristan's voice came out low and heavy. "Nothing at all. Not from Char either."

"I feel so bad for them. Owen probably hates me."

"I don't think anyone can hate you, Lex," Tristan said as he led me outside. "And it wasn't your fault. Owen's not stupid; he gets that. He just needs some time to deal with this. Like you did when you found out about your biological father."

"Like you do about your mother. How was your time with Bree, anyway?"

He shrugged. "A bit . . . awkward. But it's not over. She wants to talk to both of us."

We had followed the path to the beach, where we came upon Bree sitting on the sand and gazing out over the water. The sun enflamed her hair to a near blinding brilliance. She turned to look at us and gave us a stunning smile. But I had to agree with Tristan. It was a bit awkward. I returned her smile anyway, and Tristan and I sat down next to her.

"When the Angels first spoke of this plan for both of you," Bree said as she looked back out over the water, "I had no idea two people of this world could be so perfect for each other. I didn't fully understand what they meant. Now I finally see you two together and realize they truly did create a match in Heaven. There's no doubt you belong together."

"And not because of a stupid stone," I muttered.

Bree looked over at me and frowned. "A stone cannot create or force love, no, but it is not a 'stupid' stone, Alexis. That stone is very important, and you need to know about it. *All* about it."

I sighed. I practically hated the stone now, with all the problems it had nearly caused between Tristan and me. I didn't want to think about it and had seriously considered letting Vanessa keep the damn thing. But I couldn't deny my curiosity about it. After all, it had been implanted in Tristan's heart, and he had cut it out and given it to me, his true soul mate. Bree had called it a fertility stone the other day, but I still didn't understand its full meaning.

"Okay, so let's have it," I said.

"I have to start by saying I don't know everything about it," Bree said.

"But it's *your* stone," Tristan said. "How could you not know everything about it? Or was it your stone to give?"

Bree sighed. "No, not exactly. But before we go further, Alexis what have you been taught about faerie stones?"

I snorted. "Nothing. Tristan showed me his memory of you implanting it in his heart, and everyone's called it a faerie stone, except when you called it a fertility stone. That's all I know."

"A faerie stone comes from the Otherworld," Bree said. "It's an element of that world that when brought into this physical one, takes the form of a stone. Only a faerie can bring it into this world, and when he or she does, it's for a specific purpose. The stone is given characteristics by the faerie to serve that purpose. Each stone is unique, so it's said to belong to that faerie."

"So this one didn't belong to you?" I asked.

"Yes and no. The Angels wanted me to bring the element of fertility when I came to this world permanently. They ordered me to give the stone to the child on his third birthday, with the instructions that his heart would warm when he met his true mate. The stone would tell him she is the right one, and he is to give it to her. Only then could he produce a child."

"And he did give it to me, and we had Dorian," I said. "So is Dorian it? Did the Angels know Tristan would break the curse and Dorian could lead?"

Bree's mouth formed into a thin line. "I've been kept from the Otherworld for almost three hundred years, so I am unaware of much. But I doubt it, Alexis. I'm sorry, but I don't believe Tristan is the right one to break the curse."

"Then why do we only have Dorian? Did the stone not work properly?"

"The stone doesn't determine the gender. It only guarantees Tristan's fertility. Everything else has been part of the Angels' plan. There is a reason they gave you Dorian by himself—a purpose he must accomplish that he can't do if he has a sister—but I do not know what it is."

"But regardless, he'll go to the Daemoni," I said, my heart sinking. "And we still don't have a leader after me."

"You haven't been able to get pregnant without the stone. It must be in the possession of Tristan's true love, and then can she become pregnant by him."

"So we must recover the pendant."

"Exactly."

I looked at Tristan. "Is this why you said the Daemoni couldn't have it? You knew when we lost it that we needed it back."

"I told you I didn't remember anything at the time," he said. "I only knew it was important you had it and not a good idea for it to be in their hands."

"Is there any way the Daemoni . . . since they have it . . . can they use it?" I asked Bree.

"The characteristics *I* gave it only allow it to work with the two of you. However . . ." Bree paused. When she didn't continue, Tristan and I both looked at her with our eyebrows raised.

"However?" Tristan finally asked.

She blew out a breath. "As I said, I don't know everything about it. The Angels enhanced it, and they would not tell me how. They did something with it and returned it to me, along with the instructions. They may have simply reinforced it with their powers or . . . they may have added something to it. It could be more than a faerie stone. It could be an Angel stone."

"And you have no clue?" Tristan's voice came out harshly, as if he didn't believe her.

Bree shook her head. "I'm sorry, but I don't."

Tristan sprang to his feet and paced in front of us. I didn't understand why he was so upset. "So there could be something more to the stone, but we have no idea what it is?"

"Yes," Bree said.

"And we don't know if it's something only *for* us or if the Daemoni could figure out how to use it *against* us."

"Correct."

And now I caught up with him.

"Shit," Tristan and I both said at the same time. He plopped back into the sand next to me.

"Agreed," Bree said.

We all sat in silence for a long moment.

"But if we get the stone, I can get pregnant, right?" I asked.

"Well," Bree said, hesitantly. "Its fertility works specifically for Tristan, so he couldn't populate the world with offspring before you were even born. It doesn't guarantee *your* fertility. However, with all the Angels have planned for you and the Amadis, I am sure they have included another Amadis daughter in those plans. But right now, your chances are zero, at least with Tristan. You must retrieve the stone."

"Yes, we must. And sooner rather than later. I really don't want to fight the council again about staying with you, Tristan. I won't let them force me to Owen."

Bree stood up. "I must return to Lilith now. Just remember it may be even more important than another Amadis daughter. Considering it's a connection between the two of you, if the Angels added anything to the stone, it probably serves as some sort of protection of one or both of you. As in your lives or your souls."

Tristan and I exchanged a glance, and we looked back up at Bree, but she was gone. I sighed and leaned my head against Tristan's shoulder.

"*Ms. Alexis,*" Ophelia's voice called in my mind. Now that my ability had been made public, I'd have to get used to people jumping into my head. The good news, though: they never heard my thoughts unless I wanted them to. Well, except when Tristan made me lose my mind completely. One reason we wouldn't be staying on the island long.

Yes? I answered.

"*Mail for you. Ms. Sophia said to deliver it straight to you.*"

With tiny *pops*, three envelopes appeared in the air in front of me and dropped into my lap.

Thank you. Can you please send Dorian out?

"*Of course.*" She gave a mental curtsy and vanished from my mind.

My stomach took a nervous dip as I studied the envelopes. Who could possibly be mailing me anything? Any bills would be sent to Tristan's alias at our Florida address, and dead authors no longer received fan mail. Anyone who knew I was alive was pretty much right on this island, except Blossom. Only my name and the embossed Amadis seal marked the envelopes— not postmarks or anything else. I reluctantly opened the first one and breathed a sigh of relief.

> Princess,
> I wanted you to know I made it home. Your bush is all right, but I think I'll be staying here for a while. I hope you realize I had nothing to do with any of the set-up. But I think my sheila did. If you see the were-bitch, send her my way. I could always use a snack.

I shook my head, a small smile on my lips. Jax was home safely, which was good. And he hadn't played an intentional role in Kali's scheme, another relief because I didn't want to hate him. But Kali brought him into it and used him. That pissed me off.

The next envelope contained a second one within it addressed to me in Florida, with a Sanibel return address but no name, and a stamp but no postmark. As if it'd been intercepted somewhere between the sender's mailbox and the post office. *Strange.* With a tingle down my spine, I opened it.

> Dear Alexis,
> I need your help. I know everything about you. You are the famous author A.K. Emerson. You are also Alexis Ames, even though you gave my mom a different

name when she helped you find your house on Sanibel. Your men messed with her memories, but not with mine. I know you from a long time ago, too, and you don't look any older. You look exactly like you did nine years ago when you punched my asshole dad in the face. I was only eight then, but I remember that day clearly. Your men were there, too, and they also look exactly the same now.

Don't worry. I'm not going to the media or anything. I'm not blackmailing you. I'm writing because I really do need your help. I have an older sister Sonya who was at a friend's house the day you hit our dad. But you might remember her, because she attended almost every single one of your signings. She loved your books. I do, too, but Sonya was over the top with them and with you. She always said she was your biggest fan, always on the Internet chats and forums for your books. She idolized you ever since the day you saved our mom. You were her favorite author and also her favorite person. Because of you and your men, our mom is alive today.

If you're paying attention, you'll notice I used past tense for Sonya. She's supposedly dead. That's what Mom thinks anyway, but I've seen her. Just like you're supposedly dead but I know I saw you. As crazy as it sounds, I think Sonya has been turned. She always wanted to be a vampire and I think she is one now. Yes, I believe they exist. I think there are some living over on Captiva, and I think they're good, nice like some of the ones in your books. But they deny it. They won't help me. Only you can help me.

I cried for weeks when I thought my sister was dead and cried again when she pretended to be someone else, the time I caught her. I can't lose her, Alexis. I can't stand the thought of her being bad, of her killing people. I can't get the image of her with blood dripping from her mouth out of my mind. Please help me. You're the only who can.

On my knees begging you,
Your second biggest fan,
Heather

"Wow," I breathed, dropping the paper into Tristan's lap. "I'm not sure what to say about that."

Tristan read the letter and then said plainly, "We'll help her."

"Of course we will. But how many more will there be? Solomon and Rina swore my books were a good thing. But this . . . I made this happen, Tristan. And I'm sure she's not the only one!"

He wrapped his arms around me. "*You* didn't do this. The Daemoni did. It's not your fault they're out there. It's not your fault she went to them. People make their own choices and Sonya made hers. Fortunately for her, we can help her."

I couldn't shake the guilt, though. I punched her wife-beating dad in the face, bringing her attention to me. She read my books because I wrote them—she didn't become a fan of me because she liked my books first. She stalked me. And my publicist put a stop to it, so what did she do? Went out and found the Daemoni. Tears stung the backs of my eyes.

My hands shook, reminding me I had one more letter. I didn't want to read it. I couldn't take anymore right now. I forced myself to open the card-sized envelope and pull out the ivory stationery. I carefully unfolded the linen paper.

Alexis, if you are reading this, then you have won this battle. But do not be fooled, child. The war has only begun. We will meet again some day soon. After all, you have something that belongs to me, something very powerful, and I WILL possess it one of these days very soon.

"What . . . what does it mean?" My voice trembled. I handed the letter with the beautiful calligraphy and terrifying words to Tristan. "Who's it from?"

He glanced at the letter, taking it all in with a quick read. "Probably Kali. And my guess is it means either Owen or Dorian."

I pressed my lips together and nodded, the sting in my eyes growing. And I prayed Charlotte would get her revenge sooner rather than later. If she needed assistance, I'd be the first to volunteer.

Nobody threatened my family.

"I'm gonna kill you!" warned a child's voice.

I pulled in a deep breath and blew it out to calm myself. *That threat doesn't count.*

"You both need a spanking until you can't even sit," Dorian continued.

"What did we do, little man?" I asked, looking up at our son as he stood over us with his hands on his hips. I couldn't help the smile stretching across my face just to see him. This only made him angrier, though, as he glowered at us.

"You lied to me. You told me not to do my tricks ever again, because no one else can do them, but I keep seeing *everyone* doing their own tricks! Why can't I do mine?"

Uh-oh. "Um . . . where have you been, Dorian?"

He stared at the ground and stabbed his toe into the sand, forgetting his own indignation as guilt washed over him. "Ophelia had to do something. She said it was really important. I was supposed to stay by the big tree, but I wanted to *see*."

"What did you see?" Tristan asked as he stuffed the folded letters into his back pocket.

Dorian prodded the sand some more. "Lots of stuff. Stores and houses and people." He looked up at us, remembering his threat now. His eyes narrowed. "And they were disappearing and appearing out of nowhere. And doing crazy things. Tricks. How come *they* can do tricks but I can't?"

Tristan gave me a pointed glance. My stomach sank, but

I understood. I nodded at him, and he reached out and pulled Dorian to sit between us.

"Because your tricks are amazing and people would always want to watch them," Tristan said. "And some people, very bad people, would want to take you away from us because of them."

I gathered Dorian into a hug. "We don't ever want that to happen. We want you all to ourselves! Okay?"

Dorian giggled as I nuzzled my nose against his neck. "Okay. But don't worry, Mom. If anyone tries to take me away, I'll kick them in the knees and punch them in the balls."

"Dorian!" I said, unable to help the laugh. Then I tickled him, making him squeal. "I don't know why anyone would want you. You're such an ornery little man!"

Sasha bounded over to us, barking as Tristan and I both tickled Dorian. She jumped in circles around us, yipping and wagging her tail, just like a normal dog.

And, I supposed, if someone were watching us, they might see us all as a normal little family, playing and laughing together on the beach as if we didn't have a care in the world. A bright image I would hold onto as we carried on into the dark days ahead.

About the Author

Photo by Michael Soule

Kristie Cook is a lifelong, award-winning writer in various genres, from marketing communications to fantasy fiction. Besides writing, she enjoys reading, cooking, traveling and riding on the back of a motorcycle. She has lived in ten states, but currently calls Southwest Florida home with her husband, three teenage sons, a beagle and a puggle. She can be found at www.KristieCook.com.

Connect With Kristie Online

Email: kristie@kristiecook.com
Author's Website & Blog: www.KristieCook.com
Series Website: www.SoulSaversSeries.com
Facebook: www.Facebook.com/AuthorKristieCook
Twitter: www.Twitter.com/#!/KristieCookAuth
Tumbler: www.Tumblr.com/tumblelog/KristieCook
Google+: Kristie Cook